The Turncoats

A guard, a hunter, a duty…

THE SECOND BOOK
IN
THE THIRTEENTH
SERIES

by

G.L. Twynham

ISBN:978-1-907652-71-4

www.thethirteenth.co.uk
sales@thethirteenth.co.uk
Media Contact - Tel: 01673 849 813

Dedication

In Loving Memory

Of

Nan.P and Phil
*

This book is dedicated to Alzheimer's Society, the UK's leading care and research charity for people with dementia, their families and carers.
*

Thank you
*

Visit: alzheimers.org.uk

The Thirteenth Series:
The Thirteenth
The Turncoats

Turncoat:
1550- 60, from turn + coat;
Originally a person, who tried to hide,
or turn round the badge of their party or leader,
a traitor.

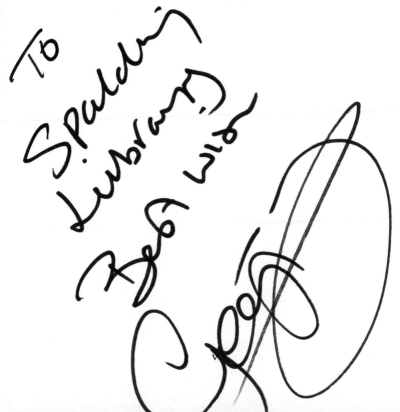

Chapter 1

The Hunter Arrives

Valerie Saunders opened her eyes tentatively, unsure of what would be waiting for her. Luckily she found herself face to face with the sleeve of a strangely familiar, yet very ugly, tweed jacket. She sighed in relief. In the early hours, when she had returned to the flat above the bookshop, she had decided not to sleep on the bed. It smelt of old men and that, mixed with the crazy seventies duvet pattern, was enough to put anyone off climbing in. So she had tried to make herself comfortable on the hard wooden floor. Cushioned by a pile of old clothes and a sleeping bag she had spotted by chance on the top of Wallace's wardrobe.

As she pulled at the sleeping bag's zip, images of her ex-boss, the aggressive elderly bookshop owner who had turned out to be a psychotic prison guard turned rogue from another planet, ran through her mind. But Wallace was no longer a problem: she now had to deal with his alter ego. "Excariot," his name escaped her lips as if to remind her that he was back here with her, in the present. Not only that, he had brought with him the spirits of a multitude of escaped prisoners who were just waiting for an opportunity to jump into the bodies of innocent humans. She may have lost to him yesterday, but she still had the satisfaction of knowing that the one person he really wanted, Lailah, was safely locked away on the prison planet of Alchany.

Rolling onto her back she looked up at a yellow stained, artexed ceiling. Her thoughts drifted for a second to how her life had changed since her eighteenth birthday party and the mysterious arrival of a tattoo. Destiny had thrust itself upon her without having the good manners to first ask her permission. Still, she had done what she thought was right, even though it had turned out to be the complete opposite. She raised her arm into the air and turned it to see the now clear patch where the tattoo had been. Then her eyes moved down her arm to her new accessory, the bracelet Gabrielle, her alien father, had left her. She really wasn't one hundred percent sure what it could do. However, having seen Excariot use his to escape her in sixteen forty-five she knew it had power and if her life continued to follow its new path she was sure to be shown, very soon, what it was capable of, possibly whilst hanging off a burning building or dodging a bullet on an airplane.

She lowered her arm and pushed herself up. A quick glance across at the cupboard door was a stark reminder that she was now the proud owner of a bookshop and a portal to another galaxy. It wasn't normal, but what was anymore?

The hardest part of this crazy situation was losing her present day mum and dad. Wyetta, Val's other mother, and her coven had reached into the future from sixteen-forty-five and caused Val's parents - and almost everyone else - , to forget her, to protect them from Excariot. So now she had one set of parents who had forgotten she ever existed, a mother she had no memory of except in her dreams, and a father, Gabrielle, she had never met.

Gabrielle had been the unlucky guard who had been sent to catch Excariot and deliver him to the Warden or, as she liked to think of him, the *Father Christmas* look-alike. Val giggled. The sound echoed round the empty flat and she stopped, feeling embarrassed and then sad at how alone she was. She had gone from 'only child' to 'lonely child' in one fell swoop.

The clock on the bedside table buzzed bringing her to the sharp reality that it was time to go to work. She made her way to the bathroom, her mind already busy with plans. She was definitely going to require some new clothes and food, and for that she would have to find some money. Popping home for a meal and change any time soon was out of the question.

At least the shower worked and the aging mirror reflected her disgusted grimace as she contemplated using Wallace's greasy comb to tame her hair, but needs must. Pulling on the jeans and t-shirt she had worn the previous day, she moved over towards the door to Alchany and pulled it ajar slightly. What if someone needed her? Maybe that Collector woman she had met last night would come and visit, she thought to herself. But she wouldn't be putting the bracelet near the portal in a great hurry after all the problems she had caused. Like the Collector had warned, "Not unless you have a prisoner," and she really wanted to stay out of trouble.

Val grabbed her trusty sword and phone from the bed and shoved them into her back pocket as images of Sam flooded into her head. He was so gorgeous. After she had fallen for Jason and felt the pain of meeting his very nice girlfriend, Fran, Sam had arrived at just the right moment. Not only was he incredibly good looking, without his gadgets she would be lost.

She headed downstairs, knowing that Wendy wouldn't be able to stay away for long. Her *'never judge a book by its cover,'* friend, Wendy Whitmore, was the girl who had added a pinch of witchcraft to her life. The one person she had spent her life avoiding had turned out to be her guardian and protector. A better friend than *her*! Val could feel her face scrunching into an annoyed frown as memories of Delta suddenly rushed through her mind. "*The traitor*!" How could she have done that to her after everything they had been through together? Friends, like family, every summer for seven years. "Stop," she said in a hushed tone. She wouldn't waste another second thinking about someone everyone had obviously forgotten and she would never have to see again.

She opened the door marked private. It seemed strange coming into the shop from this angle. Everything seemed brighter today, cleaner, if that was possible. Val gently passed her hand over the counter as if greeting an old friend. She had done a good job keeping this place spick and span, but as the Warden had reminded her she would now have to read a few of these books not just dust them.

As the mangled water cooler spluttered out a glass of water, Val couldn't even begin to imagine what was going to happen to her from here on in. When the bang came on the door she nearly threw her glass across the room. However, as she had predicted, there stood Wendy ready to start work at eight-thirty a.m.

"So much for a late start," Val said as she unlocked the door.

"Should I go?" Wendy looked shamefully at the ground.

"Shut up and get in," Val laughed grabbing her by the arm. "Do you want a coffee?"

Wendy nodded as she circled the counter and placed her bag down. "Where would you like me to begin?"

As Wendy's last word escaped her, the private door flew open. In the opening stood a young man, slightly out of breath, dressed all in black. He had jet-black hair in a military style haircut. He scanned Wendy with searching blue eyes, then grabbed her by the arm.

"Where is twenty-three thirteen!?" he barked into her face.

"Who?" Wendy struggled.

Val instantly dropped her glass and moved swiftly in their direction.

The man looked up at Val. "Twenty-three thirteen?" He released Wendy whose thrashing about hadn't even been acknowledged.

Val had her sword out and was around the counter pointing it at his throat in the blink of an eye. "What if I am? Who wants to know?" she demanded, pulling Wendy behind her.

"I'm thirty-three twenty-seven, your designated hunter. We need to go." He reached past Val's sword with ease and they were gone, a blue spark marking the spot.

Wendy was alone. She scrambled for her bag, pulled out her mobile and started to dial. "Shane, this man came and took Val. Get here now!" Wendy listened to Shane's instructions, her adrenaline pumping, "OK." She shut the phone and quickly wedged the stool from behind the counter up against the door to the flat. Picking up her bag she backed towards the main shop door, never taking her eyes away from the flat's entrance. When her back touched the cold glass of the door she turned the lock and then gradually eased herself to the ground, still never taking her eyes away from the *private* sign.

"What on earth!" Val fell to the ground, landing with the grace of an elephant on ice skates. They had arrived in an alley and Val's nostrils were immediately assaulted by the smell of food, yet she was unable to distinguish which type. There were piles of rubbish scattered around and several large bins on each side. "Who are you?" Val questioned, pulling herself up as the man walked around her looking at some strange watch attached to his wrist.

"Your landing was worse than I expected and your memory is highly disappointing. I have already told you, I am thirty-three twenty-seven, your designated hunter. Remember it. I know you are a reject, but it seems that this is going to be harder than I could have ever expected." The hunter stopped and gradually turned on the spot almost in slow motion, until he was facing Val. He raised his hand up straight and pointed to a nearby dumpster.

Val wanted to laugh; it was like something out of one of those S.A.S movies her dad had made her watch.

"In the iron box is prisoner 77294. Do you have your dellatrax with you?"

"My what a trax?" Val looked bemused.

"Your dellatrax! A guard's most important piece of equipment. It catalogues all prisoners, their abilities, strengths and weaknesses." The hunter started to look worried.

"No, I don't have one of those. What does it look like?" Val responded with a perplexed expression.

"It looks like a dellatrax. We're going to be killed! The Warden promised me this would be an easy mission." He glanced at his watch again.

"Hello, anyone in there?" Val called out to the dumpster.

"What are you doing? You are giving away our position," the hunter hissed, seeming confused by her actions.

"Rather him out than me in that thing," Val replied.

"Here it comes," he said stepping back as the dumpster sprang open.

"AHH!" screamed a very rotund, balding man as he leapt out. Val was shocked by his agility compared to his size. She reached instinctively for her sword, but it was too late. The man had grabbed her and in one compression Val was powerless.

"Assistance now!" Val wheezed at the hunter as her attacker squeezed harder and harder.

"What? We don't assist, we just hunt," the hunter shouted back at her across the alley.

He had to be kidding, she was being squeezed to death and he was seriously intending to just stand by and watch. She could feel herself getting crosser.

"Plus, if you had your dellatrax this wouldn't be happening." The hunter glared at her like a scolding parent.

Val lost it. Her knee came up with force, straight into her aggressor's stomach making him loosen his grip for one second. "Are you insane?" Val called out, managing to take a breath. "Help me!"

The aggressor had recovered quickly and was now lifting Val high off the ground, preparing to throw her.

"Sorry twenty-three thirteen, but rules are rules." The hunter shuffled back, neatly dodging Val who hurtled past him, crashing into the dumpster.

As she lifted herself back onto her feet she noticed that her bracelet had started to glow. She pulled out her sword and flicked it into the extended position and headed back across the alley. "I'll deal with you in a minute," she mumbled as she passed the hunter on her way towards the babbling maniac who was coming at her again, arms extended. Val swung her sword at him, knowing it would take at least five to ten seconds to take effect on someone of his stature. What happened next was as much a surprise to her as it was to him. She aimed at his chest and as the sword made contact her bracelet lit up like a Christmas tree, and the power through it seemed to be enhanced by one hundred percent. The man shook for what felt like a blink in time and then dropped to the ground. Val stood over his body in a state of disbelief. What made that happen?

"Well, not a bad first arrest, reject," the hunter said, surveying the prisoner and looking impressed.

"I'm sorry but you and I need a little chat. You don't just turn up and teleport me away and you definitely don't call me a reject. On this planet that's an insult."

"It is on mine as well," he replied smoothly.

"My name is Valerie Saunders," she told him, closing her sword, "and the next time you will help me, or I will take great pleasure in taking you to Alchany for extraction myself!"

The mounting tension was broken by the Star Wars theme bleating out from her mobile. "Hi Shane. Yes, I'm ok. Do you know where we are?" Val waited for his response. "Soho in London. Ok. I will be back at the bookshop in a minute, I hope," Val flipped the phone shut. "So, what do we do now?" She pointed at the motionless man on the floor.

"We should get him to your Collector before he wakes." The hunter reached out for Val and the man, the blue spark passed between them and they were off again.

They didn't arrive, as Val had expected, back in the bookshop but in the flat, just in front of the portal to Alchany. The door was still wide open from the hunter's arrival. He placed his hand in the gap and instantly the warning noises started. They stood in awkward silence but after only a few seconds the Collector arrived.

"Thirty-three twenty-seven, what a pleasure to see you and Val," the Collector said looking down at the unconscious man on the floor. "Oh, I see you have prisoner 77294," she sniggered. "How easy was that catch then?"

"Not easy at all, actually. If hunter boy here had helped I probably wouldn't have ended up with this bruise from hell on my back," Val moaned.

The Collector looked at her sternly. "He's not here to fight your battles for you; his job is purely to hunt out the escaped prisoners when they take human bodies."

"So, it's ok for me to get mangled and half beaten to death while this bloke watches?"

"Yes. Was this prisoner hard to catch?" The Collector looked back and forth from Val to the hunter.

"No, and I apologize for her complaining." The hunter lowered his head in shame.

"I'm sorry, but yes it was difficult. Maybe I will get the next prisoner to throw *you* against a dumpster." Val poked him in the arm.

"You should have had your dellatrax then this would not have happened." The hunter poked Val back.

"Well if you..." Val started.

"STOP!" the Collector shouted, cutting her short. "Enough. This prisoner is a grade one, Val. That means he is the easiest person you will ever get to arrest. He has no magical power and probably isn't too bright." The Collector placed her hand over the man's body and he started to levitate, almost as if he was on a conveyer belt. "And you, thirty-three twenty-seven, Val hasn't been trained. You will need to get her a dellatrax, and try to be patient. You know you can't leave your guard, unless they become deceased, so you need to work together." Abruptly she turned away from them and headed back through the portal.

Val and the hunter stood like chastised children, staring at the floor until she was completely gone.

After a few moments of uncomfortable silence Val chose to speak first. "Fancy a fresh start?" she asked looking at her unwanted new friend.

"Very well," he smiled back. It was the first time Val had seen him do anything but frown. She decided he had a friendly smile.

"Well we can't go around calling you hunter or thirty-three twenty-seven, so what's your name?" Val sat on the bed.

"I don't have a name; why would I need one?" He sat next to her.

"Because it will help you blend in. I will give you one." Val looked around for inspiration. Out of the corner of her eye she spotted a magazine. It wasn't one Wallace would have read. She knew exactly who this had belonged to: Delta. She must have been in the flat, visiting her beloved master, long enough to read a copy of TEEN-VOGUE. Val leaned over and picked it up. On the front cover was a picture of the actor Zac Efron and some girl.

"Who's he? Is he important?" the hunter asked pointing at the picture.

"He is almost God like on Earth. All the women crave him and all the men want to be him." She smiled; he wasn't her type; she liked the dark and secretive type.

"Then I shall take this name, Zac Efron, as my Earth name." The hunter stood up looking really pleased with his new title.

"Zac it is. Now we need to go downstairs to see if my friend Wendy's OK." Val pointed to the stairs and together they headed down. When Val pushed the door she was surprised to find it was locked. She tried her key, but with no success. Zac had a go, but still no luck. Then they heard a voice from behind the door.

"Who is it? I'm armed and dangerous!" Wendy's voice was noticeable shaky.

"Well, Wendy-armed-and-dangerous, this is your boss; now let me in," Val called. They heard Wendy pulling away whatever was blocking the door as she opened it. Cautiously, two green eyes popped around the edge.

"Oh, you're ok!" Wendy sighed with relief and allowed them back into the shop. "I called Shane. He was with Jason working on the laptop. Have you spoken to him?" Wendy asked.

"Yes, it's all fine." Val pushed Zac forward. "Wendy, this is my hunter."

"Hello," Wendy smiled politely, keeping her distance after his physical approach earlier.

"I am Zac Efron. You must be the one they say is a powerful seer." Zac actually seemed excited to meet Wendy, more so than he had Val.

"I'm sorry, did you just say your name was Zac Efron?" Wendy looked to Val for confirmation.

"Yes, I have taken the name of one of your Gods, so the reject Val tells me," Zac said with a smile.

"Enough with the reject." Val shoved Zac out of the way. "How come you know about Wendy?" she asked, walking to the kettle and switching it on.

"In Alchany we have been cataloguing your life. We knew Wendy was here to help you, and all about her powers. What makes her special is that she has a similar power to one of our Judges. The ability to see the future is a far more valuable power than anything you and I could ever dream of having."

"Yes Val, I have the power." Wendy rubbed her temples and tried to look mean.

"I agree, but for now let's concentrate on the job at hand." Val stirred their drinks and passed a mug to Wendy and another to Zac.

"What is this?" Zac looked at the mug with a confused expression.

"It's coffee. I made you white with one sugar; that combination tends to please anyone on this planet."

Wendy sipped hers trying to show Zac what to do.

"In Alchany we don't have this coffee." He sniffed at it suspiciously.

"Just drink it." Val tapped his mug with hers. "So Zac, tell me what is a dellatrax?"

"Ah yes, the dellatrax is a unique device that all guards receive at birth. I didn't know you haven't received yours yet and so for that I must apologise. I can get you one when I return to Alchany. It tells you all about your training, skills and abilities. It has lists of all prisoners past and present."

Zac took a sip of his coffee and pulled an outrageous face of puzzlement, looking closely at the liquid in his mug. He placed the mug on the counter as cautiously as if it was a hand grenade and looked at the girls. A beeping sound interrupted whatever he was about to say to them. He looked at his watch.

"I must leave. I have been summoned to an extraction." He turned to go.

"So that's it. You whisk me away, bring me back and dump me. I need to know more." Val complained.

However, Zac wasn't taking any notice of her. "I will return when I sense the next prisoner." He hurried through the private door with Val hot on his heels.

"When? And how do you know you're going to an extraction - Is it your watch?" she asked.

Zac stopped. "My what?" He looked confused.

Val caught up and touched his wrist. "This. It's a watch," she said.

"Oh. Well, yes, it tells me where, and who, but I don't have all the information, that's why hunters and guards work together. Now, please stop delaying me." Zac pushed past Val to the door to Alchany, and was gone.

"Bye, it's been special," Val shouted sarcastically, making sure she didn't get too close to the portal as she knew what could happen.

When she got back to the shop, Wendy was sitting with her drink staring wistfully into the air.

"Ok, what's wrong with you?"

"He said they knew all about me and my power, that I was special," Wendy said, as if she hardly believed what she'd heard.

Val realised that this was something new for Wendy. Val had received adoration from her parents all her life, but all Wendy had ever done was try to befriend Val; it had never been about her.

"Wendy you are special with or without your power, it just took me time to realise that, now let's get to work." She handed Wendy a duster.

They moved around the bookshop together looking at the different sections, talking about Zac and how much life was changing for them both. Some things made them laugh and others were beyond them both. There were just about to start cataloguing the Irish fiction section when the doorbell rang.

"Just coming," Val called out.

"Hurry up, we haven't got all day," a familiar voice called back.

"About time you two showed up." Val got to the counter to find Jason and Fran with two large boxes. "Thinking of moving in?"

"Dad says that it makes sense to bring the kit here," Jason told her. "So, what happened in Soho?" They put their boxes on the counter.

"Big guy threw me about a bit. I met my designated hunter, but he has popped home for an extraction and will return later. Then we had a coffee and dusted a little." Val smiled looking from Jason to Fran, who looked as confused as she felt. "To make it simpler, we caught a prisoner this morning and he was what they call a grade one, he had no magical power and the Collector told me he wasn't too bright, but it was hard work. I'm not sure I'm up to all this." To illustrate her point, Val lifted her top up to the satisfying gasps of the others as they saw the size of her bruise.

"Did this hunter guy get hurt?" Jason asked.

"He doesn't fight or help with the arrest; he just hunts them down for me. He knows when one of those spirit things that came back with Excariot takes a human's body. It's like, he's Rudolf and I'm Santa."

Fran let out a snigger, "Sorry but I have images in my mind."

"So, changing the subject, what about the boxes?" Val started pulling at the tops.

"You're obviously going to need us here, so where are we going to set up base?" Jason started to look around for space.

"Well, you can't go in the flat, it's too dangerous. The only other place is the cleaning cupboard at the back." Val pointed to the rear of the bookshop.

"You want me to spend my days sitting in a cleaning cupboard?" Jason looked from Val to the other girls. "Fine, but I will not be helping around the shop, plus you and me: fencing later." Jason pointed at Val then picked up his box and strutted off down the aisle. Fran grabbed hers and followed smiling back at Wendy and Val.

"Do you think Wallace aka Excariot kept any money here?" Val started to move the boxes behind the counter. "We will need to pay the bills and buy new stock."

"I don't know, but you probably have about fifty thousand pounds worth of stock, or more, already in the shop," Wendy responded in a matter of fact way.

Val sat back on the stool. "Are you being serious with me?"

Wendy nodded her response, visibly less impressed than Val. "My family has been in the retail industry for years," she explained. "I will speak to my mum about what we need; you just keep bagging those prisoners." Wendy grabbed a pen and paper with her duster and headed off to catalogue the books.

Val rummaged a little more and managed to find a twenty-pound note. Not a bad start, but she needed so many things. It was hard being on your own. Her mum and dad had always done everything for her. She pondered what they had been doing with their time since the spell that had made them forget her existence. Glancing over at the clock she saw it was eleven-thirty. Dad would be at work, probably having his mid-morning sandwich with the lads, and her mum would be shopping for dinner. Or would they? Now Val had gone would their lives still be the same? The doorbell broke her painful reverie and as she looked up her heart skipped to her throat.

"Morning Val." Sam walked up to the counter.

"Hi, how's it going?"

He looked amazing: crisp white t-shirt, jeans and he smelt like he had just jumped out of the shower. How could she hide her feelings? They were pouring out all over her counter.

"Are those the clothes you were wearing yesterday?" he frowned.

Please God swallow me up and let me die peacefully. "Yes. I haven't got anything else. I need to go shopping, but I was busy being beaten up and meeting my designated hunter," Val responded brushing herself down.

"Sounds exciting. Tell me more." Sam leaned on the counter and Val relaxed as she told him about the morning's entertainment.

"I can't wait to meet this hunter; he sounds fascinating. Now for the real reason I'm here." Sam opened his brown leather satchel.

"Please say it's to whisk me off my feet and take me for lunch. I'm starving," Val thought.

"Do you remember I told you I had a new gadget for you? Well, here it is." Sam pulled a small black box out of a pocket and placed it on the counter.

"You could have wrapped it." Val eagerly picked it up and opened the lid. "It's a bracelet." She held it out. It was definitely pretty but how was this thing a gadget? Plus she already had a bracelet; she was going to start looking like the queen of bling.

"Well sort of. Let's put it on. See, it goes closer to the top of your arm to keep it hidden." Sam took the bracelet as Val lifted up her sleeve.

It felt strange to Val not to see the tattoo any more.

"OK, it goes here." Sam wrapped it around her arm.

She frowned at it, still unsure of its purpose. "OK, now what?" She asked looking from her arm to Sam.

"See the gemstone on the end?"

There was a clear orange looking gem on the end. Val nodded.

"Grab it and pull, but leave enough room." Sam stood back.

Enough room for what, Val wondered. She was excited and afraid at the same time. She held the gem in her hand and pulled. It was amazing, it uncoiled at such speed. Within a second she had four feet of what looked like silver rope in her hands. "It's titanium tungsten carbide alloy, which makes it light but very strong." Sam beamed at her like a schoolboy.

"I'm very impressed, but what do I do with it?" She asked, handing it back to Sam.

"Watch." He turned the gem back and it recoiled into the bracelet. "You can use it as a rope or a whip." Sam handed the bracelet back to Val who slipped it back on her arm and covered it up.

"It's lovely thanks." Val felt pleased. "Sam, I need to tell you about something that happened today. When I used the sword my bracelet went haywire. There were flashing lights and then the sword seemed to be so much stronger than usual. Do you know why?" Val held out her wrist for him to look at it. Sam took her hand and her skin electrified, her senses going into emotional overload. How could it be that this Sam didn't seem to have the slightest interest in her and yet Sixteen-forty five Sam couldn't keep his hands off her?

"I can't really tell. If you give me your bracelet I could maybe do a few tests." He turned her hand over a few times inspecting it.

"I wish it was that simple, it won't come off." Val tugged but it was impossible. "Sorry." She gently pulled her hand away. "So what now? Are you off again?" Val held her breath unsure if she wanted to hear the answer.

"No. I have decided to spend a little more time here with Shane, but there's another reason for me coming to see you. I was wondering if you wanted to have lunch tomorrow, at my new house."

"Yes! I'm free between twelve and one." Val wondered if skipping at this point would be highly inappropriate.

"Great! Here's my address." Sam handed her a card. "I'll see you then."

"Yes, you will." Val took it and stood as still as she possibly could. She waited, hardly breathing, until Sam had left the shop, and then let out a huge squeal, ran around the counter and started prancing around the entrance. At this point Wendy, Jason and Fran came running.

"What's wrong? Are you ok?" they chorused.

"Look at her; they are playing with her mind," Fran said to Jason.

Val grabbed Fran and used her as an anchor as she came to a halt. "I'm fine, Fran, just happy."

"Well, you're going to be ecstatic in a minute. Come and see this." Jason led Val towards his new headquarters. Val walked into the cupboard and looked about her, wondering what all the fuss was about. They had placed the two boxes down on the floor, moved the mop and a couple of other things about, but there was nothing worth singing about.

"Ok Val, what can you see?" Jason pointed towards the wall in front of her. Val looked. There were shelves and a very dodgy picture of a ship.

"Nothing special." Val shrugged and turned to look at the others.

"Wendy, you found it, so you do the honours," Jason said. Wendy moved past Val and pulled back the picture.

"Oh my goodness!" Val gasped. "There's a safe." She moved to stand beside Wendy to see the brick-sized metal square jutting out of the wall, a white key pad on the front of it.

"Yes, we haven't got a clue what the number might be to open it, but it's a start."

Val moved closer. "I think I know what it is." She typed in the number twenty-three twelve and the door made a clunking sound. Val turned the handle and it opened with surprising ease. The others watched silently. Val pulled it back and there it was: a stash of money. "Oh yes, you beauty." Val pulled a pile out and handed it to Wendy, then another, then another. There were also a few pieces of paper that Val placed on Jason's new desk.

"How did you know what the number would be?" Wendy asked as she started to count the notes in her hand.

"It was Excariot's prison guard ID, just a lucky guess. So how much?" She turned to the others.

"Well I have five hundred." Wendy held out her stash.

"Same here," Jason and Fran choroused.

"So Wallace left us fifteen hundred pounds." If Val's grin had been any wider a plate could have fitted in the gap.

"What now?" Jason handed over the cash.

"Snakes and Ladders for burgers on me." Val took the money.

She shoved a few notes in her pocket and put the rest back in the safe and closed the door.

"Hello anyone there?" a voice called from the front of the shop.

"Did you hear the door bell?" Val darted a glance at the others. They all shook their heads. Jason quickly moved back to back with Val. She placed her hand on the sword but didn't want to pull it in case they were wrong. They made their way cautiously up the main aisle and as they were getting closer to the entrance the stranger called out again.

"Hello, it's Zac Efron here."

"Did he just say Zac Efron?" Jason looked at Val.

She nodded and relaxed her stance, replacing her sword into her back pocket.

"Hi Zac, what's wrong?" Val made her way towards the counter.

"We have a problem."

"Hi," said Jason. He and Fran waved in Zac's direction. His expression was unmoved as he stared at them both. They lowered their hands, noticeably uncomfortable.

"Another prisoner?" Val asked, easing the icy moment as she started to collect her belongings.

"I'll get back to the computer room," Jason started to head off.

"No, it's your dellatrax. I went to collect one for you, but it seems that it won't work on your planet; the signal is scrambled by your moon and another twenty-five in between."

"Now what?" Val asked.

"The Warden came up with a solution and the Judges have agreed. We will give you all the information you need in these." Zac moved to reveal a pile of dated looking leather bound books on the counter.

"Great, more books. How on earth am I supposed to carry them every time we get called out? The Warden didn't think this one out," Val moaned.

"They understand that. However, the Warden feels that they will be well disguised in the bookshop and that your seer, Wendy, would be a worthy reader for you. Maybe these two others could be of assistance too." Zac pointed at Jason and Fran.

"Either way, this isn't what I expected. What do you think Zac?" Val asked.

"Sorry?" Zac's expression changed to one of confusion.

"I said, what do you think? Can we work like this?" Val looked at him, waiting or a response.

"It is not my place to answer that question. Please, let us talk about you." Zac was visibly uncomfortable.

Wendy walked over to him and gently placed her hand on his arm. He looked down at her hand feeling even more confused. "Listen, we were just going to the Snakes and Ladders burger bar for lunch. Come with us and you and Val can carry on this conversation there."

"Yes mate, come on." Jason patted him on the shoulder and they all walked towards the exit gently coaxing Zac to go with them.

"Is this normal and appropriate behaviour?" Zac called back to Val.

"Very." She locked up and they all climbed into Wendy's Morris Traveller.

"Give your dad a call and get him to meet us," Val shouted over the engine noise to Jason. He nodded back.

The Snakes and Ladders was fuller than usual and Val was pleased when they managed to get a nice table tucked away in the corner. The waitress came over to take their order as Jason's dad, Shane, arrived.

"Where have you been?" Val stood up and embraced him. This was as close as she was going to get to a father figure for now.

"I have a job." He hugged her back and then went to greet the others.

"You are Shane Walker, the painter. I am pleased to meet you. I am Zac Efron," Zac bowed a little for him and Shane gave him a welcoming smile and a pat on the arm.

"Hi Zac. I hear from Jason that you're a hunter. Tell me all about it." Shane sat next to Zac and Val smiled to see her hunter relax a little. Shane had once again willingly embraced a complete stranger.

Jason called over the music, "Dad, when were we last here? I can't remember."

Val could: the exact moment, the very day, and who was with them. She remembered the plane crash and how much she had wanted to protect her then best friend, Delta.

"I'm not sure, son. Strange, but I can't remember," Shane replied.

"Burger with cheese? Veggie delight?" the waitress called out over their heads.

"I'm the Veggie," Wendy leaned over to collect her plate.

"That's Zac's," Val called, grabbing the enormous burger.

Zac's face said it all. Val could tell that he had never seen anything like this burger. She picked up her Hawaiian and started to eat. Zac looked around the table at the others, then tentatively picked up his burger. Val nodded at him and he took a bite.

She watched with interest as he chewed, concentrating on the new sensations he was experiencing. Finally he looked at her and declared, "This burger is very pleasant."

Val grinned at him. "Glad I've done something that meets with your approval."

"We have no need of food in Alchany," he told them. "We have what you call a pill that supplies us with all the nutrition we need, but this is much tastier." Zac pulled out a small black pill from his pocket and handed it to Val.

"Wow, tasty, thanks." Val smiled and popped it into her pocket. "I'll save it for later."

"That will feed you for at least three of your weekly cycles," Zac told them, shoving another hand full of chips into his mouth.

Val was enjoying everyone being there, even her new acquaintance, Zac. They would find a way to make this new system work. If anyone knew books it was Wendy; she knew the shop was in good hands. In thirteen years of waiting, Wendy had never given up on her and that meant that she was the closest thing Val now had to a best friend.

She glanced across the table. Jason and Fran were laughing together about something; she had to admit that they made the perfect couple. She had confronted the fact that her romantic feelings for Jason had been all her own and she was over that now. Anyway, they were committed to helping her and she knew how much she needed their support. She looked across the table to see Shane nodding, agreeing with something Zac was telling him, and then proceeding to slap him vigorously on the back. He was the glue that would keep them all sane. This was good; things were going to be ok.

Then it began.

CHAPTER 2

Protection

Val could feel it in the pit of her stomach: something was wrong; she didn't know what, but it was going to be bad. There were no pains like before, when she had the tattoo, but it had taught her a very important lesson: she now knew to listen to her instincts and something was definitely coming. Zac was just devouring the last chip on his plate when his watch sprang into life.

"Zac something is happening; I can sense it." Val rose from her chair. Zac was with her as lights and symbols flashed away on his screen.

Zac pointed at his watch, as if Val would understand it. "There are at least five prisoners taking human bodies now. We don't stand a chance against that many; we need to get out of here immediately."

Had they deliberately sought and found Val, or was it just by chance that they had come to rest at the diner? It wouldn't be long before she found out. Val, Zac, Jason and Shane stood together as five very large, highly intimidating men came their way from a booth across the room. They moved in close and Val could feel the tension building. The men circled them and then stopped.

"Too late for escape now," Zac said, pushing Wendy into the corner as Shane and Jason protected Fran.

"Really," Val smirked. Everyone in the bar had now stopped what they were doing and were looking at them. She pulled out her sword, but didn't extend it just yet. What was going on? Why didn't they just attack? If these were criminals, what was stopping them?

Suddenly the largest of the five men started to jerk, his eyes flickering in their sockets. Then he became rigid. There were fearful murmurs coming from all corners of the Snakes and Ladders, but no one dared make a move.

"Do I look like that when I do my thing?" Wendy whispered to Val.

"No, you look much scarier, now get back." Val pushed Wendy behind her again.

The now still giant opened his eyes and looked around him. "Where are you?" The man started to walk, however not like before. Now he walked upright with arrogance. "Ah, Val, my precious little guard, oh how I've missed you." He moved towards her, unbothered by the crowd of spectators. Jason and Shane went to move in front of her, but Val held out her hand to signal to the others that she was ok. She could sense their longing to protect her, but she knew who this was.

"Excariot, what a pleasant surprise, and what a lovely parlour trick!" Val was now almost nose-to-nose with the guy. "Once again you're too scared to meet me in person." Val knew which buttons to press.

"Listen to me, girl. I have better things to do than hanging around waiting for you. I have so many new friends here I don't even know which one to send you next." The man stepped back. "Now, let me see..."

He rubbed his chin with his index finger and thumb in a patronising fashion. "We have the daddy, and the baby..." he pointed to Shane and Jason, "...the nothing and the witch," he pointed from Fran to Wendy. "Oh, someone new! Let me see..." The man turned to Zac and eyeballed him up and down. "I do believe it's a hunter. What did you do wrong to end up on this dump of a planet with a half breed guard?"

Zac was about to respond when Excariot turned away from them all and walked back towards the other four prisoners. "You, hunter, won't be a problem, you haven't even been taught how to defend yourself," he said patronisingly without glancing back.

"Just so I know for future reference, is that true?" asked Jason.

"Yes," Zac responded. His attention distracted by flashes and he looked at something on his screen. "Val, these men are 44789, they're Grindary, and I know this fact because I helped capture them."

"How does that help to stop us from being beaten into a pulp?" she whispered urgently, wanting an answer and it needed to be fast.

"They have a weak spot, just between their eyes. I can only guess that stays the same when they take human form. You give them a direct hit in that spot and they will pass out."

"Did you hear that guys? We need to go for the forehead, between the eyes," Val said. Shane and Jason nodded their understanding.

"Ok Excariot. Well, you're the all powerful and clever blah, blah, blah, so let's get this thing done, because I was enjoying my first meal of the day," Val called.

"Do you really have to do that?" Zac flashed an angry glare at Val.

"Well, if we do die at least I won't go out a coward," Val hissed back at him, "Plus, Excariot has already killed me once so it's not like its anything new." She extended her sword. "You ready guys?"

Jason and Shane nodded grimly.

"Kill them!" Excariot cried. The body that had been housing him vibrated once more and they knew Excariot was gone. Val, seeing that he was dazed, instantly took Zac's advice. Flying forward, the tip of her sword extending, swiftly struck the first man between the eyes. To her pleasure and disbelief, Zac was right. He dropped like a dead weight. The people in the bar took advantage of the fight to start fleeing through all exits. Jason managed to get straight in with his thug and a jab to the head was an instant knock out. Shane followed suit after a momentary struggle and now they only had two left. As Val was heading towards the last two a glass came flying past her ear whacking number four a bull's-eye and he was down. Val turned in amazement to find Fran standing there.

"What! No one calls me a nothing and my boyfriend a baby," she said. Val was impressed.

They regrouped and stood together facing their remaining foe. The fifth and final member of the Grindary looked a little lost. Val put her hand up to stop the others.

"You," she pointed at him as he hopped from one foot to the other, unsure how to escape. "Run back to Excariot and tell him if he thinks he's getting Lailah back he has another thing coming."

The man took her advice and headed for the exit. They all stood in silence, taking in what had just occurred.

Apart from them, the only other person left in the burger bar was the owner, who was hiding behind the counter. "Have you finished?" he called them from his hiding spot.

"Yes, we are done, you may now come out," Zac told him.

"I'll call the police. Is anyone hurt?" The man reached for his phone.

"Do not worry. Val here is a highly qualified prison guard and we will deal with these men ourselves. Please continue with your job," Zac informed him.

"Listen mate, I'm calling the police." The man fumbled with the phone.

"Good try," Val said. "Shane, Jason, let's get these guys out of here."

"Wait! You can't take them; you will invalidate my insurance." The man was trying to dial.

"Sorry, but we have a duty to protect you and your customers," Val saluted the bar man as they dragged the four men out into the empty car park.

"So, what do we do with them now?" Jason asked, dropping the legs of the fourth man.

"We can teleport now." Zac held out his hand to Val.

"So you can teleport from anywhere you like, whenever you want?" Val asked.

"Only when it's relevant to an arrest. It's frowned upon to use an unofficial teleport for personal reasons and you know what happens when you break the rules." Val and Zac exchanged a look that met somewhere between paper work and extraction.

"See you guys back at the bookshop," Val called out. Val and Zac both touched the bodies, and Zac teleported them back to the doorway to Alchany.

Wendy stared at the spot where her friend had just been, wondering if she would ever get used to this. Then she sighed and asked the others, "Do you need a lift?"

Shane pointed to his bike, a black triumph roadster, and Jason followed his dad.

"You boys go. Me and Wendy will take the safer mode of transport." Fran grabbed Wendy by the arm as they made their way to her car.

The six bodies landed with a thud, their combined weight causing a dust cloud to rise in the flat.

"Do you think the Collector is going to be pleased with us, Zac?"

He nodded.

"Can I call her this time please?" Val showed Zac her bracelet and he agreed. She pushed her hand through the portal. It felt cold but exciting. "Warning! Warning!" Val was starting to enjoy this, but when the Collector arrived she was not wearing the pleased expression Val was hoping for.

"Thirty-three twenty-seven, Val, you have made a serious error today." The Collector's tone was cold and hard.

"But we caught four Grindary for you, look." Val could feel a burning behind her eyes. They had all risked their lives, for what?

"You allowed Excariot to trick you. Do you really think he isn't brave enough to turn up in person, Val? Are you really that naive?" Her voice was starting to strain with anger. "You did exactly what he wanted you to do. You acted like 'the chosen one', spoilt and self-important, while he attacked a coven of your witches and captured a powerful high priestess."

"How do you know that?" Val demanded.

"He sent a note through this portal with the man you allowed to escape. He will sacrifice anyone to achieve his outcome and he thinks you are so insignificant that he feels safe enough to teleport here, into your home." The Collector waved a piece of paper at her. "So, Val, who's the winner?" Val was about to speak but the Collector's expression told her that maybe now was one of those times to keep quiet. "Now, go back to work and think about what happened here today. Sleep well tonight and wake up tomorrow on the humble side of your bed!" The Collector levitated the four prisoners with her tiny hand and was gone.

Val turned to her new companion who was standing next to her looking completely overwhelmed by being rebuked, not once but twice in one day. "This won't happen again I swear."

Val walked back into the bookshop, followed by a silent Zac. She found a hive of activity. Jason and Fran were busy setting up their little centre of operations with Shane and Wendy giving them instructions.

"No, there's no socket there," Wendy pointed as Jason patiently pushed the table over to the other side of his three foot by three foot prison.

"Guys, please stop," Val interrupted. "I made a huge mistake back at the Snakes and Ladders. It seems that Excariot set us up, and managed to send a message to Alchany with the guy from the bar that we let go free." Val lowered her head. "He used the Grindary to divert our attention while he took a high priestess. He then sent a note direct to my Collector, telling her what he'd done. But he won't get away with this." Val said in a serious tone

"He was here! I thought you said that he would stay away because of the portal?" Wendy asked, looking nervously between Val and Zac for some form of reassurance.

"The Collector told me that if the door was open guards could travel through and so Excariot would stay away, but I suppose they were relying on me and Zac keeping it safe." Val tried to reassure Wendy.

"So we messed up, but he didn't spot your dellatrax sitting on the counter," Fran pointed out.

"He didn't take anything from the shop, Fran, he kidnapped an innocent woman from a coven. I think that's a serious mess up. We don't know where she is, where she came from or what he's going to do to her." Val was feeling overwhelmed by the enormity of the situation.

Zac placed his hands behind his back and started to pace. "Ok, first things first, let us all stay calm. Val, please correct me if I'm wrong. In sixteen forty-five Excariot needed the whole of your mother's coven, to open the portal to free Lailah." Val nodded. "So, if he's trying to repeat the same spell and open another portal, in theory he will need another twelve witches, to recreate a full coven. So, he won't do anything with this woman yet."

"So what will he do now?" Val asked.

"His job now is to collect more witches," Zac replied.

"Where will he get them from? I haven't seen witches for hire on e-bay," Jason questioned.

"He only needs twelve, surely that will be easy. How many covens are there in England or even the world?" Val asked.

"Well, the figure is endless. Did you know that Wicca is *the* fastest growing religion in some countries?" Wendy gave an awkward geeky smile at the others.

"How does that help us stop Excariot? He will always be one step ahead of us," Jason said.

"Incorrect. He needed Val's mother's coven from sixteen forty-five for a reason. They were special, very powerful, and Val's mother's human blood mixed with her father's twenty-three eleven's alien DNA is what made Val extremely powerful. He needs the same witches again now." Zac smiled, placing his hand on Val's shoulder.

"Well, he will be out of luck. That was over four hundred years ago; they're long gone," Wendy pointed out.

"Right, so we need to follow their trail. DNA is everything, as it is for you, Val, it will be for the descendants of the coven. If we can find them, then we will be one a step ahead of Excariot." Zac seemed focused; Val could tell he was in his element.

"When this all started, I got a tattoo to guide me, that was followed by visions of the people who I needed to save. They were all direct descendants of the witches from my mother's coven," Val replied.

"I have a question. Didn't you save your mum and the others in the past, even though they had previously died?" Fran asked.

"Yes." Val nodded.

"So surely you changed the past. Doesn't that mean you have also changed the future?" Fran now stared at the others.

"Oh my God, you're right, Fran! The repercussions are enormous." Val grabbed at Jason's chair for support and sat down.

"Not really. The judges who rule over Alchany step in and out of time whenever required and the changes afterwards are normally minimal. Your main concern now should be to find out about the witches that were direct descendants," Zac said.

"Why didn't these judges just step on in and save the high priestess? As a matter of fact, why haven't they done anything to help us?" Val looked up at him.

"The job of a judge is not to deal with petty matters of guards. They are beings who make world changing decisions," Zac responded dryly, then looked at Wendy. "You can check the dellatrax for any information on the original coven's members, and we will need to use your family history books for answers to their whereabouts."

"Oh, I'm so looking forward to getting my hands on those books." Wendy's eyes were as large as saucers as she stood up and started to make her way towards the counter.

"Seems like a good idea to me, Zac. I will introduce you to the internet and the joys of the ancestry website." Jason politely tipped Val off his chair and switched on the laptop.

"I have to get back to work. Keep me updated, son," Shane said. Jason nodded without raising his eyes from the screen that he and Zac now shared.

"What shall I do?" Val asked.

Zac looked up. "Nothing. Keep your strength for the battle ahead. We're working on it, be patient. We need information and then we will have a better chance of finding and stopping Excariot getting anymore priests and priestesses, if you allow us to get on." He dismissed Val and looked back at the screen.

"They're on the case, Val. We'll find her and I think your hunter friend is right, I don't think Excariot is going to lay a finger on the priestess. He needs her alive. Now just try and get on with what you need to do for now," Shane said as he walked away from her.

Fran looked affectionately at Val. "You know you can't actually do anything, don't you? But I think I know what might help distract you for a while." She grabbed Val's hand and pulled her down the aisle.

"I can't possibly leave. Zac needs me, don't you," Val called out.

"No. If I do I will teleport to your location," he replied.

"Lend me your car, Wendy," she called and a set of keys came winging their way over the top of the books.

"What will distract me, Fran?" Val asked as they walked down the steps to Wendy's car.

"Please don't take this personally, but you need some new clothes." Fran opened the door to Wendy's Morris traveller. Val hesitated. It felt wrong to be leaving, but she had no choice but to go, and it was actually a very good suggestion. She had no change of clothes and knew that she couldn't go on wearing the same ones. More importantly, she couldn't turn up at Sam's tomorrow in the same clothes she had been wearing today, not after the comment he had made this morning. She nodded and climbed aboard the little car.

As they travelled into town Fran was quiet, the radio playing softly in the background. The last time Val had gone into town it had been with Delta; Fran was nothing like her. They would have been chatting, or Delta would have been embellishing some story about a famous person's private life. She wished she could forget her. In time maybe she would.

Fran and Val wandered around, in and out of various shops. It was odd how Fran seemed to know more about

Val's personal preferences than she did herself. Within a very short space of time, Val had spent the little money she had and was begging for a drink break.

"Hot chocolate?" Val asked.

"Do you need to ask?" Fran sat down at a small table for two in the heart of the shopping centre.

Val was soon placing the steaming drinks in front of them. As she sat down she said, "So Fran, tell me all about you. I feel like I know nothing and yet you know so much about me." Val smiled warmly. A change of conversation would be good. She was tired of Excariot being part of her every waking moment.

"Well, my full name is Francesca Alice Tickle and if you laugh I will tell Jason you said he hits like a girl. I have been in love with Jason since the first day I met him at school, three years ago. I spend my summers with him and term time with my mum and dad. They're extremely cool. My mum is into being a mum and she is a gym-aholic. My dad is a stock and quality controller, something for a Chinese firm, so he flits between here and China. I have a fraternal twin sister called Yassmin who's a pain, but only in a sisterly way, a cat called Ginger and a Jack Russell called Sophie, and that's about it." She proceeded to tuck into her hot chocolate.

Val felt the pain of missing her ordinary mum and dad. She would have loved to sit and talk for hours about her mum's serious portion control issues or her dad's bad shirt days, but they were things of the past.

"So tell me about you?" Fran asked looking up from her whipped cream.

But Val wasn't listening. Something far more alarming had caught her attention. Across the shopping centre she had spotted a girl with her back to Val, on a pink flip top phone with a mane of long blonde hair; attached to her arm was a Gucci handbag.

"Wait here." Val made no eye contact with Fran. If this was who she thought it was she wasn't taking her eyes off her target for a second. Considering her heart had now gently lodged itself in her throat, she managed to walk steadily towards the blond. If it was Delta how on earth had she gotten back here? She walked up behind her.

"Delta?" Val said in a broken voice.

The girl turned and Val instantly realised it wasn't her ex-friend. As quickly as her heart had risen it settled again. "I'm sorry, I thought you were someone else," Val said apologetically and went to turn away.

"Stop," the blonde girl requested. Val instinctively did as she was told. "This is so crazy! A girl came up to me in Topshop and gave me this wig, bag, phone and envelope and said to wait here. She also gave me this." The girl held a wad of money out at Val. "I thought she was crazy, but what the hell it's a hundred quid. Then she said someone would come up to me and that I should give this envelope to them." The girl handed Val the envelope. It had her name on the front. She gently caressed the letters with her finger for a second. She would have recognised that hand writing anywhere. Cautiously she opened it, her hands now visibly shaking. Inside was a card that simply read: **Miss me Alien? Love Yankee xx**

This couldn't be happening. All of a sudden it dawned on Val that she had left Fran alone. She turned on the spot. Where was Fran? It was ok! She was still at the table. She turned back to the girl who saw, from the new expression on Val's face, that all wasn't well. The girl started to look for a way out, but she was far too slow. Val lurched forwards, grabbing her by the arm.

"When did she give you this?" Val's anger erupted into the girl's face, her aggression highly visible.

"Oy, you're hurting me!" The girl pulled off the wig and tried to wrench her other arm free.

"I'm going to do a hell of a lot worse if you don't give me some explanations, now."

"She came up to me, I told you, about twenty minutes ago, and handed it all to me. She told me to stay here, that you would come and talk to me. How many languages do you want me to tell you that one in?" The girl was squirming. "If you don't let me go I'm going to call security."

"Val, what's going on?"

Suddenly Val realised that they weren't alone. Her momentary lapse allowed the girl to pull free and she instantly darted away, crossing the shopping centre at full speed. Val hadn't realised how much of a scene she had made, and this wasn't a conversation she was willing to have with Fran; if she talked to anyone about Delta she could risk breaking the spell on her parents. She needed to move out of here and fast. She was obviously being watched. She shoved the card into her pocket. How had Delta returned? Where was she? She was going to be so mad with her, but Val was madder and she wasn't scared of a stupid, blonde, skinny Delta who had possibly managed to time travel from the sixteenth century all on her own.

"I asked what's going on, Val?" Fran's voice showed real concern.

"Stupid girl used to pick on me at school, so I thought it was time I showed her that I had grown up," Val replied. Fran's expression of unease didn't falter. "I would like to go back to the bookshop now." Val ended the conversation by walking back to the table, collecting her bags and heading back to the car park.

Still frowning, Fran followed hot on her heels. As they got into Wendy's Morris Traveller, Fran asked, "Many more people upset you that I should know about?"

"Not worth worrying about," Val said dismissively as they pulled out, looking out of the car window and letting the world pass her by as she thought about the possible consequences of the message in her pocket.

As they arrived back at the shop Wendy was waving goodbye to some regulars. Val had completely forgotten she had a business to run. As soon as Fran had parked she jumped out of the car and ran up the stairs.

"I'm so sorry; I should have been here." Val dropped her shopping bags in the entrance.

"They had some reserved books to collect so I just let them in and dealt with them. Don't worry, we don't want to raise too much suspicion, so being open at normal times is a good thing at the moment." Wendy closed the door behind the girls.

Val walked down to the cleaning cupboard door and knocked on it. It opened just enough for Val to see Zac's eyes peeking out at her.

"We are hiding from the people." He said gravely, signalling for her to enter.

"Wow, it's very close in here," she said leaning up against the wall.

"Was your trip productive?" Zac asked with interest.

"No." Val turned to Jason trying to change the subject before Fran arrived. "Any information on the covens?"

Jason tapped away at the laptop without even glancing at Val. "Well, no luck so far, but I've e-mailed Sam as he has access to the original drawings of the coven."

Val remembered the picture of Wyetta with their matching tattoos. She was sure Sam would be able to help; he seemed to have access through his top secret job to a great deal of useful information. When Fran walked in Jason's attention was taken instantly off Google and turned onto his dream girl. He looked up and gave her a warm smile. "Hi babe, had fun?"

Fran nodded and sat down on Jason's knee.

"Yak, love stinks," Val thought to herself.

"I'm sorry, Val. Do you require to be seated on me?" Zac looked from Fran to Val.

"NO!" Val replied sharply. Zac looked taken aback by her reaction.

Jason and Fran burst into laughter. Val couldn't help but follow. Even Zac smiled, though he was still confused by the peculiar habits of these strange people.

Wendy came to the door, attracted by the noise. "What's so funny?"

"You had to be here." Val grabbed Wendy by the arm. "Tell me, my young apprentice, how many sales have we had today?" she asked as they headed back towards the counter.

"Well, it's not life changing, but for the time we managed to open, it's ok. Val, I have been making a few calls. My mother says that we can create a protection spell for the bookshop to stop Excariot coming in."

"Really? That's fantastic news. What do you need to do?" Val felt very relieved.

"Well, there's a dark moon tonight and that's considered a good moon to work against aggressors, but it is also very unpredictable." Wendy picked up her bag. "I still have time to pop to the *Mystic Box* to pick up some supplies and be back here in time to work on the spell later this evening, if that's ok?"

Val agreed and handed Wendy some money from the cash box. "Will this be enough? I don't know how much magic costs these days."

"That'll be fine. I'll be back later. And, Val, don't worry; everything will be ok." Wendy called goodbye to the others who were heading up the aisle and she was gone.

Jason and Fran arrived at the counter, "On that note I'm whisking my girlfriend away for a romantic meal of meat, vegetables and gravy that my dad has just prepared. We'll come back later," Jason said pulling Fran by the hand.

"If you need us, text, and any more school bullies just walk away. You can do it," Fran advised as they left.

Val looked around at the empty shop. In one action-packed day she had been abducted by a hunter, caught five prisoners, lost a high priestess and received a mysterious note from her ex-best friend. Eventful would be a good word to describe it.

"What should we do now?" Zac asked, looking like a lost puppy.

"We need a chat. I have a dilemma and I need your help." Val walked around Zac, who once again looked uncomfortable at being asked his opinion on anything, and flicked on the kettle. "I have a personal problem that I don't want the others to know about, but it could be dangerous. I have a criminal who needs arresting, but here on Earth we have to have a very good reason to capture and hold anyone. So, I guess I'm just going to have to watch them until they make a mistake." Val poured boiling water into two mugs.

"What crimes have they committed?" Zac took the mug she offered. "The worse crime of all: betrayal." Val took a sip of her coffee and sat on her stool.

"Are you talking about the traitor Delta?" Zac asked, sipping his coffee and politely put it on the counter.

"What?" Val spat a mouthful of coffee across the counter.

Zac, who was on the receiving end, looked at her in utter astonishment. Was this some other weird ritual? He was just about to reciprocate when Val jumped up and passed him a handful of tissues.

"Oh, I'm so sorry!" Val apologised. "It's just that you gave me such a shock. I didn't think anyone else knew about Delta. How do you know about her? Where did you get that information? You mustn't tell anyone about this." Val pulled the card out of her pocket and passed it to Zac to examine. "She sent me this today, almost in person."

Zac swallowed the mouthful of coffee he had been preparing to fire at Val and examined the card. "She says little. We have information on her in Alchany. I'm sorry that she betrayed you. I have images of her and I will keep a close guard to make sure that she does not try to enter the shop. Do the others know her?"

"They did, but when I came back from sixteen forty-five it was like she had never existed. When I mentioned her name they all looked at me like I had gone crazy."

"Ok. Question: you travelled back with Excariot and Delta to the time of the original protection spell, is this correct?" Zac was walking again, something he seemed to do whenever he had to think something through. Val nodded as he glanced at her and he turned to walk in the opposite direction. "But, when you returned, this Delta was left behind?" Val nodded again. "Ok, the answer is there. When guards travel through time you create a type of time-line. Excariot travelled with you and, as he returned to the present before you did, he travelled back on the same line. Then you returned; you were the creator of the time-line and so on your return it was closed. So, your friend..."

"Ex-friend," Val chirped up.

"Yes, ex-friend. She missed her chance; she became a nothing; lost in the past without having ever existed. She is what we call forgotten."

"So, if I understand you correctly, what you're saying is no one remembers Delta because I came back and she wasn't on the same ride." Val had a lump in her throat. How could this be happening?

"Yes. She has never existed. She is gone from your time, and is now forgotten. But my main concern is how she got back. To our knowledge only the Judges have the ability to step into time without magic, and without negative physiological outcomes."

"When you say negative, what exactly do you mean, because I've done some serious time travel recently and if my eyeballs are going to fall out I want to know."

"Excariot is a very ingenious person and he had four hundred years to prepare for something the judges do on a day to day basis. You aren't going to have any problems as you aren't human. Your friend, Delta, may not be so lucky. I can't tell you how it will manifest in her as we have never heard of a human successfully travelling through time." He sighed. "You are all so technologically backwards on this planet. Another thing that surprises me about this Val is that you're ex-friend, if she is here, has done something remarkable in a time when your technology was extremely basic." Val had to agree, they had had nothing; her mother only had one chair. Then an idea hit Val like a thunderbolt.

"She had Wyetta! I didn't have time to warn Wyetta about Delta. Could she have gotten the coven to return her to our time?"

Zac nodded. "It's possible; they managed to send you somehow. If I'm honest we have tried several times to study how the coven sent you to the future, but we still can't work out how they did it. I will ask for some assistance when I return to Alchany, but for now we must take care that Delta doesn't cause us any problems."

"I'm sorry to say I think she will be trying to make lots of problems, but if I have you then it will make it easier to keep the others safe." Val picked up Zac's coffee and handed it to him. "If you want to fit in you will need to drink this." Val opened the private door. "I'm hungry. Let's order a take-away." Val picked up the phone and was pleasantly surprised to hear a dial tone. She punched in the numbers of her favourite Indian take-away.

"Mum," Wendy called through the shop.

A happy "Hello," came back to her as her mother appeared from behind the vegetables. "Have you been to the Magic Box?" she asked.

"Yes I have. Raven sends blessings and here are all the ingredients." Wendy opened the bag.

"Good, I will gather with the others at the bookshop at midnight. The dark moon will cover us. It's unpredictable, but we should have enough power to create a protective circle around the shop." She took the bag from Wendy and placed it on the counter. "Come, eat something, you will need all your strength."

Wendy smiled and followed her mother. She knew she was right: working with magic could be exhausting.

As Wendy tucked into the vegetable stew her mother had prepared, she sat in silent contemplation. It felt strange coming back to her mum's shop from Val's. Who could have predicted that just yesterday, after a lifetime of following Val, trying to befriend her, endless training, constantly being reminded of her duty as guardian and how everything was on her shoulders, that it could all change so quickly? This was the first time in her life that talks of guarding Val and Wendy's failure hadn't been drummed into her during mealtime. Her mum had gone to call the coven and she was alone. She liked it. It felt as if the way things should be had finally arrived, and she would now be allowed a time of peace.

Jason parked his bike and he and Fran made their way up the drive to his dad's barn conversion. Shane had bought the property the year before his wife Elizabeth died. It had the most amazing studio with views across endless fields. It was here, in the attic, that Shane created his masterpieces. Jason unlocked the door and walked in, throwing his keys into a delicate glass bowl on an antique table by the front door.

"Jason," Fran's disapproval resounded in her words.

"What?" Jason shrugged. "Dad," he called into the dark house.

"Up here," Shane called to them. Jason knew he would be *up there*.

"Dad, are you going to have a break?"

"Maybe later. There's dinner for you both in the cooker."

"Ok." They knew better than to try and drag him away from his art.

Val had created a picnic area in the bookshop for their dinner and as Zac finished up chicken korma, mushroom rice, poppadom and pickles he found himself leaning back with a deep look of satisfaction across his face. "This food is truly wondrous. I have never eaten like this before. Do you feast like this often?"

"I used to do it every Friday night, but I suppose we can make it our new ritual. The guard and hunter's curry night." Val raised her glass of water into the air just as there came a knock at the door. Val jumped up and walked her now satisfied body towards the door to be greeted by, not just Wendy, but Fran and Jason.

"It's magic time." Jason made strange hand gestures behind Wendy's head.

Fran pushed him in. "I'm so sorry Wendy, but Jason missed out on maturity when they were handing it out."

Wendy turned to Jason and grabbed his hand. Startled, he stopped dead, blocking the way "If I wish, Jason, I can make you run around the streets of Arcsdale telling everyone that you are a little girl and you want your dummy. Would you like that?" Jason stood statuesquely still and then, slowly, he shook his head in response. "So, are we going to mock a power, about which you have no knowledge or understanding, and that has survived thousands of years through hidden scripts written in the blood of innocents?"

"No," Jason replied shakily.

Wendy let his hand go. "Good choice." She grinned and they all started to move into the shop, slightly more subdued than before.

"Can you really do that?" Val whispered into Wendy's ear.

"No, but it's a good lesson to learn: sometimes you have to fake it till you make it."

As Wendy walked past her, Val smiled; Wendy had a dark side that she actually quite liked.

"Ok scary lady, tell us what we need to do." Val asked.

"We will need to make room for the coven to fit in here," Wendy looked around the area just inside the entrance door, the biggest clear space the bookshop had to offer. She pointed to the idle book trolley and then the old reliable, mangled water cooler. As Jason and Zac started pulling things out of the way a knock came at the door. Val turned to see Wendy's mother standing there with a group of strangers. She moved quickly to let them in.

"Good evening, Wendy's mum," Val held the door as they all came in.

"You must call me Belinda, and a good evening to you, Val." Belinda made her way over to Wendy who was already positioning black candles in a circle. As the others entered, they all found a way to touch Val, whether with a pat on the hand or a tap on the arm, and wished her "Merry Meet".

Seeing that Val was looking uneasy, Wendy came over to her, wearing a softer than usual expression on her face.

"Everything is going to be ok, Val. These people are your family now. As a Witch you are amongst your own."

"Why do they keep 'merry meeting' me?" Val whispered.

Wendy started to chuckle.

"What?"

"They mean exactly what they say. 'Merry meet' is our way of saying hello. We don't always use it as it would bring too much attention to us, but when amongst our own we can speak freely." Wendy placed her hand gently on Val as a sign that all was good.

"So in this day and age you still have to hide your greetings?" Val felt confused and concerned.

"You will learn that we'll never be completely accepted, ever. We have more freedom now, but when others don't understand there can only ever be fear. Our only mission in life is to simply support the environment in which we have been given the gift of life. We try to work with the ebb and flow of our precious planet and moon. As a group we look after our own and never intrude on others. But please don't think that all witches are good. There are those who bring us into shame and it's these few who make our existence now, and in the future, one that will always survive behind closed doors and with secret greetings. Now, let's get you some protection." She handed Val a black candle and beckoned her over to join the other witches.

Fran, Jason and Zac positioned themselves behind the counter, their expressions enough to let Val know that they weren't going to get in the way. Belinda had set up a table display in the corner and the people who were circling her had started to chant just like her mother's coven had in the past. Val followed Wendy, gripping her candle firmly. She wondered if it would melt under the heat her hands were starting to create. She was getting very warm; maybe it was the volume of people in the shop. Wendy led Val into the centre of the circle and made her face Belinda. Then she moved back, joining the other witches who were now holding hands and circling a lot faster than before, repeating a name over and over again. To Val it sounded like they were chanting Brigit or Brigid.

Belinda leaned in towards her table and lit her candle. Suddenly and without warning, the others came to an instant standstill and the quiet rained down on them.

Belinda began to speak, her voice little more than a whisper.

"To this fire Brigid come; Goddess, sister
we are one.
By this dark moon with no light, hear me
mother on this night,
In this place and on this ground, may
protection now be found."

Val didn't know whether to rip off her clothes or throw herself at the water cooler. Perspiration was pouring down her back. She looked around to see if the heating was on the blink, but no one else seemed even close to breaking a sweat. Then they started again and this time Belinda joined them as they circled Val. This felt familiar, like the time she had done the spell to protect her parents. She started to relax as their song intensified.

Then it happened. She didn't know how or what caused it, but she was on fire. There was a gasp from all present and Wendy had to bring them back to the chanting. The flames seemed to skip up and down Val's body; her candle began melting over her hands and dripped onto the floor of the shop. The chorus reached fever pitch. Val could feel her heart beating inside her in time with them like a drum, growing, growing, growing in intensity. She was heady with the power surging through her. Then, as suddenly as before, they stopped.

Belinda stepped towards a now flaming, Val. "As it is, so be it done!" She expelled the words on a powerful breath that seemed to push Val backwards; it was as if Belinda had blown her out like a simple candle on a cake. Her fiery cloak had disappeared.

She looked around. Once again everyone in the circle was starring uneasily at her.

"Let us not forget whose presence we are in. What did you expect?" Belinda addressed the others in a stern tone.

They all nodded, then, as if embarrassed by the deep silence, they began to speak all at once. They walked around kissing each other on the cheek and patting Val on the back. Perplexed, not understanding what had happened, Val turned to look at Jason and Fran who were moving around putting things back to normal. They had been witness to Val's crazy experience, yet they all looked as if nothing unusual had happened. The only person who seemed disturbed was Zac, who was still behind the counter and staring at her with an appalled expression.

"Are you ok?" Val moved towards him, careful not to get too close.

"You are different. I have never seen a guard do that. How... why can you do these things?" Zac actually looked scared of Val.

"Actually that's the first time I have set myself on fire without assistance, so it's all new to me." She grinned, trying to make light of the situation.

"Guards use their hands as weapons, but I have never seen such power. No wonder Excariot needs you. It seems that a witch mixed with a guard is a very powerful reject." Finally he lost the scared look. "Coffee?" he asked.

"Zac, you read my mind." Val was pleased she had at last impressed him.

She felt a light tap on her shoulder. "Excuse me Val, but we must be making a move. We have done the best we can do and this spell should stop Excariot from entering the shop. However, his power is great and he has his own magic so we will have to keep our fingers crossed." Belinda embraced Val. "Merry we meet and merry we part, Val, so that we may meet again." Belinda placed a kiss on Val's cheek.

"Yes, all of that and come back whenever you want," Val replied.

"Come, it's time to leave." Belinda beckoned to the other witches and they all followed her out.

"I will see you in the morning if you're sure you're ok," Wendy said, also preparing to leave.

"Well, I'm feeling a little safer and a lot cooler now," Val responded. "Do you think the wax will come off the floor boards?" she asked as she followed Wendy to the door.

Wendy laughed and shook her head in mock despair, then followed her mother.

"So, our turn now," Fran pitched in as she grabbed Jason's hand and dragged him towards the exit.

"Are you sure you're ok, because we can stay?" Jason asked.

"No, I'm fine. Go home and rest. I'll see you all in the morning." Val pushed them out locking up behind them.

She turned out the lights and headed upstairs, ready to get some sleep. Then something occurred to her and she turned to Zac who was following. "What do you hunters do at bed time?"

"I should stay here tonight just in case Excariot returns." Zac said.

"What exactly will you do if he does? You don't fight so you will become the hunted, not the hunter. Go back to Alchany. We can talk in the morning about what has to be done next. I'll stay here with the door open so you can return if any escaped prisoners decide to hijack any more bodies. Ok?" Val was tired. The day had been one of the longest she could remember, and she had been through a few odd days recently. Now she just wanted a little time alone to take it all in.

"If that is what you want me to do, then I will." Zac walked up to the portal. With one glance back he was gone, leaving only a brief shimmer on the face of the gateway.

"Bye." Val waved at nothing and smiled. She ran a bath and laid out her new clothes on the bed. She still didn't want to sleep in it so another night on the nest she had created was the only other option.

She sank into the warm water amongst a mountain of foam, thanks to some ancient bubble bath for old men. She knew she would smell like her granddad afterwards, but who cared. She started to wash and noticed her bare arm. There was no tattoo. The one thing that had been constant was now gone. "Time for change," she told herself as she washed her arm clean.

She got dried, dressed and into her new pyjamas behind the door, just in case the people behind the portal could see in; she wasn't brave enough to close it just yet.

Then, lying on the floor next to the bed, she flipped the switch and the room became cloaked in darkness. She very much doubted that she would fall asleep, but she barely lasted sixty seconds before she was snoring like a baby.

As her breathing deepened, a figure came through the portal. Moving cautiously in the darkness, it moved to the bed next to Val and sat down.

CHAPTER 3

The Connection

Opening her eyes Val realised that she was looking at a highly polished pair of military style boots. Her prison guard instinct kicked in and she leapt to her feet. She would have taken her visitor by surprise had she not forgotten that she was inside a sleeping bag; as quickly as she rose she fell. Luckily a pair of strong arms grabbed her, saving her from an undignified sprawl over the wooden floor.

"Good morning, Val," Zac said as he pulled her to her feet.

"What are you doing here so early? Is there a problem?" Val started to pull off her bag.

"No, I just thought an early start would be good," Zac lied. "You have much to learn and I have much to teach you." He offered Val his hand as she clambered out of the bag.

"First juice and cereal, then we go and find our missing priestess." Val pointed to the kitchen. Pulling a carton of orange juice and a box of cereal from the cupboard, she filled two glasses and two bowls. Zac watched with great interest as she poured milk over the cereal. Putting it all on a tray she headed back to the bed, pushing her clothes to one side so they could sit and eat. Zac was really getting into the consumption side of things Val thought, watching him clean his bowl. The orange juice was not such a success and his pained expression spoke a thousand words. 'Note to self: orange juice will not to be on the menu again,' Val joked.

When they had finished, Val handed Zac the keys to the front door. "You go downstairs while I get ready."

"But what if..."

"OK, stop talking. I need to get changed and I am going to do that alone. Nothing will happen and anyway, Wendy will be here any minute." He took the keys begrudgingly and did as he was told.

She looked at the clothes she had purchased the previous day and wondered what Sam would like best. Then she pinched her arm. "Get real," she whispered as she picked up the trusty t-shirt and Jeans.

Val headed downstairs to find Wendy and Zac, already buried in her dellatrax.

"Morning Val. Did you sleep well?" Wendy smiled over the top of a huge leather bound volume.

"Yes thanks, first dreamless night I've had in a while. What is our next move, oh clever one?" Val asked Zac.

"We need to connect our links as soon as possible. It will help us work more efficiently."

"Uh?" Val shook her head. "Links? What links?"

Zac reminded himself to be patient, but Val really didn't know *anything*. "When a guard is born he is connected with his hunter and from the beginning they are together for the vast majority of the time. Obviously we have never had a female guard so things may have to be slightly different for you and me."

"Slow down, cowboy. What is this connection business, because you are *so* not my type," Val said feeling worried.

"First things first. We must connect our signals." Zac lifted his sleeve to reveal a bracelet. Its appearance was similar to Val's, but instead of being in a V shape it simply circled his arm. "And what is this *type* thing you speak of?" Zac looked from Val to Wendy.

"Oh, bracelets, good." Val let out a sigh of relief. "The type thing is just something we say when two peoples' DNA doesn't quite match."

"Right," Wendy nodded impressed with Val's answer.

"Irrelevant. We must get on." Zac moved towards Val and held out his hand.

"So we just touch bracelets, then?" Val had butterflies in her stomach. This felt so odd and yet she knew that it had to be done.

She pulled up her sleeve to reveal the bracelet her father had left her. Her hand gently moved towards Zac's, then she stopped. "Will it hurt?"

Zac shook his head.

Val reached for his hand and they were connected. She could feel the floor falling away as if she was in an elevator, yet they were both stationary. All she could sense was what seemed to her to be Zac's heart. She knew it was him. He reached into her soul. They were all alone in the universe and their bracelets where making the strangest noises and flashing happily away in sync. She couldn't get over the fact that she felt so at one with him; it was like he was the brother she had never had. They really were connected.

Then it stopped. The lights, the noise the sense of connection gently faded, and Val felt the floor returning. Instinctively they released each others' hands.

"Is that it?" Wendy looked between them. As far as she could tell, nothing had happened, yet Val and Zac were just staring into each other's faces as if something very important had just taken place. Then Val shook her head, almost as if waking from a dream.

"Are you seriously telling me you didn't see any of what just happened?"

Wendy shook her head.

"It was amazing; we were truly connected." Val turned to Zac who was almost back. "Come on mate, I see now that I have a lot to learn, and some witches to find." Val pulled him over to the books and they all sat and studied the morning away.

Fran and Jason arrived around eleven at which point the shop was open and quite busy with the usual bookworms.

"Hi guys," Fran greeted them, adding to their pile of books with a few of her own.

"What's all this?" Wendy enquired, starting to pick through them.

"Jason received them in a parcel this morning, from Sam; something about local history." Fran walked off towards the cupboard as Jason came in with another pile.

"Where does this guy get his stuff from and doesn't he sleep?" Jason dropped them on to the counter.

"Wow, these books are really old," Wendy said stroking the covers gently.

"You make me glad I'm a geek." Jason smiled and walked off after Fran.

"Where is this Sam?" Zac asked. Val sensed his apprehension on the subject.

"He's moving here to Arcsdale. Don't worry; he's just a really cool guy who gave me my sword and the stuff that Jason uses to track me. He's Shane's best friend, if that makes you feel any better, and I'm going to his house for lunch. So on that note I'm off."

Val stood grabbing her bag. "Are you ok to close the shop over lunch and open up this afternoon if I'm not back in time, Wendy?"

"Is that a joke? Look at all these goodies." Wendy's eyes didn't leave the books as she gave Val a dismissive wave.

Val could see that Zac wasn't at all pleased to see her go, but she still had to have a life. Anyway, Sam might have some valuable information to pass on.

"You can contact me on my mobile if you need me." She waved her phone at him, turned and left. The bus ride was pleasant. Just leaving the shop and not having to try to capture someone made a pleasing change to the recent full on approach.

She jumped off the bus, checking the card he had given her one more time, and walked along the road towards his new house. Luckily Arcsdale wasn't that big and she was familiar with the area. As the address came into view, Val saw Sandy the TVR parked with tender loving care on the driveway. She had to admire the size of the place. Whatever Sam did for a living, he clearly earned a pretty decent wage. Making her way to the front door she instantly recognised that it was made out of cherry wood in a classic design. She gently passed her hand over it. Her dad had taught her well. She rang the doorbell and waited patiently.

It opened and there he was, her personal dream guy. Today he was wearing jeans and a black skin tight t-shirt. A million questions shot through her head and then she pulled herself back to reality.

"Val, I'm so pleased you could make it. Come in." Sam stepped to one side to allow her in.

"How could anyone smell that good?" she thought to herself.

The entrance was as beautiful and impressive as the exterior. Val looked around her at the open gallery staircase leading to what seemed like an endless landing. The floor was a classic slate and made it seem almost as if she had been transported back in time. There were few pieces of furniture, but each one was well thought out and placed perfectly. Attention to detail was obviously a priority for him.

"Sam, your house is breathtaking; actually it's close to perfect." Val complimented him as they walked down the corridor.

"It's nearly finished. They're still making a few minor changes, but I'm really pleased with the outcome." He pushed open a door and they walked into the kitchen. Marble surfaces, a sheet glass wall and the minimalist design gave Val shivers down her spine.

"I don't think I've ever been in a more exquisite room in my life." Val walked to the glass wall to admire the garden. "Sam, it's just such an amazing work of art. Who built this?"

"This man did," Sam answered. Val turned to look as he opened a side door. "How's it going today?" Sam asked as he shook Val's dad's hand.

"Morning. Not much more to do," Mike greeted him, and then spotted Val. "Sorry, I didn't know you had a guest. I can come back later." He smiled awkwardly at Val and turned to leave.

"No, Mike. Please come and meet my friend. She was just admiring your work. No, let me rephrase that; she was telling me it was almost perfect." Sam glanced across at Val who was starting to feel faint. Mike crossed the room towards her. If she had been a little braver she would have thrown herself through the glass wall in an attempt to escape.

"Thank you. That's a big compliment from such a young lady. What exactly is it that you like?" Mike wiped his dusty hand down his shirt and offered it to Val. She could feel the pain of tears burning behind her eyes. This was too much. She reached out and their hands joined. An overwhelming feeling of safety and love flushed through Val's body. She just wanted him to wrap her in his arms and tell her it would all be ok, like he had when she was a little girl. But that would never happen again and this was not a good position for her to be in.

"Hello?" Sam said waving his hand in her face, snapping her out of the trance she was in.

"I'm sorry," she said releasing his hand. "I thought the Cherry wood front door was breathtaking and this glass wall," Val turned, almost like a robot, towards the wall, "is a touch of genius." She could smell his aftershave; it was his favourite *Hugo Boss*; she had bought him a bottle for Christmas.

"That's impressive. You obviously have a good knowledge of buildings and thank you for the compliments."

Val nodded her acknowledgement as Mike turned to Sam. "Sam, I just came to tell you that the garage is nearly finished. On that note I will leave you to admire my work." He turned back to Val. "Sorry, I didn't catch your name."

"It's Valerie." She was still unable to move. He was going to leave and that would be it. She was no better off than Delta: forgotten.

"What a coincidence. My grandmother was called Valerie; it's not a very common name. Well, it's been a pleasure meeting you and I hope you like everything you see," Mike chirped, pleased with his new fan. As he walked away with Sam, Val leaned on the cool marble counter concentrating on taking one breath after another. It felt like her whole chest was about to collapse with the pain. How could this have happened? What were the chances of Sam getting her dad to build his house? Then she remembered her mum telling her about some important cash job her dad had won. Sam had been the one all along. Her dad had known Sam for months. She realised she had to calm down or Sam would know something was wrong. She took a few deep breaths and stood up straight Just as Sam came bounding back in.

"He's such a nice guy; seemed impressed with your knowledge," he said as he made his way over to a black double fridge and pulled it open. "OK, what do you want to drink? I have Pepsi, juice, tea, coffee or just about anything else you can think of."

"Pepsi sounds great," Val replied pushing up the corners of her mouth to create the impression that everything was ok. She would have to see the good in this situation. She had just come face to face with her dad and he definitely hadn't remembered her. Sam also obviously didn't have a clue who Mike was, so the spell had definitely worked.

"I have prepared us some food in the dining room. Follow me." Sam handed Val a large glass and she did as she was told.

Another room and yet another stunning design. She now felt guilty that she hadn't realised it was her dad's work. It had his signature written all over it. Along the length of the room was a sturdy oak table, leading to French doors that opened out onto an elevated patio. She had always felt that her dad's greatest creation was Delta's house, but this definitely topped it. Then she saw the spread on the table. This guy could cook! She was starting to think that he was too good to be true, but she must remember that this was the Sam of the future, not the Sam from her past. There were no romantic ties here and she must keep that in mind.

He pulled a chair out for Val to sit down. "So how's it all going?"

"Well, apart from meeting my hunter who's turning out to be a great guy, catching a load of prisoners at the Snakes and Ladders, and casting a spell to protect the shop, it's quite boring. Ah yes, and let's not forget the high priestess that was kidnapped by Excariot yesterday. But you know about that and thanks for the books." Val shoved a piece of celery into her mouth.

"A spell to protect the shop... Did Wendy and her friends do that for you?" Sam seemed interested and so Val began to explain as they chatted over lunch, and for a short while she felt at ease.

Sam had cleared away the table and gone to get the puddings. Val was standing in the dining room's open patio door when the doorbell rang. "Val, I have my hands full, can you get that?" he called through.

"Ok," she replied, making her way to the front door.

To her surprise, Zac was standing on the other side. "What are you doing here?" She was annoyed that he was disturbing her normality.

"We have to work. Now." Zac grabbed her arm. The blue spark flickered and they were gone.

Wendy ran down the shop towards the centre of operations, also known as the cleaning cupboard. "Jason, Fran, help."

"What's up?" Jason asked, opening the door. He could tell by her expression that something was happening, and it wasn't good.

"Zac's watch thing just started to purr, then he stood up and poof, blue spark, gone. Not even a goodbye. You don't think he'll do anything silly, like try to go it alone?" Wendy asked in an exasperated tone.

"First let's check on Val." Jason grabbed his chair and span to a halt in front of the laptop. "Looks like she's still in Arcsdale." As he spoke the computer sprang into life, numbers flashing and whizzing across the screen. "I take that back. Zac has obviously found her." They all watched patiently for her to re-appear.

CHAPTER 4

The Price of Fame

Val landed, as usual, on the ground, knees first this time, christening her new jeans in soft wet mud.

"What exactly are you doing?!" she yelled at Zac who landed as if he had just jumped off of a five-inch curb.

"Our job." Zac grabbed her arm, lifting her to her feet, then placed his finger on her lips to keep her quiet.

"Get the hell off of me! I'll shout if I want to. I was having lunch. Can't I even have five minutes away from the chaos?" Val shoved Zac's hand away and finished brushing herself down. "Ruined. I just put these on today. I'm not made of money, you know. I don't even know if I have a washing machine." Val was so mad that her face glowed beetroot red.

"Duck!" Zac called, but it was too late. Two middle-aged women of medium build, dressed as if they were out hiking, launched themselves from behind a bush and landed on Val's back. She collapsed back onto the ground with a startled 'poof' of expelled air. If she had been mad before it now intensified tenfold as she rolled in the mud trying to escape the two crazy brunettes who were trying to finish her off with their fists.

This time, Val didn't have to wait for that warning sensation in her arms and hands. She simply knew she was going to blow these ladies away. They were responsible for ruining her first date with Sam. She scrambled to her feet and turned to tackle them, but one reached forward, grabbing her ankle and pulling her down again, while the other struck her repeatedly. That was when she snapped. She swung her arms around yelling "Off!" and a powerful gust of wind escaped her palms, hurling both her assailants across the ground, through several bushes and, for the time being, out of sight. Her powers were growing in intensity and her speed and confidence in her ability were increasing along with them. Val leapt to her feet, calling to Zac to follow. As she began to run she turned, only for a split second, to make sure he was keeping up.

"The eagle has landed," Jason said.

"Where are they?" Fran and Wendy asked in sync.

"The Yorkshire moors."

"That's not good. Isn't that one of those Godforsaken places where people get lost and no one can find them because there's thousands of miles of nothing?" Wendy was starting to look pale.

"Hey, Val can teleport, don't worry. I'll give her a call." Jason pulled out his military style phone and dialled her number.

"Is that big enough for you?" Wendy asked. Jason smirked sarcastically back at her as he held the device to his head. To their surprise a phone started ringing in the shop. Jason hung up and tried again. The same thing happened. Wendy ran into the shop to find Val's bag vibrating under the counter.

"It's all here, chunky phone, ear piece and her sword. She's out there alone," Wendy wailed.

"She has Zac," Fran pointed out.

"So she's all alone," Jason replied.

Val spotted a derelict stone building on the horizon and headed for it as fast as her Converse trainers could get her through the thick pink and green heather and waterlogged holes. Zac was still following. All she could pray for was that they would make it there before the maniacs got to them. Val collided with the front door at speed; luckily for her it flew open with ease. She waited for Zac to enter, then thrust it shut. She looked around frantically for something to bar the door with. Spotting only a half broken chair, she grabbed it and shoved it under the door handle.

With her back against the door, she lowered herself to the stone floor of what seemed to be the main and only room. She sat still, panting and desperate for oxygen. Fumbling in her pocket she pulled out her personal mobile. "Please God let there be a signal," she whispered. "Hi Jason. Yes, I'm fully aware that I left everything in my bag. I was supposed to be having a quiet lunch. Now is not the time to tell me off. We're in some sort of abandoned building, but where?"

"Val I need to speak with Wendy," Zac whispered.

"What for?" she snapped.

"She has the answer to our problem. She can look in the dellatrax."

Val knew he was right and handed the mobile to Zac.

"Please, allow me to speak with Wendy," Zac said into the receiver and waited patiently. "Hello, you need to go to the dellatrax and look for..." Zac looked down at his watch, "...prisoner 148702, and speed would be appropriate at this point."

"For heaven's sake, Wendy, please hurry up!" Val shouted from behind Zac. "And it's fine for you, it's not you they're after." She pointed angrily at him.

"I'll stay here. Now go," Jason said watching the screen.

Wendy ran down the aisle towards the books with Fran close behind her. "Which one Fran?" she asked.

"I don't know! Look at them all."

There were at least twenty large volumes on the counter and there was nothing distinguishable about any of them. Fran was worried that they couldn't do this.

Wendy picked up the one nearest to her. Throwing the top cover open she just stared at the page. "I don't know what to do. Zac said I could do this, but he was wrong," Wendy flapped.

Fran had to do something quickly before Wendy went into complete melt down. "Give me the phone, Wendy," she ordered. Wendy willingly passed the phone to Fran.

"Zac, we need your help. Wendy doesn't know what to do."

Zac started to talk and Fran nodded and made knowing sound effects as Wendy just looked blankly at the pages. "Right. Wendy, Zac says that the dellatrax is like a life force; you can read it, but you can also sense it. He says you need to sense prisoner 148702. You can do this,"

"Sense prisoner 148702? We should have practised this. I like to study; I'm very good at studying."

Fran realised from Wendy's jabbering that this wasn't working. "Anything else that could help us, Zac? Zac..." Fran's heart literally skipped a beat. The line was dead; they had been cut off. She needed to make a decision quickly: to tell or not to tell Wendy that they were alone.

"What's he saying, Fran?" Wendy asked.

Fran put her hand up to motion Wendy to be quiet. Meanwhile she nodded as if she was receiving important information. "Ok. Zac says to use your special powers…that thing you did at the hospital."

"I can't control it, Fran, surely he realises that. It only happens when there is something in the future for me to see."

"Wendy, how does a dead Val and Zac sound to you? Can you see that? Now do it!" Fran was still faking holding the phone to her head.

Wendy placed the book she was holding down on the counter. She allowed her hands to float about an inch above the leather cover and closed her eyes. "I can't promise this will work as I…" Before she could finish the sentence, her body started to shake violently, although her hands were fixed over the book.

Fran stepped back, her jaw almost dislocating. Val's power was awesome but this was scary beyond words.

Then Wendy stilled. Her eyes were pure white so Fran knew that it was show time. Slowly she pulled the phone away from her head. Wendy lifted the cover and the pages started to turn, flying at a velocity no normal person could possibly achieve. As Fran watched, symbols began to peel off the page. They rose into the air and turned into neon blue holograms, floating around Wendy and the book. Fran made out symbols that resembled the one on Val's tattoo. If it hadn't been such a tense moment she would have said it was pretty.

Wendy's body suddenly became completely rigid and she hadn't blinked since she started. The pages seemed to slow and then stop. She looked and there, on the open page, was prisoner 148702. "Bingo!"

Fran looked down at Jason's phone, pressed re-dial and then started to pray.

There was an immense thud against the door. Their attackers had arrived. Zac had lost his signal and was wandering around the room, as instructed by Val, holding the phone up high, looking for some strange lines to indicate that he could make another call. "Primitive!" he kept shouting as another bang came. Val was holding the door shut with only her own bodyweight and that of the chair, and the two women outside weren't as tired as she was right now. Just as the third collision struck the phone started to ring. Zac looked nervously from the phone to Val.

"Green button! Press the green button!" Val screamed.

He looked at the phone and smiled as the penny dropped. "Fran! Have you found the information we require?" Zac asked as he started to walk towards Val.

Val shouted at him, "No! Don't move! You'll lose the signal. Stand still!"

Zac froze. "Yes. Yes. Oh, those two. I remember reading about them. Not a good story, they..."

"ZAC!" Val was ready to blow as another jolt almost knocked her clear of the door.

"Sorry, Val. Fran, please give me the information I require." Zac listened intently, visibly processing everything that Fran was saying, then shoved the phone into his pocket. "These two are a pair of cargo thieves. They stole from all over the galaxy and we had great difficulty catching them. They are Chellemi. Fran says that in the dellatrax it says their weakness is their obsession with guns, gold and precious gems."

"Great. I will beat them to death with my purse. Oh no, I don't have one. Or I could club them with my diamond rings, of which I have even less. What good is this information to us?"

It was too late. With one massive final blow, the door blew Val across the room. She struck the wall and collapsed onto the floor. The Chellemi were in and they quickly made their way to Val's body.

They seemed to move as one in an almost feline fashion. The darkest haired of the two, bent down close to Val's face. "We have been sent to destroy you, guard, and the fact that you are a female and the daughter of Gabrielle has made the price on your head even greater." She flicked her tongue out, tasting the air and Val could smell her rancid breath. The two women then proceeded to brush against each other's arms in celebration, almost like cats. Val felt completely repulsed.

"Wait," Zac called from behind.

"What do you want, hunter?" They looked at him in disgust.

"I have something greater than money or the life of this pathetic guard for you." Zac reached into his pocket and pulled out a bracelet.

"You would give us a portal key for the life of this thing?" The dark haired women asked, kicking at Val with the edge corner of their boots.

"It's no good to me now, but it would be to you." Zac waved it at them and they seemed hypnotised by it. Turning towards him they moved as one in his direction.

"How can we trust that it will work?" The leader of the two women held out her arm towards it, but not quite reaching it, scared to touch it.

"You have my word as a hunter." Zac stepped forward, holding it closer to them as they recoiled nervously.

"Then the deal is done." The woman snatched the bracelet and they huddled quickly together in the corner of the room examining their prize.

"Zac, what are you doing?" Val grabbed his hand as he pulled her to her feet.

"Making sure you live to fight another day." The blue spark passed between them and they disappeared.

Zac arrived back at the door to Alchany to find Val had landed upside down on the bed. "Move. We need to get ready," he said. "And remind me that we must work on your landing; you come across as childlike when you arrive in such a manner." He held out his hand to help her rise.

"I'm trying!" she snapped pushing him away.

They entered the bookshop to find Fran holding a glass of water for Wendy. Relief flooded her face when she saw they were safe. "You had me worried, guys. Wendy had to go all psycho to find what you wanted."

"Psychic, not psycho." Wendy lifted her head and beamed at Val.

"Val has no time to talk. Show me where her things are and the page with the Chellemi on it," Zac said.

"Excuse me. I can speak for myself. So, what's going on?" Val rummaged in her bag and retrieved all her gadgets. She flicked out her sword to check it was still working then shoved it into her pocket.

"They will come as soon as they find out the portal is here," Zac warned them, scanning the information in the book. "Then they will attempt to kill us all. They have amazing strength and give no value to our lives. We only escaped because I gave them a key to our universal doorways, all over the galaxy. Aha..." Zac was now tapping his finger on the page. "This is how we can stop them."

Val looked over Zac's shoulder to see a hideous image of a slimy looking, half-human half fish creature. "Is that what they really look like?"

Zac nodded.

"Wow, gross. So what do we need to do?" Val asked.

"It says that the original guard who captured them used a trap. He and his hunter cornered them and used a slig-lock to take them back."

"I'm sorry, a slig-what?" Fran asked as Wendy finally stood up.

"A slig-lock is a powerful force field. You see, the Chellemi are very clever, cunning and hard to catch and, as I said, they put no value on life, so they will kill us all unless we can make a trade of sufficient value."

"I think we get the 'they will kill us' part now, Zac." Val needed him to stop talking for Fran and Wendy's sake. "Does the book tell us how to create this slig-lock thing or not?"

"We need a conductor of energy and a supply. They seem to have a problem with the thing you call electricity. I presume that is because in their original form they are 96.8% fluid."

"That's not good news because we Earth people also have a problem with that thing we call electricity. What sort of risk are we going to need to take?" Val asked.

Zac moved around the counter and headed for the door. "A large one; they're here."

Fran and Wendy moved towards the door behind Zac and watched as the two very angry women made their way up the street towards the shop.

"Hey, what's going on? I saw you were back. How did it go?" asked Jason, choosing that moment to emerge from the cupboard.

"Not good," Val said taking off the bracelet Sam had given her. She flicked it out, watching it uncoil rapidly and then relax by her side.

"When did you get that?" asked Jason.

"Yesterday. Now help me set it into a circle on the floor and then get the others back behind the counter."

Val stepped to the side of the water cooler and flicked out her sword. Jason laid the lasso style bracelet on the ground and went to the door.

"Come on guys, Val has a plan." Jason grabbed the girls and led them behind the counter.

"Open the door, Jason; we can't afford any damage," Val called over. "Zac, you stand on the other side of the circle, ok."

Zac did as he was told. "What's your plan..." he asked, but he was too slow and the women burst through the open doorway.

"You," the women closest to Val pointed at Zac, "where's the portal?" They stepped forward. Luckily both entered the circle at the same time. Val stepped into view and gently placed the tip of her sword onto the bracelet. She was apprehensive, not sure what would happen, but she just hoped that her small knowledge of science was correct and she had created a conductor. She need not have worried. Her father's bracelet plus the sword touching the Sam's bracelet made a powerful combination and the sparks started to fly.

The Chellemi stared around them, then they began to laugh heartily. "You are pathetic. Are you going to dazzle us to death with your light show?"

Val responded confidently, "No, I'm going to show you how not to mess with electricity on planet earth." Her free hand came back and she grabbed the water cooler. "Zac, run," she called as it started to fall.

The two women in the circle were not so confident now. They stood no chance. The cooler crashed down and the water gushed across the floor in seconds. When it entered the circle it had the desired effect and the two women started to shake and shudder. Their screams were stomach curdling. Val pulled the sword away as they fell to their knees into a pool of water and sparks.

"Zac, get them upstairs," Val ordered.

He touched both women and disappeared. Val picked up her bracelet turning the gem as Sam had shown her and watching as it resumed its original form.

"We will be back in a minute," she reassured the others as she ran up the stairs to join Zac who had deposited the bodies in front of the portal. "Call the Collector," she ordered and he placed his hand through the portal.

"Warning! Warning! Prisoners in transit," the portal called out.

"Like we didn't know," Val whispered sarcastically.

Meanwhile Zac was panicking. He desperately searched the bodies of the two women for the bracelet. When he finally found it, he quickly placed it in his pocket and glanced nervously at Val.

The Collector arrived before he could say anything.

"Good day Val and thirty-three twenty-seven. Or would you now prefer me to call you by your new earth name, Zac?" She looked from one to the other. It was amazing how she was at least a foot smaller than them, yet Val always felt like she was looking up to speak to her. "I see you have captured prisoners 148702 well done. I also hear you have created a spell to protect the shop. Very good indeed, if it works." The Collector placed her hand over the women and elevated them in preparation to take them away.

"Just a minute. I need to ask a question. Aren't these humans? Aren't they just possessed by your prisoners' spirits?" Val felt nervous questioning the Collector, but she needed an answer. "So what exactly happens to them? After all, they could have families. These women could be mums, wives or sisters."

Zac now looked as uncomfortable as she was feeling. The Collector pivoted in her direction, still holding the women with what seemed like no effort at least three feet off the ground.

"Yes, they are humans and our key objective is to never harm a human, taken by a prisoner's spirit or otherwise. I take it you want to know exactly what is about to happen to these women?" The Collector raised just one eyebrow.

"Yes and the men yesterday," Val said, ignoring Zac who was looking at her with a pleading expression.

"That's ok, Zac, Val wants answers. We take them back to the prison. Firstly they go for an extraction to make sure our prisoners are safely removed and put back where they belong. Then they are wiped clean of their memories and returned to their point of origin. Anything else I can help you with?" The Collector looked steadily at her but Val could see that she was uneasy with the line of questioning. Neither

Val nor Zac spoke. "Good." She turned, leaving them once again, alone in the flat.

They both took a deep breath and exhaled at the same time, the tension released. "Ok Zac, I need more answers. Who brings them back? Is it the judges?" Val pleaded unable to let it go that easily.

Zac looked to the portal to make sure the Collector had completely gone. "No, they have a special group who return prisoners to their places of origin when they are in their new bodies ready for release, and they can also return the humans," he said uneasily, looking every so often towards the portal as if someone might jump through at any second. "Some call them 'the Returners' others call them 'the Darks'. We don't get to see them as it would put us at risk. The humans go to the extractors, as the Collector said, then the Returners clean any memories they have of their experience and place them back here. We don't interfere with them. They are a group apart from the rest."

"So up until the point they are returned, the humans will know exactly what's happening to them?" Val felt disturbed that those poor women today had been high jacked, then electrocuted. Now they would be extracted, then they would have their memories wiped, all because of Excariot's emotional issues.

"Yes, but you cannot get involved. They are alive and so we have done our job."

"Ok. Next, why is it those women trusted your word like that?"

Zac made his way over to the bed and sat down, his expression visibly emotional.

Val joined him. "What's wrong? We're a team, if you can't tell me then how can I trust you?"

"Everyone knows, even criminals, that hunters don't lie. The bracelet would open portals all over the galaxy, that's true."

"So, where did you get it from?"

"It belonged to my guard and this is the thing I didn't tell the Chellemi: it will only work for someone with the same strand of DNA." He held the bracelet pensively in his hand. Val placed her hand gently on his. He flinched momentarily then relaxed again. "We were connected at birth. We worked together as *one* for two hundred and thirty-six of your earth years. We were as close as a hunter and a guard could be." Zac moved the bracelet between his fingers. "Then it happened. It was a dark night and we were just out checking a local hot spot for a little action when I found a nest of Tucklets, level six. We were far too confident; we walked straight into a trap. He fought bravely and I tried to get some back up for him, but they were too late. He received a fatal wound and within minutes he was gone. I took his bracelet as I didn't want anyone else to have it. The Collectors just assumed the Tucklets had stolen it. It's all I had left, Val. Please don't tell them; they will take it from me." Zac's voice was beseeching.

"*We* are one now, it's our secret. I'm genuinely sorry you lost your guard. We have been connected for only a few hours so I can't begin to imagine what it must feel like to lose someone you have been with for that long." Val patted Zac's hand and they sat, just for a moment, in united silence.

"Ok buddy, enough information for one day. Let's go see how the others are doing." Val stood to the sound of her mobile phone breaking into song.

"Here." Zac passed it to her.

It was Sam. "Oh Sam, I'm so sorry about earlier. Zac came for me and I had to work; you know how it is." Val had forgotten all about her quick departure from her lunch date. "Oh, you tracked me. You'll be telling me I'm on 'Google View' next. Yes I know it's for my safety, but," Val pushed Zac as she chatted. They went downstairs where the others were clearing up. "Yes Sam, your gadgets did come in handy. Ok, I'll see you there." Val flipped her phone shut.

"Everything ok?" Fran enquired.

Val nodded.

"What about those women, will they be ok?" It was as if Fran's mind was on the same wavelength as Val's.

Val nodded and hoped that would be the end of the questions. It would take far too long to explain, and she knew that they would be no better off knowing about the returners or the extractors.

"You're extremely muddy." Wendy pointed at Val's soiled clothes. "We need to open; you go get cleaned up. I'm sure we'll be fine without you for another couple of minutes." Wendy pushed Val back towards the flat as Fran opened the door once again.

"Are you guys sure. Because we don't have to open?" Val looked for support as she looked down at her now brown jeans. How annoying. Now she would have to find the washing machine.

"And let that evil man Excariot and his minions win? Never!" Wendy replied with determination in her voice. "Anyway, you have bills to pay, and wages."

"Fine. I'll be back in ten." Zac started to follow. "NO." Val put her hand out to stop him. "This is alone time again, just like earlier. Stay." She closed the private door behind her.

"Come on, Zac, let us men hide in the cleaning cupboard," Jason said heading down the aisle.

Fran busied herself around the shop, placing things back on shelves while Wendy found a safe place for the dellatrax under the counter. It would be easier to keep the volumes there; at least they wouldn't get sold by mistake. She was the first to hear the doorbell. Standing up from behind the counter it must have looked as if she had appeared by magic to the young man who entered.

"Hello, I was wondering if you could help me please?" He smiled at Wendy. She thought how odd looking he was. He was different; something wasn't making sense to her. She couldn't take her eyes off him. Was it his messy blonde hair or his emerald green eyes? Could it be that lovely scent he was giving off? Maybe she should speak but nothing was coming into her head just yet.

"Are you alright?" he asked politely.

Wendy was still staring. Then her brain joined the rest of her body. "Welcome to the bookshop," she mumbled.

He responded to her much slower than was normal, exaggerating each syllable as if Wendy was foreign or something. "I-need-a-book," he said, making open and closed signs with his hands as a visual aid.

Wendy was now blatantly aware of the fool she was making of herself. "Sorry, it's been a long day, what were you looking for?"

He gave a relieved grin. "Oh, ok. I was looking for something by Umberto Eco,"

"*The Name of the Rose*, a classic. Good choice and I do know that we have a signed first edition. I wanted it myself but you can't have everything." Wendy took a breath in her babbling and found herself blushing uncontrollably.

"Very impressive. My name is Daniel," the young man said.

"I'm Wendy." She circled the counter as Fran came into view.

"Hello." Fran moved in. "Is everything ok, Wendy?"

"Perfect. Please come this way." Wendy led him down the aisle.

Val ran upstairs, throwing her clothes across the room, then dived into the shower. Alien prisoners could attack at any moment. It was completely apparent that they all knew where the bookshop was and they would come looking for her if necessary. She scrambled in and out of the shower in record time and threw on another set of clothes, forcefully tugging at her wet mess of hair. She was worried that the others wouldn't be able to cope if something or someone happened. If Zac had lost his guard after two hundred odd years, what chance would they stand without her, after just two days? She must hurry.

Val came bursting through the private door back into the bookshop. "Miss me," she sang to no one. The shop looked empty. Had they all been kidnapped? She needed to find Zac and then get help. She was starting to put plan together in her mind when she heard laughter coming from one of the aisles. She moved towards the sound, but before she could close in on the fun, Fran was there to stop her.

"Don't you go any further," she grabbed Val's arm and led her back towards the counter.

"Did I just see what I think I saw?" Val questioned.

"Yes, and I'm as disturbed as you. She's our Wendy. I hope he buys and disappears." Fran tutted as she put the kettle on and pulled out some mugs. "Tell me, while we are on the subject, how did it go with you and Sam?"

Val felt all her tensions release as she thought about him. She sat down on her stool; a dreamy expression in her eyes. "His house was my dream house. He can cook as well as iron. He smells gorgeous, looks amazing and makes something inside me go soft like marshmallows over a fire." She sighed dramatically. "But he's not interested in me. In any case, I don't have time for that sort of stuff." Val folded her arms defensively, ending the discussion.

"If you say so, Val, but you have to ask yourself: what if he doesn't agree with you?" Fran shrugged her shoulders, gave Val a mug of tea and grabbed another pile of books off the counter. "Changing the subject slightly do you think many more prisoners will come to the bookshop? I'm worried about damage. Do you know if we're insured?"

Val shrugged her shoulders, "Insured? I haven't a clue."

"I'll check with Wendy when she's free." Fran turned and headed off.

Val was very glad that she had responsible people here to help her. She had never paid a bill in her life. She lifted the tea as the doorbell rang again.

When Val saw who had come into the shop, her hand shook so much that she was forced to place her mug on the safe surface of the counter.

"Good afternoon, I hope you can help me," said Eva, as she walked towards Val. "I have a reservation on a book and I was wondering if it was in stock yet?" The most shocking part was she said it all in perfect English. Val didn't know what to say. Only three days ago Eva had given birth to a baby on the floor just two feet away and could speak hardly a word of English and yet here she was, ready to take her place on Countdown.

Val eyed her warily. "Right. Well, I've just taken over so I'm not sure about reservations. Why don't you have a browse while I call one of my colleagues?" Val got to her feet. "Wendy," she called.

Eva nodded and walked off down one of the aisles. Val didn't know what women were supposed to look like three days after giving birth, but Eva was as slim and toned as a 'Girls Aloud' member.

"Are you ok?" Wendy arrived with *that* guy she had just met.

"Yes, never been better. There's a lady here called Eva. She has a reservation, but I'm not sure where we keep them." Wendy gave no sign of recognising the name.

"Yes, I found the catalogue earlier. All the reservations have been ordered and should arrive in the next few days," she said nodding at Val, then smiling up at the man who was standing very close to her. "Anything else?"

Val shook her head.

"Then I will introduce you. Val, this is Daniel." Wendy gazed at the strange looking blond guy who was now also blocking Val's way.

"Hi Daniel. Get what you were looking for?" Val had never been any good at small talk.

"Yes thanks. Wendy has such an amazing knowledge of this place. You are very lucky to have her." He didn't know how close to the truth he was, and Val had every intention of keeping it that way.

"Thank you," she responded, not bothering to smile at him. She really didn't like the look of him, but was that because he was showing Wendy some attention?

"So that's one hundred and ninety-five pounds please, Daniel," Wendy said.

"A bargain," he replied handing her the cash. Maybe he wasn't so bad after all Val thought.

"Please come again. It's always nice to meet someone who has a deeper understanding of literature," Wendy gushed, blushing furiously.

"I will be back very soon." He picked up his bag and walked backwards, never taking his eyes off Wendy till he reached the door. As he opened it he looked back one more time.

"I think I'm going to be sick." Val made vomiting noises into Wendy's ear.

"Stop it! Oh, you're so immature!" Wendy pushed Val towards the flat. "Didn't you have something to do, like save the world," Wendy said just as Eva reappeared.

"Any luck?" she asked.

"My colleague here says that they will be here in a few days," Val said. She could see by Wendy's expression that if she hadn't remembered the name, she definitely remembered Eva's face. She discreetly squeezed Wendy's arm, looking at her with an expression that said 'don't say a word'.

"I'll come back later in the week then. Thank you for your help." Eva turned and left them.

Val wasn't sure exactly what had just happened. It was as if Eva was a different person, not Brazilian any more, although she did look the same. So why had she changed?

"That was the girl! She was here. I remember her! She got beaten up by Excariot," Wendy exclaimed excitedly. "Why doesn't she remember us?"

"The witches cast a spell so that anyone who had seen me, except you guys, would forget me; I would have been in too much danger,"

"Oh yes, I see. Wow! That felt so weird." Wendy went to get a drink. "I could do with a copy of that spell. I'll go and tell Fran and the others."

"Ok," Val agreed, starting to run questions through her mind. Eva had originally drawn Val with one of the symbols on her tattoo, which meant that she was a descendant of the original witches. "Oh my God!" That meant that Eva was one of the people Excariot was trying to get. And she had just let her go back out into the world for him to capture.

"Wendy, faster," she yelled down the shop. "Get the others. She's one of the high priestesses!" She hurried to the door to see if she could still see Eva. She scanned the street but nothing. She stepped out onto the path, looking desperately in both directions. There was no sign of her anywhere. "You idiot," Val hissed kicking the wall.

"Yes, you are," a young voice came from the alley next to the shop.

Val turned with a start. She could just make out the silhouette of a young girl.

"Should you be there? It's not safe," Val told her.

Slowly the young girl came into view. She was like one of those porcelain dolls with golden ringlets in her hair and a perfect complexion and her lips were like a small rose on her pure white face. She was wearing a delicate silk dress that almost reached the floor and tiny white shoes. Val was left breathless at her appearance: she was almost angelic. "Where are your mum and dad?" she asked concerned for the child's safety.

The girl moved a little closer; for some strange reason she walked like a man. She stopped, looking Val up and down, her jaw moving as she chewed something. Disturbingly the stuff she was chewing was black.

"Are you alright?" Val asked.

"I think disappointed just about covers it." The little girl turned her head and spat something dark and disgusting onto the pavement.

"Hey what are you doing?" Val jumped in disgust.

"It's tobacco. What would you like me to do, swallow it?" The little girl laughed a deep gruff laugh - much deeper than a little girl should have. She then proceeded to reach inside her dress pocket and pull out a tin. Popping the lid she pulled out a brown shredded substance and shoved it into her mouth and started to chew again.

"God! Stop! That stuff will kill you." Val grabbed the tin from the girl's hands. The girl looked up at her, her eyes visibly tearing up. "No, look I'm sorry, but this stuff is for adults and you're just a child. How old are you?"

"Twelve. Please let me have my tin," she sniffed and then the tears started to roll.

"I'll give it you back if you promise to go home." The girl nodded and wiped her eyes on her sleeve. "Ok." Val handed her the tin.

"Sucker," the child laughed.

Val didn't know how to deal with this. "Just go away. What's wrong with you?" She had completely forgotten why she was out here. Ah yes, Eva. Well, any chance of her still being around was gone. Now she was stuck with psycho kid.

"You're looking for the witch," the girl said confidently.

"How do you know about that?" She wondered if the girl could be possessed by a prisoner; it wouldn't surprise Val and it would explain the tobacco habit. It wouldn't be the first time they had used children against her.

"Because," the girl spat again, "I am the first, the oldest of them all and I want to join your team."

CHAPTER 5

To Trust or Not to Trust

"You may be the oldest, but I'm not getting the impression that you're the wisest. Why on earth would you choose to take the body of a twelve year old girl?" Val asked.

"Hit me." The girl spat yet another mouthful of tobacco, which landed perfectly on Val's trainer.

"You're mad. That's disgusting, and I'm not going to hit you, you're just a little girl." Val stared at her shoe indignantly.

"First prize goes to the dumb guard," the girl laughed, pulling her tin out again. "Listen, I don't have much time," she said as Wendy, Fran, Jason and Zac flew around the corner.

"Are you alright?" Zac asked, eyeing the girl with a concerned expression.

"Well, sort of," Val looked at her shoe.

"I'm sorry, do you need a group hug before we can continue?" The girl asked nastily.

"Ok! Firstly the attitude needs to stop if you want to join us," Val responded.

"Since when do we take on minors?" Wendy shot a horrified glance at Val.

"She's not your average girl, are you? What's your name?"

"Flo," the girl gave an innocent wave and curtseyed to them.

"Flo is supposedly the oldest of the oldest, or something, and she wants in; she knew about Eva," Val said.

"Please tell me this is a joke. The oldest don't exist; it's a myth, a story." Zac kept his suspicious gaze fixed on Flo.

"Listen to me hunter, I was travelling the galaxy before your line had even been started, so back off." Flo pushed out her chest.

"So what are you doing here?" Zac stood his ground. He needed more proof than that to believe that she was who she was saying she was. He pulled out his watch and started to scan her.

"You can put that thing away; there are no records of my existence. That was the deal I made with the Warden." She straightened her dress like a little girl would. "We need to get indoors; Excariot will be looking for me." She started to head past them into the bookshop.

Val grabbed her by the arm and brought her to an abrupt halt. "What do you know of Excariot?"

"Ow, that really hurts!" Flo hissed. "I will tell you everything, but not here, so you have two choices."

Val wasn't letting go. She pulled her into the bookshop with the others close behind. "Talk and fast."

Flo pulled out of Val's grip, straightening her dress again and scanning her surroundings. "Nice place you have here." She went to the counter and made a sorry attempt at leaning on it like it was a bar. "If you want my help and information, madam, you won't touch me again, understood?"

"Let's get one thing clear. We aren't going to trust you until Zac tells us you're what you say you are. Now, let's hear what you have, and it had better be good." Val made her way behind the counter and sat down. The others stood on guard around the girl.

Zac stopped doing his checks, paused then spoke. "I have no record of this prisoner, but one thing does concern me: she's dead."

"What!" Wendy jumped back. "Oh my God, she's a zombie or a vampire."

Fran gave her a withering look. "Don't be silly. You read far too many books."

"The body I have was that of a girl who was about to pass away. That's true, but that's my speciality."

"Sorry, but a speciality is egg fried rice, not dead bodies," Jason remarked.

"Well, let me explain for the slower of us here, which seems to be all of you," Flo said, glaring at them. "I can jump bodies. That's why the Judges sent me here originally. They wanted to know if spirits could take other life forms. I'm one of a handful of my kind and I agreed to finish my existence here in exchange for freedom from the prison. So, for hundreds of years I have been here as Flo, not bothering anyone, until he arrived." Her forehead wrinkled as her pretty face was marred by a scowl.

"Are you referring to Excariot?" Val asked.

"No, the Easter Bunny," she hissed. "Yes, Excariot." Her expression was visibly getting darker by the second. "He changed everything. He killed and trapped for pleasure and then he found me. He knew who I was, and he used his witch to capture me."

"What?" Wendy chipped in, looking offended. "He killed witches, that's true, but they didn't work for him."

"Look, I know you children must find this sort of information hard to digest, but if you are going get upset or offended by what I have to say, maybe I made a mistake coming here." Flo turned as if to leave.

"No, stay, tell us more." Wendy put her arm out blocking the exit. "It's just a hard pill to swallow." She lowered her hand and Flo leaned awkwardly against the counter.

"Ok, so where was I? Ah yes, prisoner. So, I have worked for Excariot for the past four hundred years give or take a few. Sometimes he leaves me alone for a while, but recently with the arrival of you," she pointed at Val, "I have been extremely busy."

"Me, what do you have to do with me?" Val looked mystified. "I have never met you before."

"Well, firstly that water cooler scalded like mad, then you tied me up; you really should have taken the baseball bat with you. Then there was the time on the plane, that really scared me. Do I need to say more? Oh no, let's not forget the day you set me on fire!"

"You! You were the one who made me save all those people so Excariot could release Lailah!" Val leapt to her feet, enraged. This little girl was responsible for everything.

"I just told you I didn't have any choice. Which part did you miss? The witch has power over my actions. Well, she did until the other day when you changed everything."

"Sorry that doesn't wash with me. We all have a choice, and what changed the other day?" Val enquired.

"When you went back in time you altered something because the witch's orders have all changed. She doesn't even look at me anymore."

"I don't care. You are trouble with a capital 'T' and I think you need to go back to Alchany." Val stood up.

"Stop," Zac stepped in. "I believe her. There were a group of people who were imprisoned for a crime against their planet. The stories say it was thousands of years ago, when Alchany was just starting. It has been said that the judges chose to send a few of these spirits through the portals to find new planets to use. If what Flo says is true and she's been trapped under a spell, which is also a possibility, then we need to move with caution. I also have to add that I have never seen any spirit take a dead form; it's quite a unique ability." Flo was nodding in agreement with Zac's words. "I have also seen people on Alchany murder, destroy and commit atrocities just to follow orders without the influence of any magic. So let her tell us how she can help and maybe we can learn, instead of just following in Excariot's footsteps."

Val glared at Zac. "This thing hurt me and many other people, including children. You think we should just let her off?"

"No, but you must learn to listen before you judge, then you will become a good guard."

His words hit Val Like a betrayal. She wanted to scream into his face, but deep down she knew that he was possibly right. She took a deep breath. "Ok, but I'm only doing this for you."

"Are we all done with the talking about me and not to me?" Flo asked.

"You would do well to show my guard a little more respect; she has awesome powers," Zac commanded.

"Ok, just been here a long time, hunter." Flo raised her hands in submission. "You're right. I have been at the end of this girl's power and she has had Excariot shaking in his boots. All I want is for you to finish off Excariot and his witch and let me get on with my existence as I did before."

"What do you have to offer us?" Val asked.

"Information. I'm still trapped on the inside and he already has three high priestesses, and he's planning to catch more every day. He just sends a couple of prisoners out to distract you and sends a couple more to pick up a witch. He isn't even breaking a sweat. Can you say the same?"

"Maybe not." Val had to admit if this little girl was telling the truth it could really work for them. "So why on earth would we trust you?"

"Look, I don't care about you, or him; I care about me. But you're the only ones strong enough to oppose him so what choice do I have?" "A disturbingly honest speech, but before I take my people into a situation recommended by the oldest and wisest, I want proof. I want to know where, when and with whom he's going to attack next, and it had better work out," Val told her.

"Easy. Tonight, eight p.m. Be at this address and be ready." Flo handed Val a folded piece of paper. "I heard him saying he was sending in the Bendicks. They hunt in groups and he has at least four waiting to attack, so don't go unprepared. You will find them on your dellatrax under 6339." Flo opened her tin, shoved a handful of tobacco into her mouth and headed towards the door. "I need to leave; it has taken me far longer than I would have hoped to get such a simple message across."

"How should we contact you if we need you again, or if this all goes wrong and I have to deal with you?" Val called over.

"I will be back. Don't worry, everything will work as long as you don't go in there emotions first." Flo headed to towards the door, but Jason was blocking her way. "Please?"

Jason looked over her head to Val who nodded in agreement for her release.

"Thank you." She stepped around him, opened the door and, never looking back, walked out.

They all stood in silence for what seemed like an eternity. Then Jason asked, "Did we just have a conversation with an ancient, dead, twelve-year-old, tobacco chewing girl?"

"Yes, I think we did." Val said, shaking her head in disbelief at what had just happened.

"That was *the* weirdest thing..." Jason muttered.
"How long do we have before we have to be at..." Val opened the piece of paper. "....the warehouse behind The Party Shack, for priestess pick up?"

"About three hours. It's time to close up and we need more hands," Wendy turned the sign on to the closed sign.

"I'll call my dad." Jason pulled out his mobile.

"I'll try Sam." Val dialled but it went straight to answer machine. "Hi, it's Val. We have a problem with a child, several Bendicks, I think that's what she said, and a missing priestess. Assistance would be most welcome. We will be at the warehouse behind the Party Shack at 8 p.m. Bye."

"So, as you feel so strongly that we should trust her, tell us a little more about Flo," Fran challenged Zac, who was flapping around the dellatrax.

"Well, I thought it was all a myth. We heard stories of the oldest in training. Apparently they were sent all over the galaxy to find planets that spirits could inhabit. Until tonight it was just a story." Zac pulled a large volume onto the counter and started flipping pages.

"Why them? And why was Flo in prison?" Wendy wanted to know.

"Well story says that Sliyig, the leader, was planning to take over a planet when the Warden caught up with him. It's said that they had a battle that lasted days."

"I'm sorry, but the Warden looks like Father Christmas; I can't imagine him attacking anything but a cream cake, so it must be a myth," Val sniggered to herself.

"Show some respect!" Zac snapped, visibly irritated. "The Warden has lived for almost eight hundred years; he has captured some of the most dangerous criminals that this and the Ballany galaxy have ever seen." He turned more pages clearly annoyed.

Val backed off it feeling uncomfortable; it was obvious she was in the wrong.

After a moment he continued. "They were imprisoned for eternity, but the story goes that the judges decided to use their ability to jump bodies. This child Flo can go from one body to the next, which could be me, you or Val. So under no circumstances can we take any risks while Flo is about."

"What about Eva? How do we get her back?" Jason asked.

"The good news is she had a book reserved. If she manages to stay out of Excariot's grip she will be back here to collect it in a couple of days," Wendy replied.

"Do we have that much time?" Val looked to the others.

"We don't have any choice. We only have a few hours to get ready for this next arrest and I need Wendy to help me. Here is an image of Sliyig." Zac turned the book towards Val and the others. He was a man of huge stature, just like the men who had attacked her only a few days ago. He had thick black hair and a muscular body, with a square chin and wide set neck. Not someone you would consider arguing with.

"He doesn't look like an alien." Val said, studying the image.

"Just because he's an alien doesn't mean he's any different to me or you Val. You have so much to learn it makes my head spin." Zac rubbed the back of his neck as if he was tired.

"What's wrong?" Val asked.

"I'm unsure, but I'm not feeling at peak condition." Zac sat down on the stool. "Wendy come and connect with the dellatrax. I need you to locate prisoners 6339 so we can find out more about these Bendicks."

Wendy started to flick through the pages.

"I said connect." Zac pushed Wendy gently.

"I'm off. I can't do the white eyeballs thing." Fran headed towards the cupboard, with Jason hot on her heels.

"We'll get directions to the Shack," Jason said as they disappeared.

Wendy stood nervously with her hands floating over the volume of the dellatrax that Zac had on the counter. Zac's face twitched then, for a change, it transformed into a grin from one cheek to the other.

"Ok, what's so funny?" Wendy asked placing her hands down by her side.

"I'm sorry, but you all try so hard. The dellatrax would normally be attached to the guard at birth and they would interact naturally with it. Obviously Val can't do that, but you have a gift that works perfectly in sync with it. So, just relax." He took her hands and placed them on top of the book. "Feel it. It's alive. Forget everything you think you know about books. These volumes have all the knowledge; they are created of living things and so they are alive."

Val, who was standing, watching quietly, saw Wendy's expression start to soften as Zac held her hands.

"I can feel it. It's like its talking to me." Wendy's face lit up. She threw the cover open and started to flick, stopping every few seconds to touch the page again. Then she stopped. "Here." Wendy pointed to prisoners 6339.

"That's it." Zac patted her on the arm affectionately.

"Can I do that?" Val asked.

"No. You need to learn how to land first," Zac replied.

Wendy grinned at Val like the child who got a gold star.

"I'm trying my best." Val was just about to start an assault of whining when the door opened and in walked Shane. "At last someone who loves me just the way I am." Val grabbed Shane and he reciprocated with a hug. "Come in and I will tell you everything that has happened." She grabbed him by the arm and started to pull him down the shop.

"Hi Zac, Wendy and bye," he called.

Val spent a few minutes telling Shane about Flo and Eva, who he remembered well. Then she filled him in on tonight's little assault on the Bendicks.

"So, do we have any idea what these Bendicks can do?" he quizzed her.

"Wendy and Zac do," she huffed.

"Hey, Dad, I thought I heard your voice. Ready for some fun?" Jason bounded up and hugged his father.

"I'm sorry to be the party pooper here guys, but I'm concerned about our safety. What happened at the Snakes and Ladders was out of our control, but tonight you want us to walk into an organised fight with four aliens. I'm not happy. I need more answers from Zac before I let any of you go."

"But..." Jason started to contest.

"No son, end of conversation."

Zac and Wendy were deep in talk when the others came back. They had obviously found who they wanted and were making notes as symbols floated in the air.

"Is it just me or can you guys see the 3D light show going on?" Val asked.

"Same as before," Fran replied. "Although it's much prettier this time." She reached out to one as it passed through her fingers.

"Hello." Shane interrupted their conference.

"Sorry, we were making plans." Zac stood up. Wendy followed and the holograms disappeared.

"So what's with the lights?" Val was intrigued.

"Oh, Wendy is doing that. The dellatrax likes her and she has a vast knowledge of Theban, one of the languages we use."

"That's great Zac, but I need some more information before I send my son and his girlfriend into a dangerous situation."

"Yes sir, I understand, that's why they aren't going. Wendy is going to create a spell for us to protect the high priestess. As soon as we find her we will be able to cloak her from Excariot and his spirits and she will be safe. Only myself and Val will be in danger."

"Great," Val replied mockingly.

"No, you need to give me more information before you take Val. There are four of these things so she tells me and at the end of the day I'm the only adult here so I need to look out for her."

Val felt a lump forming in her throat.

"Shane, I have over two hundred years of experience and this is Val's duty. She has no choice. Nevertheless, your emotions are touching," Zac replied.

"And I have eighteen years as a dad, which you have no knowledge of, so give me more information or I will be taking Val home with me tonight." Shane was serious and they could all sense it.

"Yes, of course. Look at this: Prisoners 6339." Zac tapped the page. "Bendicks are quite a high level prisoner, but they only have one ability."

"And that would be?" Shane enquired.

"They can cloak themselves,"

"What, like Harry Potter?" Jason asked.

"Who is Harry Potter?" Zac looked for support.

"Stop it." Fran pushed him. "What exactly does this cloak thing do?"

"They can become invisible."

"That's not so bad, no death rays coming out of their eyes; I think we should be ok," Val proclaimed confidently, but Shane shook his head. "Look Shane I know you're finding this hard, but I trust Zac and I'm still here, ok."

"I want to look after you, I can't do anything when you disappear, and it's a hard pill Val."

"Sorry to interrupt; has anyone noticed the time?" Wendy pulled at Shane's arm and looked at his watch. "It's nearly seven already. We need to get ready." She was right. Val started to get her things together.

"We need to go to the Magic Box for supplies." Wendy grabbed her bag.

"I wish to come and see this place." Zac decided, following her.

"Ok, we'll wait here for you to return." Val smiled although she felt a little put out. He was *her* hunter and why was Wendy so special? It was her dellatrax and *she* should be bonding with it, no one else. She waited until they had left and Shane, Jason and Fran had all gone to squeeze themselves into the cupboard, then she pulled one of the dellatrax volumes onto the counter. "Ok, feel its life force," Val said to herself. She placed her hands over one of the pages, surprised that she instantly felt a tingling sensation. "Not so hard after all," she thought.

That was when it all went wrong. Val's hands slammed uncontrollably onto the book and some invisible force held them there. Images flashed aggressively around her head. Not the soft neon blue that Wendy experienced, but shades of black, sharp and ugly in form. This wasn't how it was supposed to be. Her eyes started to cloud over, but she couldn't wipe them as her hands were now stuck to the pages. Suddenly everything went black. There was silence. She was alone, somewhere she had never been before and she could hear voices.

"How did it go?" the man asked. Val knew who it was straight away: Excariot.

"They suspected nothing," a female voice responded.

"Will they trust you?"

"Yes. They have no reason to doubt me, Excariot. Now let me get on with what I have to do,"

"Release the Bendicks and get the priestess here now," he shouted into the darkness.

Once again Val could feel herself moving. The book suddenly released her hands and she dropped to the ground with a large enough thud for the others to come running.

"What happened?" Shane gripped her under her arms and lifted her to her feet.

"Excariot has let the Bendicks out and I think Flo is a double agent!" Val looked around for her sword. It was on the counter ready to go. She shoved it into her back pocket. "I need to leave now. He has sent out the Bendicks and that means that the girl is already in danger." Val didn't know what to do. She had no hunter and no tattoo. What good was she on her own? "Damn!" She felt useless. Then she thought about what Zac had said. This was her duty; it was about time she started to embrace it.

Everything Zac did he seemed to do as second nature. She had never seen him stop and think about how he was going to teleport, he just did it. Maybe she just needed a little more confidence in her ability.

"Shane, I'm going to save the priestess. Please tell Zac where I have gone." She looked around her; at the others who were staring back with blank expressions. They obviously believed it about as much as she did.

"Do you want a lift?" Jason asked.

"No, I think I will teleport thanks," Val replied, trying to sound confident. 'Come on, disappear,' she thought. As the seconds ticked by the situation was becoming more and more awkward. Val felt crosser than ever. She had heard Excariot sending the Bendicks out, and that girl was going to be in danger: a situation that she was supposed to be getting her out of. Oh, and then there would be Zac with, 'trying to teleport on your own, we need to work on your landings, blah, blah, blah'. Well, she may as well give up because the only thing she could do was electrocute people and fall flat on her face.

Fran broke the silence. "Thinking of going anytime soon or should I put the kettle on?"

Val was really mad now; she was making a fool of herself. It was entirely her real parents' fault. If they hadn't met... She looked down at her father's bracelet. That was the answer! She reached out and held it, just as Excariot had when he had come back to the future from sixteen forty- five. A blue spark appeared and she was off.

CHAPTER 6

Invisibility!

She let the feeling of the journey wash over her. Success! Zac would be so proud of her, she thought as she hit the wall face first, before falling backwards and landing flat on her bottom behind a pile of boxes. "Ok, must keep that one to myself," she whispered.

She knelt up, looking over the top of the brown cardboard wall into a very empty warehouse. Why would a high priestess be seen dead in a dump like this? It had to be trap. That Flo was going to get it next time Val found her.

She froze when she heard a grating sound coming from the corner of the warehouse. She peered into the shadows and then a crack of light appeared as a door opened. A young woman entered, looked warily around her and pulled the metal door shut. Making her way to the centre of the building she crouched down and started to write something in the thick layer of dust that had settled on the floor. Val stood up; this would be easier than she had thought. She would get the girl and teleport her back to the shop, and Zac would give her a brownie point.

"Hey, you," Val called.

The woman looked up, startled at the voice and the presence of another person.

"Hi, I'm Val. I know who you are and I'm here to help you." Gosh, it was starting to feel like the old days. She clambered over the cardboard and took a step towards the girl. She wasn't sure how, but the next thing she knew she was on her knees in the dirt, wondering why her back hurt.

The woman looked panicked by Val's new position and ran for the door. She screamed when a man materialised in midair, blocking her way. He grabbed her arms and held on to her.

"What did I tell you? They can cloak," came a voice from behind her." Zac had arrived just in time to watch Val failing. "Get up," he ordered, pulling her to her feet. "The others are safe at the bookshop, but you need to get her back." He shoved Val towards the struggling woman.

"Pleased to see you," Val grunted, pulling out her sword. Almost immediately she was struck again, from the side this time - no warning, not even heavy breath - and she was on the floor again.

"Please try and sense them," Zac begged, watching anxiously.

"I will try, but I'm not the sensing one." She pulled herself up again. In the time it took her to stand up they had struck her again and down she went. Zac was waving his arms and Val's ears were actually starting to ring. While she sprawled on the floor waiting for the world to stop spinning, the three Bendicks who had been cloaked appeared. She was surrounded. They were all identically dressed and had clearly been working on a building site nearby.

"We don't need to cloak ourselves with this little girl," one of the men laughed derisively.

Another tapped Val with his boot.

Val pulled herself onto her knees, anger that they were laughing at her starting to overcome the pain.

"Stop right there!" A new voice echoed across the empty warehouse. Val looked up with a start. It was Sam, and behind him were Jason, Shane and Wendy. Three of the Bendicks instantly cloaked themselves again; the one holding the priestess dragged her into the corner.

Jason, Shane and Wendy looked bewildered. "If we can't see them how do we fight them?" Jason asked.

"Sensei here says we need to sense them," Val shrugged pulling herself onto her feet.

"I note mistrust in your voice, Val," Zac looked insulted.

"Nothing personal, but you choose the worst times to teach me a lesson," she said extending her sword again and circling. "Have you got the spell, Wendy," Val asked as she jabbed into the nothingness. Wendy waved a small pouch in the air. The men were still surrounding her.

Val was suddenly stuck across the face but this time she was half expecting it and managed to only fall to her knees.

"That's enough!" Her anger flared and the frustration in her voice shook through the air. Her stomach was in knots. She needed to stop this before these Bendicks made her look any worse in front of everyone. She took a deep breath and she pulled the energy from her stomach. It bolted down her arms, slamming her hands, palms down, flat onto the floor with such power that it shook the ground. It took a moment for her friends, who were struggling to stand on the trembling ground, to realise what she had done. A thick cloud of dust had rose and through it they could clearly see the Bendicks' silhouettes.

"Now," Sam called running forward, pulling out, to Val's surprise, a sword like hers. Shane was already face to face with one dusty man and felled him with one expert blow. Sam had another cornered; with his sword to help him, he too was winning. Val jumped to her feet and ran at the priestess, but the Bendicks that had her and had been in plain sight, now disappeared. Val span around, her sword ready and her free hand facing palm out in front of her, set to release whatever may come. She felt more confident now. And then, without realising how, she sensed him. He was to their left. She could feel his breath on her neck. She pivoted and landed a jab straight into the centre of his face before he had a chance to move, and he was down.

She grabbed the priestess by the hand and ran towards Wendy and Jason who had been left on guard. "Give her the potion," Val ordered.

"What once was seen, be now forgotten." Wendy tipped what looked like a handful of ash on the woman's head and the battle was over. Sam and Shane who were still in mid-fight were astonished when the Bendicks came to an abrupt halt.

Val looked around her; they had gone from brawl to nothing in just a few seconds. The stillness was quite eerie.

"Why have they stopped?" Jason asked.

"Well, my guess would be that they don't know who they are looking for any more; Wendy's little spell has worked," Val responded. Sam prodded one of the Bendicks with the tip of his sword, moving him with small shocks towards the others who were suffering from various injuries. "What now, Zac?" Val turned to look for her hunter and was shocked to see him just staring blankly at her. "Are you ok?"

"Get them tied up and let's go." Zac pushed past Val and started to wander around the perimeter of the interior staring at his watch. Val did as she was told, which was quite easy as the men were now being restrained in a corner by Sam.

"Zac says I need to tie them up. How glad am I to see you." She patted him on the arm.

"You were lucky. Wendy and I came together from the Magic Box; and Jason and Shane came on his bike. Zac wasn't at all happy that you had travelled alone."

"Well, he will have to deal with it. What can we tie them up with?" Val watched as Sam pulled some plastic cord out of his pocket and started to bind the men together. "Oh, question. Where did your sword come from? I thought that was my thing?" Sam roughly jerked two more hands together. "Ok, what on earth makes you think I'm going to come into a situation like this unarmed?" Sam looked at her, tutted and then passed her the four Bendicks, all neatly tied together.

"Well, I thought mine was special." Val touched his arm.

"Come on, Wendy, let's get you home." Sam walked away.

"If that's it, me and Jason will get off. We left Fran on her own so we need to get back to the bookshop. See you when you teleport back." Shane pulled Jason in close as they headed out.

They all left as quickly as they had arrived, leaving her alone with Zac and the Bendicks.

"I'll see you there," she called.

"We must leave now," Zac came over, grabbed Val, and in an instant they were back in the flat, outside the portal. Luckily for Val, the Bendicks were good at landing and because she was holding the arm of one, she arrived in the upright position for a change. She hoped Zac would notice, but he already had his hand through the portal. The Collector arrived to find them all standing waiting as if for a bus.

"Good job! Four Bendicks if I'm correct." The Collector looked them up and down. "The Warden will be pleased. How did you get them?" She looked genuinely interested for a change. Val was pleased, but Zac was grumpy and impatient, looking at his watch as if the Collector was wasting his time.

"Val created a dust cloud to make them visible then the humans, Sam and Shane, fought alongside her. The witch, Wendy, cast a spell to hide the priestess while Jason protected her, and that was it," Zac said.

"Right, well done." The Collector didn't even have to touch them. They did as her tiny hand commanded and were gone.

"I will see you later." Without further explanation, Zac walked past Val and disappeared through the portal, just seconds behind the Collector.

Val stood there, unsure of what had just transpired. Zac had never been so visibly distracted. He had left and she had no idea when he would return. Clearly something was upsetting him. But what? She needed to find out; he was her hunter after all. She stepped closer to the portal. She hadn't travelled to Alchany since her first visit and wasn't sure if this would hurt, or even if she would arrive in one piece.

She placed her hand onto the mirror-like image the portal reflected into the room, and her hand slipped through. "It's now or never..." She pushed forward and was off. It felt faster than her normal teleporting. She could feel her body coming apart. Just as she was starting to worry, she was thrown out on the other side. It was like shooting out of one of those rapids she had ridden on at a water park as a little girl. She didn't know whether to whoop or cry.

Unfortunately she landed on top of five very small people. She jumped quickly to her feet. "Er, sorry about that." She started to pick them up. She felt like a giant. They were very annoyed and brushed themselves and each other down, grumbling and rubbing at imaginary bruises. At that moment it dawned on Val exactly what they were. "You're Collectors," she announced, pointed at them, waving her hands about like a tourist.

"And you are the reject," one of the men replied venomously.

"Thanks," she grinned as they all stormed off in different directions.

This wasn't exactly going to plan. She needed to find Zac. She looked around spotting a mixture of characters: more Collectors, and some strange creatures of various shapes, sizes and origins. She would have been completely freaked out if she hadn't already seen the pictures in the dellatrax. The Collectors seemed to have them under their control. This was clearly the next step in the process and must be where the Collector came before taking the prisoners for extraction. Out of the corner of her eye she spotted Zac going through a door on the other side of what she could only describe as an open space with more little people in it. She followed, trying her hardest not to step on too many of them. She reached the place Zac had excited, but the door had gone. She placed her hand on the wall looking for some kind of edge that might indicate a concealed door, but there was nothing.

"Bracelet, reject," a Collector sneered, waving her arm at Val. "Thanks," she called politely. She hadn't wanted to thank her; 'reject' was still an insult, but she had been brought up to have good manners.

She placed her hand with the bracelet onto the wall and, as if by magic, a door opened. She went through it: into chaos. There were what she could only imagine to be guards and hunters everywhere. The only thing that distinguished the two was the fact that she recognised Zac's style of clothing. She spotted him on the other side, having what looked like a heated debate with a man who looked like the hunters, but was wearing a different uniform, its red top making him really stand out in the crowd. She started to wade through the guards and hunters towards them.

Zac stopped in front of the man he knew as his Mechanic. "We need to talk, now!" he said in a very agitated tone.

"Good..." he looked down at his chart, "...evening, I believe on Earth."

"I want answers and I want them fast," Zac's voice was getting louder.

"Alright if we can't be civil, what's the problem?" He looked back down at his board.

"I was out with my guard when I saw this signal." Zac held his watch out to the Mechanic.

He looked at it half-heartedly. "That's not possible; it must be faulty." He pushed Zac's hand away.

"I saw it with my own eyes."

"Are those the eyes the ones that the Warden has on a warning, and got you sent to Earth to baby-sit the freak?"

Zac ignored his feeble attempt to goad him. "Look at it, it's not faulty. You are looking at exactly what I just witnessed on Earth in some dirty warehouse." He pushed it back again under the Mechanic's nose. "I want answers. How is it possible that I received a signal for a Judge on Earth?" Zac shouted, twitching with agitation. He stopped when he realised that silence had fallen around him.

The Mechanic was now looking past him to something of even more interest than a Judge on Earth.

Zac turned to see Val standing a few feet away with guards and hunters just staring at her. "This had better be good," he hissed. "This is not over. I want an answer," Zac said, turning back to the Mechanic before heading towards Val. "What are you doing here?"

"Wow! Two rejects together, what a joke." One of the guards laughed openly at them.

Zac took Val's hand. "We need to leave. Now." He pulled her along.

The same guard pushed in front of them. "Wait. Sorry, what is your name now? Oh yes, Zac. Let's have a chat with your precious reject, guard." He stood in front of Zac, forcing them to stop.

"Look thirty-three twenty-six, I just need to get her back home. We don't want any trouble." Zac tried to move around him, but the guard wasn't going to give in that easily and side stepped.

"What can your precious reject do, *Zac*?"

At this point Val had had enough. She had been called reject five times in as many minutes and her hunter was being bullied by some second rate guard who was particularly ugly in her opinion. Zac was about to start another round of 'please let us pass' when Val moved in for the strike. Taking her sword out, she moved swiftly around Zac, pulling him back, as if they were dancing.

"Zac's reject guard can do this," she said, slipping the tip of her sword under his chin. As she moved in closer to his face he began to shake with the tazer. She felt the others start to move away from them and she felt empowered. "Then she is going to do this," she continued, smiling sweetly at him while her knee came up hard into his stomach. He bent over, completely winded by the blow, and dropped to the ground. There was a communal gasp of shock. They had never seen anything like her before and now they had to doubt whether what they had been told about her was true.

"Would anyone else like to chat with the rejects?" Val challenged them as she closed her sword and popped it neatly into her back pocket. There was silence. "No? Then we will be off to catch a few more of those prisoners." She bowed and kicked the guard, who was now quivering on the ground, with the corner of her shoe. Zac squeezed her hand and she squeezed his back and they headed out, entering the portal together. When they arrived back at her flat they were both standing a little taller.

"Ok. Now you can tell me about this Judge thing you were shouting about." Val sat on the bed.

Zac looked uncomfortable. "This must be our secret, as you call it. Like your friend Delta,"

"Ex," Val added.

"Yes ex. When you were fighting with the Bendicks and Wendy created that spell to disguise the witch so no one would recognise her, I had a signal on my watch. It was only for a split second, but I know it can't be wrong. It was a judge. And if there is a Judge here on Earth, something is really wrong and we need to know about it." Zac was doing his pacing act.

"So how close would a Judge need to be for you to get a reading?"

"I'm not sure. Their energy is so strong, and it was literally a split second burst." Zac stopped and slumped down on the bed next to Val. "Do you think I'm crazy?" he looked at her.

"No, I'm just so pleased that you're a reject like me." She patted his hand.

"Yes, that is another story, but we have more pressing issues like Excariot and his witch. And how come you didn't want to wait for me and teleported yourself?"

"Well, on one the hand I was just a little sick and tired of feeling like I have nothing to offer. Wendy does the magic stuff and Wendy works my dellatrax, and I just wanted to get your attention. You're *my* hunter. We bonded, no one else." Val was beginning to realise how silly she sounded.

"You must learn that you are more vulnerable when you split your emotions, between what you call ego, jealousy, fear and all the other strange things you humans suffer with. To work well and to receive the desired outcome you must be focused and trust that everything I do is to make our job easier."

"So we're a team then?" Val searched Zac's face for an answer.

"Like you said, we are connected; there is no power stronger than our link. The dellatrax is just a small part of your ability; Wendy is powerful and you should just be happy that you have her."

"Ah yes, and on the other hand, the dellatrax: I used it! That's how I got the message about the girl, and that's why I left in such a hurry. I thought she was in danger."

"No more than you going in alone. Tell me more while we have a coffee." Zac patted her on the shoulder. "We must go and see the others." He stood up and then lurched to the side unexpectedly.

"Zac! What's wrong?" Val tried to grab him, but he was too heavy. He started to shake violently and then collapsed onto the floor.

"Shane! Jason!" Val screamed at the top of her voice, holding Zac's head in her lap. "Please help me, Shane!" Val kept screaming until she heard the private door fly open.

"Val what's wrong?" Shane was calling as he pounded up the stairs.

"It's Zac. He's just collapsed. Help him, please Shane," she pleaded.

"He doesn't look good. We need to get him to a hospital," Jason said as he came up behind Shane.

"Not as easy as you would think, son; he's not human remember." Shane felt Zac's wrist for a pulse. Wendy and Fran, who had also arrived in the room, could do nothing but watch Val and Zac's plight.

"Help me get him up," Val demanded.

"What are you thinking?" Shane lifted him.

"I have to take him home." She was already standing with Zac's limp arm over her shoulder.

"We can't follow you there, but with Zac like this, who's going to protect you?"

Shane's concerns were Val's too, but she needed speed at this moment, not doubt. "Just help me."

Shane and Jason helped her to the edge of the portal she had only moments earlier exited. Taking the strain of Zac's weight, she signalled for them to move back. "I've got you," she whispered in Zac's ear as they passed through the portal. This time she entered with confidence.

CHAPTER 7

The Traitor

Val, still holding tightly onto Zac's limp body, landed on top of a group of Collectors. She didn't care much as they had cushioned his landing. She lowered him gently on to the polished floor.

"You!" she grabbed a Collector, who was struggling to get back to her feet. "Help me now," she demanded, holding her by the arm. This was clearly not a request and the Collector saw that her only option was to assist.

"Call the Mechanics!" the small woman shouted. The others started to bustle around, passing on the message. She gently put her hand onto Val's. "Please, Val, you're hurting me."

It was the unexpected fact that she knew her name that made Val release her. Slumping down to Zac's side, she pulled up his head and placed it gently on her lap. She stroked his hair and she whispered into his ear, "Someone's coming; you'll be ok. I won't leave you, you're my hunter, I need you."

"Twenty- three thirteen," a large man called into the crowd.

Val quickly got to her feet. "We're here, hurry." She waved her arms frantically, but unnecessarily; now she was standing it became apparent that she was the only person over four feet tall. The Mechanic waded through the Collectors with no regard for their wellbeing. Val watched them disperse, mumbling complaints under their breath. His uniform, like the man Zac had been speaking to earlier, was a different colour: in this case a bright canary yellow with a thick black band around the middle.

"Right, what do we have here?" He leant down with what looked like one of those luminous disco sticks. Gradually he moved over Zac's lifeless body. Val watched as it flashed all the colours of the rainbow. He tutted a little and then huffed. She had never seen anything so ridiculous in her life.

"Aren't you going to get him to a hospital or something?" Val asked, agitation in her tone.

"I'm sorry, but we don't save people here. If they are going to make it then they will; if not, we dispose of them and move on." He carried on with the light show.

"You can't be serious! He belongs here. He's one of your hunters." At this point Val was considering damage control as her stress levels were beginning to spiral.

"Look, twenty-three thirteen, I just do my job same as everyone else here. He's not going to die, although there is something wrong. I will take him to his quarters and you can watch over him there, ok?" The Mechanic stood up and, using the light stick in one hand and what looked like a small silver plate resting on his palm, he levitated Zac.

"You do that. There's someone I need to talk to first," Val replied. She was going to sort this out. As she walked through the Collectors, forcing them to scatter yet again, a million thoughts were slamming though her head. No one cared about anyone on this planet. They were just employees with no health benefits. She placed her bracelet against the wall and walked into the chaos of the guards and hunters on the other side. She wasn't sure what she was going to say, but she was going to get to the top and to do that she needed directions. Reaching out she grabbed the first person she could get her hands on: a thin hunter with flaming red hair.

"Oy!" He started to struggle, but thought better of it when he saw who had him, "What do you want reject?" he grunted, distain in his tone.

"The Warden." she pushed him forward.

"You can't be serious. He won't see you without good reason." Val ignored the certainty in his voice. She wasn't going to listen to anyone until she had answers.

"You have two options. You can show me where he is or I'll use my magical powers on you. I will make your eyeballs swell until they explode in your head." She pulled him to a standstill, pressing her face close to his. "So, what do you choose?"

"You can't do that," he responded nervously.

"Try me." Val invited, breathed heavily into his face. '*Fake it till you make it*' better work, Wendy, she thought.

"Fine, but don't say I didn't warn you," he said, turning and beginning to walk away, clearly expecting her to follow him. Unwilling to release his arm, Val lurched after him. They walked for what seemed like an eternity, up and down corridors of prisoners in boxes. He stopped and pointed at a wall. Then, pulling himself free, he stalked off, indignation in every line of his body.

"Bye and thanks," Val called out. She looked at the huge wall in front of her. Was this the right place? For all she knew this could be the men's toilets and he had just gotten some serious revenge on her. This was actually much scarier then she thought it would be. She placed her bracelet on the wall: nothing. She swiped her bracelet again, still nothing. What now? Then, when she was on the point of walking away and finding someone else to guide her, a crease of light appeared and the door opened slightly. She pushed it gently, then stepped inside. The Warden, his back to her, was looking over his balcony onto the madness below.

"Yes, Val?" he asked without turning.

Val straightened, an instinctive response to his undoubted authority, almost as she would have done when going into the headmaster's office. "It's my hunter, he's hurt and no one will help us, I don't understand," she gabbled, shaking with fear. She placed her hands together so that the tremor wouldn't be visible.

"We have too many people here to care for the individual; we would have to dedicate far too many resources; it would not be productive." He talked in an even, almost bored tone and still didn't turn to acknowledge her.

"All these people put their lives on the line for you and you just let them die?" Val launched her challenge, trying to sound as calm as possible.

"Enough time has been wasted on this useless conversation!" he snapped. "I humour you because you are different, but it's your fault that your hunter has been poisoned, Val. Go home and deal with your mess and do not come to me again with trivia." At last he turned, his expression one of extreme annoyance. He raised his hand and, before another word could escape her lips, she was gone.

Val landed on her feet, taking a step to bring herself to a halt. If front of her Shane and the others were standing around the bed. Her arrival drew their attention.

"Hey are you ok?" Shane reached out.

"Zac is sick and they won't help me." Her eyes started to fill up.

"He'll be ok," said Wendy moving to one side so that Val could see Zac. He was awake.

"Oh!" Val threw herself at him, wrapping her arms around his neck, tears pouring down her face. "The Warden told me this was my fault, that you have been poisoned."

Zac lifted his head slightly. "It seems that your food is not very good for me," he said feebly, then lowered his head again.

She was horrified. She had never even thought about it. Poor Zac had consumed every take-away available on Earth, mixed with ten gallons of coffee. "I'm so sorry. I didn't know I was hurting you. How long will it take for you to get better?"

"The man who delivered him said it would take about three days for him to make a complete recovery," Fran tried to be reassuring. "And can I please add 'how big was that man'!"

Wendy nodded in agreement.

"The Mechanic delivered him here?" asked Val.

"Yes. Literally you went through and he was back; took about thirty seconds," Jason said. "You've only been gone for about five minutes."

"But I met with the Warden; I must have been in Alchany for at least a half an hour."

"You did what?" A weak voice spoke up.

"I went to see the Warden about making you better."

"Oh, we are in so much trouble now." Zac shook his head and sighed. "You must understand something, all of you. I was created to do a job. I'm not your friend or your brother or sister; I'm a hunter. Look at your animals. They do their job for the collective group, but if one falls behind they carry on and another in the pack takes their place. You must not worry about me and you must never go to the Warden about me again." Zac turned over, facing away from Val, and pulled the covers around him.

"But let me explain I..." She felt a hand on her shoulder. Shane shook his head signalling for them all to leave. Val stood up. "I'll come back soon," she whispered to Zac's back. They headed down to the shop in silence.

"Give him some time to rest; he will see things differently tomorrow, Shane advised.

As they trooped back into the shop, Val saw a young woman standing on the other side of the counter.

'Not more people,' she thought. "Hello," she greeted her politely as Wendy walked past her and put her arm around the stranger's shoulders. It took Val a moment to register who it was. "Oh, you're the priestess from the warehouse," she said, smiling for the first time for ages.

"Yes, she is, and we have been waiting here patiently," Sam butted in handing the girl a mug. "Now I have to go. I have an appointment."

Val wanted to talk to him, but he was in a noticeable hurry to get away.

"Ok, we can talk later," she said, waving as he left the shop, annoyed by his obvious lack of interest in her, or Zac's well being. Her smile disappeared again.

"Sorry I've kept you waiting; we've been a little busy. I'm Val," she greeted the woman.

"Hi, I'm Lucy," she responded, sipping nervously at her drink. " Lucy Carlton."

"Do I know you?" Val was suddenly overwhelmed with a gut feeling she had seen her before.

"I don't think so." She gave and uncomfortable smile.

"So, first things first, what were you doing in the warehouse?"

"It was the site of our ancestors' pagan burial ground and I was going to make an offering like I do every month. Then you appeared and that guy grabbed me, and now I'm here. So, can someone please tell me what exactly is going on?" she glanced from one to the other.

"Ok, you're a witch," Val stated.

"I prefer Wiccan, but yes," Lucy nodded.

"Me and Wendy here are also Wiccans, and stuff," Val added waving her hands dramatically. "We're now going to tell you a story that will make everything you know sound bland in comparison. But one thing I can promise you is, if you don't listen carefully and you tell anyone what we're about to divulge, you will be in serious trouble." Val smiled although it still sounded like a threat.

"Is there an option B?" asked Lucy nervously.

"No, just listen." Val proceeded to tell her all the information she felt was necessary.

Lucy's eyes grew as big as saucers and she sipped nervously at her drink.

"So you see our dilemma. We need to keep you and the other priests and priestesses safe, but now Wendy has cast the spell on you, that problem should be solved." Val waited for Lucy's reaction.

Lucy paused for a second, absorbing all the information, then spoke. "Your life sounds extremely complicated and I'm sorry this is happening, but don't forget I have been hiding who I am for as far back as I can remember. If it wasn't a coven meeting it was the passing of books of spells hidden behind false covers. So a little more underground existence shouldn't be a problem. Having seen the reaction of those builders today I'm sure that Wendy is a very competent spell worker. However I can't stay here; people will start looking for me. It's my fiancés birthday and I'm expected at his party." She placed her drink on the counter. "I'm allowed to leave, aren't I?"

"Yes, of course, but here's my number, just in case you need us." Val scribbled her mobile down on a scrap of paper.

"Thanks, for everything." Lucy smiled at the group.

"You're welcome," they all chorused as she made her way out with Val.

"What have you got him?" Val asked, making polite conversation as she walked Lucy to the door.

"Funnily enough he loves reading, so I got him a first edition James Joyce 'The Dubliners'. Maybe next time I need a book I'll come here."

After Lucy had gone Val, wandered back into the shop, looking thoughtful. "Why did that book sound familiar," she asked herself. Then: "Oh my God!"

"What's wrong?" asked Fran from the counter.

"Lucy! I thought I recognised her. Do you remember the very first time I teleported, Shane?"

"Yes. It's not something I'm likely to forget."

"She was the one. She came in for that exact same book. Her hair was lighter, but it was her. It's really true:

we need to find the people I saved. Wendy, have a look in the records to see if we have a phone number for Eva. We need to get her; she is definitely on the list." Wendy started to leaf through the record book. "In the meantime, I'm going to check on the patient."

"Hold your horses, Val. What time would you like us to sleep?" Shane asked, looking amused.

"What?" Val looked confused.

"It's now nine-thirty in the evening. I have a business to run and you will expect Wendy back in the morning. Jason and Fran have jobs to do at home, so how much longer will you require us to save the world today?"

"I don't mind," Jason grinned. Fran slapped his arm.

Val looked perplexed then appalled. "Oh, I am so sorry! I didn't realise... I was just so focused. Wendy, look for Eva in the morning; Jason, go and do your jobs. I'll see you all tomorrow."

Val knew Shane was right they all needed a break.

"Good, now you go and rest too; you have a fencing lesson at seven a.m," Jason said. As she locked up she felt her body start to relax. She made her way upstairs on tired legs to check on Zac. When she arrived he'd fallen asleep. 'So hunters do sleep,' she thought to herself. 'Well this guard is going to join you, whether you like me today or not.' She lay down next to Zac on the dreaded seventies sheets and slipped off into a deep sleep.

The morning came far too quickly. Val woke to find Zac still sleeping. She put her hand over his nose just to make sure he was still breathing. She got up realising that for the first time she had actually managed to sleep on the bed, although those sheets would, without doubt, have to go.

A juice and some toast led to a shower and change of clothes. As she tugged at her unruly hair with Wallace's comb, she observed her face in the mirror, and her mum's eyes stared back. Val smiled for a second as she thought about how her Uncle Matthew always joked that she had her dad's chin, just before pretending to punch her on it. It hurt just thinking about them. Why was she doing all this? What was possessing her to carry on with this madness? Was it all because of a super powerful prison warden who had her name and address, or was it the power to travel to far off galaxies? No. It was revenge; she knew it was. Revenge for her real father, and for having to lose her mum and dad. It wasn't a comforting thing to know about herself, but she also knew that she wouldn't stop until Excariot was in a very small box. Because of him she hadn't seen her mum now for four days. It was as if she had gone on some crazy holiday that would end at any minute. Then she could go home, get her clothes washed and have dinner. A lump started forming in her throat. Why hadn't she appreciated them more? Still, there was no time for that now; she needed to get to Shane's for a fencing lesson.

She hurried down the main street. When she arrived her eyes were drawn to the window. There, just as it had been when she first saw it, only a few weeks ago, was the zodiac circle. She smiled thinking back to her first meeting with Shane and holding onto the fact that if he had turned her away she would never have made it to this point. She tapped on the door.

Jason, his eyes still sleepy, let her in. She followed him into the gym where her kit was waiting for her.

"You ready for this?" he asked lifting up his epee.

"As ready as I'll ever be." She saluted him and they fenced.

It was at least forty-five minutes before he would let her stop for a rest. Her arm hurt and she was extremely thirsty. She knew better than to question Jason now. He took this very seriously, wanting her to get everything right.

"No, step back!" he shouted, hitting her leg. "Salute." He pulled of his mask. "Well, let's pray you're better at your boxing tonight." He walked across the gym, closely followed by Val. Placing his mask on the glass table he handed her a towel and a bottle of water. "What do you have planned for us today?" he swigged from his bottle.

"We need to start finding all the people I saved when I released Excariot. They're the key to stopping him this time."

Shane walked in as the clock struck nine. "Morning Val, you look…" his eyes wandered over her, "…sweaty. How's Zac?"

Val grinned sarcastically as she pulled off her fencing uniform. "He was still asleep when I left, but I'm on my way back now, so I'll see you there later." They both nodded their agreement and she left hurriedly and headed back to the bookshop.

The sun was now awake and shining down as she made her way up the main street. Shops were opening and people where going about their day-to-day lives. Val glanced across the street at a boutique called *Spring*. She had seen it a million times before, but today things were different. Behind the glass an assistant was standing back admiring a girl in a mirror. Val thought it was odd, clothes shopping so early and looked more closely.

Her heart thumped when she saw a familiar mane of long blonde hair. It took a moment for her to recompose herself. This really was no good; she couldn't spend her life freaking out every time she saw a blonde. If Delta was back then she would have to come and find her, because she was busy. At that moment, the blonde turned to receive the adoration of the assistant face to face, and Val's worst nightmares came to life. The early morning shopper *was* Delta.

Driven by the determination to confront her, Val stepped blindly into the road. A horn blasted her ear, forcing her to step back. "Why is it that the minute you want to cross the street every car in the country arrives?" She cursed the traffic, hopping on and off of the pavement with Delta still in her sights. Laughing with the girl, Delta grabbed another dress and headed towards the changing area, just as the traffic finally broke its snake like chain. Val dashed across the road and crashed through the pretty pink front door of the boutique, startling the assistants and another girl who was browsing the racks.

"Hi. Blonde girl. Where did she go?" The speechless assistant pointed towards a doorway at the back of the shop. Val ran at it, its swinging motion allowing her easy entrance. On the other side were four cubicles all with beige curtains. Each one shut. She couldn't call out because the last thing she wanted was more attention. However, she wasn't prepared to wait. She moved to cubicle one, tentatively pulling back the curtain. There was no one there. She took a step to her right and pulled back number two; still no one. Three held no more luck. All there was left was four. Val didn't feel the need to pull out her sword, it was only

Delta. She jerked back the final curtain with a look of satisfaction at catching her so easily, and came face to face with a girl trying on a top. The girl screamed at the top of her voice covering her bra with her new garment. Val waved her hands in front of her eyes trying desperately to apologise, then she worked her way out backwards glancing again into each cubicle, but there was still no sign of Delta. The door flew open and the assistant, although feeble looking, arrived, fully prepared to protect her customers. Val pushed her to one side as gently as possible and ran out of the shop.

Val wanted to scream, "where are you?" at the top of her voice, but it stayed a quiet hiss in her throat. Delta was definitely back and something had changed. She needed to get back to the others quickly; they could be in danger, and Zac wouldn't be able to protect them.

As she got closer she could see that the shop was open. Worryingly, Wendy was pacing the pavement outside. Maybe something was wrong with Zac. Val started to run even faster towards her.

"What's wrong Wendy?" Val gasped.

"Everything! This has never happened to me before." Wendy was spinning in circles.

Val grabbed her and stopping her turning. "Tell me what's wrong. Is it Zac?"

"No, he's still asleep; I just went to check on him." Wendy pulled out her mobile and showed the screen to Val as she started pacing again. Val wanted to read it but she was aware of how exposed to Delta they were out here.

"Let's go in and we can talk." She looked around for any suspicious signs, but it was all clear.

"What am I going to do?" Wendy slumped on the stool putting her hands over her head which she then placed on the wooden counter.

"Ok, let's have a look." Val pushed the button and the screen lit up.

Hi Wendy, it was really nice meeting you the other day at the bookshop. I hope you don't mind me texting you like this but I was wondering if you would like to go to the cinema with me this evening Daniel.

"Oh, a date with a real boy." Val pushed the phone back towards Wendy's hair that was spreading all over the wooden surface. She wasn't sure what to do for the best. "Do you want to go?"

"I don't know. I have never been out with a boy. I don't know what possessed me to give him my number in the first place. I think I felt sorry for him. He's new to the area and he was all alone." Wendy fumbled on the counter, took her phone and shoved it back in her pocket.

"Ok, the question is, do you want to go? Forget everything else. And I can't believe you have never been on a date."

"Val, you have been my life for the past thirteen years, that's it."

If she hadn't felt guilty before about Wendy's sacrifice, she sure as hell did now. "You have to go. If you didn't like him it wouldn't be bothering you this much."

"My mum won't let me. She'll say I need to do some craft work and spell preparation."

Now the truth was coming out. "Listen, tell your mum you're sleeping over here. You can get what's his face to pick you up here and she'll never know." Val smiled tapping Wendy's head. "Come on, then you can stop over after you get back and be here to go to work at the crack of dawn. Plus, if it's awful, you can ring me and I can say I need you back at work asap."

Wendy lifted her head up just enough to see Val. "Should I do it?"

"Only you can answer that question. Can you see the future?"

"No. A true clairvoyant can rarely see their own future, but I think I'm going to go for it." She smiled, sat up and pulled out her phone. "What should I say?"

"Yes, thanks, pick me up at seven." Val leaned over Wendy, making sure she did it.

"Sent!" Wendy looked very pale for a few seconds and then the silence was broken by the entrance of Fran.

"Morning girls. What's going on?" Immediately sensing something important happening, she looked enquiringly from Val to Wendy. "What have you done?"

"Wendy is going on her first date with that guy that came in."

"Daniel," Wendy supplied with a shy grin.

"Ahh!" Fran squealed her delight then ran round the counter and hugged Wendy. "Too cool! Where are you going? Tell me everything. Let's polish and gossip." Fran grabbed Wendy and a duster and they disappeared down an aisle giggling like silly schoolgirls.

Val made a drink and took her place behind the counter. As she lifted her mug the doorbell rang. And in walked her mum.

Val gripped her cup hard. This wasn't happening. Her mum had never been in a bookshop. Her idea of reading was 'hello magazine' and the 'Bible'.

"Hello, I'm sorry. I was wondering if you could help me?" Susan made her way over to the counter, looking around and taking in her surroundings with a confused expression. "I received this invitation in the post to a cookery display at this address today, but you're obviously a bookshop, so I'm feeling a little confused." Susan placed the invitation on the counter, smiling warmly at Val.

Val just stared at her, the heat in her cup growing in intensity. After seeing her dad yesterday she had thought it couldn't get any worse, but it just had. Susan was still waiting for an answer. "I'm sorry, it's clearly a mistake. Please accept my apologies. I hope you haven't travelled far." Val stood up. She needed to get her mum out of the shop before anyone noticed her.

"So this is a first edition bookshop is it?" Susan looked around. "I saw the sign outside and should have realised it was too good to be true, I mean, a free cooking display in Arcsdale," she tutted.

Val placed her bubbling brew on the counter and made her way around to Susan. "Yes utterly ridiculous," she responded and was just about to open the door to guide her mum out when she noticed a figure on the other side of the road. It was Delta. This time Val could see her clearly, and she wasn't going anywhere. She looked just the same, but what did Val expect? They had only been apart for two nights. Val felt a gentle hand touch her arm as Susan tried to pass. She flinched. "Just a minute, I think I know what this is all about." Val pushed the door shut looking up at the bell in annoyance as if it was faulty. Then taking her mum's arm, she led her gently back towards the counter. "Think Val Think," she had to stop her mum leaving the shop. Delta had evidently set them up. "Fran, can you come here please," she called, knowing she needed help. Fran appeared as if by magic from one of the aisles.

"Yes boss." She waved at Susan. "Hi."

"This lady needs to see our first edition cookbooks," Val knew this would capture her mum's interest.

"Really, what sort of cook books?" Susan asked as she followed Fran down the aisle.

Val had to deal with Delta quickly; she wasn't going to let her get away this time. Her mobile started to ring. The display told her it was a withheld number. She answered.

"Hello."

"Hello, Alien." Delta waved from across the street. Val glared back at her from behind the glass door. "Miss me?"

"Like a hole in the head, Delta. What brings you back here? I thought I left you in my past." Val spat down the line.

"Sticks and stones, Val, that's not nice. You left me to die so I'm the one who should be a little ticked off, don't you think," Delta retorted in her slick American accent.

"You watched me die, so maybe not,"

"Triviality. You're just being picky now. Anyway, back to the now. We need to move on and start over."

Val couldn't believe what she had just heard. Had Delta said she wanted to start over? Val's voice was quiet. "Are you serious?" She genuinely didn't have a clue what angle to come from.

"Heck no. I'm going to make your life a living nightmare. I'm going to hunt you down every day, toy with you and your friends and possibly pick them off one by one. Then I'm going to take great pleasure in killing you." Delta's voice was steely cool. There was no hint of emotion or concern in it and Val knew this was serious.

"If you touch my parents or any of my friends there will be nowhere you can hide that I won't find you." Val could feel her throat physically tightening with her anger.

"I would never hurt your parents. They were kind to me; it's not their fault they got dumped with you." The line went dead. Val watched Delta close her mobile and then a large articulated lorry passed, blocking the view completely. When it had gone, Delta was gone too. Val was just about to run out of the shop when she heard a voice from behind.

"Val, are you ok?" It was Wendy.

"Yes, never been better." She turned to go towards the counter just as Fran reappeared with Susan.

"Val, we have found some amazing stuff. This lady has just brought three books of original recipes."

"Great, keep up the good work. Thank you for your purchase and I'm sorry about the mix up." Val needed to get away from her mum. In her gut she knew that Delta wouldn't hurt her parents. Delta was turning out to be a lot of things, but Val's mum and dad were like her own. However, she could be leaving them open to Excariot if she didn't get away from her soon.

"It was a pleasure meeting you," Susan held out her hand and Val took it, not wanting to make a scene. "Thank you for looking after me. You know, it's really strange, but I feel like we have met before, though I'm not sure where. You look familiar. Are your parents from around here?"

Val felt panic take over. She actually wanted Delta to burst in now and kill her, to stop the pain in her heart getting any worse.

Val coughed to clear her throat. "I'm sorry, but I'm orphaned, and I'm not from around here, so I don't think you know me." Val felt tears starting to form behind her eyes. She wanted more than anything at this moment for her mum to hug her tight, to stroke her hair and tell her, as she sipped one of her special hot chocolates, that this crazy world would one day be a much better place. She felt Susan's grip relax.

"I'm sorry; I'm too nosey for my own good." Susan turned and followed Fran to the counter. Val stood still watching her, all urgency gone. She just wanted to watch. Her mum took her bag thanked Fran and headed out of the shop. Val could only pray that she would never come here again. She took a deep breath. She needed to talk to Zac.

"Are you ok?" Fran asked. Wendy might be the one who could see the future, but Fran sensed things about people. "I'm fine, just going to check on Zac," Val smiled. If she could just make it upstairs without any more incidents she would be ok.

Wendy arrived at the counter duster in hand. Behind her the door opened and the bell rang again. Susan was back.

"Please, forgive me, I forgot to put my number on the back of my cheque." Fran smiled and handed it back to her. Susan wrote on it, waved politely at the girls and then paused for a moment, as if in thought. Val felt sweat starting to form on her top lip. Was Susan remembering her? Could she break the spell? Surely not; she was just her mum. She had no magical powers, apart from making fairy cakes. "You delivered my newspaper a couple of days ago," Susan said nodding to herself. "That's where I've seen you before."

"No you're mistaken, I don't do a newspaper round. I have a bookshop. I'm sorry, I have to get on." Val hurried away, closing the flat door firmly behind her. If this continued Susan was going to get herself killed or possessed, one of the two.

Val prayed the others didn't hear her sobs. She tried to be as quiet as possible, but it was all too much. She sat on the bottom step and let it all out. Then, after a moment to recompose herself, she went to check on Zac. He was still in bed, but at least he was awake.

"Hello, have you forgive me yet?" she asked sheepishly, her red eyes adding to the apologetic look.

"There is no need for forgiveness; no official crime was committed." He looked at Val with a confused expression.

"Ok, so can we be mates again if I promise I won't go back to the Warden and ask for help?"

"Very well," he smiled looking relieved that this was settled.

"So, juice?" Val asked then realised what she had done. "Sorry, no more drinks. Do you need me to get you any food pills from Alchany?"

"No, I have enough to last me a few of your calendar weeks, and I think we should steer clear for a while." Val had to agree. They had both made quite a bad impression on their last two visits.

"We have a problem. Delta was here and she threatened to kill us all. We need to be on high alert. She is completely crazy, Zac."

Val lay down on the bed, buried her face into the pillow next to him and started once more to cry.

Zac was uncomfortable with all this emotion. He pulled himself up a little. "We will find answers in the dellatrax. Jason and the others are very good at protecting themselves. Just because they are not as powerful as you, it doesn't mean they are weak. Now please stop that thing you are doing"

Val wiped her eyes and nose on her sleeve. "Yes, but she could attack at any minute." She curled up into a miserable ball on the bed, not bothered whose sheets they were or how they smelt.

"Is there any reason why we must hide this Delta from the others?" he asked.

Val knew that the best thing to do would be to tell the others, so they could protect themselves, but she just didn't know what would happen. "I think they will be safer if they aren't worrying." She wiped her face again.

"I will do as you say, but if a blind man could see the edge of the cliff he would stand a much better chance of not falling, don't you think?" Zac dropped back exhausted.

"I'll think about it."

They laid side by side in silence until Zac's watch sprang into sudden life. He tried to sit up but failed abysmally.

"What's going on?" Val asked.

"A prisoner has just taken form. We need to go."

"Zac you're no good to me. You can't even stand up. You need to stay here and get well." She started to collect her things together. Earpiece in, sword in her pocket. She was ready for action and it was still only ten-thirty in the morning. She wasn't nervous at all. She needed to stop thinking about her mum and Delta and this would be a good distraction for her. "I'm coming." Zac tried to pull himself up. Val was quite surprised that he actually made it to the sitting position before he collapsed again. "I'm coming," he said again.

"Just because you say it, doesn't mean it's going to happen." Val leaned over him to look at his watch. "Ok, what am I suppose to do because I don't read alien." She waited for an answer.

"This is your fault twenty-three thirteen: Zac have a coffee, Zac have a burger and oh, let's finish Zac off with that thing you called a curry!" His attempt at being cross was quite feeble.

"Ok less of the number calling. Now tell me where I'm going because someone apart from you needs my help."

"I don't understand your insults and I'm not letting you go alone. What about Jason or that Sam person? You could take Shane."

Val was touched by his concern, but getting more annoyed at his lack of cooperation. "If you don't tell me in ten seconds I will tazer you until you pass out, then I will leave you outside the Warden's office, dressed as a clown!"

"Fine, but before you go you must get Wendy here. Please." He looked so pathetic that Val agreed. Making her way to the top of the stairs she called down for Wendy. "Come up and you had better bring a book with you. Is Jason here yet?"

"Yes he is. Are you going out?" Wendy answered.

"Well I suppose you could say that." Val turned and headed back to Zac. "Ok, everyone is ready. Please let me go now; it could already be too late."

He held up his watch towards Val. "Hold my hand."

Val reached towards him. Their hands touched. The blue spark passed through Val and she was gone.

Once again she landed on her feet, needing only a small step to adjust her balance. "So unfair. Where's a hunter when you have a perfect landing?" she whispered, pausing to take in her surroundings. She was indoors, in quite a large room with ample light from beautiful sash windows. It was furnished as if it was a show home, with everything in its place, and it was too clean. Val pulled out her sword and started to make her way towards a closed door. Actually it was the only door and so now it was her only exit.

CHAPTER 8

Eyes Down for a Full House

"Hi," Wendy called as she ran up the stairs, her arms full of books.

"Hurry," Zac responded feebly.

"What's wrong Zac?" Wendy looked around for Val who had called her only moments ago.

"Val has gone. You need to find out who she is going to meet." He looked at his watch. "Find me prisoner 44798."

"I need to tell Jason what's going on." She ran to the stairs shouting the facts down to Jason who instantly headed for the cupboard.

"Ok, you said 44798." Wendy flipped the top page and placed her hands on the book.

Val placed her ear to the door. She strained to hear what might be happening on the other side, but there didn't seem to be any sound at all. Her hand reached down to the handle and cold metal filled her palm. She turned and pulled gently and the door came soundlessly towards her. She found herself looking at another equally pristine room.

"Hello." She smiled to hear Jason's voice in her ear.

"Hello mate. Where exactly am I?" She paused waiting for an answer.

"We seem to be having a few problems here, Val. I can't get a lock on your location. The computer is going mad. I've sent Fran up to Zac and Wendy to see if they can give me anything, but at the moment we are riding blind, sorry."

"Have you tried to call, Sam?"

"No answer, but I'll keep trying. Now what's going on?"

"Well, it looks like I'm in the house of a person who is petrified of dirt and personal belongings; or it's one of those show homes." She moved out of the next room onto a landing.

"I need something. I feel lost not knowing where you are. I'm going to try Sam again. Don't do anything."

"Ok." Val ignored Jason and moved slowly down the landing towards the staircase.

Back at the bookshop, Fran ran up the stairs to find Wendy doing her hologram act, watched by Zac who had propped himself in a sitting position against the back wall. "I need info. Jason has a problem; he can't find her."

"I knew this was the wrong thing to do." Zac said, shaking his head. "Something will happen to her and it will be my fault."

"44798. It's a Summari," Wendy announced. "So what can the Summari do?" She and Fran looked at Zac for answers.

"Pass me the book," he demanded. Wendy placed it gently on his lap.

"You need to hurry." Fran started pacing, waiting for information to take back to Jason.

"Yes it's here. The Summari." Zac looked up. "We have a problem."

Fran groaned impatiently. "Zac, we always have a problem. Just tell me what I need to tell Jason and hurry up."

At the top of the stairs Val came to a halt. She was feeling the pressure. Knowing that Jason didn't have a clue where she was had left her confused. And Sam wasn't answering his phone when she was in danger. How dare he!

"Val, it's me, Fran."

"Any news? I could really do with some information," Val whispered.

"Not good I'm afraid, and when I say afraid, I really mean that. You're coming up against this thing called a Summari. They are quite rare. They cause you to hallucinate, so you need to make sure that it doesn't touch you. It's something to do with an acid that their skin secretes. Zac said if it comes in contact with you, you would start to hallucinate instantly. Why don't you just come back and we can go catch this thing when we have a better chance of success?"

"Look, I have my trusty sword I'm sure I can keep it at arm's distance. Don't fret; just find out where I am."

"So as you can see, this is the main reception room, Mr Crow." The woman's voice came quite clearly up the stairwell. "Please call me Excariot," a man's voice replied smoothly.

"Oh hell, this is not good," Val whispered. "Fran, get upstairs with the phone now. Excariot's house hunting." Val's stomach was in knots. She leaned against the wall for support. This was the last thing she had ever expected. Who was the woman? Was she the one Val was supposed to help? If so, how could she beat Excariot?

"Would you like to see upstairs, Mr Crow, oh sorry, Excariot. That's a strange name. Is it foreign?" The woman asked as they headed up the stairs.

"Well, it's from such a distant place I'm sure you wouldn't know where it was, but please, less about me and more about you. What part of Brazil are you from, Miss Alvarez?"

"Please call me Eva."

Val caught her breath. So he was with Eva. She could hear them making their way up the stairs.

Zac spoke calmly into the phone. "Val, please return now. You are making a big mistake."

"Too late. They are coming upstairs and I'm stuck." Val turned towards the closest door and opened it, unbothered by what might lay behind it. The only other option was a 'show down' with Excariot. She stepped into what turned out to be the bathroom. "What's going on?" Zac asked, but Val was far too close to the others to speak; he would just have to wait until she was alone again. In the meantime, she needed to save Eva; the poor woman was like a fly in a web.

"Do you have a family, Excariot? Is that why you are looking at such large properties?"

"No, no direct family, just lots of visitors," he responded.

"Yes tied to walls," Val thought to herself.

"This is the bathroom." The handle started to turn. Val stepped back knocking into the bath. The door opened.

Eva walked in first. "ARHH!" she screamed when she saw Val. Eva was visibly shocked, but not as much as Excariot seemed to be.

"Long story," Val said, grabbing Eva's hand and taking advantage of the fact that Excariot was so surprised to see her, she push him onto the toilet unit and ran. This would have worked if Eva hadn't pulled in the opposite direction.

"Let go please," Eva cried as Excariot stood up behind her.

"Val, teleport now!" Zac shouted.

"Please come with me. That man is a very bad person who wants to hold you captive. You must remember me; I'm from the bookshop." Val extended her sword with her free hand; she needed to keep Excariot away.

"Please teleport!" Zac shouted again. Val pulled her earpiece out, throwing it on the ground. Zac shouting down her ear wasn't helping.

"Miss Alvarez, stay still. This person is obviously crazy. Please let her go, little girl. You can take me instead." Excariot smiled.

"Yes take him," Eva exhaled still trying to pull her wrist free.

"Look Excariot..."

"How does she know your name?" Eva stopped pulling quite so hard.

"I know his name because he has tried to kill me on several occasions in the past, and he wants to do the same to you." However Eva was still not prepared to trust Val.

"Please Val, I didn't try to kill you, that's an exaggeration." Excariot shrugged. It took Eva a few seconds to register what he had just said.

"Do you want to run now?" Val asked.

"Yes but..." Before Eva could say another word, Val felt a hand on her wrist. She turned as soon as she felt the contact to see a slim, dark haired oriental woman. Val gazed into her eyes. They were violet. Val thought how pretty they were and then she slowly started to drift away.

Clouds of candyfloss came towards her and as they passed over her she found herself sitting at a table with her mum and dad. As always there was enough food to feed a small battalion. Susan made her way to her side. "Honey you need to wake up." She gently stroked Val's forehead.

"No, it's ok, Mum, I think I want to stay here just a little longer." She reached out for her mum's hand.

"Sorry, but it's time to go back." Susan kissed Val softly on the cheek and as it contacted her skin so her eyes opened.

She was now lying on the ground out in the open, looking into Sam's eyes. Beyond him was a starry night sky.

"Hello my love. I need you to teleport." He leant down and placed a gentle kiss on her lips.

Val knew instinctively that this was her Sam. She was so tired. "I love you, Sam, please don't leave me here alone," she whispered, shutting her eyes once more and drifting off into what felt like a deep sleep.

Through the strange fog in her mind, Val could hear voices. There was screaming and shouting, and then she felt herself being lifted off the ground. She wanted to open her eyes, but nothing seemed to be happening. Now she could distinguish Shane's voice, telling Jason to call an ambulance. Fran was crying. She knew it was Fran because Wendy had a different tone when she was upset. Val wondered what was going on. Why were they panicking?

Val was desperate to talk, but her throat wouldn't work. She tried to wriggle one of her fingers, but nothing happened. She needed to tell them about Excariot and that he most likely had Eva now, and they needed to do something fast.

Sirens started in the distance then got louder and louder. Val felt herself being lifted onto a stretcher, heard the paramedic reassuring Shane, saying that they could only help her if they got her to the hospital. She heard them saying they had never seen anything quite like it, but there must be a logical explanation. Val listened to the chaos raining down on her. They asked for her parents and Shane explained that he was her guardian. Then came a series of thuds and jolts and she knew she was in the back of the ambulance with Shane holding her hand tightly.

As they travelled he talked to her about how much he cared about her, told her that he would never forgive himself if something happened to her. She allowed her mind to drift again, hoping it would go back to her mum and dad for one last moment, but it didn't, she just slept.

"Please, someone tell me what's going on." Zac demanded from the bed. He could hear the confusion downstairs, but was still not strong enough to stand. He waited, looking at his watch. After what seemed like an eternity Wendy arrived in the flat. "Where's Val? What is happening, Wendy?"

"Calm down. It's going to be ok." Wendy sat down on the bed. "We still aren't sure how she got back to the bookshop, but at least she did. Until the doctors can give us a little more information we can't tell exactly why she is in the state she is in, but at least we have her, not Excariot."

"The Summari touched her, that's what happened. I need to get to her. Your doctors will not know what to do. Get the books and take me to where she is now. That's an order." Zac pushed himself up, but fell back again.

"Look, our doctors will do the best they can for her, and you aren't strong enough for anything,"

Zac knew Wendy was right, but he wasn't going to give up that easily. They couldn't afford to both be out of action. "Will you please get the book with the blue cover, just so we can take a look?" Zac smiled as he had seen them do when they wanted something.

"Ok," she trotted off.

Zac took a few deep breaths, he knew this was going to leave him weak, but it had to be done. Wendy came back book in hand. "Thank you. Please hold it open for me?"

Wendy settled on the bed and did as he asked. Before she knew what had hit her he had her arm and she felt her stomach being wrenched out of her body and shoved back in as she landed with a violent jolt on a grey plastic floor. The retching was actually not the worst part of the experience.

"Please forgive me. You will be fine. The feelings of unwell will pass quickly," Zac said.

Wendy lifted her head up and muttered. "You will have feelings of unwell when I get my hands on you. What the hell are you doing? And where on earth are we?"

She soon realised they were in a hospital room. Zac was resting against the wall, looking exhausted. Still looking very sick, Wendy wobbled over to him. "Why have you brought me here?"

"This is the closest I could get you to Val without bringing attention to us. You must do the rest. Take the book and find her. She needs to connect with the dellatrax, it's her life force. Now go, she doesn't have much time." Zac slumped onto the floor and Wendy realised he had done this with the last of his energy.

"I'll do it and then I'm coming back for you." Wendy felt for a wall for support. No wonder Val always landed on her backside she thought. After a few moments she was steady enough to make her way out into the busy corridor, trying to make the very large old blue book under her arm look as inconspicuous as possible. She decided reception would be her best option.

When Val woke again she was in Wyatt's hut in the woods. It was daytime now and she was alone. Why was she here? Did her mum need her? Or maybe Excariot had sent her there. She stood up and made her way out towards the familiar pond. There wasn't anyone in sight. It felt strange, eerie; she looked towards the woods. Had they all gone for a meeting? She started towards the trees but had taken only a couple of steps when a man emerged from between two bushes. Val was immediately struck by his unusual appearance. He was almost angelic, but although he was smiling at her as he approached, Val felt nervous. She wanted to hide behind someone, but that wasn't an option.

"Hello V," he said. His voice left her heart thumping; it was as if he was speaking straight to her soul.

"Hello," she replied in an inaudible voice.

"Things aren't going so well for you are they?" He moved closer and reached out his hand, touching her gently on the arm.

"Well, I've had better days, but we're coping,"

"I'm sorry about all this mess you have to clean up. It was never my intention to cause you so much pain and trouble." She found she couldn't tear her eyes away from his. "You need to listen to me now, V; your friends are going to help you but the final battle is for you alone." His expression became serious and Val began to feel uneasy. He walked past her towards the pond and looked into the water. Slowly Val came up next to him and gazed in. Their faces, seen together in the reflection, made their resemblance uncanny. And then she knew.

"Are you Gabrielle?" she asked, hardly able to breathe.

He sighed and nodded.

"But you're dead." Val stepped away from him.

"To you and Wyetta I am, but that has no relevance in this place." He took Val's hand. "You must not lose sight of what's important, V. I was so focused on Excariot that I left you and your mother open to him and his ways."

"Why can't I come back in time and save you? I bet I could do that." Val's voice was full of desperation. "I know I could do that."

"Because sometimes we are meant for other things, things greater than our own wishes. You need to learn that. I made a choice. If I changed that choice I would bring shame upon my existence. This thing you call life that you grasp onto so desperately is only as good as you make it by your actions. Some of your people only see a single grain of sand; others see an ocean of life. You would do well to remember to never change anyone who has had honour thrown in their path. Now I'm going to leave you once more, but now you know that I'm proud of you. Remember that and do not break under Excariot's pressure. You, my daughter, were sent here for a greater reason than any of them know. Only the fearful try to change their reason for being. Are you afraid?"

"Sometimes."

"Don't worry. I am with you always." He took Val's wrist and held her bracelet, and she understood. Then Gabrielle placed his other hand on Val's arm; she jolted as if stuck by an electric volt. "It's time to wake up." He let her go and started to walk away towards the wood.

Val tried to follow him, but something was stopping her. Something was pulling her backwards. "Gabrielle!" she screamed. But he just kept walking away.

Wendy turned a corner and spotted her friend. "Fran! Fran!" she didn't want to shout and attract attention, but she knew time was of the essence.

Fran ran to her. "How did you get here so fast? Um, I don't mean to insult you car, but..."

"Zac teleported me here. I need to get to Val now." Wendy flashed the book at Fran.

"Let's go witch girl."

Jason was guarding the door. "Wendy! How...?"

Fran raised her hand, signalling him to be quiet, then went into the room where Shane was sitting at the side of the bed, still holding Val's lifeless hand. Jason came in behind them and locked the door.

"What's going on girls?" Shane asked, sensing their urgency.

"Zac got me here, *just*. Now I have to wake Val up." Wendy sat down next to her. "She looks so pale," she said placing the book on Val's chest.

"Wow, these books never cease to freak me out," Jason announced.

"Shh!" Wendy grumbled at him. The dellatrax was already buzzing. Black holograms, very different to Wendy's, were spinning at great speed around Val's body and head.

They were all watching patiently, waiting for something more definite to happen, when the first knock came at the door.

"Hello, it's Dr Maxwell here. Please unlock the door."

"This thing better hurry up," Shane voiced everyone's thoughts.

"Just a minute!" Fran called, hunching her shoulders as if to express the lameness of her actions.

"I'm going to have to get security if you don't open this door!"

"Come on Val, fight," Shane pleaded.

The dark holograms gave a single vivid flash of bright neon blue, causing them all to cover their eyes. When they looked again the holograms had disappeared. At last Val reacted, releasing an elongated scream, her back arching then dropping down onto the hospital bed as she was forced back into to consciousness.

"Val." Shane grabbed her shaking body, stopping her from falling to the floor.

She opened her eyes and was instantly thrown into intense pain. The light of the room was so bright. Where was she? She scrambled up, pulling free from Shane, panicking that she was in even more danger. As her eyes adjusted to the light she saw first Shane's worried face, and then all the others looking back at her.

"Right, I'm getting security," called the voice through the door.

"Just getting it now," Jason answered, trying to buy time by rattling the handle. "Doors in hospitals, hey."

He popped his head around the edge. The doctor pushed past, unimpressed with being locked out.

"When did she wake up? Why didn't someone inform me? If you don't mind I need a minute with my patient." The doctor glared at them over his glasses.

"Yes let's go." Wendy grabbed the book off the bed and signalled for Fran and Jason to leave.

"Don't worry, I will stay with her," said Shane. Wendy grabbed Jason by the arm before he could protest and they exited, leaving the doctor to begin examining Val.

Val looked from the doctor to Shane. Was this real? She really had no idea what was happening. After a few minutes the doctor had finished. "This is extremely strange. All her vitals are normal. I'm going to get my colleague." He glared at Shane. "Don't lock the door."

Shane nodded dismissively, his full attention on Val.

"Ok little lady, where have you been?" Shane held her hand tightly.

Val placed the palm of her other hand gently onto Shanes cheek. He was real, that's all she needed to know. "Well, I was at a house and Excariot and Eva were there. Is that bit real?"

He nodded. "We just couldn't get a hold on your whereabouts."

"Then I was having dinner with..." she paused to choose her words carefully, "...some friends and then I saw Sam." She blushed.

"We don't know about that bit. You were in the house then you disappeared. We had no contact with you. I thought the worst had happened and the next minute someone was calling us because there was an unconscious girl in the doorway of the shop, and there you were on the floor. We don't know how you got there. We can only assume you managed to teleport back." Shane was as close to the bed as he could physically get; Val remembered him saying he was her guardian.

"Thanks for looking after me." She gave him a hug and as she pulled away she could see intense sadness in his eyes. "What's wrong?"

"Val, you're just a kid. I know you need me to be strong for you, but I have lost so many people and this is getting harder by the day." Shane shook his head as if to get rid of the thoughts. "Sorry, so it seems you got touched by this acid skinned thing then."

"Yes, and I lost Eva. I'm pretty sure now that Excariot will have her so we need to be stepping up our game. Where's Sam? I need to know why you couldn't track me."

"I'm meeting him this afternoon. I'll tell him to pop in and visit you."

"You aren't thinking I'm going to stay here are you?"

"Val, you have just been though something none of us understand; you need to be monitored; you're unwell,"

"Speaking of the unwell, who's looking after Zac if you're all here?"

"Ah yes, that's another problem."

But not one they had to wait long to find out about as Jason walked in carrying Zac in his arms followed by the girls.

"What did you do?" Val said crossly.

"What was necessary? Now please return me to the bookshop. This place disturbs me; everyone is sick," Zac whispered.

"I think we will have to get you out of here through the front door mate," Jason said.

"No, I will get us home." Val stood up.

"Wait a minute, you have just been in a semi-coma and now you want to teleport home?" Shane seemed annoyed.

"Look, we need to get Zac out of here and I feel fine." Val turned to Jason. "Please put him on the bed. Together we can get home." Jason did as he was told. Val stepped towards him. "Missed me buddy?" she winked and placed her hand on his. The blue spark passed between them and they were gone.

"That's so unfair. This is costing me a fortune in petrol, Dad," Jason moaned.

"I think I would rather drive." Shane pushed his son towards the door. Let's get back to work."

"I can second that," Wendy chipped in.

Val landed next to the bed, dropping Zac down onto the covers. He looked terrible. She had no idea how he was supposed to get better. The Mechanic had said three days, but he looked worse than he had before.

"Ok, what's going on?" A familiar voice asked from behind her. It was the Collector.

"I didn't touch that portal." Val turned around raising both arms in the air.

"No you didn't. However, you did teleport and so, if you don't have a prisoner for me, I need to know what you're up to."

"I got touched by a Summari and ended up in hospital, and now we are back. And that's it,"

"That's wonderful for you but you don't have a prisoner and you teleported. Has Zac not explained to you that you don't return unless you have a prisoner or you're dead? That doesn't leave much room for misunderstanding, does it?" The Collector used her most patronising tone.

"I tried, but I couldn't get her this time, so I will go back again tomorrow. Anyway, look at Zac. He's no good to me like this." She moved so the Collector could see him lying on the bed.

"I see. He does look unwell," She moved over to the bed. Pulling a small piece of glass out of her pocket she placed it to her eye. Making her way around the bed she inspected Zac up and down. She made a tutting noise and a variety of huffs and sighs then put the glass back into her pocket. "I think I can help. There's a blockage. I have dealt with this problem once before."

Val thought about all the food inside his body and understood what she meant.

The Collector placed her tiny hand over him, raising Zac onto his feet. Val wondered if she could do the same for her, her back was starting to hurt from carrying Zac. Although he was now upright he was still hanging like a puppet on strings.

"What are you going to do to him?"

"This." The Collector snapped the fingers on her other hand and Zac instantly went rigid. Val was scared. Then she clapped her hands together. Zac bent violently in the middle and dropped to the floor.

Val leapt to catch him, but was too slow. "What the hell's your problem? Was he not ill enough already for you!" she spat at the Collector.

"It's ok Val. I feel much better." Zac lifted himself up smiling at her.

"What's going on?" Val jumped back.

"His blockage has been cleared. Now, get the job done and I will return for your prisoner." The Collector turned leaving Val and Zac sitting on the floor together.

"So, how're you feeling?" Val beamed at Zac.

"Annoyed, with you. What were you thinking of going up against Excariot without me?" Zac stood up like nothing had ever been wrong with him.

"I have taken him on before. I just didn't expect to get jumped from behind by hallucination girl," Val also stood up and, for a moment, the two looked as though they were squaring up for a fight.

"How did you get back here?" asked Zac.

"Shane said some old lady found me on the street. He thought I had managed to teleport."

"Incorrect, my report shows your second teleport was from the hospital." Zac started pressing buttons.

"So how did I get back here? I'm sure Excariot wasn't kind enough to drop me off."

"At this moment I have no answer for you. Right now we have work to do. We must get the Summari." Zac reached out for Val's arm, but she pulled it away before he could get to her.

"Listen Zac, I love teleporting with you, it's just oodles of fun. Nevertheless, you need to start telling me what we're doing because this grab and disappear business is really not ok." Val stood with her hands on her hips.

"Sorry. Are you prepared to go to work or would you like a little time to get ready?" Zac grabbed Val's arm and they were gone.

They arrived in sync and Val immediately turned to look around her, pulling out her sword instinctively. Her hand rose naturally to call on whatever power she needed. Zac scanned the area and kept close to her side. They walked as one down the back street that held their prisoner. Val turned to look at Zac who pointed towards a doorway. Val could hear her heart pounding, could feel the adrenaline rushing down her body. This was actually quite exciting. Zac turned the handle of the dark, dirty door and shoved it quickly inwards. Val stepped into the entrance with her sword leading; she wasn't going to get caught out again.

There was no one there. The room contained an old wooden table, a dull lamp and no windows, which made the room look seedy, as it was daylight outside. Val stepped cautiously forwards. Zac turned and they were back to back again, ready for any outcome. They moved towards the table, turning slowly in circular movements. Val noticed Zac tapping on his screen again. He concentrated for a moment then he pointed silently at a wardrobe on the far side of the room. They moved forward. He nodded at her and she took a step back while he threw the door open. There, crouched in the cramped space, was the woman who had sent Val into happy land. She leapt at Val, hands outstretched, ready to send her to cloud cuckoo land again. But Val was ready. With one swift movement of her hand she created enough energy to pin the woman to the wall without making contact. Stepping forward, she jabbed her with her sword. The woman screamed, then writhed until finally falling lifeless to the ground.

"Boo-yahh." Val turned to Zac. She felt extremely smug.

"What?" Zac's expression clearly showed his confusion.

"Sorry. It's a word that means 'We Rock'." She punched him playfully on the arm. "Now let's get this thing home." She reached out, careful not to touch the woman's skin. Zac grabbed her and they were gone.

CHAPTER 9

Love is in the Air

For a change the Collector was pleased with them. Val was more impressed with their teamwork. She and Zac seemed to be getting more and more connected. This hunter thing was starting to make sense. She could almost see why he didn't fight. Although she would still need a little time to get used to his strange ways, this could just work.

They headed down to the shop where they found several people at the counter and Wendy busy serving. It was as if everything that had just happened was part of her morning break.

"Zac, you're better!" Wendy cheered throwing her arms around him in a friendly embrace. He looked like one of those kids being smothered by an overfriendly relative. Wendy released him aware of her overflow of affection.

"You didn't have to work this afternoon Wendy," Val told her.

"Well, I have nothing better to do. I'm sleeping here tonight if you hadn't forgotten."

Val could have kicked herself. She was so wrapped up in being a guard that she had completely forgotten about Wendy's date with Daniel. Then Jason appeared.

"Where have you been? I saw you disappear, but I couldn't contact you." Jason seemed quite annoyed with her. Then she remembered she had dropped her earpiece intentionally.

"Jason, chill out, they're here and all in one piece. Were you thinking of eating any time this week?" Fran came over with a sandwich in her out stretched hand.

"Wendy, I'm sorry, I did forget your date, but I was hallucinating so everything has been a bit odd. Don't worry, there's nothing to stop you going." She gave Wendy a quick hug.

"Jason, I lost my ear piece. I'll make sure I get a new one from Sam, and Fran, give me that sandwich before I bite your hand off." She grabbed the food with relish, not realising until now just how hungry she was.

"What time is it?" Zac asked.

"Three-thirty," Wendy responded.

"Do you wish to do some work?" he asked Val.

She couldn't believe her ears. She had had a fencing lesson at 8 a.m, spent the morning in hospital, had only just teleported back from catching a Summari, and now he wanted her to work. "What exactly did you have in mind?" Val shoved another mouthful of bread in.

"Well, you have little control over your powers, we should work on them."

"Ok," Val nodded. What could go wrong?

"Can I watch?" Jason asked eagerly.

Val looked to Fran for approval. She nodded and turned to walk away.

"I need you back here for five, Val. We have to decide what I'm going to wear tonight," Wendy said. Then Val saw the cogs of her mind turning. "Sorry, forget that last one. Fran!" Wendy called, "I need some help with what to wear." Grinning, she trotted down the aisle.

"I should really take that personally, but I don't." Val frowned at the men as they headed out onto the street. "So where are we going?"

"To the tattoo parlour. That is where you do your training is it not?" Zac looked confused.

"Yes Zac, it is." They walked along the high street. Val could see Zac taking in everything. Nothing got past him. He was a real hunter.

Jason pulled Val around pretending to push her towards the road; as she screamed he pulled her back in.

"Why do you do this to Val?"

"It's just harmless fun, Zac," Jason reassured him.

"So, if one of your metal vehicles hits her she will die. How is this entertaining?"

"Ok, just ruined my fun." Jason moved away from Val and stood on the other side of Zac so he could stay out of trouble.

"Here we are." Val took Zac's arm and as they started to cross the road the doors to the parlour opened and out came Sam. Val remembered Shane saying he was going to see him later.

"Sam..." Jason greeted him and then stopped. "Wow, what happened to your face mate?"

"Stupid garage door fell on me. It seems that it wasn't put on properly," Sam said, giving Val a cold look. He had a lump on his forehead and several scratches on his cheek.

Val was annoyed that he would even think of accusing her dad of shoddy workmanship. "I'm sure you just did something wrong," she retaliated.

"Yes, I put my face in the way," he snapped back.

"That was a severe miscalculation on your behalf," Zac stated.

"Really!" Sam went to walk past them.

"I lost my ear piece earlier. Would it be possible to get another one?" Val asked before he could escape.

"Come to the house later; I have a spare," he said, not even looking at her, then walked away. She didn't know whether to be furious, upset or just grateful. She knew that old Sam was in love with her, but this one was in the process of beginning to hate her. It was like having a relationship with twins. The problem was, nice Sam was in sixteen forty-five, so she really couldn't count that as a realistic option. Maybe she should just forget the option of any relationship with any Sam. Knowing her luck she would end up having to let him go, or he would turn out to have a girlfriend.

"Come on mate." Jason nudged her.

"Yes, you were just looking into the sky. What is that all about?" Zac pushed her through the door.

"Sometimes we do something called daydreaming. It's when you think about something happening; something that hasn't happened yet, and may not ever happen. But no one can stop you from wishing it would."

"So this Sam makes you daydream about things you wish would happen, but may not?" questioned Zac.

Val's cheeks filled with heat and she definitely didn't need a mirror to tell her what she looked like. "No, I was thinking about training, now let's get on." She pushed past him.

"So what did you wish would happen with your training," Zac persisted.

"Hi Shane," Val moved away from Zac in the hope that he would stop his questioning.

"What are you doing here?" He looked up from the forearm of a stunning looking woman with the reddest hair Val had ever seen. He was in the process of adding another tattoo to her collection and Val admired the fact that she wasn't even flinching.

"Training," Jason smiled pulling Val along. "Come on," he pushed her through the door.

Zac stood transfixed by the woman's beauty. "Your hair is a colour I have never seen," he walked up to the woman. "What are you painting on your body?" He looked closely at her arm.

"Hi," she replied looking up. "It's Rock'n'Roll Red, and this is a Viper." She smiled at him.

"Rock'n'Roll red! Amazing! I once saw a double suncross that resembled that colour. It only happens once every three thousand years and..."

Before Zac could get himself into any more trouble Shane stepped in. "Zac, training." He pointed him in the direction of the door.

Zac walked towards it, still looking back at her.

"Bye Zac," she smiled, "I'm Holly by the way."

"Goodbye Holly of the Rock'n'Roll red hair. May our paths cross again." He pushed the door and was confronted with three more doors. Before he had time to start a technical scan for Val her head popped round the middle one.

"Come on, stop messing about." She grabbed his arm.

They walked in and Jason was already in the gym working out. Val took her jacket off and moved over to the clear floor area. "What now?" She bounced on her feet playfully around Zac.

"As a guard you're expected to understand your power and use it with precision at all times." Zac walked around her. "You're required to do your utmost to never injure a prisoner during the arrest, as this may be held against you as a negative count," Zac told her.

"So what does a negative count do?" Val was still bouncing playfully.

"A lot. Three negative counts and you will be extracted."

Val stopped, her arms dropping by her side. "Are you serious? Extraction?" Her expression changed to one of horror.

"It's never happened, but the quicker we get you in control the better." Zac raised his hand. "I want you to push my hand."

Val walked over to him and pushed his hand. "Ok."

"NO! With your powers." He pushed her back.

"Oy," Val was annoyed. If he wanted power she could do that. Her emotions getting the better of her, she slammed him with a gust of wind that threw him several feet across the room. Jason had no choice but to stop his training when Zac arrived between him and his slam man.

Zac stood up and stamped back to Val. "NO! Push." He pushed her again.

"Are you trying to wind me up?" Her temper was at boiling point; a ball of fire started to form in her hand. As she lost control of her senses, it started to grow up her arm.

"Val, stop!"

Jason's voice brought her back to reality; the flames petered out.

"This is no good. You have no control; you must learn." Zac was clearly annoyed.

"Then stop pushing me," she retaliated.

"Excariot will kill you if you don't learn how to behave. He was a guard and one of the best, and he will trick you into losing your life. Now push," Zac ordered.

Jason quickly stepped away from Val.

"Alright." Val raised her hands in submission. "Understood, sorry. I just find it hard to control these... these powers." Val lifted her hand and concentrated on the centre of Zac's palm. She could feel the energy inside her rising, almost like a kettle boiling, but she stopped herself and Zac's hand popped back.

"Better." He gave a half-hearted smile.

"How's it going?" Shane asked walking up behind Val.

"We're getting there, I think," she replied. Shane made his way to the percolator poured himself a cup then stopped to watch.

"Again," Zac ordered.

Val was ready for a small push.

"Did you see Sam?" Shane asked innocently.

Val's small push instantly turned into a blast. Zac flew across the room again.

"Sorry," she said apologetically as Jason lifted him off the floor. Why they had thought it a good idea to attach your powers to your emotions was beyond her. Just the thought of Sam made her stomach twist in knots.

"My fault." Shane raised his hand. "I distracted her." He took his coffee and headed off towards the glass table.

Val and Zac spent at least an hour practising control over her power, pushing his hand over and over. In the end, boredom got the better of her. "Please can we stop with the pushing? I think I get the idea," she sighed.

"Yes it's my turn." Jason threw her a pair of boxing gloves.

She groaned. "I take that back. I can do push." She looked to Zac for support, but he was already talking to Shane.

"Thanks buddy," she called.

"Let's do it." Jason pushed her with his gloves. Val didn't have much choice but to get on with it.

They sparred until Val begged to stop. "If I duck one more time I'm going to look like one. Please stop. You do remember I was in hospital this morning." The sweat was pouring down her back; her arms were throbbing with the strain. She had even contemplated being sick at one point.

"Very impressive, Jason," Zac enthused.

"Thanks mate."

"Jason has won several trophies for his boxing," Shane swelled with pride as he bragged about his son. Gasping for breath, as they all puffed out their chests around her, Val wished she was somewhere else instead.

"Val you had better get back to the shop. Wendy will be going out on her date soon." Jason pointed at the clock.

"Yes, let us go back to the bookshop." Zac headed to the door, with a very damp Val on his heels.

"Tell Fran I will pick her up soon. I need a shower first." Jason called after them, slinging a towel over his shoulder.

They arrived to find the shop closed, yet the door still open. "Hello," Val called as they entered.

"Hi," Fran called back to them. "Just give us a second."

Val and Zac stood patiently by the door.

"Presenting for your delight, the adorable Miss Wendy Whitmore." Fran stood back and there she was.

Wendy was wearing a beautiful knee length dress in cream, with small black flowers in a sweeping design down the front. Her hair was up and Fran had obviously taken time in doing her make-up. She looked stunning.

"Oh Wendy, you look amazing," Val said in genuine admiration. She went to her, intending to give Wendy a hug.

Wendy put her hand up. "Sorry, but you stink."

Val looked down at herself. It was true, she did stink and she looked a mess. Her t-shirt was stained with sweat and her jeans were covered in marks.

"What if he doesn't come?" Wendy looked anxiously from Fran to Val.

"I will arrest him. And you look perfect," Zac said.

"Extreme but acceptable," Val agreed.

The moment was snapped by a knock at the door. Val opened it and there stood Daniel. He actually looked as smart as Wendy; it was almost like a date from the nineteen fifties.

"Good evening." Daniel looked her up and down quizzically,

"Boxing." Val defended her appearance.

"Indeed." He looked past her and spotted Wendy. "You look breathtaking! Are you ready?" His face reflected just how perfect this moment was.

"Yes." She took the hand he offered. "I will see you guys later. If you need me…"

"We won't need you. Go and have fun." Val opened the door for them. "Where's your car?"

"There." Daniel pointed to what Val could only describe as another old heap, much like Wendy's old heap.

"It's a Standard Vanguard, in black. You know they were named after HMS Vanguard, the last of the British

Navy's battleships. I love it." Wendy ran down the stairs to look in the window.

"I hoped you would." Daniel put his arm around and opened the door. She stepped in and then waved at them, smiling widely.

They watched them pull away. After they had disappeared around the corner Val turned to take her aching body back into the shop. Then she spotted Fran.

"Are you crying Miss Tickle?" Val put her arm around Fran's shoulder.

"Maybe. It was so romantic. They looked so sweet together, almost made for each other." She wiped a tear away as she pulled away from Val. "Val, get a bath."

"Yes fine, I'm going. Jason said he would pick you up from here."

"That's fine. I'll start walking. He never gets anywhere quickly, especially when he's with his dad. He promised me some romantic fish and chips tonight so I'll pick them up on the way." She waved goodbye and hurried off along the road. "Well, just me and you." Val smiled at Zac. "Fancy watching me eat some food?"

"No, but do I have any other option?" Zac asked as Val locked up the bookshop and made her way towards the flat.

"Not unless you have a hot date. I saw you looking at that girl at the tattoo parlour."

"I will not have this conversation with you. It was simply that I admired the colour of her hair."

"Uhu," Val giggled.

They headed upstairs. Val started to run a bath and noticed that Zac had followed her into the bathroom. "Listen very carefully Zac. You can't come in when I'm in here, not under any circumstances. If you do I will blow you through the wall and set you on fire. Do you understand?"

He backed away slowly. "What if a prisoner takes form?"

"Then you knock on the door and I will come as quickly as I can, ok."

Val followed him to the door, locked it and went back to her bath. Disturbingly she was starting to like the old man bubble bath. She watched almost in a trace as the bath filled. She yawned, but tiredness was something she was beginning to learn to live with. She threw her now smelly, dirty clothes onto the bathroom floor, feeling the tiredness washing over her as she sunk down into the warm water.

She leaned backwards placing her arms on the side of the bath for support and closed her eyes for just a second. Then her brain told her that she had just spotted something on her arm. Val tentatively opened one eye. "NO!" she screamed, "NO! NO! NO! NO!"

There was a frantic knock at the door. "Val! Val. Do you require my assistance?" Zac asked.

"I don't believe this! I've got another tattoo. This is not happening." she grabbed the soap in a vain attempt to wash it off. "Where did it come from?" She stood up stepping out of the bath and grabbing a towel.

"Val, please open the door?"

"Zac, I'm fine. Just wait a minute." She pulled at her arm, twisting and turning the flesh. At least there was only one tattoo for now. It looked like a backwards J with a v attached to it. Had Excariot done this to her or was it perhaps Wyetta sending her a message? She rubbed herself down vigorously and threw her clean clothes on.

Opening the door she came face to face with a very concerned looking Zac. "What is it?"

Val pulled up her sleeve to reveal the symbol. It was the same size as her Theban V. Zac pulled her skin and then smiled.

"What are you smiling at?" She demanded, irritated by his know-it-all grin.

"It is a training symbol," Zac explained.

"What do you mean a training symbol?" Val looked down at the letter.

"Well, sometimes we have a path to follow and it is marked out for us. For the more needy, the Judges give symbols of guidance."

"I'm sorry! Did you just call me needy?" Val pushed past Zac making her way to the kitchen. "I'm not in *need* of any symbols to tell me that my life is hell." Val slammed the kettle onto its stand. Zac stayed at a healthy distance.

They both jumped when an unfamiliar voice called out from the flat. "Thirty-three twenty-seven are you there?"

Zac hot tailing it out of the kitchen. Val followed him. They found a woman standing near the portal. She was the colour of night. Her skin was so perfect that Val felt she wanted to touch her; the feeling was almost uncontrollable. She stepped forward, mesmerised, but Zac's arm held her back.

"Don't get close to her," Zac warned, pushing her back slightly, then addressed the woman. "Is it my time? This is not a good moment; my guard needs me."

"First contact must be made." The woman reached out to take Zac's hand and they started to walk away.

"Just a minute. Where are you going?" Val demanded.

The woman guided Zac towards the portal. "Thirty-three twenty-seven's Ranswar has arrived. They are to meet this night for the first time."

Val knew exactly what she was talking about. Lailah had been her father's Ranswar. "Oh, ok when will he return?" The woman's eyes were a gorgeous honey gold colour. It was no surprise to her that Zac was being so docile; she wanted to go as well.

"He will return if he is needed tonight; if not it will be in the morning."

"That's fine." Val was almost drunk on the woman's beauty. Zac didn't even look back and then they were gone and Val was alone and feeling surprisingly romantic. It was as if she had been slapped by cupid.

Now her pal had gone the silence in the flat was unbearable. She didn't want to be alone and she needed to find out what the symbol on her arm was. Val knew who would help her. She picked up her phone and dialled Wendy's number. It went to answer machine. "Of course," Val hissed. Wendy was on her first date. She would try Fran. Once again she got an answering machine; Fran was on a romantic fish and chips date with wonder boy. Who was left? "Ah yes, Sam." She giggled. The man who was driving her to distraction with his hot and cold attitude. But how would she get to his place? All forms of transport had gone out on one galaxy or another for a romantic evening. She could feel her emotions starting to get the better of her. Her heart was starting to beat faster. Why didn't this Sam love her? She was going to find out right now. She grabbed her bracelet; a blue spark appeared. And she was off.

Arriving at his front door she stopped for a second to contemplate what she was about to do, but her emotional imbalance was enough to keep her going. She knocked firmly on the cherry wood front door, stood back and waited. Her head was beginning to feel like a gold fish was swimming between her ears. To her satisfaction, the door opened without delay and there stood Sam. He was wearing tracksuit bottoms and a vest; it was obvious he wasn't going anywhere.

"Hi, you're here for your..." He was cut short as she pushed past him.

"Well, if you're asking..." she wasn't sure at this point whether to punch him or kiss him. Walking directly into the kitchen, Val made her way to the fridge, opened it and pulled out a Pepsi. Pulling open the lid she started gulping as if she hadn't had a drink in weeks.

"Are you ok, Val?" Sam caught up with her.

"What do you think? Wendy has a new boyfriend, Mr Daniel." She bowed. "Fran and Jason are so very in love and now Zac has to slip off for the night to meet his Ranswar, which is short for alien girlfriend. I'm left at home with another tattoo. But don't worry, apparently they're just for the needy who can't quite work out their destinies." Val slumped against the fridge, slipping down its cool black front until she was sitting on the floor.

"Have you been drinking?" Sam moved over to her.

"No!" Now she was more annoyed than before. How dare he accuse her of being drunk.

"Can I see your arm please?" Sam sat next to her.

"Look," she pulled up her sleeve. "Happy now?"

"I recognise that symbol." He stood up ignoring her moodiness and left the room.

"Yeah, run away. Who cares about Val's needs?" she called after him. She chugged on her can until it was all gone, then sat, unprepared to leave her precious spot on the floor.

Sam came back with a book in his hands and sat down next to her. "Look, it's the letter A in Theban."

She made herself look. He was right. "Great, maybe they're trying to teach me the alphabet." She stuck her head between her knees and heaved a great sigh. Her brain wanted her to do one thing and her body another. She needed to stay in control, but she wasn't sure how long she could keep this up.

"I don't know, but it's here and we need to know how you got it." Sam seemed blind to her emotional state. "This could be a magical tracking system of some sort." Sam touched the tattoo, tracing the outline of the letter with one finger, and that was it. His contact with her skin sent the message for her body to take over. Before Sam could do anything to defend himself, Val turned on him and got him pinned up against the fridge.

"This is your fault! You've broken me. You loved me. You called me your love. I was something in your life. You protected me; you were prepared to die for me, and now here we are and I can't tell if you even like me. But you can't hide how you feel when you touch me, Sam. I know you feel the same way." Val was breathing fast; her face close to his. She could feel him holding his breath under her grip. She felt completely out of control.

"Val, I don't know what you're talking about, but this is not ok." He was trying desperately to stay calm but she could tell he wasn't succeeding. Her senses were out the window, but she knew exactly how he was feeling about her in that moment. "Please Val!" Finally he pulled away from her.

What was she doing? She pulled back, slumping into a kneeling position. "Oh my God, Sam, I'm so sorry. I don't know what's wrong with me." She bent forward resting her head on the kitchen floor. "I'm spiralling," she sobbed.

"Talk to me. I can't help you if we don't talk." Sam helped her to sit up then hunkered down beside her.

"It hurts so bad, Sam."

He put his arm around her, but stayed silent, waiting for her to go on.

"We lived another life together and you loved me; you were my soul mate, I know you were. And now... now, here we are and I have memories and you don't."

"I'm so sorry," He pulled her in close.

"It's not your fault." Val looked into his eyes. Knowing he understood, she put her head onto his chest.

"So, was I brave?" he asked.

"Very. You saved me from Excariot."

"Really. Wow! That's good news"

"Please don't tell the others; they wouldn't understand." She wiped her face.

"It's our secret," he assured her gently. "Now let's find you a new ear piece, that's what you need isn't it?" He knew how to make a girl feel better: a replacement gadget. He helped her up and they headed out to the hall, up the stairs and along the landing.

They came to a door. It looked like all the others, nothing special.

"Open the door," Sam said stepping to one side.

"Chivalry really has died." Val tried to turn the handle, it didn't budge. "Ok, funny it's locked," she said looking for a keyhole.

"No, it's made the same way as your sword." He reached out to turn the handle, which proceeded to light up in recognition of his hand.

"Impressive!" She followed him into a room which lit up automatically as they entered. The walls were bare, but she knew that she would only see what he wanted her to see.

"Yes, isn't it?" Sam agreed. He walked over to a drawer and pressed the front, and it slid open. Inside was a collection of boxes. He moved them around until he found the one he wanted. "Please don't lose this, ok," he said, handing it to her.

"Well, I try to stay safe but it doesn't always work," she said pushing the little box deep into her pocket. "So, are you hungry?"

"Yes, as long as you're cooking." If she was honest after her funny turn she was ravenous. It was odd, even though telling him how she actually felt, had felt like the worst thing to do, she was relieved that he knew. Now all she had to do was accept that he wasn't her dream Sam, he was just a great guy.

"What's that noise?" Sam asked.

"Me." Val pulled the phone out of her pocket and flipped it open. "What's up, mate?" Val's expression started to change. "No, she left the shop to come to you." She fell silent again, listening intently. "I'm coming," she said after a moment. "Listen to me, Jason, don't panic. I'll find her."

"What's wrong?"

"It's Fran. She never made it back to Jason."

CHAPTER 10

Missing Persons!

Val put her phone back in her pocket and stood for a second processing all the information Jason had given her.

"Are you serious?" Sam asked.

"Very. He said that he went to the bookshop on his bike about ten minutes ago and there was no one there. He called her mobile and there was no answer. I called her earlier as well, but I thought she was with Jason. I need to get to him now." she was just about to teleport.

"Stop, wait a minute. Where are they? I can help look for her," Sam started to open drawers revealing various gadgets Val had never seen, plus his trusty light sword.

"Jason and Shane are at the parlour, meet us there," she responded and was gone.

Val arrived at the gym, knowing she would be in trouble for making another unofficial jump, but that didn't matter when a friend's safety was at stake.

"Any news?" she asked Jason who was prowling up and down.

"Thank God you're here. Where's Zac?" Jason looked around fretfully.

"He had to go back to Alchany." Now wasn't the time for Ranswar explanations. "Do we have any clues? Have you called Fran's parents?" she asked.

"No. She seems to have disappeared into thin air," Shane said as Jason continued pacing while trying, over and over again, to dial her number.

"Maybe I should wait at the bookshop; she may go back there," said Val.

"Maybe we should call the police." Jason started to dial.

"Son, I've told you we can't do that. You know what would happen to Val if they found out about her."

"No. Call them. I will work from my end with Sam. Anyone who can help us find her should be on board." Val stepped into Jason's path. "We will find her, Jason, I promise you that." She could feel tears welling in her eyes, he looked so completely lost. The mighty boxer felled with one punch to the heart and it hurt her to her core. He nodded and started to dial. Val grabbed her bracelet and teleported back to the bookshop.

She arrived to darkness and silence: no Wendy, no Zac, nothing. She was completely alone, not a feeling she was accustomed to. She needed to get Zac, but how? She had already broken the rules three times so what difference would it make if she did it again? She decided to go to Alchany and get him back. She flicked the lights on, meaning to go straight upstairs, but her attention was drawn to the counter. There, on its dark wooden top, was a stark white envelope, with her name on the front. "Delta," she hissed. How had she gotten into the shop? She held it in her hand for a moment; even the touch of it made her uneasy; she knew this wouldn't be good news. It opened easily and its contents were just as bad as she had feared. She found herself looking at a picture of Fran, tied to a chair. She turned it over and on the back was written: **A promise is a promise, Alien.**

Val pulled out her phone and rang Jason. Things had just taken a turn for the worse in more ways than one, but at least she knew who had Fran. "You need to come to the bookshop now with your dad. I know who has her. No, I can't explain over the phone." She flipped the picture over in her fingers. "Tell the police it's a false alarm. Get rid of them. Tell them she has turned up. And trust me." She hung up and headed towards the flat; she needed to get ready.

As Jason and Shane arrived at the bookshop so did Wendy, returning from her first date with Daniel. She stepped out of the car, romance fresh in her cheeks, like a flower that had just been allowed to breathe its first breath of spring. She glowed with happiness. Daniel followed her as she made her way over to Jason who hadn't noticed her arrival.

She tapped him on the shoulder. "Hey, you, gone blind?"

Jason turned. "What?" He spotted Daniel and carried on towards the shop, Shane close behind him.

"Shane, what's wrong?" Wendy was clever enough to know by now that something was going on. She stopped, turning towards Daniel who almost fell over her. "I have to go." She put her hand on his chest to stop and support him at the same time.

"Oh, but I thought..."

"Not now." She walked away from him and towards the real world waiting for her behind the bookshop doors. Daniel watched her go, then he retreated to his car and left.

"Ok, what is going on?" Wendy asked.

"Fran has gone missing, and we now have this picture of her," Shane passed it to Wendy.

"Oh no! When did this happen? Why didn't you call me? Jason, we will get her back." Wendy was shaking so Shane removed the picture from her hand and put an arm around her tiny frame.

Val stood behind the counter suited and booted, ready to go. "I need to go and find Zac first."

She had barely spoken the sentence when he walked though the private door. "Zac! You're back early." Val was pleased she had been able to avoid going through the portal, but she was also concerned that he was back so soon.

"The Ranswar that was selected for me did not find me suitable." Zac seemed matter of fact about his rejection, but Val knew it was a little bit of show.

"Well, her loss and we need you here. Things are not going well. Fran has been taken and I know who's done it, but they don't," Val pointed to the others.

"You know? Tell me now! What's wrong with you?" Jason shouted at Val.

"Because it's not that simple," Val spoke softly; she could tell Jason was at breaking point.

Zac turned the picture around in his hand. "I see. So it's your ex friend Delta. I warned you about this; they are going to need all the information you can give them if they are going to get through this."

"I know and I..." Val was interrupted by the bell as Sam walked in.

"Hello, I guessed you might be here." He walked straight over to Jason and put his arm around him. Jason lowered his forehead onto Sam's chest. "Well get her back, don't worry mate."

Val knew that if she allowed them to remember Delta it may put her parents at risk, but enough was enough. "Wendy, I need you to do something really important for me. Long story short: I had a friend. She was a traitor and she betrayed us all. When I came back from sixteen forty-five you guys didn't remember her. Zac told me that was because she didn't come back with me on my timeline, and so she became one of the 'forgotten'. I left it alone thinking this particular ghost would never come back to haunt me, but I underestimated her greatly. She is the one who has Fran and I need you guys to remember her. Now can you do anything to make that happen?"

"Wow, information overload, Val," said Wendy, heading towards the counter and the dellatrax. "One of the chapters is about a memory restoral. It has something to do with the people that have been taken by prisoners and then have to return to Earth."

Val could have kicked herself. The Collector had told her all about it. "Yes! You're right. Zac, can we allow them to remember Delta from the information you hold on her? We need to move quickly."

"It against regulations! This could be a trap. I warned you." Zac was rubbing his neck, visibly uneasy about what they were about to do.

"Listen, my girlfriend is out there possibly being tortured by some thug, so please forgive me if I don't give a damn about your regulations," Jason looked like he was going to launch an attack on Zac, but Sam had him by the arm and pulled him back.

"Wendy, do it." Val knew that they didn't realise that Zac was only trying to protect her. It was far too much to explain. Wendy rummaged behind the counter and pulled out one of the books.

"It says that all those who want to remember need to touch this entry in the dellatrax together." Jason was at her side in a blink, hand on the centre of the page followed by Shane and Sam. Wendy placed her hands with theirs and the light show began. Images danced over them all. Val felt a churning in her stomach. What if they didn't remember Delta? What if it went wrong and the dellatrax wiped all their memories. A little late for that thought now.

The colour changed from blue to red, and then to a deep purple. It was the most extraordinary display to watch. Then, in the gap between them, an image of Delta appeared. It was like watching a movie rewinding at speed. Val found it extremely painful to watch. As the film started to fade into a blur, so the light show seemed to dissipate. Sam was the first to look up. Val waited patiently for a reaction. They all stood back in silence.

Wendy was first to speak. "Don't do that to me again."

Val looked at the ground. They had every right to be angry with her. "I'm sorry but..."

Zac came to Val's side. "Val did nothing to you. She had no control over you forgetting Delta. She could have told you everything but it wouldn't have made sense because it no longer existed in your memory banks." Zac looked serious, ready to argue with anyone who wanted to question his decision.

"It's ok, Zac." Val placed her hand on his arm. "Look, I'm sorry I couldn't tell you, but I'm not sorry that I left her there."

"Neither am I," Jason spoke up. "Now I remember her and what happened on that night I agree with your decision, but all I care about now is getting Fran back.

Is there any way you can find her with your equipment, Zac?"

"No, she isn't in my prison banks. So, unless a prisoner takes form to capture her, I can do nothing."

"She's with Delta and that means there are no prisoners. From what I have seen of her, she's working alone and is extremely annoyed with me."

"How did she get back then?" Sam asked.

"We don't know, but whatever she did it must have had some serious power behind it. It took Excariot a whole coven plus me to travel through time."

"Maybe she isn't alone then," Sam suggested what Val didn't want to even contemplate.

"Hello! Fran. Please." Jason's voice was now full of despair.

"I understand, mate, but we need to know what we could be walking into and from what Val has just said it could be very dangerous." Sam was right, they didn't have enough information, but they needed to move fast.

"Let's look at the picture. Maybe there are some clues on it." Shane started to inspect it closely.

"Ok, everyone, please take one of these." Sam pulled a small box from his pocket with what looked like pinhead badges.

Wendy picked a purple one out. "What are they for?" She put it onto her dress.

"So we don't lose you as well." Sam handed one to Shane, Jason then Zac.

"I have no need of this device; I am a hunter." Zac held it back out to Sam.

"You are and a very good one, but we aren't, so do me a favour and put it on." Zac did as he was told, looking concerned at Sam's words.

"I just can't see anything to help us: white walls and a standard chair; there are no defining points to the image." As Shane passed the picture back to Jason a violent knock came at the door causing them all to jump. Wendy squealed with shock. Val looked out into the darkness but the lights cast a reflection on the glass so it was hard to see who was there.

She made her way to the window and pressed her nose to the glass. Now she could see Flo on the other side. "It's Flo. Should I let her in?"

Flo banged again loudly. "I can hear you, you idiot. Let me in!" Val opened the door and Flo pushed past.

"You're a nice little girl!" Sam said sarcastically; pushing her past him gently.

"She's not a girl," Zac responded.

Sam shook his head as if not surprised.

Flo pointed at Jason. "You're the reason I'm here. That little trollop Delta is back, and she has your girlfriend." Everyone looked at Flo in amazement.

Jason crossed over to Flo, grabbing her forcefully by the arm. "Where is she?"

Flo winced and let out a cry. "Do you want me to help you?"

He released her, but stayed close.

"Listen carefully. Excariot knows Delta's back. She has been leaving him notes all over the place, but he hasn't managed to find her yet, not even the witch has. Then tonight he got this picture." Flo held up an identical picture to the one Val had received. She turned it over, revealing an address on the back. "He is going to send some Daymars to try and get rid of Delta once and for all. He's not stupid enough to go himself. So, now you know where she is, go and get the girl before him." She grinned at them, seeming pleased with her offer.

"You say not even his witch can find Delta, so Delta must be powerful," Wendy commented.

"Yes, he's also very displeased that you escaped from the Summari, Val. He came back injured, but he won't even talk about what happened. I heard through the grapevine that there was some sort of heated fight."

"A fight?" Zac asked, but Flo chose to ignore him.

"Anyway, back to tonight. Excariot has located another high priest and he's sent me to go collect this man from some weird location. I know we had a deal for me to tell you about these collections, but I thought that maybe saving your friend was a priority today. Plus he suspects there's a turncoat in his midst, so I need to tread carefully." Flo looked up at the others for a reaction.

Val scratched her head. "Let's just take a moment. You're saying that there was a fight and Excariot got wounded, although you can't say by whom or how, and we have an address for Fran but you're off in the opposite direction to capture another innocent high priest. Are you asking us to ignore you?" Val looked for support.

"Well, it would take some of the heat off me." Flo shoved a hand full of tobacco into her mouth.

"That stuff will kill you," Sam said.

"Don't worry, she's already dead," Val replied.

Jason grabbed the picture from Val's hand and headed towards the door. "I know where I'm going."

"No, Jason, wait. We need to work out how we're going to tackle everything. Flo is off and we need to get Fran back, but we need to be a united front or we don't stand a chance."

"Val, this situation you're in means nothing to me, but Fran does." He pulled the handle.

"STOP! Listen! Our Daymars have just taken human form: Prisoner 16059. They are already where Fran is." Zac shouted urgently, getting everyone's attention. "Wendy, get the books open; we need information, fast." Glad of something positive to do, she headed behind the counter.

The shop door banged shut as Jason disappeared through it.

"I'm going with Jason." Val hurried after him.

"No, I'll go." Shane ran past, helmet in hand. "You go with Zac and make sure nothing happens to her till we get there."

"I'll man the computer and stay here with Wendy." Sam waved them all off as he headed towards the cupboard.

"But I need you," Val whined.

"We need to move out. Do you have everything?" Zac asked impatiently, his hand hovering ready to teleport her.

"Yes, but what about Flo?" She looked towards the little blonde girl standing at the counter.

"There's only one Fran and there are more priests and priestesses. Let Flo get this one to prove to Excariot that she isn't this turncoat person. Let's get your friend back. Jason is a vital member of your unit, and without her he is lost."

The last thing she saw as they teleported was Wendy grabbing a book and running after Sam.

As Val landed she felt Zac pull her to the ground and slap his hand over her mouth. Holding her down, he leaned over her body. If his weight wasn't bad enough, the fact that she couldn't breathe made things a little more confusing. Zac looked down into her eyes, his hot breath blowing into her face, making her blink uncontrollably. She realised they must have landed a little closer to the action than expected, so she didn't do the usual complaining. Slowly Zac lifted himself off of her, easing the pressure of his hand over her lips so that breathing became slightly less painful. She nodded in his direction to confirm she understood that things weren't going so well. As he released her, she heard footsteps on the other side of what they had landed behind. She reached her hand out to touch something that felt like very poor quality wooden shelving, mass-produced, and possibly pre-packed. If they were ever captured and tortured with furniture questions she would definitely get out alive.

"Do you recognise where we are?" Zac whispered.

Val pulled herself into a sitting position, knowing she would be hidden by the shelves. She peeked over the top and caught her breath. "Toy r Us," she said, ducking back down.

"What?"

"We are in a very large toy store. Here on Earth we give toys and play with our children."

"There is no need for your sarcasm; we have forms of entertainment on Alchany."

"Sorry. So the place is full of shelves with stuffed teddies and Barbies. We'll never find Delta," Val sniggered, then stopped realising how inappropriate it was.

"Will there be a problem with these teddies and Barbies?"

"No." He really was an alien.

"Hello." A familiar voice whispered into her ear. She smiled. Sam was there with her.

"Do you know where we are?"

"Lanron," he responded.

"Ok. So Jason and Shane will be here soon. Zac, we need to get ready because Jason isn't going to go for a quiet entrance."

"I agree. Wendy has found the Daymars... she's so good with these books," Sam gushed.

"Hi Val," Wendy called from the background. "Prisoner 16059. The Daymars are sort of like scorpions. They have armour for skin, which is impossible to penetrate unless you have a telactic horn, something a little bit like a curly dagger."

"Zac, do you have a telactic horn hidden in your uniform?" Val looked at him with expectant eyes.

"No!" Zac let out a nerdy snigger. "Do you know how rare they are?"

"No, and I don't care," she hissed back at him. "Did you hear that, Wendy?" she whispered in the hope that Wendy would come back with an earthly alternative.

"Shh," Zac placed his finger clumsily against Val's lips, making her look like a strange fish. She rolled her eyes, unsure what was happening, but following his lead. He pointed towards the shelving that covered them and Val heard a deep cough come from the other side. Her heart suddenly started to race; this was real. Fran was here somewhere and she needed to save her. For the first time since they had arrived she knew her friend's life depended on her, and that was an overwhelming weight to bear. She pulled out her sword. It may not work on the solid skin of the Daymars, but she didn't yet know exactly what was on the other side of the shelving.

The bang happened with no warning. It was like a bullet going off and for a split second, Val feared the worse. She peered over the shelves to see that the noise was Jason who was coming through the double doors. He had arrived a lot quicker than she had hoped and he wasn't going to be quiet or patient, and she was sure he definitely didn't have a telactic horn in his pocket.

"We need to act now. Jason's here and he's not going to take any prisoners," she said to Zac. She extended her sword and jumped up to see Jason and Shane running towards them down the main aisle. What she hadn't spotted was the man coming in from the right hand side. The first she knew of him was when a very large fist connected with her face. The initial pain wasn't too bad; it was the crunching sound her nose made that was more worrying. She could tell it was bleeding because when the man's fist withdrew, it was covered in blood: her blood. She staggered back into the supportive arms of Zac. At least he was there to catch her, even if he didn't fight.

"Pay attention!" he scolded her. "Don't let your emotions distract you." He said unsympathetically, pushing her back out - towards the man's returning fist. If her face was going to survive the experience she needed to react.

Her duck was perfectly timed. His hand missed, flying past her head and ruffling her hair, causing him to lose his balance. As he staggered over her, she came in close with an upper cut, aided by alien magic. No one was going to make her nose bleed twice in one evening. He fell backwards but no one was there to stop his flight and he crashed into the shiny plastic flooring with a thud. He grunted when a shower of 'tickle me Elmos' landed on him.

"Good," Zac called from behind her. She would deal with him later, now she needed to get to Jason who, with Shane, had another large man on the ground.

"Where is she?" he screamed into his face.

The man laughed. Jason was just about to show him how much he didn't appreciate that when a store room door flew open and out walked three women. "Daymars," Zac told her, pointing at them. "Look at that armour; you can see it, even in human form."

Val wiped blood from her face with the hem of her t-shirt. She needed a sponsorship; that way she could have a new top for every occasion. As they came into the florescent lighting Val could see what he meant. Their skin looked like shiny black metal. As they came closer, the man who was pinned down started to panic. He managed to push Shane off and scramble to his feet, bursting past Val and running in the only direction he could: towards the women. He obviously hadn't heard of telactic horns or Daymars. What followed was very quick. The first girl moved into a single leg squat. Her other leg came across the man's shin. Val heard it crack. This wasn't going to be pretty. He crumbled to the ground, screaming in pain. The female returned to the walking position without even breaking her stride.

"Wendy, I need some help and fast. These women are going to kill us." She looked anxiously towards Jason and Shane. They wouldn't stand a chance against these women.

"Ok, it says here that they have the ability to withstand bullets. Wow, that's cool."

"Are you serious?" Val yelled.

"Fire!" Sam shouted almost deafening Val. "They are subdued by fire."

"Fire?" Val looked at Zac. "What about the women who own the bodies? Will I hurt them?"

"No. The human form should be protected until extraction," Zac answered.

"Should?" Val blurted. She knew she could do it, but would it be enough? Only time would tell and the time was now. She pushed her sword into her back pocket and focused all her energy on the nerves in her stomach. A small flame appeared on the palm of her hand, but it wasn't big enough or quick enough. The Daymars were on top of them and Val feared the worst. She tensed, expecting pain. Then a hand grabbed her from behind and in an instant she was teleported across the room. Zac did have his uses.

She opened her eyes to see one of the women striking Shane. To her horror he fell to the ground and stayed there, his body seeming limp and lifeless. Jason leapt onto a set of shelves to avoid one of the others. Val ran at the woman closest to Shane, no thought in her mind other than the need to protect him.

"YOU!" she screamed, getting the creature's instant attention. The anger she felt now, had only been equalled the time she had thought that Delta was dead. Without any effort from her, her body raised off the ground and fire exploded on both her hands. This was power beyond anyone's imagining, including hers. She threw a massive bolt towards the woman closest to Shane. When it hit, the woman screamed once, then froze. It was as if her chemical compounds were shorted out by the flames. She became completely rigid, cooked in her own armour.

The other two women didn't fare any better. Flames fired from Val's hands, causing toys to fly through the air and filling it with the overwhelming smell of singed fur.

Finished with them at last, Val came to a standstill only feet away from Shane's still unconscious body.

She lifted Shane's wrist and felt for a pulse. He was alive. "Zac, you stay with him, teleport out if necessary," Val ordered and he knew better than to cross her at this moment. He wasn't even sure if she knew her hands were still on fire.

"Jason! Me, you, out back. Sam, Wendy - silence." She pointed towards the large set of swing doors the women had been heading for. They had metal detectors on each side of them and a sign above them. Val now had a good idea where Delta had put Fran. They pushed through together as her flames petered out. Jason closed in. He wasn't scared, she could sense it. Fran was so lucky.

"Where are we going, mate?" he asked as they walked past a wall full of board games.

"I think she'll be in the toilets, but don't expect her to be alone." The ladies' toilets lay five feet ahead of them. When they reached the door, Jason nodded at her, and she pulled out her sword and extended it. Whatever was behind that door, this finished here and now. Val moved in front. She kicked the door with her foot, allowing it to swing open once. In the crack she saw a very scared looking Fran, tied and gagged, and guarded by three large men. Where did they all come from? 'Giants for hire.com'? Jason pushed past her, lost in the sight of Fran. It would be no good to even try to stop him.

The first man who came at Jason received a great deal of the anger he had been holding inside. His huge mass fell limp after the exchange of a few blows, then Val tazered the next guy, her bracelet flashing contently in sync with her sword. She smiled grimly as he also fell to the ground where he twitched and writhed. However, the last one wasn't going to go down so easily. He struck Jason across the face and had him on his knees before Val could get to him.

"Stop!" she yelled. The man was shocked at her reaction and whilst still holding Jason's hair he came to a halt. "Enough. We want Fran and you're alone. If you leave now I promise you won't get hurt." She was pointing her sword at his face. He looked nervously between the two of them. And then decided to take the offer. Val didn't care about this man. He was an employee and no wage could match her anger. She had what she wanted. He released Jason who leapt to his feet and ran to Fran, throwing himself on her, kissing her face with his bloodied lips. Finally reminded by Fran's frantic grunts and expressively rolling eyes, he pulled frantically at her ropes and released her. Val watched the last man starting his dash for freedom.

Jason pulled down Fran's gag. "I'm so sorry. It won't ever happen again. I love you. I'll never leave your side. Tell me if they hurt you. Please talk to me." Jason had now almost completely covered Fran's face in kisses.

"Thought you'd decided to keep me tied up!" she managed a small joke. "I'm fine. Are you ok?" Fran rubbed her wrists as Jason finally managed to free her feet. Then she quickly pulled his face in close and kissed him. "I knew you'd find me," she whispered, tears filling her eyes. She tried to stand, but it was all too much and she collapsed back onto the chair. Jason scooped her up into his arms.

As he walked past Val, Fran held out her hand. Val grabbed it and Fran held onto her tightly. Shane was now sitting up rubbing his head while Zac pulled the stone women closer together.

"Fran!" Shane stood when he saw the small group approaching, and embraced her and his son. "Thank goodness you're safe."

She gave a weak smile in his direction. "I could do with a hot chocolate."

Suddenly Val was overwhelmed by the realisation of how close she had come to losing a very good friend. All the bravado and anger of the last few minutes disappeared and her eyes filled with tears. Not wanting the others to see this sudden sign of weakness, she tried to move away. Fran tightened her grip.

"This is not your fault, Val," she whispered. "There was this girl, blonde thing who needs a good meal if you ask me. She seriously hates you, but we won't give in to her. She needs a good sorting out and she's going to get it!"

Val gave a watery smile and nodded, too emotional to trust her voice.

"We can tell you all about her back at the book shop." Jason winked at Val and pulled Fran in closer. Clearly he wasn't going to let her go any time soon.

"You only have the bike here, how will you all get back?" Val asked.

"If it's safe to speak, Sam's on his way," Wendy's voice rang in her ear.

"Sam's coming. We will just wait till he gets here." Val winced as she dabbed her painful nose again. Shane came over and took her chin between his fingers, gently turning her face from one side to the other.

"I think you've been lucky. It's doesn't look broken, just painful. You're going to look extra specially attractive tomorrow." He put his arm around her and gave her a gentle squeeze. "You ok?"

"I am now we have Fran back." She smiled weakly. This was all starting to take its toll on her. Her day seemed to be filled with fighting and stress. She felt at breaking point. "We have another prisoner," Zac announced.

"Are you serious?" Val's look of despair was lost on hunter boy.

"Yes, we need to get these Daymars back to the Collector and go." He was absolutely serious.

"She's done enough Zac; she's just a kid." Shane's concern was also wasted on Zac.

"Now!" Zac pulled the three stone women close enough for them to be teleported in one go.

Val looked at the others, resignation in her eyes. She was so tired she wondered how she could possibly do anything else today. "See you back at the bookshop." She placed her hand on Zac and they were off.

Fran glared at Jason. "Put me down." He lowered her to her unsteady feet. "This is just ridiculous; Val can't carry on like this. It's going to kill her. She's being pulled in a million directions at a hundred miles an hour." Fran looked between the two men that stood protectively on each side of her.

Shane nodded in agreement. "What can we do?"

"I don't know, but there has to be another way. Maybe some other guard could take over. Surely there are better qualified people than her?"

"I have to say that when she lost it today, Dad, she was scary. It was as if seeing you on the ground sent her into some sort of power surge. She was awesome! Maybe she is *really* special. Even Zac looked shocked when she threw those massive fire balls."

Shane looked at his wrist. "So that explains my burns. Well, we need to sit down and think about what we can do, but first, let's get out of here."

Jason put his arm around Fran and they made their way back to the exit they had broken in through.

Delta watched them leave. "Well, that was entertaining." She looked over her shoulder. "The war has started and we have thrown the first stone."

A voice answered from the darkness. "Yes, but they got her back and now you have lost four of your followers."

"You have enough money. Anyone will follow you, plus someone has to be a scapegoat for breaking and entering. Call the police and make sure they get here quickly." She flicked back her hair.

"Yes mother, but..."

"Do I have to tell you again?" Delta raised her hand for silence. "She left us to die; your father left us to die, and I was the only one who loved you. No one came for us and we have made our way back to the future. You're as powerful as her and don't you forget it. Our time will come. Plans are in place. I will get them back for what they did to us, do you understand," her voice tight and agitated.

"Yes Mother."

"Good, now make the call."

Chapter 11

Promises, Promises

Val and Zac stood outside the portal with three stone statues. "Can't we leave these here and just go for the next prisoner, then we can deliver them all at once and the Collector will be so pleased with us." She wasn't sure how to tell him she had teleported five times already this evening and that she was more than positive she would be in some serious trouble.

"Ok. Let us find Wendy and see who prisoner..." he looked at his watch, "...103774 is."

They left the figures behind and hurried to find Wendy who was in the cupboard looking at her mobile phone with a blank expression.

"Hello," Val whispered trying not to make her jump. She failed; Wendy jolted, almost falling off her chair.

"You're back!" She stood and hugged Val and smiled at Zac - she knew he wasn't too keen on the touching thing.

"We need you to do some more of your magic, but first, why are you staring at the phone like that?"

"Daniel, he sent me a text."

"If he has upset you, I can sort him out," Val said.

"No," she laughed. "He wants to see me again tomorrow."

"That's good, isn't it?" Val was confused by her reaction.

"Yes, if you're a normal girl, living in a normal world, it's just peachy. But I'm not, I'm the guardian to the most powerful witch of all time, and I read an alien book, and I've never been on a date until tonight, and now I'm looking at number two in less than twenty-four hours."

"Just take it one day at a time, Wendy. He seems like a nice guy and he has a weird old car just like you, so you're obviously made for each other. Love doesn't always come easy; if it's worth having you will find a way. Say *yes* and we will work the rest out. Now, tell me about prisoner 103774." Val touched Wendy's shoulder and gave her the famous Valerie Sheridan Saunders "everything is going to be ok" smile.

Wendy looked down at the dellatrax and out the corner of her eye caught a glimpse of a blue flash as Val and Zac vanished.

Val was surprised when they arrived in the great outdoors. They were on what looked like a coastline and the dark mixed with the cold air made it feel particularly eerie. "Wendy where are we?"

"The screen says Dover. Your prisoners are Valangar. They love water and like to drown people, from the inside out, so my advice would be to stay away from the sea. No joke intended."

"Thanks." As Val's eyesight adjusted to the dark, she realised that staying dry was going to be top of her list. They were about ten feet from the edge of the white cliffs of Dover. Val had visited them once with her parents when she was little and she was just as scared of heights now as she had been then.

"Over there," Zac pointed. They made their way cautiously, following the edge of the cliff. "It seems very high," he said.

"You think so?" Val responded holding onto his arm.

"Well hello." A voice came out of the darkness. Val strained to see figures in the distance. "Not exactly the best time of day to be walking so close to the edge, is it?" another voice said. They came closer; Val wasn't sure if she was seeing double. She rubbed both eyes together to clear her vision, but no, they were identical twins.

"It's them," Zac whispered.

"Are you guys out here camping, because you know it's not safe to be walking so close to the edge and you look really young?"

"What's going on?" a man called out.

"Nothing," one of the twins responded.

"Girls, come on back to the camping ground. It's not safe out here." The man jogged up to them and Val recognised him instantly. It was Max, the man she had rescued from the underground caving incident. Of course! He was the high priest; he looked exactly the same. Val remembered he worked for the Navy or something.

"We were lost and the girls were giving us directions," Val explained as Flo waltzed up between them.

"Oh well, come back to the camp site with us and we will help you out." Max was still a gentleman. As he turned the twins grabbed him one on each side. "Girls, don't be silly." Max pulled at his arm but the girls weren't letting go and they were extremely strong; far too strong. "Hey, you're hurting me," he said looking confused.

"What are you playing at?" Val's asked angrily.

"You said you would stay away if I helped you, so why are you here?" Flo spoke softly but with an unmistakeable hint of a threat.

"We got information that prisoners had taken human form. We came to investigate," Val responded.

"The man is ours. Leave before it gets ugly. No harm will come to him." Flo was about to leave, not interested in any further discussion.

"No, this is not acceptable. You don't get to tell us who we can or can't arrest," Zac shouted, starting to get agitated. "Val, we have Fran. You can save this man. Please take action."

"You, stupid hunter. You told her to let me do this. How quickly you forget." Flo shoved her chest out at Zac, like a man, as if she was challenging him to fight.

Val really wasn't sure what to do. Wendy came to her rescue. "Can you hear me?" she whispered into Val's ear."

"Yes, are you ok?"

"Yes. When you made the promise to Flo it was to help you keep someone on the inside safe. You have no choice but to walk away from this. We still have time to stop Excariot."

"But Max…" she struggled with her decision, hearing Max calling for help while the twins dragged him into the darkness. "Flo, if one hair on his head gets damaged before I get him back, you will pay." She poked her in the chest.

"You're doing the right thing." Flo smiled smugly, brushed down her dress, then walked off towards the twins.

"What are you doing?" Zac grabbed Val's arm.

She shook him off and glared at him. "What I need to do. There's a saying here on Earth: 'keep your friends close and your enemies closer'. Take me home." She was glad it was dark, that way he couldn't see the tears streaming down her face.

"No." Zac said before he disappeared.

"Immature," Val shouted into the dark. She twisted round just in time to see Flo, the twins and Max teleport. Funny, Flo's spark was green.

"How did I get here?" Val sat down on the ground, the cool grass below her, and looked up at the star filled sky. The moon was hardly visible and the sea breeze was salty-smelling. She would have to go back, she knew that, but just for a minute she wanted to sit and take a breather. She knew Zac was right: she should never have allowed Flo and the twins to take Max. Letting an innocent person be taken away while she sat back and watched. Zac was very unhappy with her, but he would get over it, and Flo was right: he had said it was ok. So actually *she* had every right to be annoyed with *him*.

"Val," a voice in her head interrupted her musings. It was Sam.

"Hi."

"You ok?"

"No, but what can we do?" She felt her throat tightening as the tears flowed again. "Is Zac back?"

"Yes, he's with Jason. He's in a bit of a mood. What's going on?"

"We had to let someone go. We made a deal with Flo and when the time came he didn't want to go through with it."

"And you did?"

"Please don't have a go. I'm feeling terrible as it is and my nose really hurts. He was calling for help and

I watched them take him away. What's wrong with me Sam?"

"Only the greatest soldiers can leave a man behind in order to choose the path they know will be for the greater good of all. You did the right thing. Please come home." She could hear the concern and honesty in his voice.

"I'm on my way." She placed her hand on her father's bracelet and was off.

The flat was empty apart from the three statue women from toys r us.

"Hi ladies, thinking of popping out?" Val giggled; she would never lose her sense of humour. It kept her sane. She headed to the bookshop where she found Fran being introduced to Delta through the magic of her dellatrax.

Fran stepped back from the book. "Ok, no wonder she was such a bundle of fun." Fran looked exhausted. Jason helped her to a chair and passed her a hot drink.

"Hi, how're you feeling?" Val knelt down by Fran's chair.

"I've had better days, but I know who my friends are now, and Wendy told me about Max. We will save him won't we? I feel so guilty."

"I promise you we will; I just did what I had to do to keep you safe."

"Yes, and now we have to go and face the Collector. She is *not* going to be happy," Zac interrupted huffily. "I will get ready for her arrival." He stomped off to the flat.

"Yeah, yeah." Val patted Fran's knee. "See you tomorrow."

"Yes, bright and early." Fran stood and Jason led her out the shop, Shane following them.

"Well if that's all for today, I think I need a rest," Wendy said. She looked tired too. Sam offered to take her home, but she turned him down insisting she had her car outside. Val waved from the top of the outside steps as he escorted her to the vehicle.

As soon as Wendy had driven off, Sam came back up the steps towards Val. They were alone. He moved closer to her and, as much as she didn't want to feel the way she did, it was almost like her heart was beating its way out of her chest.

"So what are you doing now?" he asked, moving another step closer.

She was pleased she was holding onto the door or she may have collapsed. "I have prisoners to hand over."

"And after that?" One more step. If he came any closer they would be touching. His eyes were level with Val's. They looked darker at night, like pools of ink on a pure white page.

"Nothing."

"Would you like to have a coffee?"

"Yes," she replied, as he stepped up the last step. The shop door flew open allowing Val to fall backward into the shop. Sam grabbed her hand before she had time to reach the floor. "Sorry," she said blushing, pulling herself back up. "Will you wait for me here?" she asked.

He nodded in response.

"Ok, two minutes." Val had to stop herself from falling over the counter and knocking herself out on the private door. It was like a scene from the chuckle brothers she thought despairingly.

Maybe telling Sam about her feelings for the other Sam wasn't such a bad thing after all. Possibly it was just what was needed to move them on to the next level in their friendship, like having a coffee. Oh, what was she thinking? He probably just wanted to ask her some nerdy questions about her powers. He was as interested in her as she was in football.

She made her way up the stairs to find an impatient Zac tapping his foot. "Don't say anything to me. You left me all on my own out there." Val shoved past him. He followed her, obviously still sulking. Val flashed her bracelet over the portal and they steeled themselves for the Collector's arrival. The warning signals started, but they didn't sound the same as the ones she had grown used to. She could swear that it had just said something like "Guard arrest". Zac looked nervously at Val. They both knew something was very wrong but neither of them had time to move an inch. The portal opened and a young man stepped into the flat.

"Twenty-three thirteen, you are here by arrested for the crime of hiding a known criminal from the Warden and Judges of Alchany, and for the excess use of teleportation for personal reasons. You will escort me to the prison, where you will stand trial for these charges."

"What? I wouldn't hide a criminal. What are you talking about?" Val was confused.

"She has done nothing of the sort, and I have teleported with her every time. She hasn't used excess teleports," Zac responded dryly.

"Oh, no, that's true." She looked at the ground in shame. "But I don't know any criminals and I think I would know if I was supposedly hiding one." She could feel her chest beginning to tighten.

The guard moved forward and placed what looked like a glowing circle from his bracelet over Val's wrist.

"I didn't know I could do that."

"Val, when did you teleport?"

"I went to see Sam, and then to get Fran. I just couldn't help myself. When you left with that woman I was out of control."

"Enough talking has taken place. Thirty-three twenty-seven you will wait here for your Collector to arrive, and you will cover this position until a suitable guard can be sent to replace this thing." He pushed Val towards the portal.

She had no choice but to go. When she looked back the last thing she saw was the fear in Zac's eyes.

CHAPTER 12

In the Eyes of the Law

Zac watched Val fade into the portal; his world felt like it had fallen completely apart. Why hadn't she told him about her little teleporting issues? He had warned her what would happen. Why was she so difficult to work with? His last guard hadn't been this problematic. He looked around the flat. The reality was sinking in and he had no idea what to do. Then he remembered the Daymars; they would get him the Collector. She would help him. He placed his bracelet on the portal. The usual sounds rang in his ear and the Collector arrived.

"Something really bad has happened to Val..."

She raised her hand for Zac to pipe down. "She is in holding at the moment, and I'm unable to communicate with you about this issue. You need to look at the people you have been mixing with. Maybe a little girl who is older than her years has all the answers." The Collector moved her tiny hand and three solid statues rose obediently off the ground.

Zac knew exactly who she was talking about: Flo. The Collector disappeared from sight and he ran for the stairs. He didn't know how he was going to solve this problem, but he wouldn't give up on her.

When he reached the bottom of the stairs Zac became aware that there was someone still in the shop. The lights were still on and there was a strange mumbling sound, as if someone was speaking. He pushed the private door violently in the hope of scaring any intruders.

"Good God!" Sam gasped, nearly falling off his stool. "What on earth are you doing Zac?" He straightened himself up. "And where's Val?"

"She was arrested for helping the old one, Flo, and for teleporting without permission."

"What do you mean arrested?" Sam stood up.

"They have taken her back to Alchany to be placed in holding. She will be put on trial at the first opportunity. I have been told to wait for my replacement, which gives me the impression that she will be extracted." He took a deep breath. "I don't want that to happen to her. She is annoying, unprofessional, lacks discipline and has many other negative personality traits, which I won't list, but she wanted to save my life so much that she risked going to the Warden for me."

"I understand." Sam rose from his stool. "I need to know what you want me to do and how I can help you."

"We have to find Flo. The Collector gave me a clue as to why they had taken her and it was her."

"Funny you should say that because when she was here last I planted a tracking device on her. I never was one for trusting little dead girls who chew tobacco. So, let's go find our friend." Sam and Zac headed to the cupboard.

Val's arrival was reminiscent of previous times, except she was now the criminal and the Collectors were glaring at her for a completely different reason. What was going to happen to her? She was scared, there was no doubt about that. She had never even been in detention before; now she was a prisoner on an alien planet. How had her life become this messed up? She had a real mixed bag of emotions going through her head as the guard dragged her along. Scared came top, annoyed that she had allowed herself to teleport the way she had, especially after Zac's warning and, last but not least, she was sad to think that she might never go home. He eyes started to fill up but she fought the tears back. She wouldn't be weak in front of these people.

"Here is your quarter. You will stay here until your trial." The guard unattached himself and pushed Val into a tiny luminous glass cubicle. A see-through door closed behind her. The walls and ceiling started to move and lasers shot out, surrounding her body. Then the cell and walls adjusted their height and width so all she could do was sit on a bench as wide as her bottom and look out at the world passing her by. She placed her head against the door and started to beg that someone, anyone, would come and get her out of here.

Sam and Zac found Flo quickly using Sam's tracking device. He said she wasn't that far away and Zac was eager to leave.

"Which one is she?" Zac starred at the computer screen. "Who's that?" he pointed at a cluster of lights.

"That's Shane, Jason and Fran. They're at home."

"So this one is Flo?" He identified a single light.

"No, that's Wendy." Sam pointed to the last light. "There's our friend, Flo; she's about four miles from here."

"Sam, do you want to come with me?"

"I wouldn't miss it for the world. Let's go."

Zac grabbed Sam's arm and they were off.

Their arrival was slightly messy as Sam was obviously unpractised in the art of landing.

"Is this your first time?" Zac enquired, patting Sam's back as he bent over gagging.

"No, I have teleported with Val before, but the journey was very short." He raised himself to full height and took a few deep breaths.

"Where are we?" Zac looked at his surroundings. There were far more books here than in the bookshop. They looked clean and smart, on light coloured shelves, in military style rows.

"It's a library. Why would Flo be in a library?" Sam looked around. The emergency exit lighting gave them enough illumination to see their surroundings quite clearly.

A child's voice rang through the air. "No, it's not a problem. I said it was all going to plan. Trust me; I have been doing this for hundreds of years."

Zac signalled in the direction of the voice and to his pleasure, Sam clearly understood. They moved together towards the flickering lights that seemed to be emanating from the computer section of the library.

"She's being dealt with, and she's growing in power every day. The time to strike is close at hand, just a few more days; be patient!" Flo clicked the mouse and the screen went dark.

Zac was on the aisle behind her and ready to pounce. Sam wasn't as tolerant.

"Flo," he called, standing up and moving from behind the books to stand in front of the little girl.

"Arhh!" she squealed jumping up. As she attempted to escape she found herself running into the arms of Zac.

"Hello Flo. You and me have a little trip to make."

Zac knew he had to get her to Alchany if he was to stand any chance of getting Val back. He grabbed her arm, teleported and arrived back at the bookshop. To his utter disbelief he was completely alone. He looked around. What had just happened? Where was Flo? He teleported straight back to the library where he found Sam struggling to hold on to a wriggling twelve-year-old girl.

"What happened there?" Sam asked as Flo struggled.

"I don't know." Zac's expression matched his confusion. He really had no idea.

"How did you find me, you imbecile?" Flo screeched at Zac.

"That's none of your business. Tell me why you didn't teleport."

"Because, idiot, a hunter can't teleport a human corpse. God! Do they teach you nothing nowadays?" Flo spat at him.

"We need to get you to Alchany, now. How do we do it?" He roared, shaking her.

"You can't. I'm never going back to that prison."

"Zac, what are we going to do?" Sam was feeling the strain of restraining her.

"I don't know. We need her. Without her they won't let us have Val back."

"Then we need to find a way." Sam shoved Flo back down onto the chair she had been sitting on. "You may be dead, but I'm betting there is something you can do to help us, because if there isn't, I will make sure you wish you were alive." Sam's patience was also running very thin. He pulled out his sword from his back pocket and flicked it open.

"Look I'm really sorry about your guard, but I really can't go back to Alchany, unless one of you has a guard's bracelet, which you don't." She grinned smugly.

"Big mistake!" Zac pulled his guard's bracelet out of his pocket. Sam held her down while he shoved it onto her wrist.

Val wasn't sure how long she had been sitting in her cell when the guard who had locked her up returned. He tapped on her glass. "The Warden will deal with you soon." Val just stared at him. They weren't going to break her that easily. Then the Collector arrived. Val felt her heart skip, she was so glad to see a friendly face. Standing up, she pushed herself at the glass and knocked trying to get her attention.

The Collector flashed Val an evil glance. "Good evening," she greeted the guard. "So what's happening to the reject? What a disappointing batch of DNA she came from. First Excariot, then her." She shook her head. He nodded in agreement.

"How dare you, you evil, short, bossy, mean..." Val hissed. She would have continued but the Collector was taking no notice so she knew she was wasting precious energy. She sat back on her hard bench. At this point the guard left and the Collector was left starring at Val.

She came close to the door. "I will forget the things you just said as I know you're frightened." She reached out and touched the glass, her face softening. "How can I protect you as I promised your father, if you keep breaking the rules?" Val could see her eyes misting up.

"What do you mean?" Val reached out and touched the other side of the door.

"I have been a Collector for a very long time and I have always been responsible for the twenty-three line. I lost your father and Excariot in one blow; it was the worst thing to happen, but I carried on, as we all do when we lose our guards. Then they told me about you, and I knew it would be hard, that you would mess up. I just didn't expect it to happen so quickly. You have to prove to the Warden that you really didn't know that you were doing anything wrong, and I have to leave you."

"Please don't go." Val begged. "Please, I promise I'll be good. I'll try harder and do everything you tell me. Please don't go." Her body was now pressed against the glass, and tears were streaming down her face.

"I have to. Be brave. Your father was one of the greatest guards I have ever had the pleasure of looking after, and I know somehow you will get through this." She removed her hand and walked away to the sound of Val pleading her to stay. Her heart sank. What chance did she have?

Val sat digesting this new information. Her Collector had been her father's Collector, and Excariot's. She found it so hard to imagine them ever having worked together. Family almost. Uncle Excariot. She let out a laugh. It almost felt right in this moment of madness to have a little bit of humour. If she was going to be extracted at least her real parents would never know she existed. That was some consolation. She reached down into her pocket and pulled out her mobile phone. "No signal." She searched the numbers and found her mum's. This might be her last message. How long would it take to get to Earth from this distant galaxy? She hoped never. She started to type.

Hi Mum and Dad. Well, you'll never guess what I've been up to! No really you won't ☺ but I miss you. I want to come home. I never realised how much you meant to me, yet I thought I made it clear every day. If I could come back I would listen when you talked, I would take the time to be more understanding. It's not easy being a grown up and you don't have all the answers. So I just wanted to let you know, I love you both to the stars. xxx

She pressed send, closed her mobile, put it back into her pocket and sat waiting for her fate to play out.

Sam arrived first, his knees smashing into the bed as he fell backwards onto the bedroom floor. Not exactly the entrance he was hoping for, but at least he didn't feel quite as sick as before. Zac followed, arriving perfectly poised and Sam now understood why Val got so annoyed. It was like being the clumsy kid in the playground.

"Let's go." Zac said as Sam got to his feet, rubbing his sore knees.

"Where's Flo?" They asked in perfect unison

"Evil, little, Sliyig!" Zac hissed. "We have been tricked and now she has the bracelet." Zac kicked the bed. Throwing his arms over his head he crouched down on the floor, ranting in a language Sam couldn't understand, which was just as well considering what Zac was calling Flo.

"Look, she's not here, so we will track her again."

"And do what Sam? Tell her she's a naughty little girl?" Zac looked at him, sarcasm spread all over his face.

"Tell me what we need to do, Zac. Val is still through that door and I want her here as much as you do. So what do we do?"

"I don't know." Zac pushed his head further between his knees.

"Get up!" A woman's voice suddenly snapped at Zac. "You're not the prisoner, Val is. Get yourself together. Didn't the last time you lost a guard teach you anything?"

Zac jerked upright to find the Collector glaring at him. He stood instantly to attention and said, "Sam, this is the Collector."

Sam held out his hand and she reciprocated by shaking his.

"Help me, what can I do?" Zac pleaded.

"Don't give up. You are trained to look for things. Try and work out why Val did what she did. You warned her, I warned her and yet, for some reason, she still felt the need to teleport."

"She came to see me," Sam told her. "To be honest it was very odd. She told me that everyone was with someone and she was alone. She told me I had loved her in sixteen forty-five and that I had saved her life. But it wasn't that that struck me as odd, she seemed drunk and I don't think she drinks; I've never seen her drink."

"Where were you Zac?" The Collector looked confused.

"I was having a first meeting with my Ranswar."

She shook her head thoughtfully. "I don't remember anyone telling me you would be off duty or that there was any such meeting."

A moment of silence fell over them all as reality started to dawn.

Eventually the Collector spoke, "Zac, I think you need to come with me. Sam, it was a pleasure meeting you and I hope to see you again." She headed quickly towards the portal with Zac hot on her heels.

Sam was left alone in the flat.

A knock came at her prison door. Val jumped. She must have fallen asleep momentarily. She checked for drool. She wasn't going to her extraction looking a mess. This time it wasn't a guard, but a very serious looking man. Maybe he was the extractor.

"Time to go." He passed his bracelet over her door. It slid open smoothly and Val stood, her heart beating so hard that it was aching. Were these her final moments? Her head swam with fear. She started to walk out but her legs had turned to jelly and she found herself falling onto this strange man. He held her steady until she was able to stand.

"Sorry," she mumbled through a mouth dry with terror. But she was *not* going to give them the satisfaction of seeing how terrified she was. She straightened her back and tilted her chin up. "We must leave now."

They headed down the huge corridors towards whatever her future held. The prisoners' souls, mere wispy lights in the walls, were a stark reminder of where she might find herself in the very near future. It dawned on her that they were on show as a warning. It was a little late for her.

"Wait here." The man passed through a door, leaving her standing in the corridor. She could run, but where? She could hide. But how could you hide if you didn't know where you were in the first place? Maybe he had left her alone so she could drive herself insane before she even got to see the Warden.

"Come in." A face appeared around the edge of the door. Val followed, slowly, nervously, feeling sick, but still holding her head high. Her heart was now pounding so fast that she actually expected to have a heart attack.

"Twenty- three thirteen, is that correct?" a woman in a black suit looked over the top of her screen at Val.

"Yes, but you can call me Val if you like."

"Just a simple yes or no."

"Yes."

"Daughter to Twenty-three eleven, is this correct."

"Yes, and..."

The woman looked sternly at Val.

"Yes."

"Do you admit to teleporting unlawfully for personal reasons on three separate occasions?"

"Well, I'm not sure it was three, if you count the Valangar it may have been less." She realised what she was doing. "Sorry, yes."

"Do you admit to partaking in a conversation with one of the old ones and not reporting it to your designated Collector on two separate occasions?"

Flo! So, she was the prisoner that they said she was protecting. "Yes."

"Then we will proceed." The woman stood up, moved over to a wall and another door opened. She signalled to Val to follow her. This was it. Her soul was going to be pulled out through her ear. To her surprise the Warden was on the other side, sitting at his desk.

"You may leave," he said to the woman.

"Hello," Val said in a timid voice, quaking with fear.

"You have admitted to both charges, Val. What should I do with you?"

"Ground me for a week with no pocket money." She looked for a glimmer of hope in his expression, but there was none.

"I had high hopes for you, but I was wrong. I will sentence you to..."

"Let us in!" A voice shouted from the other room.

The Warden rose from his chair, looking confused. "What's going on?" he demanded. A door flew open and there stood Zac, the Collector and the woman who had come to take Zac to his Ranswar. "What is the meaning of this?" the Warden demanded. "You are already in my bad books," he pointed at Zac.

"We understand that things haven't gone smoothly, Warden, but I implore you to listen to what we have to say," the Collector stood forward and spoke boldly.

"I have known you for too long not to listen, but it had better be good or you will all be dealt with." He slowly lowered himself back down onto his chair.

"This Ranswar has been working against us." Zac pushed the girl forwards. "At the time of Val's unnecessary teleporting it has become apparent that we were being lured into a trap. It seems that I was never meant to meet any Ranswar. I was brought here under false pretences by *her*, to make sure I could not help Val. Val and I were subjected to the oaken berry scent. If you know of this then you will understand that Val wasn't herself when she teleported."

The Warden looked enraged. "Speak girl," he pointed at the Ranswar.

"I would rather die than tell you anything." She stood very still, brave and proud. "Guard." the Warden said, his voice was so low that Val wondered how anyone would possibly hear that summons, but seconds later a door opened and a guard entered. "Take her away; we will deal with her later."

The girl turned to look at Val. "She's coming for you and you can't stop her." She laughed as the guard dragged her off.

"Why me, why can't she be coming for you?" Val asked Zac. "I'm the needy one." She pulled up her sleeve to reveal her tattoo. "Warden, this tattoo is for children who don't know where they're going, yet you allow this woman to come to Earth and abuse me and Zac. So much for control."

"Be silent!" The Collector snapped at Val, frightened that she would condemn them all with her rash words.

"I'm sorry." Val lowered her head.

"No, this should never have happened, but it doesn't change the fact that you have been mixing with one of the oldest."

"About that," Zac stepped forward. "Val met this child and was taken in by the offer of help, but I, as her hunter with far more experience than her, should have put a stop to this from the start, but I also lived in hope of some support. The situation on Earth is far more complicated than we could have ever imagined. Val is fighting constantly armed only with the knowledge of a fledgling." He looked at her and his expression softened. "She doesn't question what I tell her to do and she fights a battle that isn't hers. She will catch Excariot, of that I have no doubt, but surely, trying to use an offer of help isn't a mistake. And it worked until tonight, when myself and another Earth person called Sam were tricked and betrayed."

"Sam," Val whispered.

"Is this true?" the Warden looked at Zac with testing eyes.

"Yes, I was unwell, as you know, for several of their Earth hours and Val fought Excariot alone and was wounded. We need time to adjust to our position and she is working as hard as she can."

"Collector." The Warden's voice was stern.

"Yes." She stepped forward.

"This situation is not satisfactory. You will be responsible for the mistakes or misunderstandings of these two from this moment on. I will deal with the rogue Ranswar myself."

She nodded in agreement.

"You," he pointed at Val, "will continue to learn you job on Earth. You will do as your hunter says. Be sure that if you make any more mistakes I will extract you myself and put you into one of your human rodents to live out your days. Is this understood? Twenty–three thirteen, you are free to leave Alchany and return to your position on Earth. Do so quickly and without speaking. Zac, you will return with her and my warning goes to you to too: keep her out of trouble or you will be the flea on the back of Val's rodent form. Do I make myself clear?"

They both nodded. Val was starting to believe that maybe she would survive this.

The Collector understood that they had saved Val by the skin of her teeth and now she needed to get her out of the way - fast. "Move!" she hissed into Val's ear. Val jumped, still in shock, but didn't move. Zac pivoted on the spot, grabbed Val and moved her out of the room as quickly as he could. They hurried down several corridors without exchanging a word. Then Val stopped dead, like a mule refusing to walk. "What just happened?"

"You survived. Now we must get you home." Zac could tell she was in deep shock, but he couldn't allow her to break just yet.

"Get her out before word gets round. Go." The Collector patted Zac.

"Thank you."

"Don't thank me. My life is on the line as well now and I will be watching every little thing you do." The old Collector was back.

"We won't let you down." Zac assured her, propelling Val through the guards' area, which was quite quiet for a change. From there they went into the Collectors sector, and then back through the portal to Earth.

"Val!" Sam jumped up from the bed as they arrived, and threw himself onto her as she stepped into the room.

She was beyond words and simply rested her head on Sam's shoulder. Sensing her deep need for human contact and comfort, he pulled her as close as possible. Solid, earthman, that's what she needed.

After a minute, he pushed her back a little, still holding her by the arms and asked, "What were you playing at, teleporting when you shouldn't, you fool?"

"So much for pleased to see you," Val huffed, in an attempt at her old humour.

"It wasn't her fault, Sam. We were both intoxicated by a berry that only grows on the planet of the Ranswar's. For this reason alone Val did and said the things you heard."

Sam looked almost saddened by this news. "Well, I knew it was odd, I said that all along. Ah well, as long as we know that then…"

Val stepped closer to him and looked deep into his eyes. "Everything I said was the truth, Sam. The berries just made me a little more forward in my method of delivery." She carefully kept any feeling out of her voice. She had just returned from potentially having her soul extracted. Now wasn't the time to back track on her emotional issues.

"Oh, well, that's good then." Sam blushed and for a moment Val could see what he must have looked like at the age of ten.

"Should we call the others?"

"No, leave them; they have enough to worry about with Delta. Let tonight be between us. It's finished. I have learnt my lesson. Sam, you need to go home and rest. Zac, you need to bring me up to date on what happened with Flo."

"Val, just sleep for now. We can talk about Flo another time." Sam lowered his hands from her arms and just kept hold of one hand. "Come on, see me out so you can lock up."

"Yes, ok. Zac I'll be back in a minute."

"You know, Zac made a massive sacrifice for you tonight, Val. If I had any doubts about him they are well and truly gone." Sam reached the door first and pulled it open, Val still attached to him.

"He's really great. I know he thinks I'm a bit of a letdown at times, but we're a good team, plus we're connected."

"What do you mean connected?"

"Do I hear a note of jealousy?" Val laughed as she pushed Sam into the shop. She hadn't realised how much time had gone, but the sun was just about to consider waking and she would only have a few hours before the others came back again.

"No." He slipped down a couple of stairs then pulled himself back up to Val. "I nearly lost you tonight, before I even had the chance to understand you as well as the old Sam did."

Val's heart was singing in her ears so loudly it was hard to define his words. "Perhaps we have been given a second chance. Maybe we need to take advantage and start again from the beginning."

He nodded.

She needed to know him much better before she could have anything close to what she thought had existed between her and the old Sam.

She realised how very tired she was. "So much to think about."

"And no rush," he told her, kissing her cheek. "Things will work out the way they are supposed to, if we just let them"

He sounded so very wise. "Good night or good morning?" she asked. "I'm not sure any more."

As Sam walked down the steps, their hands slowly parted. She stepped back inside the shop and pushed the door shut, watching as Sam walked backwards towards Sandy, smiling at her.

Val locked up and wandered back up the stairs. Wasn't it odd how bad situations sometimes lead to good ones? Zac had proven that he was prepared to walk the mile to help her and she now knew the Collector had also been her father's Collector. Best of all, Sam had feelings for her. However, she was more than aware that she was walking a fine line with the Warden. Any more mistakes and he would be coming down on her like a ton of bricks. The way things were going it was a price she would probably have to pay. "Here." Zac offered her a mug as she flopped down on the bed.

"So what happened with Flo?" she asked.

Zac looked at his shoes. "I gave her my bracelet," he admitted in an almost inaudible voice.

"What?"

"I gave her my guard's bracelet. She tricked us." He sat down next to her, his shoulders slumped with the enormity of his mistake.

"Oh Zac." Val was horrified. "I'm so sorry you had to do that. Is this going to cause problems?"

"The lying, evil urchin said she would help us. Then, when I teleported, she wasn't there. Did I say she tricked us?"

"Yes. So what's the damage? If she gives the bracelet to Excariot what can he do with it?" Val sipped her drink appreciatively; coffee had never tasted quite as good as it did now.

"He could access the portal, although Wendy and her friends have put a protection spell around the shop so hopefully he can't get in, which should win us a little time. But trust me, if he has the bracelet he will see it as a green *go* light," he said.

"Excariot already has a bracelet. Why would he want another one?"

"Because bracelets are coded and made for each individual, so, like you, if he uses his to pass through a portal, everyone would know he was coming. Using someone else's bracelet confuses everything."

"Right..." she said doubtfully. "So why does Gabrielle's work for me?"

"Because you come from the same DNA. Each code comes from a unique strand. If your DNA matches, then you can use the bracelet."

"If Excariot can use your bracelet, does that mean he comes from the same DNA as your guard?"

"Yes." Zac stared at his hands.

Val could tell this line of questioning was making Zac very uncomfortable. He looked more tired than usual.

"We will continue this conversation after we've had some sleep, ok?"

He nodded in agreement.

"One last thing, listen to me, you're a mad man for giving the freaky little traitor your bracelet, but I love you for it. No one has ever done anything so amazing for me! Thank you."

She placed her coffee on the floor and snuggled down on the bed. She would try to save the world again in the morning.

"What do you think the others are doing?" Zac asked.

"Sleeping!" she said. "Just like we should be doing."

Her eyes closed as she drifted off. Zac sat on the end of the bed his eyes gradually closing . He too slept, but only lightly: enough to recover; not enough to be off duty.

After Wendy left the others, she went for a walk by the local stream. It always felt good to be in touch with the elements when she was confused. The memories of Delta had made her feel angry. She had been able to feel everything that Delta had felt about her and the woman made her stomach churn. Although she already knew that Val and Delta had never liked her, that was nothing compared to actually feeling a person's negative emotions for you. Anger churned in her gut. How dare Delta think those things about her without even knowing her, and the things she had done to Val were unforgivable. Adding to her disquiet, she was also finding the situation with Daniel more than she could possibly understand.

Feeling a little better after her walk, Wendy allowed her car to drift to a halt outside her mother's shop, hoping she wouldn't detect her arrival. Carefully, she opened the door, praying the alarm was off. The aim was to get in and not be noticed by her mum as she was supposed to be sleeping at Val's.

Even in darkness she knew every shelf and every stand. She took a few steps: nothing; she was almost home and dry. She had joked once that she could restock the shelves with her eyes shut and now, even in the dark, she moved around the aisles with confidence, as though she had an invisible map.

There was only supposed to be one thing in her life: Val, but tonight had been a dream. Daniel had taken her to the perfect restaurant; they had laughed about the same things and he was just perfect. Then she had come back to the madness of the bookshop and Fran going missing. How could she make this work?

Maybe she should tell her mum about him. She let out a laugh, and then stood still, listening to see if she had woken her up. There was no noise; she carried on towards the back door into the house. Something she did know for sure was that her magical abilities had grown and she felt more at one with everything. She wondered as she very carefully opened the door if it was anything to do with the dellatrax. Zac had said it was at one with nature so maybe it was helping her get more in touch with what she already understood of the universe working as one. So much to think about and so few brain cells left after too many hours working, fighting and reading, and she badly needed to sleep. She reached her room undetected by the parental radar. Taking off her dress she slipped into bed and fell into a deep sleep.

Fran lay awake looking at the clock. Jason had fallen straight to sleep: typical of him. She was sure he could sleep though a train going through the room. She had put on a brave face for everyone tonight, but now she was alone in the dark she wept. When she had been grabbed from the street, she had no chance to protect herself. Her abductors hadn't hurt her, but just not knowing what was happening was enough to drive her crazy. She had just kept praying; praying that Jason wouldn't give up on her; that she would make it through this horrific ordeal in one piece. When she was with Delta she hadn't known who she was. She knew now, but she didn't need those revived memories to tell her that Delta was evil. Never in her life had she felt more vulnerable; she had feared she would never see her parents or her sister again. Details of Delta's past were not the only memories that had been restored. After all she had been through, nothing hurt Fran as much as knowing that Val had been so in love with Jason.

She held her mobile phone tight and sent another message on Facebook to her sister.

"So, what ya doin now? :P"

"RAMDOM STUFF SIS!"

"Missing you misses xxx"

"Want me to visit u?"

"No, no probs, luv U, kiss the oldies 4 me."

"Adios crazy chic xxxx"

Fran closed her phone and held it close to her heart. She needed to step up her game, learn a little self-defence and maybe a trick or two from Sam.

Shane sat in his attic, looking directly into the eyes of his dead wife Elizabeth. "So, how's it going," he asked, smiling at her portrait and relishing the bittersweet feeling that her beauty always stirred in him. As always there was no response. "We had a very interesting day today. Fran was kidnapped and I got knocked out. You would have laughed at me. I think I'm getting a little long in the tooth Beth." He started to place base colours on a canvas he had prepared. "Val's a very brave girl for her age and you would have loved to have seen Jason. I know I shouldn't gush about our son getting into a tight situation with aliens, but he was very impressive. He loves Fran so much; seems like they will be together forever, just like us." He put colour on the board with fast, assured strokes.

"I worry..." He lifted a glass of water, swirling his brush into a whirlpool. "...about the side effects. I know I did the right thing and I know she will never know, but I still have Jason to think about. I need to put things in place for him. I know that when the time comes, Beth, he will understand." His sweeps became more aggressive. "And that madam, Delta, how could we have forgotten her? She seems to have us all sussed out. She had Fran and was trying to cause a fight before we knew what was going on. Someone will have to deal with her and quickly. Anyway, my love, I'm off to bed for a few hours. Fully booked tomorrow at the parlour and London is demanding more paintings by the adorable Elizabeth Reed." Shane raised his glass to the portrait. "So, see you soon." He plopped his brush into water, placed his pallet on the table, switched out the lights and headed for bed.

The Collector looked at all the scurrying bodies, her family working hard as always, day in and day out. She had heard stories of how it had been before: their home, the place her kind had originally been taken from to become the Collectors. They were special. It seemed that they were among the few who could control the aggressive aliens and move successfully through the portal without assistance. It was an honourable job, but she had never known any other life, she wondered sometimes what it was like on her planet and if she would ever return. Being around Val created strange emotions in her. Val was not like her father; he would never have broken the rules. She gave a small laugh. Who was she trying to kid? Gabrielle and Excariot were always breaking the rules. They were just lucky not to get caught. Well, until Excariot fell for that woman. She was bad news from the day she arrived. Val not only acted like her father, she looked like him as well and because of Val, today she had acted against the system, and from what she could tell they had won.

"Collector." A woman of similar build and appearance came up to her.

She automatically put all thoughts to the back of her mind. "Yes," she answered.

"You have an arrival at portal thirty-seven."

The Collector moved back into her world once more.

Sam pulled up outside his garage; the door opened smoothly at the push of a button. He entered the house through the kitchen

Why had he let himself fall for her again? If the first time hadn't been painful enough, here he was four hundred years later and still no wiser. He lifted his top to check his bandages. His skin was still badly bruised. Why had he interfered? She didn't need him. She had Zac who was a good hunter, if a little unpredictable, but that was good: he matched Val's irresponsible side. Together they would get into endless trouble.

He had thought he might have to blow his cover tonight, thought she was lost to the Warden. Things had got out of hand too quickly. When he came across Flo again, she would feel his full power. No one took a guard's bracelet and got away with it. He dabbed his scars with a damp t-towel from the kitchen. Getting to Val in time had been sheer luck. Excariot hadn't been expecting him and the element of surprise was all he had needed to get her out. She had literally had minutes before the Summari would have left her in a coma for life.

However, he needed to move with more caution in future. He was spending too much time with them and he couldn't afford to be discovered. If he was, he knew what the consequence would be. That wasn't an option.

He also needed a bigger car. He would go and look on the internet. He loved having money and cars were his passion. He would concentrate on finding something new, and that might help him to stay away from Val. He nodded to himself as he poured a glass of water from the fridge and took his tablet. Hopefully this problem would be resolved soon and things would go back to the way they were before.

CHAPTER 13

Double date

Val woke to find Zac sitting, back completely rigid, on the end of her bed. His eyes were shut and he was obviously asleep, but he was looking very creepy. She pulled herself up quietly and crept to the bathroom. A shower would go down a treat and she could count bruises for a laugh. She locked the door behind her, throwing her clothes on the floor along with all the others that had accumulated over the past few days. Luckily for her she still had some clean ones, but she was going to have to get some more soon, or possibly work out how to get this lot washed. She showered and dressed quickly, ready for another day of fun and antics, and poking at her new tattoo. "Needy," she grumbled.

When she exited she was greeted by Zac who was awake and ready to serve her a very odd-looking drink.

"Morning," she greeted him as he passed her the steaming liquid. "Should I ask what this is?"

"If you want," he answered, heading into the bathroom.

"Ok, what?" she called through the crack in the door.

He shut it in her face and raised his voice so she could hear him through the solid wood. "It's what I consume to stay in peak condition. It has a mixture of what you call herbs and leaves. It helps clear out all blockages and returns energy to the person drinking it." She heard the water starting to pump again.

She moved away and sat on the bed to consider whether she should drink it. She stuck her nose in the mug. Sewage came to mind, but if Zac said she would feel at the top of her game for drinking it, then he must be right. She sipped, holding back the urge to gag. "Ok, Val, pinch your nose," she told herself. She pinched and tipped and within a few short gulps she had downed the lot. "Zac, that's officially the most disgusting thing I have ever drunk in my life."

Zac emerged from the bathroom. "It's probably the best thing you have ever had."

"No, my mum's hot chocolate with..." Val stopped herself, fighting the surge of sadness that came hot on the heels of the memory.

"Hot chocolate? What is this?" he asked sitting on the edge of the bed.

"Just a hot drink that I like." She raised a smile hoping he hadn't heard or understood what she had been talking about. "I wonder where everyone is. It's nine o'clock and I haven't heard any noise from downstairs." She stood, placed her mug in the sink and, followed by her hunter, made her way to the shop.

"There is no one here. Do you think they're in danger?" Zac's expression was one of genuine concern.

"Let's go check the computer before we panic." Pulling up the lid of the laptop she waited impatiently for it to load. The welcome screen lit up and she realised straight away that they would need a password. "Let's get my phone." She headed back to the counter just as her mobile sprang to life. She could hear the Star Wars theme music through the cloth. She fumbled with the zip. Maybe they had all been captured by Delta.

"Yes," she said in a breathless tone.

"Morning Val. I have a problem," said Wendy.

"Are you hurt? Does anyone have you?" Val asked, her imagination running riot.

"No! What are you talking about?"

"There's no one here. Zac and I are worried about you all. What's happened?"

Val heard Wendy giggle on the other end of the line. "What?" she enquired frowning.

"Val. It's Sunday. Unless you need my help to save the world, it's my day off."

Val let out a sigh. "Thank goodness for that! I thought I was going mad. So what's the problem?"

"Daniel wants to take me to the cinema today and I really want some support, so I was wondering if you and maybe Zac would like to come. Then he would be there if there were any problems and you could go."

"Alright, we'll come - as long as it's not a sloppy love film, I hate them."

"Yes, anything. We'll pick you up at ten. Thanks Val."

"Right Zaccy boy, you and I are going out," Val announced, tucking her phone away and grinning at her hunter.

"Is there a problem? Is Wendy safe?" Zac's concerned expression made Val feel sorry for him. He was so single minded that he never thought about relaxation or enjoyment.

"No. I completely forgot it was Sunday."

"The seventh day of your solar cycle."

"Yes. The shop doesn't open today so we're going to town," she chirped, patting him on the back.

"I'm sorry, why is the shop not opening?" he asked, once again confused.

"Because today is the day of rest. Don't ask any more questions."

"Just one more. Why a day of rest? You hardly do anything, then you sleep. Why do you need rest?" The worst part of this was he was deadly serious.

"When God created the Earth and the Universe and everything in it, it took him six days, ok. Then, on the seventh he was a tad on the worn out side and decided to have a day off. So out of respect for his hard work we take a day off."

Zac started to laugh. "Are you telling me because someone in your mythical history worked for six days creating the universe you all think you deserve a day off?" His shoulders were shaking with suppressed laughter.

"Listen to me mate," Val poked him in the chest, which brought him to a stiff halt. "I need a day off and you are going to spend it with me, without laughing about my God or anyone else."

"Fine, as long as I'm with you, let's go and rest." He shrugged, then shook his head, clearly still mystified by the strange ways of this alien planet.

Val got her things ready and shoved them all into her bag. Zac came down to the bookshop wearing his trusty black uniform. "We need to get you some more clothes," she told him.

He looked down at his attire. "I see nothing wrong," he responded indignantly.

Val headed out, locking up behind them. "You see nothing wrong with anything," she murmured.

They were still indulging in their verbal jousting when Wendy arrived with Daniel already in the front of the car.

"Look, just try and behave normally. Daniel knows nothing about us and I want it to stay that way."

"I am normal. You're the one with the issues," he responded.

They were both grinning like Cheshire cats as the car doors opened.

"Hi Guys. Zac this is Daniel," Wendy introduced them, wondering why they were wearing those frozen grins.

"Welcome Daniel." Zac thrust out his hand. Wendy turned with an expression of panic across her face. Val hunched her shoulders and got into the back of the car praying silently that they would survive. Why, she wondered, had she been stupid enough to think that this would work?

"Welcome back at you Zac," Daniel shook his hand seeming unfazed by this odd young man in fancy dress.

"He's foreign," Wendy whispered over the roof to Daniel.

"Oh, that explains the clothes." He gave her a thumbs up.

The journey to the cinema was going well, Val thought. If she could just make sure no one spoke for the whole way then it would be perfect.

"So Wendy, are you, like Val, also resting in the name of your God's job?"

All eyes turned on Zac; even the car swerved.

"I'm sorry Zac." Wendy pulled the car straight again. "I'm not sure what you're trying to say."

Val stared out of the window wondering whether it would be better to simply throw herself out of the moving car, or teleport again. Even extraction would be better than this.

"Today is also your day of rest...."

Someone had to shut him up.

"Zac, I don't worship God as such. I worship the Goddess, and I don't think she took a day off like God did." Wendy smiled into the rear view mirror.

If Val thought it was already bad, Wendy had just ranked it up a notch. "Well guys what film are we going to watch?" she asked, trying to bring them back to something that might sound normal.

Daniel turned to face her, looking strangely calm. "Wendy said you liked nerdy films so I got tickets to the new Transformers movie."

"Thank you Daniel, and thanks for the nerdy," Val jokingly pushed Wendy's seat. At least she would be able to enjoy the film, a good film, as her world fell apart and her sanity dribbled out of her ear.

When they arrived at the cinema Zac's face lit up. He had never been anywhere like this before. It was like taking a child into a real sweetshop for the first time. He walked around touching the posters and watching everything people were doing. Val kept a good grip on his arm. Her concern was that he might attempt to talk to a stranger about how they didn't have this on his planet, or did they worship the God that gave you a day off?

Daniel collected drinks, popcorn, nachos and candyfloss. He obviously liked Wendy a lot and Val needed to remember that this was her moment and try to keep Zac to a minimum of weirdness, and pray that no prisoner took form before the end of the film.

"This way." They followed Daniel to the screen and took their seats. Val made sure Zac was positioned on the aisle seat.

He was hopping around in his seat, looking backwards and forwards like an over-excited kid. Val grabbed his wrist and pulling him down. "Look, I know you're excited, but you need to calm down. We really don't need you bringing any attention to yourself at this point, ok." She patted his arm.

He took a deep breath. "Val, this is a wondrous experience."

"I know and I want you to enjoy..." Val stopped as the lights went down and the curtains went back. Wendy handed her two pairs of 3D glasses. "It's in 3D!" she grimaced. "Zac you need to wear these glasses to watch the film." She handed him a pair.

"No. I have no ocular problems, but many thanks."

"It's not because of your eyesight; it's in three dimensions. Oh, just put them on." She forced them onto his nose, which sent him off on another 'Where's Wally' moment staring at everyone through his new glasses.

The film started and everyone went quiet. For a couple of delusional moments, Val thought that it could be possible to actually relax. She settled in her seat, sipped her water and grabbed a nacho off Wendy's lap. Through the darkness the Transformer on the screen came hurtling towards them. Zac Jumped up, his feet on the chair and his hand over his face.

"Stop it!" Val grabbed him.

"I must keep you safe." He threw himself over Val. What a stupid time for him to get the idea of saving her. She had almost got a broken nose yesterday and he hadn't flinched, and now a 3D image pops out a screen and he's her knight in shining armour. Her drink went flying into the air and everyone in the cinema seemed to jump with them. Water spilled all down her trousers.

She stood up, "Zac, out, now!" Grabbing him by the arm she pulled him out of his seat and into the aisle and down the steps as another character leapt out of the screen at them.

There were hissings and mutterings directed at them from all over the cinema. Disturbingly some people looked at her with sympathy as she dragged her clearly dysfunctional charge up the aisle.

"Are you angry? I'm so sorry about the mess," he apologised as they exited the screen.

"No, but you're drawing far too much attention to us." She pulled his glasses off with a furious jerk. "It was crazy of us to come here. Let's just go home."

Wendy hurried through the doors after them. "Hey, are you ok?" she pulled on Zac's hand.

"Yes, I'm sorry I have let you down. Please tell Daniel I am unable to stop and need to return to the bookshop," he said in a heartbreakingly sad voice.

"Val, stop being so mean. You come with me, Zac." Wendy held his hand as she dragged him back to the film.

Val flapped her arms in frustration. "Seriously, someone is going to end up in tears here," she warned.

Wendy placed Zac next to her, pushing Val out to the edge. Daniel smiled awkwardly across at her. She actually felt quite sorry for him. He was stuck with them. Well, if he stuck with Wendy after this he really did like her.

The beeping of a mobile phone rang out; Val looked around in annoyance. She hated nothing more than people who didn't switch off their phone. It only took a second.

"Is that you?" Zac whispered.

She looked down at her bag. "Yes! Sorry, sorry," she apologised. Now everyone was looking at them again. She quickly pulled it out. She had a text. She needed to see what it said. It couldn't wait and anyway, everyone there already wished they had chosen a different day and time to come to the cinema; opening a text wasn't going to make them hate her any less. She flipped it open. The message had come from an anonymous caller. Maybe it was Sam. She opened it.

Hi Alien. Isn't it entertaining – you go to the cinema to watch a movie about aliens ☺ I suppose it makes you feel at home and I see you have a few new friends. More fun for me! Kiss-kiss Delta.

Val felt her body starting to shake with adrenaline. Delta was watching them. She knew they had gone to the cinema. Val felt her anger building and knew she needed to move out of here before something went wrong. "Wendy, we need to leave here now," she voice commanded.

Wendy wasn't stupid; she understood instantly that whatever had just arrived on that phone wasn't good. "Daniel, I'm not feeling well. I think I need some fresh air." She stood, not giving him time to ask her what she wanted to do. Val grabbed Zac's hand, pulling him up while trying to survey their surroundings. If Delta was in the theatre, she couldn't see her. One thing about Delta was that she stood out in a crowd, even in the dark.

"Are you alright?" Daniel asked Wendy as they all made their way to the reception area.

"I need the bathroom. Will you come with me?" she asked Val, who nodded.

"Stay here," she instructed Zac, like a newly trained puppy.

"Just here." He pointed to the spot he was standing on.

"Don't be silly," she replied as they disappeared into the ladies.

"So what's going on?" Wendy whispered, looking around to see if anyone was in there.

"Look at this." Val handed Wendy her phone.

"Oh, this is not good. What do we do?"

"We get out of here as fast as we can. She's obviously watching us, plus now Daniel is on her radar. Do you know where he lives?" Val started to look into the empty cubicles.

"Yes, I picked him up today. It's a house on Queen Street, very big, very impressive actually."

"Then we need to get him home."

"Oh yes, and remind me next time to invite Fran and Jason," Wendy chipped in as they left the toilets to collect the guys and leave.

Val showed Zac the text during the very quiet journey to Daniel's house. It was as if they were waiting for a bomb to go off. As they pulled up, Val had to admit that his house was very nice. She could see his old, or as Wendy would call it, Classic car in the drive. Next to it was a shiny new BMW sports car.

"So, that was short but sweet. I will call you to see if you're feeling any better," Daniel said as he got out the car, turning to wave briefly at Val and Zac on the back seat.

"Don't worry, we will look after her," Val replied, feeling guilty that this had to happen.

They watched Daniel head up the drive as Val's phone beeped again.

Do you think it's safe to let the boy go? Look what happened to Fran ☺

"Wendy, call him back. Now! Get out of the damn car and call him!" Val was desperately trying to climb over the seat.

"Daniel, come back!" Wendy screamed as she struggled with her door. He turned looking at her with a confused expression.

"What's up?" he headed back to them. "Are you going to be sick?"

"Get him in the car," Val pulled out her sword. "She's followed us here." Val jumped out, her mobile phone in hand. "Shane, where are you?" She turned, looking at all the cars and surrounding buildings. "It's Delta. She's following us. Stay at work, we're coming to you. Get Jason and Fran there now."

"What are you doing Val?" Daniel protested as she pushed him back into the car. "Oy!" He didn't seem at all impressed with her weirdness. "I don't want to come across as rude, but you're weird, and your foreign friend is even weirder." He tried to stand but Val dived into the car and plonked herself on his lap. "This is highly inappropriate! Wendy, please understand that I don't want this girl to sit on my lap."

"Daniel, shut up! She's trying to save your life." Wendy waited for the door to close and drove off as fast as her Morris traveller could go.

"What's going on?" Daniel demanded, trying to shove Val onto the floor between the seat and the dashboard.

"You have no choice, but to tell him he's in danger, Val." Zac advised from the back.

"Right. Yes, Daniel, I'm not really who you think I am. I have a secret agent chasing me because I'm an MI6 agent working undercover."

"In Arcsdale, in a second-hand bookshop!" Daniel raised an eyebrow.

"I thought that would sound good, but it really was lame. The truth is I'm half alien, half witch, and my evil ex-best friend, who I left in sixteen forty-five to fend for herself after she helped kill me, is trying to kill you because you're dating my friend here."

"I think I'll go for the MI6 agent. Now let me out of this loony bin so I can go home, or I'll call the police." Daniel was about to do something Val knew he would regret and so the time had come to put an end to his journey.

"Sorry," she said as her sword extended in front of Daniel's eyes. She touched him as carefully as possible; she only wanted him out until they could get him back to the tattoo parlour. It was swift and he only shook for a few seconds.

"I can't believe you just did that!" Wendy yelled over Daniel's limp body.

"I had no choice; get us to Shane's," she demanded. There wasn't much room on the one seat in the front. She leant her body the best she could against the door of car and looked out the window wondering when this was all going to blow up in her face.

Jason and Fran were already waiting for them outside Shane's. "Hello strangers," Jason called out cheerfully.

"A hand would be good," Val replied as she fell out the car in an attempt to hold Daniel's body up.

"Here." Jason pulled her to her feet. She pushed him backwards. "Not me you fool, Daniel."

"Is he dead?" asked Fran.

"No, just unconscious." Val jangled her sword.

Fran tutted. "You so have the advantage on everyone."

"Hey Wendy, how are you?" Jason enquired, casually pulling Daniel's body out of the car. Zac climbed over the car seat to grab his feet.

"I've had better Sundays," she announced.

"When?" Jason grinned at her.

Wendy thought about her response. "That's disturbing. I can't think of an answer. Just take what could have been my first real boyfriend indoors so he can wake up and dump me."

Jason pulled as Zac lifted, and Daniel was out. Lucky for them it was Sunday and the high street was empty or it might have looked like they were moving a corpse about. Wendy locked the car and they all piled into the tattoo parlour.

"Morning Shane," Zac greeted him.

Shane was working on a large man who seemed undisturbed by the body coming through.

"How's it going Brad?" Jason tipped his head.

"Good." The man looked up. "I remember the days when me and your dad could..."

"That will be enough information, Brad. Put him out back Jason, to sober up," Shane said not lifting his eyes away from the amazing golden eagle he was crafting.

"Shane, why do you work on this day? Do you not worship any God or Goddess?" Zac asked as he helped carry Daniel away.

That made Shane look up. "Ok, who is messing with Zac's brain?"

"Believe me, if I could have predicted his reaction, I would never have even gone there." Val pushed the door with her back as they carried Daniel into the gym.

They placed him onto a gym mat in the corner, out of harm's way, and sat down at the glass table.

"We have a big problem. Delta is stalking us, big time. She knew we were in the cinema and she knew we were dropping Daniel off. That's why we had to bring him with us."

"How does she know what you're doing?" Fran asked.

"I'm such an idiot!" Jason slammed his hands on the table. "Your phone! She's got a phone! Don't you remember? Sam gave us all a phone. She can track you anywhere."

"Oh my God, you're right. I never thought about it." Val pulled her own bulky phone from her bag. "What do we do with them?" She placed hers in the centre of the table; Jason put his down next to it.

"Is that Wendy's new friend?" asked Shane, joining them. "Is there no one we meet that you don't electrocute, Val?"

"Where's your phone, Dad?"

"Here." He pulled it out of a pocket inside his jacket. "Why?"

"Delta has been tracking Val with the phone Sam gave her."

"She's a clever little madam. Someone needs to sort that girl out." Shane shook his head in disbelief.

"We need to call Sam. Maybe he can scramble them." Val pulled out her phone.

"Not going to happen; he's had to go away. Something about a job with 'no comms'. Sorry." Shane could see the disappointment in Val's eyes.

"What does 'no comms' mean?" Zac enquired.

"He won't be in touch. Probably got an important client. You can never predict with him."

Val felt her heart sinking into a place she didn't like the idea of. He had a job to do and so did she. She wouldn't hang around moping over some guy who disappeared without even a text to say goodbye.

"So what do we do, flush them down the toilet?" she asked Shane.

"First thing, switch them off."

Wendy and Fran turned the phones off. "We all have mobiles; it's just Val that wears the tracker." She glanced down at her necklace. "We can keep in touch for now with our personal mobiles, but I think the necklace has to go. That's what she's following." Val quickly removed it, handing it to Shane who proceeded to stand on it. "She more than likely knows you're here. We need to move."

"We can go to my house if you like," Wendy offered.

"Great. You guys go to Wendy's. I'll close up and leave a message for my other customers, but we need to get Val out without Delta seeing, or she could follow her."

"Excuse me, can someone please tell me what's going on?" Daniel suddenly appeared behind Jason, wobbling slightly from side to side.

"Daniel!" Wendy exclaimed, running over to put her arm around him for support.

"I see our new friend is awake." Shane gave him a hearty pat on the back as he walked towards the parlour. "Wendy, bring your car around the back to the fire exit," he said.

Daniel was helped to the table by Wendy and Fran and was now sitting, looking from one to the other.

"I'll be back in a second," Wendy jangled the keys to her car at him and ran out.

"Well, you see this is what we were trying to tell you before, but you just wouldn't listen. So my advice would be to pay very good attention." Val placed her foot on the chair next to Daniel and leant forward, holding the palm of her hand out in front of him.

"I'm sorry, but if you think I'm going to believe that you are an..." Daniel stopped dead, his word hanging in the air.

"Proof enough?" Val asked as her hand flickered with the flames that now engulfed it.

"Don't!" Fran moved in between them. "It's not his fault. This is a crazy world we live in, and we should have kept him safe."

Val shook the flames out on her hand. "He's got no choice now, so he'd better get used to it. At least till we catch Delta."

Fran spoke to him. "Daniel, I was like you, but you have to understand that what Val has to do helps to save people's lives. I don't have fire springing from any part of my body, thank goodness, but I'm part of this just like you are now. Delta, the girl that's after us, is a traitor. She betrayed us and left Val to die. You need to hear the whole story, then, if you want to leave, you can." Fran placed a gentle hand on Daniel's. "Jason get us a drink. Let's just take a moment to tell him, and then we can all head out." She's amazing, Val thought to herself. Yesterday she was tied to a chair and today she's the rational voice for the group.

"Five minutes." Jason tapped his watch as he walked over to the fridge and pulled out a few cans.

Val and Fran sat patiently explaining what was happening to them. Val explained how she had met Shane, Jason and the others, about the tattoo and how Excariot had tricked her into freeing him. She told him about travelling back in time to stop Lailah, Excariot's true love, from being freed and how hundreds, maybe thousands, of prisoner sprits had been released from her real home, Alchany, and it was now her job, along with her hunter, to return them, with the help of Wendy of course.

He kept nodding very slowly and Val wasn't sure if this was a nervous reaction or just because he really was taking it all in. Then she told him about Delta, how she had been her best friend, or so she thought, and the betrayal that had made her leave Delta in the past. She explained that Delta was now back in the present, ready to wreak havoc, and that Daniel had just made it onto her hit list. She told him that she had every intention of keeping him safe, but he had to work with her. He became noticeably calmer, but made no comment.

"Ok, so he knows everything then?" Wendy asked, returning from parking the car out the back ready for their escape.

"So, you're an alien witch?" Daniel finally found his voice and pointed at Val. "And you're her hunter from another planet," he pointed at Zac. "You're her boxing and fencing instructor." He pointed at Jason. Then his finger turned towards Wendy, "And you're her guardian, and you work the dellatrax thing that helps her when she's up against the alien prisoners who escaped in the past, and you're a pure witch."

Wendy didn't move, no nod, nothing, she just looked at him.

Daniel stood up and walked over to her. "I can see why you didn't tell me; I never would have believed you. Surprisingly being shocked and dragged off has shown me one thing."

"What's that?" Wendy's voice was trembling.

"That my first impressions were correct."

"Which were?" She was now physically shaking.

Daniel took her hand. "That you're the most amazing person I have ever met."

Val and Fran both made gushing noises.

"And that maybe we need to get to a safer place."

"Good, someone who makes sense," said Zac, making his feelings known.

"Then to Wendy's it is," Fran said as they all piled out.

Jason walked alongside Daniel. "By the way, she zapped me as well; the strange tingling goes in about twenty-four hours."

"Good. I was a little worried about that."

Shane came to make sure they got away safely. "All ok?" Shane looked at Daniel.

"Yes."

"Dad, we're going to Wendy's. I will call you later. When you get home, text so we know you're alright."

"Right." Shane agreed.

Jason's bike was already parked out back as he had cleaned it that morning.

"Jason, would it be possible for me to go with you?" Zac eyed the Harley Davidson eagerly.

"Fran?"

"My pleasure." She waved them off then she and Val jumped into the back of Wendy's car.

Val felt better now that they were all together. She still wasn't sure about Daniel, but the poor bloke hadn't asked to be Delta's next target so she couldn't be too annoyed with him. They set off and she watched the empty streets, wondering where Sam had gone so quickly and what would be their next move.

"Val." Fran broke her daydream.

"Yes."

"I need to talk to you about something." Val could tell by Fran's body language that this wasn't a comfortable issue.

"Ok, I'm all ears."

"When I got my memories of Delta back, it was quite an intense experience." She looked firmly to the front of the car, as if direct eye contact would be a problem.

"Are you alright?"

"Yes, it's just that I got more than I bargained for. To put it bluntly; I could remember, and feel, more than I should have."

"Is there a problem?" Val was now concerned at the direction this conversation was taking.

"I don't know. You will have to tell me the answer to that." She turned to Val with tears in her eyes. "I know you're in love with Jason and I just don't think I can compete if he finds out." A single tear ran down her cheek.

"Oh Fran, I'm so sorry! It's true I did like Jason, I won't lie to you. He's one of the coolest guys I had ever met. I was going to tell him how I felt, but that was the day I met you. That hurt! I felt like my heart had been broken, but this is the part you have to understand: he loves *you*. I knew that from the second I saw you with him. It's in the way he looks at you, the way he's always hanging on your sentences, no, your words. I would love to think that one day I will have someone who feels that way about me, but Fran, you have no worries there."

She wiped her eyes. "Do you really, honestly think that?"

"I saw the fear in his eyes when you went missing; there was no one or nothing that could have stopped him coming for you. He took on those aliens like they were just objects to be removed. Trust me on this one; you're made for each other." She passed Fran a tissue from her bag.

"Just one more thing, and I'm sorry if this hurts you, Val, but I need you to know. Delta always hated you. There was never anything good about your friendship. When she looked at you it was with the eyes of jealousy and bitterness. I don't even think Excariot knows what he has unleashed with her."

"Thanks for the heads up. I definitely need to know that. It's like I'm waiting for her to shake out of it, like it's just a bad dream."

"It's definitely one of those."

"We're here," Wendy called over the noise of the engine.

"Is your mum in?" Val asked.

"No, the coven is having a meeting tonight so she's travelling to Norfolk. She normally stays for a few days, but she can't do that now that I'm working at the bookshop, so she'll be back tomorrow."

"Sorry, but she will have to fight me for you." Val pushed Wendy in through the door followed by Fran and Daniel. "Where's Zac and Jason? Surely they would have beaten us here?"

"Knowing Jason, he can't resist showing off."

Zac had wanted a go on the bike from the minute he saw it. Something in his gut wanted to go fast, and the bike looked like it could. Now, seated on the back with the cool air hitting him he understood why Jason loved it so much. They glided around the corners completely in sync. Every so often Jason would look back and Zac would nod that all was well. His life had been all about being a hunter and he had never questioned that until the incident with his guard. Yet now, as if in answer to all his doubts, he was free, free to do things outside the prison walls. He felt the bike slowing then coming to a halt. He didn't want it to be over, but he had a job to do - and it wasn't this. "Thank you, Jason." He handed back the helmet.

"Any time. We really need to teach you how to ride this baby." Jason propped the bike on its rest and dismounted, placing both helmets on the back. They walked into Wendy's to find the girls and Daniel all sitting at the table chatting.

"Any more texts?" Jason asked.

"No, it seems that we have beaten the system for now, only problem being how do we stop the wheels turning?" Val put a grape in her mouth.

"Well, what exactly does this person want?" Daniel asked.

"Me dead." She shoved in a piece of apple and crunched down hard on it.

"Does she have powers like you?"

"No, Excariot has powers like me; he's the other one who wants me dead." She went for a strawberry this time.

"How can you eat when two people want you dead?"

"Well, it's not new news so I have gone past the too sick to eat phase."

"Plans, that's what we need, and let's not forget Excariot please; he is still our biggest threat," Zac said starring at his watch.

"Problem?" Val stood up, readying herself.

"Not sure. It's definitely a very odd signal." He pressed a few buttons, and then waited. "I'm getting a mixed warning sign. I think we may have a serious situation."

Daniel let out a snort. "Serious! Are you joking? More serious than this?"

"What's wrong Zac?" Wendy was now crossing the room.

"I can't split the signals. Wait, if this is correct, almost four hundred prisoners have just taken forms."

"You're joking me!" said Val. "How do we fight four hundred prisoners?"

"We don't. There is no way we could win. Excariot's covering himself. He's putting a large part of his army out so that we don't know which way to turn. He wants us to react, to make a mistake because we're panicking. Also if he's also having problems with Delta he could be sending out scouts to look for her."

"Four hundred seems a little exaggerated, don't you think?" Daniel asked.

"Why? She found you and Val, she's been taunting Excariot, she kidnapped Fran here. I don't think you can ever underestimate your opponent." Zac continued pressing buttons.

"Jason, text your Dad, he needs to know what's going down." Val started to pace. "Any ideas at this point need to be voiced, because I think we're in trouble."

Wendy walked over to the telephone. "I'll call my mum. If they're working as a coven tonight, then we might possibly get a little bit of extra help."

"Good idea."

"I need the laptop. We need to go to the bookshop. Do you all have the pins that Sam gave you?" Jason asked.

"I don't have one," said Val.

"Then take mine," Jason handed his to Val.

"What about you?"

"I'm going to take Fran and she already has one. We will come back here as soon as we have the stuff we need."

"Stay safe." Val hugged Fran.

"Jason, we need at least one volume of the dellatrax here, can you bring it?" Zac asked.

"Consider it done. Watch the girls."

As Fran and Jason left, Val got a sinking feeling. Her instincts were telling her that things were going very wrong, that as hard as they might fight, it just wouldn't be enough.

Wendy came back looking puzzled. "That's odd! She said that they had too much to do, that she will check to see if we still need help when she comes back, in the morning. I can't believe she would say that."

"Maybe she really has too much on. I'm sure your mum must have a good reason. Let's see what we can do from here," Val reassured her.

"I still think it sounds odd."

Val did as well, but she wasn't going to make them any more nervous. Then her phone bleeped. If Delta had found them here, she was going to give herself up. It was another text. She opened it ready for anything.

Who is this?

Val looked at the phone not sure what to do next. What if it was a trap? Maybe if she answered, Delta would be able to find them by the signal. She flipped her phone shut. Everything and anything was a potential trap. "What do we do now?" she looked to Zac for guidance.

"We wait. If my calculations are correct the main body of the prisoners are here in Arcsdale. They seem to be around the centre and nearby streets. They have arrived in such large volumes that it's almost impossible to distinguish one from the other." His concern was visible.

"Are we going to die?" Daniel asked.

"No, not today," Val comforted him. The poor lad had walked into hell on earth. If he knew nothing he would be so much better off.

"Val!" Zac called.

"What?"

"Is this normal?" He pointed at Wendy whose eyes had turned completely white.

"Grab her before she falls." Val ran towards Wendy, but she needn't have worried, Zac was a lot faster. Wendy started to convulse but he was there to catch her, holding her close.

She started to speak. "*The time has come, battle, war, death and revenge. You are wrong, if you change the past you will break the future.*" Wendy became limp in Zac's arms. Daniel helped Zac to put her on the ground, making her as comfortable as possible.

"What did she mean, someone's going to die? You just said no one was going to die." Daniel looked panic-stricken.

"I'm sure it's some psychic metaphor for rebirth," Val replied.

Wendy's eye's started to open. "Val, where are you?"

"I'm here." She bent down holding Wendy's hand. "What did you see, mate?"

"Excariot," she took a deep breath. "He's going to kill me."

CHAPTER 14

Intergalactic talks

Wendy sat on the floor with Zac's arms wrapped around her tiny frame. Her face was buried deep into his chest. Daniel stood by watching. Val knew that this was serious. Wendy's predictions were not only extremely scary, they were also totally accurate. The shop phone rang, breaking the uncomfortable silence.

"Should we answer that?" Daniel asked.

"Who has this number?" Val added tensely.

Wendy looked up. "Every person with a Yellow Pages. This is a shop."

Val started to breathe again. Of course it was a shop. How silly of her. "Do you want me to get it?" she stood up, releasing Wendy's hand. She hurried over to the vibrating nineteen fifties style, grey phone, her hand hovering over the handset.

"Yes of course. My mother still has a business to run," Wendy pointed out. Val picked up the receiver.

"Hello Val, how's it going?"

"What do you want Excariot? We're sort of busy at the minute," she replied.

"We need to talk; I think you know what about."

"Sorry, I don't normally have a latte with my enemies before I send them packing back to prison." Val could never understand why she goaded Excariot quite so much.

"Ok, you need to pay attention little girl or you'll be the next one in a box." He was starting to rise to her bait. "I have released a large number of my minions into Arcsdale. They're looking for you, every last one, and when they find you they have one order. I'm sure I don't have to tell you what that is."

"Would that be around four hundred minions? That's how many there were at my last count. Anyway, why on earth would I want to talk with you when you have so many people out to get me? And If you're ringing me, and they haven't found me yet, does that tell you anything about the intelligence of your followers?"

"My followers are waiting for my instructions," he hissed annoyance oozing in his words. "I hear you have a hunter. Bravo, at least there will be someone to watch you die. He won't save you and you know it, actually he won't even attempt to help. But less about your problems and more about mine. I want Lailah back and you and I both want rid of our little friend, Delta. True or not?"

"She's a pain, but she's no longer a problem to us." Val wasn't sure about the direction the conversation was taking. She covered the receiver and mouthed Delta's name and the others nodded in acknowledgment.

"Val, dear Val, you really have no idea what's going on with our friend Delta, do you? Listen to my offer one more time, very carefully, because she is wielding a power as big, if not bigger than the both of us put together. You lower the protection spell around the bookshop and I get Lailah, and together we can destroy Delta."

"Just a second, I need to speak with my friends." Val put the phone down.

"Why did you hang up?" Daniel looked confused and panicked at the same time.

"Daniel, one thing I know for a fact: Excariot can't be trusted. He just asked me to let him into the bookshop to release Lailah, his 'psycho love puppy', promising me he would then help me destroy Delta. Do you know what makes me different from him?" Daniel shrugged. "Not a lot actually. Excariot and I come from the same DNA pot, and he's like that one relative you never wanted and hate when they turn up at your birthday. But the difference between us is this: I'm good. I know there has to be a way around this and if he's scared enough to release four hundred prisoners then yes, Delta is super powerful, but that doesn't mean I'm going to turn on what I believe. We have been betrayed too many times to trust anyone outside our circle. So, if you want to leave now I will completely respect that. It doesn't make you less of a man in my, or anyone's, eyes. This isn't your fight, its mine, and if you want to go with him, Wendy, then go. This is going to get very ugly."

As the last word escaped her lips, Daniel, who was standing only a few feet from her started to convulse. Val and the others had seen this before. Instinct took over. Val pulled out her sword, dashing around him to protect Wendy who was still on the ground in Zac's arms. She raised her hand as what looked like a miniature wind started to swirl in the centre of the store, between them and Daniel.

Daniel stopped shaking, shook his head and surveyed his surroundings. He looked from Wendy to Zac, and then he glared across at Val. "That was rude. This offer will expire in exactly two hours. You had better choose me because if you don't, not only will you have to deal with Delta, but this time I won't fail."

"Why go to all the bother of visiting, Excariot? It would have been so much easier to call one-four-seven-one." Val taunted him over the ever-growing winds that were whipping up a mess in the store.

"You deserved Delta," Excariot hissed and Daniels body dropped to the floor.

Val slowly lowered her hand and as soon as the wind died down, she dashed over to see how he was doing.

His eyes flickered open. Val helped pull him into sitting position. He rubbed his head, totally confused. "What just happened?"

"Our buddy, Excariot, decided to use you as his mobile phone." She patted him on the shoulder. "I think now would be a good time for you to leave. Take Wendy with you and get as far away from here as you can." Val gave Daniel her hand and helped pull him up.

"No! How dare you make that decision for me?" Wendy used Zac to help her stand and face Val, fury in her eyes. "After all I've been through for you; you would let me go just like that, without a second thought. My whole life has been dedicated to you, and don't you forget that the dellatrax only works properly for me. So no, you don't get to let me go. In any case, *I'm* the one he's going to kill."

"Don't say that," Val snapped. "He's not going to kill any of us."

"I want to stay with Wendy," Daniel spoke up.

"I don't think you have any choice, Val. I have told you before that you must trust them to look after themselves." Zac was right, she couldn't be responsible for them and she couldn't tell them what to do either, and it was true that Wendy was the only person who could really work the dellatrax.

"I just want to keep everyone safe," she whispered, not trusting her voice. "It's not that I don't appreciate you, Wendy. It's just....it's just that I am *so* scared for you, all of you!"

"We know and I absolve you from any responsibility for my safety," said Wendy, smiling now.

Val took a deep breath. "Well, if you're staying, we need to make some plans, Excariot said we had two hours to make up our minds, so that probably means that he won't attack for two hours. He's obviously putting everyone in position. That gives us a little time, but it doesn't solve the problem of Delta." Val started to pick up the debris from the mini tornado, mumbling to herself about powers and mess. "We need to go to the bookshop while we still can," she announced finally.

They all agreed.

"Wendy, text Jason and tell him and Fran to stay there, that we're coming."

Jason rode through the streets with caution, keeping his speed down, aware that anything could lie around the next corner. He could tell Fran was scared by the way she was squeezing him around the middle.

As they got closer to the bookshop he noticed an unusual number of people, dotted in groups all along the street, and they all seemed to be looking at him. It was like one of those cheap zombie movies. He started to feel very uneasy. These were obviously the prisoners, but why weren't they doing anything?

They found a large group had gathered in front of the entrance. Jason pulled up, but left the bike ticking over, just in case they needed a quick getaway. Fran pulled up her visor.

"What are you going to do?" she asked still holding onto him for dear life.

"I get the feeling they either aren't after us, or something bigger is going on. They have had ample opportunity to knock us off and no one has made any moves yet. Trust me baby, let's go." Jason switched the bike off and pulled out the keys shoving them into his pocket. Fran held his hand as tightly as she had held his waist and they headed towards the door. The group at the doorway parted placidly and allowed them to enter.

"See I told you we would be ok. Looks like Val is getting it all sorted from her end," Jason said as Fran's mobile sprung into life.

"It's a text from Wendy. Something about them coming here; that we have two hours before Excariot's followers attack. They want us to stay put. Well, that shouldn't be hard. So much for Val's got it under control," she said.

"Then let's get ready the best we can. Come on." They headed for the cupboard.

Val and the others left Wendy's mum's shop; they too noticed straightaway that they were being watched.

"What's your plan?" Zac asked her when they were all safely in the car.

"Not sure, but at least in the bookshop we have control over the portal. Do you think the Warden will send us any back up?" She asked him, sure she was clutching at straws, but if she didn't ask now it would be too late.

"I suppose I had better tell you why I'm here and then you will understand how things work in Alchany. I told you I was on a hunt when my guard was taken from me by the Tucklets."

Val nodded.

"What I didn't tell you was what happened next. I called for backup, as you know, and it was denied. They didn't feel that it was worth the risk to come and help us. They told me to leave him and return. Val, we had been together for so long; I couldn't abandon him. I took his body and gave him a decent burial, removed his bracelet. Then I went looking for his killers. The Warden demanded that I return. I hunted for several days and night, but to no avail. In the end I had to go back; to shame and accusations that I had deserted my post. The Warden put me on extraction duties. It wasn't until you came along that he asked me if I wanted a second chance. So, if you want to know if they will help us, the answer is no. But if you want to know if I will stay with you till the end, it's a yes."

"Cool." Val held his hand and they travelled in silence. What could anyone say at this point? They arrived to the same welcome as Jason and Fran although now it wasn't quite as tame. Some of the prisoners recognised Zac and began to jostle him. Luckily for them Fran was waiting at the door and they managed to get inside safely.

"No need to push," Val called back at them through the glass door. "Alien prisoners! They have no manners. How's it going, Fran?" Val grinned at them, she needed to keep morale up. She got her warped sense of humour from her dad; he always made her mum laugh when things went wrong.

"I'm really scared," said Fran.

Val hadn't been expecting Fran's blunt answer. She put her arm around her shoulder. "Look at me, Fran. Me and Zac here, we're going to protect you and Jason, and if we are in serious danger, I promise I will teleport you all out."

"Val, you know the price that comes with unauthorised teleporting," Zac butted in.

"Listen to me; they will have to catch me first. It's my fault that these crazy psychos are all over town, but I will deal with it. Wendy, why don't you start on the dellatrax? See if you can find any information for us."

Wendy nodded, pulling Daniel behind the counter with her.

"We have a problem, Fran," Jason called from his little room.

"What's new, mate," Val called, hurrying to the cupboard.

He moved his chair to the side as they all piled in so they could all see the screen. "Look at this. There is an alarm going off on the screen and I don't have a clue what it means. I can see that we are all here and Dad's there, but there is another signal over here, that's flashing." Jason pointed to the flickering dot on the screen.

"That's Flo," said Zac.

"How do you know that?" Jason seemed slightly bemused.

"Sam planted a tracking device onto her,"

"Well ok. So why is she flashing?" Jason asked, hoping Zac would also be able to answer that question.

"I have no idea," Zac shook his head.

"Well at least we know it's not one of us. So what's going on?"

"Let's get you up to speed." Val sat down and started to explain. Meanwhile, Fran got a call on her mobile. She mouthed to them that it was her sister Yassmin and walked out of the cupboard.

"Hi Yass. What you up to on this sunny Sunday?" Fran gave her best 'nothing is wrong' performance. This fell on deaf ears as usual. "No, everything's fine. I hope you're not coming here. Go home. I don't want to see you. No, I'm not being weird. Me and Jason get no time to ourselves. I don't want to see you here, Yass, do you understand? Good. Now hang up and do something interesting with your life. I love you. Tell Mum and Dad I love them too." She hung up. "Stupid sisters, no telling them," she told Val who had also come back into the shop.

"If it's any consolation, I'm scared as well," Val said.

"A little," she grinned. "You know Jason and I won't leave don't you? And he believes you can do this. Please prove him right."

"You can't imagine how much that means to me," Val hugged Fran, then they headed back to the front to find Wendy opening the door.

"What are you doing?" Val started to run but it was too late, the figure was inside. Val pulled her sword out. Behind her the water cooler started to tremble, the new bottle beginning to boil.

"Stop!" Wendy yelled.

The urgency in her voice got through to Val and the water settled to a gentle simmer..

"It's my mother," Wendy said calmly.

Belinda, Wendy's mother, seemed completely unfazed by her dubious welcome and merely waited patiently for things to return to normal.

"I'm so sorry," Val slithered to a standstill inches away from her. She retracted her sword and the water in the cooler stilled.

"It's fine. I'm just pleased you want to protect my daughter so ferociously."

"I thought you were going to Norfolk, Mum," Wendy said, giving Val time to recover from her embarrassment. "You said you wouldn't help us, so what's changed all of a sudden?" her irritation with her mum plain in her challenging tone.

"Well, after you rang me earlier I was concerned that things we're getting too much for you and I wanted to help anyway I could." She floated over to the counter. "Who is this young man?"

"This is Daniel," Wendy replied, still watching her mum with cautious eyes.

"I'm pleased to meet you Mrs Whitmore," Daniel said politely.

"Call me Belinda," she simpered in a totally uncharacteristic manner.

Val was now starting to see things from Wendy's point of view and feeling very uneasy. She had only met Wendy's mum a couple of times but right now she seemed a little odd.

"Hey, good news we have an answer to the question.... Oh hello." Jason joined them. "How are you Belinda? Sorry to interrupt, but I've just been on the phone with my dad and he tells me that the reason Flo's flashing is because she hasn't moved in a prolonged period of time. It's so soldiers know if another solider is dead or inactive, for example if they are captured."

"So what you are saying is that Flo's either been taken prisoner or hasn't moved. Couldn't she just be asleep?" Val asked.

"No, this is a stillness that comes with death or being tied up very tightly."

"Wow, lucky girl," Belinda giggled.

"Are you serious?" Fran turned to her, shocked.

"Grab her!" Wendy yelled suddenly, lunging for the counter.

Val only had a split second to register what was happening.

Belinda stepped back as Wendy hit the counter. "Wow, I'm just in shock that you lot have made it this far. Watching you idiots all together makes my skin crawl. No, I take that back, it makes Belinda's skin crawl."

"Flo!" Val leapt forward, but Flo had now positioned herself perfectly behind Wendy who was dazed by her impact with the counter. She pulled Wendy in close and held a weapon that looked like a metal tube at her neck. Val hadn't been able to get near to her.

"Back off chosen one," Flo laughed. "God, I've missed saying that. You have become no fun at all since you turned all guard like."

"Is Belinda dead?" Jason asked the question on everyone's minds.

"Don't insult me, little boy. I can get into anyone I choose. I could be your dad or her mother," she pointed at Fran. "My power is beyond your planet's comprehension. I was your Prime Minister for a few days, but I got bored"

"Wendy, don't panic; this woman isn't your mum," Val said.

"Do you think!" Wendy hissed at her.

"Sorry." Val pulled out her sword. "Do you want to say anything before we send you back to Alchany where you belong?"

"Well, if you want poor Belinda to go through the extraction process, then go ahead. You know how much it hurts, don't you, Val?"

"I'm not going to listen to you. I know Belinda would want me to take you back to prison." Val moved forward another step.

"That's probably true, but do you know what I can do to her before you get me to the portal? I have the ability to remove all her memories. I can make her forget that she's a woman. She won't remember Wendy-pops here and it will all be your fault, Val. So, you give me Wendy and I think I will take the dellatrax for a little light reading, how does that sound to you?"

"You must be insane if you think I would do that." Val's eyes never moved away from Flo.

"Tick-Tock hunny. How long did Excariot give you? Two hours. Not long when you have four hundred prisoners waiting to break down your door."

"How did you know there were four hundred?" Zac interrupted.

"What relevance does this have to anything?" Flo retorted angrily.

"Excariot didn't give us a figure, yet you know how many. How?" Zac was moving forwards towards Flo and Wendy.

"Because I was with the witch when she cast the damn spell," Flo snapped.

"What spell? You don't need a spell for a prisoner to take form; they do it as individuals. This is the work of magic, isn't it?" Zac was so close that he could have grabbed Wendy at this point.

"Don't be stupid, you pathetic hunter." She had noticed his proximity and started to back towards the door, pulling Wendy with her, Zac still stalking her.

"Does the spell wear off in two hours, Flo? That must be some seriously powerful witch to create a spell that big and potent and keep it up for two whole hours." Zac was relentless.

A knock at the door, distracted everyone; they all turned to look. In that instant, Zac grabbed Wendy and pushed Flo backwards. Jason ran to open the door to Shane who was surrounded by aggressive prisoners. He was holding Flo's real body in his arms.

"Surprised to see this?" Jason said to Belinda's possessed body as Shane came in.

"You people are impossible!" Flo screamed at them.

"No, nothing is impossible. We're a just a tight-knit fighting machine." Val went to peer at Flo's body. She had to admit that, in that state, Flo looked angelic.

"Put her down or Belinda gets the brainwash." Flo backed into the corner.

"Now you know, we all know, that you need this body. You can live in her forever, but you can't do that in Belinda's. So we need to do a swap. You take your body back and leave Belinda without harming a neurological connection in her head, or we destroy this body."

"You wouldn't. You're not allowed to harm humans. I know the rules." Flo aimed her weapon at them from her corner, she pivoted on the spot, pointing at them one at a time.

"Flo, this little girl is already dead and as much as this situation is freaking me out I will do whatever is necessary to protect one of my guardians." Val flicked her hand; flames engulfed it. She then walked purposefully over to Shane who placed the child's body on the ground.

"Are you serious?" Fran was looking from Val to Shane, "this girl was once alive; she deserves some respect."

"Not the time for this, Fran." Val raised her hand allowing flames to skip up her arm. Then she brought her hand down towards the little girls dress.

"Stop! Alright, I'll go," Flo spat at them. Val pulled her hand back, but only enough to stop her dress singeing. "You're sick, do you know that?"

Belinda's body fell towards the counter; Wendy grabbed her, with Zac's assistance.

They all looked at the real Flo, waiting for her to do something.

"Do you think she's in there yet?" Val poked the little girl. "God, she's freezing cold."

Just then Flo's eyes opened, like shutters being pulled back. There was no gasp for air as Val had been expecting. Her chest didn't move up or down as a normal person's would. She sat up looking at Val with eyes filled with pure hatred. "We will win. You are a waste of space."

"Tie her up and gag her. You are a very unpleasant little girl." Val stood up.

"Wait, you said if I left Belinda..."

"I didn't say I would let you go, did I? You're a turncoat – that's what you called it. I trusted you and I nearly got extracted because of you. So now you are going to stay here until we get attacked, and then I will use you as a shield against those thugs out there. Tick-Tock Flo." Val patted her head.

Jason lifted Flo to her feet and with Shane's help they carried her to the cupboard to find a chair to attach her to.

"Wendy, is your mum ok?" Val asked.

"I'm sure she'll survive, thanks to you Val. What do we need to do now?"

"Magic. If Excariot is using a witch to work his power over the prisoners, maybe we can turn it back on him. But first let's get your mum a drink. Fran, would you mind?"

"No problem and I knew you wouldn't hurt that little girl."

"Fran, I'm sorry, but I would have burnt her to ashes before I let Flo take one single memory from Belinda's head." She was deadly serious and Fran could see that; she wasn't sure how she felt about it.

"If your mum's here do you think we stand any chance of breaking that spell before our time is up?" Val asked.

"We can try."

"You will need to move quickly, the crowd is growing restless." Zac pointed to the doorway where angry faces were peering in at them. "How long do you think we have left?"

"By my calculations about forty minutes, not long at all," Val replied.

Belinda spoke for the first time. "Val, I owe you my life. That thing took me on my way to the coven. I remember everything. I'm so sorry, Wendy; I wanted to scream for help, but I couldn't."

"Don't worry Mum," Wendy hugged her.

"Thank you," she touched Val's arm.

"You're welcome Belinda, but I really wouldn't thank me just yet as you have been deposited in close proximity to hell. We have four hundred prisoners closing in on the bookshop and no idea what to do. At least we know a spell has created this situation, but it's obviously a very strong spell. Do you think we can counteract it or break it, using only what we have here?"

"To counteract a spell isn't difficult. The complicated part is knowing who to send it back to. All we need is a mirror and the name of the witch." Belinda responded.

"So you're saying that you can stop this with a mirror? That's great, but how do we find out who the witch is?" She looked at Zac. "You know there's only one way we are going to find Excariot's den. We have to agree to his offer. We let him think that we are going along with his plan so we can find out who this powerful witch is."

"No. You're crazy! We'll never come out of this alive." Zac was walking away from her towards Fran. "Please tell her to stop talking like this. You are her friend, do something."

Fran looked at him, feeling as lost as he was. "Do you think that anything any of us says will make any difference to her when she's made her mind up?"

"I'm sorry to interrupt, but how does you letting Excariot into the bookshop help us find out who his witch is?" Daniel asked.

"We make him help us destroy Delta before we let him in. We only need a look at her or him; let's not forget it could be either. I will give myself over to him freely for talks."

"And how exactly are you thinking of doing that?" Zac asked her.

"Like this." She walked to the front door and tapped on the glass. A very angry looking man who was picking his nose, stopped to look at her.

"What?" he spat at the glass.

"Take me to your leader," she grinned. "No time to analyse. Get working on that spell and I will see you all very soon."

"You can't do this! It's insane! She's lost the plot. Someone stop her," Fran pleaded frantically, heading for the door.

"It's the only way, trust me. I'll be back so get ready." Val touched Fran's hand, opened the door and walked into the crowd of prisoners. It looked like a million hands were grabbing her as they led her towards a car that was conveniently just pulling up outside the bookshop.

"I take it he was expecting me," she said to a finely built man who opened the car door for her, closed it behind her then got into the driver's seat. He didn't respond, but just waited for her to put on her seatbelt then pulled off. As they travelled she wondered how this would all turn out. She was worried about the others. The pressure of their safety was starting to get to her. She had genuinely thought they had lost Belinda, and Wendy's premonition of Excariot killing her was too much for her to live with. She needed this to end and quickly.

Shane came back into the bookshop to silence, Jason behind him. "What's going on? We have Flo tied up. What's the deathly hush for?" he asked looking around, "Where's Val?"

"She has given herself to Excariot so that she can find out the name of the witch. We need the name to break the spell," Zac supplied the answers.

"Are you serious?" Shane was looking at them in disbelief. They all nodded. He took a deep breath, determined to be positive for their sakes. "Ok, so the stupid girl has gone insane, though from what I have seen of Val, I know that she doesn't do anything for no reason. She has come face to face with that murderer before and won. So, what does she need us to do?"

"We need a mirror," Wendy answered him.

"Then do it. Zac, she still has a pin on so you and Jason can track her. Let's find out where Excariot is. Come on people, let's not make her choice a wasted one, get moving." Shane wasn't sure what good any of this would be, but it was better than everyone falling apart.

Val seemed to have travelled several miles before she felt the car start to slow. To her surprise they were in a suburban street full of nice houses. The one they stopped in front of had a 'for sale' sign outside. "Did evil move often?" she thought to herself. The man opened the car door for her; as she climbed out she instantly saw the onlookers. They were in the background but were prominent enough to be a noticeable force.

The front door opened and there stood Excariot; all he needed were slippers and a pipe. This was a joke. Where was the secret hideout, the underground cave? She was completely taken aback by this approach. He almost seemed civil.

"Val, how are you?" he greeted her at the door.

"Freaked out would be a good expression." She walked past him into the house.

"Why? How would you like me to live? You stole my house and my business; I have to rest somewhere." He actually sounded sorry for himself.

"So how did you get this house then? Stocks and bonds?" she asked as he escorted her into the kitchen.

"No. I killed the family that owned it and buried them in the garden. It saved on the paper work." He poured himself a glass of water from a large American style fridge.

"I'm sorry, but you're crazy." Val started to head back towards the door, but a large man stepped into her path and held his hand up to stop her. She looked him up and down and decided to turn back.

"I was trying to make this experience pleasant for you. Why couldn't you just be grateful? No, you just have to moan, just like your whiney little friend, Delta, although I obviously underestimated her."

"Ex."

"What?"

"She's my ex-friend. Now, let's get down to business. Before we lift the spell on the bookshop I want to know exactly what you have planned, and I want to see the witches you're going to give me upfront."

"I don't remember saying I was going to give you any witches."

"Yes you did, just before you told me how we are going to get rid of Delta before I hand Lailah over to you." She smiled.

"DONT MESS WITH ME GIRL!" Excariot bellowed into Val's face, slamming his glass onto the counter. "I will snap you in half like a twig." Val could feel his energy pulsating. He raised his hand and her feet were off the ground, her throat tightening under his pressure.

Then he stopped, as if he remembered why she was there. "Fine. I won't need them, when I have her." He lowered her to the ground, dismissing the situation with a flick of his hand as if it had never happened.

Val was shaken, but she needed to keep it together a little longer. "So, let's go see my reward. I want to make sure they're still alive," she said.

"Very well let's go." He signalled the large man to follow them as they headed back towards the front door.

She knew this could work, but she must keep him calm.

The bookshop was a hive of activity. Wendy had the mirror and Belinda was searching for candles. Daniel was guarding the door, ready to call for help if anyone tried to enter.

Wendy walked up behind him. "I'm so sorry you had to be involved in this. I never wanted you to be part of this crazy world. You were supposed to be my moment of sanity." She looked down at the ground.

"Wendy, I know I have only seen you a few times, but you are the kindest, most caring person I have ever met. I'm the one who's sorry that we couldn't have had more time together before all this happened, then it wouldn't sound so corny when I told you I think I might be falling in love with you." Daniel placed his finger under her chin and lifted her face to his. "Life throws us some strange situations; believe me I know, but love seems to be able to rise above it all and make even the ugliest situation seem bearable." She smiled at him and they stood guard together.

Shane, Jason, Zac and Fran were all cramped into the cupboard with Flo. "She was there, Dad." Jason pointed to a street on the map. "Then she disappeared. It's just like the time that hallucination thing got her."

"Summari," Zac said.

"Yes that thing. Excariot must be covering her signal. So now she's lost again, and all we can do is wait."

Shane pulled out his phone and started to text.

"Who are you texting?" Fran asked.

"Sam."

"I thought he was out of communication, Dad?"

"Son, sometimes you have to break the rules, and this is one of those times. We need to get that signal and he is the only person who can do it." He sent the message.

Val followed Excariot out into the street. They were walking towards a wooded area. Was he seriously going to take her to his tree house hideout? This got more bizarre by the minute.

"Sometime today would be good, Excariot,"

"Did your father never teach you that patience is a virtue?" he asked.

"No, because you killed him," Val responded.

"Oh yes. Sorry about that," he laughed.

The wood seemed dense now she was close to it. As she passed through the trees they started to fade. It was like one of those optical illusions she had seen at school. There was no wood, just a doorway into a huge building. It was like an aircraft hangar. How on earth had they managed to hide something that large on the edge of a street?

"Where are we?"

"In my domain." Excariot turned towards her. He opened his arms as a woman ran up and dutifully pulled off his jacket. "You have to realise something, Val: on this planet we are gods, we are the elite and no one can touch us. When Lailah joins me she will be my queen and we will rule everything and everyone."

"Why would you want that?"

"What?" Excariot looked perplexed. "Why wouldn't you want that?"

"Well, I don't tend to see many happy politicians on the news, and being a royal seems a tad like hard work, so why would you want to dominate a planet that suffers from famine and wars? People here fight over parking spaces and fences that are a centimetre over their boundary line. Doesn't seem like much of a catch to me."

Val surveyed her surroundings. There were far too many prisoners to even attempt to attack Excariot; she would have to teleport out for certain.

"We don't want your people to live here. Do you know how many prisoners there are on Alchany? We could fill this planet in one fell swoop. You could be part of it." He was very serious and Val knew that he meant every word.

"So what's stopping you having a planet of prisoners, apart from me and the lack of a portal?"

"Delta, she's been causing problems. She has access to our technology and has been using it. She needs to be stopped, now. Here we are. Meet your little witches." Excariot pointed to a cage. Inside it she saw Max, Sarah, the girl she had saved from the burning building, Paul, the mute guy from the plane, and Jenny, the girl who she had knocked out with the baseball bat. They were all huddled in the corner, visibly petrified. As soon as they saw her the women started to cry. Sarah broke free and pushed up against the side of the cage.

"Please let us go. I want to go home." Her fingernails were bleeding and snot and tears were running down her face. Max came up and pulled her back into the corner, shushing her into silent sobs.

Val felt her heart breaking, but she couldn't let their fear and pain affect her. She would get them out in due course, but for now she was just pleased that he only had four. "So, when you say Delta has our technology, what exactly is it that she's doing that's such a problem to you?"

"She knows at all times where we are and what our next move will be. She appears and disappears at will. This isn't normal. She has returned from the past where you left her, and she threatens to put a stop to my plans. I won't have that. To my knowledge she also holds you responsible, and wants you dead, which puts us in the same position."

"Yes, so what are we going to do about her? If I had a plan I would have done something by now." Val shrugged.

"We need to bring her out into the open. At the moment she's cloaked. I don't know how, but she has managed to conceal herself from my informants."

"Don't you mean your witch?" Val continued walking around the cage trying to ignore the fact that Excariot had come to a sharp halt.

"How do you know about her?"

Bingo, Val thought, it's a woman. "I have my sources and I have been told that she's extremely powerful, but not as powerful as my Wendy."

"Wendy, your little guardian, powerful?" Excariot let out a full hearty laugh.

"She's really good; she's stopped you getting into the bookshop."

Excariot stopped laughing. "Yes, she has. I will take off my hat to her for that. But my prized possession is far more powerful."

"So why doesn't your *prized* possession break the spell over the bookshop, if she is so amazing." Val knew this could potentially aggravate the situation but she needed to draw the witch out.

"Because you have the power of the portal to back up your magic, the same as I had when it was mine."

"Ok, so say I agree with you. I get Delta, you give me the witches and I let you into the bookshop. Is that the deal? Then you release all the prisoners on Alchany and they take over Earth where I become a princess over a bunch of villains. Oh yes, and they won't try to kill you or steal everything from you at the first opportunity?"

"Listen to me!" Excariot was starting to breathe heavily again. Val could see the veins in his neck throbbing. She needed to keep this under control for just a little longer. "With your witch and mine we will be able to control them all as we have today."

"I'm sorry, but I think you're wrong. No witch is powerful enough to hold all six point eight billion humans under their control. This plan won't work, and you sound as nutty as Delta. What about the Warden? Do you really think he's going to let you get away with this?"

"I have answers to all questions, but I don't have to answer to you." He seethed, rubbing his hands together in a nervous manner.

"I'm just trying to be realistic here. If I'm going to risk the lot it's going to have to work, and I'm sorry, but I don't think you can pull off something this big, Excariot."

"No, but I can." A voice echoed into the huge hanger behind them.

Val turned to see Excariot's witch.

CHAPTER 15

The Judge

Val's mouth dropped open. It was Eva. Eva was Excariot's witch! It didn't make sense. She had been in the house, the shop, everywhere. Val had even seen her visibly scared.

"Hello Val, welcome to our humble abode. It's so lovely to see you again and so soon. Best if you close your mouth though." Eva placed herself next to Excariot.

Val shut it. "I would love to say the same, but considering I saved your life, I'm not feeling the love here, Eva." She was definitely in shock.

"May I remind you that you left my child over four hundred years ago with a blonde bimbo who now wants to destroy us all. So the 'not feeling the love' issue is mutual."

"Fair play, I did dump your child. Almost as fast as you did," Val said. "So the Brazilian accent and the estate agent act, all fake?"

"Well I'm from Brazil, and I did work as an estate agent once, but yes, I'm sorry it was all an act, although my ancestors were part of your mother's coven. That's how I came to belong to Excariot." She looked at him with the eyes of a loyal Labrador.

"Sorry, did you just say belong?"

Eva ignored Val's comment and carried on. "From what I hear, you don't think I can control a world full of criminals with magic."

"I have my doubts, Eva." Val needed to keep them talking just a little longer. She expected the guys would have her co-ordinates by now, and she would be able to come back with them to get the prisoners out, as soon as she had told the others who the witch was. They were never going to believe this one.

"Well, let me comfort you with the knowledge that I can." Eva beamed at Excariot.

"But you can't get Excariot into my little old bookshop. Is that why you came in? To see if you could crack the spell from the inside and *oh no you couldn't*," Val said proudly.

"Do not mock my witch." Excariot stormed towards her, his real nature exploding through every pore.

Val had what she needed: a name. Now she wanted out. She grabbed her wrist to teleport.

"Stop her!" Excariot ordered. Eva recited a few simple words and Val's escape was instantly halted. She found herself falling flat on the floor. Val grabbed her bracelet again, but this time she didn't even start to teleport. She realised that she was in serious trouble, and so were the others.

"Pathetic creature! Did you think we would trust you? Now you will all pay for your mistakes. You see Val, when Eva was with me before and you went back in time, she was a potent witch, but since you saved her ancestors you made her lineage so much more powerful.

You helped me once again." Excariot let out a laugh. "And now you will stay here like a good little guard and wait for the end, and maybe pray for it to be swifter than last time."

Excariot grabbed Val by the throat, lifted her clean off the ground and flung her like a doll against the hanger wall. Her body smashed violently into the concrete and she was knocked unconscious.

"Something's going on out there," Wendy said. She and Daniel were still standing guard when the crowd started to part. She looked to her mum who was standing at the counter, mirror in hand. "Mum, I'm getting a bad feeling about this."

"So am I, but if Val has gone, then it's down to us to keep the portal and our people safe." Belinda stood straight. Her heritage had taught her to never back down. "Call the others; it's time."

Wendy ran to the back of the shop. "Shane they're here, and it's not Val." He nodded and together they all left the cupboard. Jason closed the door behind him, grabbing Fran's hand and holding it tightly. They were all scared. Surely no one walks towards their end without fear in their hearts he thought. "I love you," he whispered into Fran's ear and she turned to kiss him on the cheek.

"I know."

"I love you son, and you Fran," Shane said, rubbing Jason's hair as he placed a kiss on Fran's head. "Remember that whatever happens here son, your mum and I will always be with you."

Jason shook his head, unable to speak. As they reached the bookshop window the scale of the problem was apparent. The four hundred had more or less all arrived at once.

"Please let me teleport you out of here," Zac pleaded with Shane.

"Zac, the portal needs us and if Val has given herself then we owe it to her and everyone else to at least try."

"It has been a true honour serving with you," Zac said.

"Son, it's been fun." Shane's huge arm pulled Zac in as he allowed the emotion to flow though him. "Looks like our Val hasn't made it, so we do what she would have done. We defend the bookshop the best we can until we can't anymore." They all chorused their agreement with Shane's words. "We are the last defence on this planet from that nasty little worm Excariot and his so called witch, no offence ladies." He raised his hand at Belinda and Wendy, who acknowledged him. "I think Val would be proud of our decision, so let's kick some alien butts." They all chorused a war cry. This was it, time for battle.

"Forgive me Wendy," Daniel turned to her.

"What's wrong?" She searched his face, but before he could answer there was no more Daniel. A red spark flashed and he was gone.

Wendy didn't even have time to deal with the shock. As the light from Daniel's spark faded, the front door cracked under the weight of bodies pilling thuggishly against it. They were in.

"Don't kill them. We will use them later!" a women voice called over the rabble.

"Eva?" Wendy looked over in confusion.

"Yes me." She glared at her. "You and I need a little chat." She pulled at Wendy's cheek like she was a five year old. Belinda launched herself at Eva but she didn't even get close. Two body-builders pulled her away, leaving Wendy standing face to face with Eva, still trying to come to terms with the fact that Daniel had just vanished into thin air. Not that things like that should surprise her any more.

Eva called out over the noise. "Mr Walker, if you would stand still I'm sure you would love to be reunited with your little friend, Val, very soon. We promise to keep you all alive if you stop fighting."

Shane knew they were totally outnumbered, so he called to the others to stop. Fran was holding a very large book over some odd looking man's head; Jason had a woman by the neck.

"Good choice. Now take them to the others." Wendy watched helplessly as they were all dragged out of the bookshop. "Wendy, Wendy, Wendy," Eva patted her cheek. "Where's my dellatrax? I have been waiting so patiently for it."

"Forget it! I'm not telling you anything." Wendy stood proudly in front of Eva.

"Torture her mother!" Eva called. Within seconds Wendy could hear her mum's screams from the street.

"Fine. Here. Just stop it." She pointed to the other side of the counter.

"Emotions make you weak every time. Pity you can't be on my side, you would have been amazing. Is there anyone else we need to know about?" she asked. Wendy shook her head. "No? Ok, leave a few guards around the place; we're taking the bookshop back. It's time to go to your new home."

Val opened her eyes to find Max looking into them, and he was far too close for Val's liking. She pulled herself backwards and he mimicked her, also pulling away.

"Are you ok?" he asked from his now safe distance.

"Where am I?" She looked around, realising all too quickly that she was in the cage with them. She raised her hand pulling what seemed to be a ball of fire out of the air.

"Don't move." Sarah held up her hand to Val.

"Don't you want to get out?" Val asked.

"Yes I do, but in one piece. The witch has done something to the cage. We can't do any type of magic. If we do we get these pleasant little shocks."

"Fine." Val let her hand go out. "So what's the plan? Do you have one?" She searched the empty, tired faces and realised they were in deep trouble. She sat back against the edge of the cage and started to think about what was happening to the others. Had they found her location?

"Get them in, but leave her and her out here with us." Excariot's voice echoed out.

"Yes master," a woman responded. Val turned to look. To her dismay the gang was being led towards her.

Fran spotted Val first and broke free from the woman who was pulling her by the arm. "Val, you're alive." She ran at the cage throwing her arms through the gaps and grabbing Val. "We thought you had been killed for definite," she sobbed.

"Thanks for the vote of confidence, Miss Tickle." Val returned the complicated embrace.

"Get up!" The woman was angry that Fran had escaped and pulled her back onto her feet.

"Just do as you're told. The cage is under a spell, so I can't help," Val said and Fran nodded her understanding. Then the cage door was opened and Jason, Shane, Zac and Fran were forced in. They all fell onto Val, hugging her, even Zac.

"I know you thought I was dead, thanks." Val pulled herself in close to Shane who put one arm around her and the other around Fran.

"Well, what a cosy picture. Don't you just look like the happy family?" Eva mocked from the other side of the bars.

"Eva, we don't have time to play. Come and do what you need to with this thing." Excariot threw Wendy to the ground with one hand and sent Belinda tumbling after with the other.

Wendy was still holding tight onto one of the volumes of the dellatrax. A strange looking figure who had been following her, deposited the other volumes in a pile on the floor next to her. She looked up, tears and dirt streaming down her face. When she spotted Val, the corners of her mouth lifted. "Hi," she whispered.

"Excariot, if you harm her I swear..." Val screamed across at him.

"What? Will you kill me? Will you send me to prison? They've tried all that. So what are you going to do to me?" Excariot made his way to the cage.

"I will make you wish that you had never been born." Val was up with her face pressed against the metal.

"Pathetic. Next!" he shouted at the others in with her. "No, no one's got a better threat for me. Bored now. Let's get this world domination started." He walked away.

Val needed to stall him. "You can't; you don't have all the witches," she called.

"We don't need any witches. If you had taken the time to learn anything from your troubled hunter you would know that all I needed was Wendy."

Val turned to look at him. Zac wore an expression of total confusion. "I don't understand." He shook his head.

"Ah yes, you're not exactly the best catch are you, but you know that when a guard connects with his dellatrax at birth they are sorted. That those who are gifted may be trained for upper levels."

Zac's expression started to change, as if a very slow light bulb was starting to glow in his brain.

"So, my little hunter, Wendy here has all the makings of a Judge and you know it!" Excariot said seeming particularly pleased with himself.

"She can't be a Judge! She's not from Alchany," Val called.

"Irrelevant. It's never about where you're from; it's about who you are. She has spent her life perfecting her craft. She has focus and has studied the books, and she has the gift of future sight. With a little help from me and your friends here, Wendy has been able to make a connection with a completely unique dellatrax, which she will now use to rip a doorway through time and get Lailah. How does that sound?" Satisfaction written all over his face, he walked away from them.

Zac's mouth was open like a goldfish on freeze frame. Everyone could see that Excariot was right. Wendy had spent her whole life dedicated to her people and her mission. They knew she had spent more time than anyone else studying and connecting with the dellatrax and all in theory to help Val. But it wasn't, it had been to empower Wendy.

"Val, I could have collected up your twelve witches plus you in one night. I never needed them or you. I just needed our little friend to have enough time. And here we all are, so now the light show will begin," he said as he reached Wendy. Eva pulled her to her feet.

"Before you do whatever it is you think you're going to do to me, can I ask one question?" Wendy's frail voice echoed. "Why Daniel?" The tears had now dried and mixed with dirt; she resembled one of those aborigine warriors before a battle.

"Who?" Excariot looked at her with a blank expression. All of a sudden Val realised Daniel wasn't there. Had they done away with him?

"Why make me fall in love with a guard? Well, I'm guessing he's a guard or a hunter because he teleported right in front of my face. So why make me fall in love? How does that help you?" Her voice was growing in strength and pain at the same time.

"What is she talking about?" Excariot looked around for Eva.

"I don't know." She looked just as foxed as him.

"Are you trying to mess with us?" Excariot reached down for Wendy's thin arm and pulled her in close.

"He was at the bookshop. A red spark flashed and he was gone, just like Val."

"What?" Excariot looked at Eva.

Zac pulled in a deep breath and grabbed Val's arm tightly. "What's going on?" Val whispered. "You're hurting me." Zac seemed uninterested in her complaints.

"That child, the one you took to the past and left with Delta, do you know who it belonged to?" Zac's face had gone pale.

"Yes, he was Excariot's and Eva's child. Oh my God! Daniel is Excariot's child. But how?" Val couldn't feel the pain any more. Her head was starting to spin. "How could this have happened?"

"You told me he would die!" Excariot dragged Wendy over to Eva. "You said that there was no chance he would survive back then. You lied to me!"

"I saw it in my premonition, I swear to you," Eva was visibly cowering now.

"I wanted that child dead and now he's here, and he is the reason why Delta has all this power. You will pay for this, you worthless witch." His hands struck out and Eva fell to the ground. "Now you." He shook Wendy. "Open the time portal, before I kill your mother." He pointed at Belinda who was on the floor. "I will deal with you later," he spat at Eva.

Wendy looked at the others inside the cage; her eyes filling with tears once again as she picked up one of the volumes. She turned over the top cover and placed her hand on it. The holograms instantly started to skip and dance around her body. Excariot watched with great satisfaction.

Val noticed Eva was still on the ground, looking over at her. She wanted to hate her, but looking at her life, and the fact that Excariot saw her as a possession, made Val feel pity. Eva started to lift herself up and Val saw that she was chanting something. Val understood that Excariot's outburst was going to work in their favour, that this was the straw that had broken the camel's back. Excariot had taken it one step too far this time.

Eva's eyes started to darken. Val tapped Shane with her foot. "I think we might just have got us a ticket out." The same way Wendy's eyes went white, Eva's were now completely black. Her hand rose, moving in the direction of the lock, and then lowered again, and Val knew they were free.

Wendy was in the centre of the hanger. The book she had been holding was starting to levitate under her hands, each hologram growing in size and ferocity. They spun around her increasing in speed and velocity until Wendy was almost invisible.

Excariot watched from the sidelines, holding Belinda at bay with his foot. He looked extremely pleased with himself and Val was going to take great pleasure in removing that look.

"Can she really do this?" Val whispered to Zac. To her dismay he nodded. "Then we need to move now." She reached out for the door of the cage, and pushed. To her delight and relief it opened with ease. "Come on," she signalled to the others.

When Max came to exit she grabbed his arm. "Listen Max, these guys are exhausted; it's going to get messy. I need you to take care of the others and head out. We will find you later."

He nodded in agreement. "Will do. Come on," he signalled to the others and they moved off towards the exit.

Luckily for them, all the people left in the hanger were completely mesmerized by Wendy. Val, Fran, Jason, Shane and Zac made their way along the wall to a large pile of crates, probably filled with old books, Val thought, and perfect to hide behind. Val peeked over the top. "What do we need to do now?" she asked Zac.

"We need to break the connection between Wendy and the dellatrax, and I have to say I told you so. I knew there was a Judge on Earth."

Val gave him a quick pat. "Yeah, well done you. Now let's save her." She stood up and walked towards Wendy.

"Does she ever think about what she's doing?" Zac asked Shane.

"Nope," he smiled back.

Val could only think of one way of stopping Excariot and making sure Wendy survived. "Hey, you know, you should have guessed I would get free." She turned to look for Eva, but there was no sign of her. "Damn, your witch didn't want to stop around to watch me beat you again." Val pulled out her sword.

Excariot looked away from Wendy. Realising the cage was now empty he pulled Belinda off the ground. "How many times should we dance this dance? The sword thing is becoming tedious." He turned, lifting his hand to throw her, but Val was ready and she counteracted with a massive gush of wind. She was nearly close enough to shock Wendy.

"Well, well, we have learnt a lesson or two since we last met," he mocked.

"Does annoying come naturally or do you have to practise in the mirror," she asked, lifting her hand into the air and creating a flame on her fingers.

Excariot laughed. "Did someone want a light?" He looked around as his followers and laughed.

"No, I don't like smokers!" she said as her body combusted into flames. Excariot stood back, overwhelmed with the intense heat. Belinda screamed, trying desperately to pull free, yet Excariot seemed unaffected by her attempts.

Val had what she wanted; he stepped away from her. The doorway to Wendy had opened slightly; however what she hadn't spotted was what had been happening to Wendy.

"Val, get her!" Shane called from the boxes. She turned to see Jason vaulting over the top. Then she looked towards Wendy, who had become completely consumed by the holograms. She started to run to her when something hard struck her from the side. It was Excariot, wielding a hefty length of wood. She stumbled, reaching out, but there was nothing to balance her. The flames diminished and she landed hard on the floor.

"No!"

Val heard a scream from behind her. Looking up she saw that Fran was running as well now. She felt the hairs on her body stand on end; as she looked up to see what resembled a tear in the atmosphere opening above Wendy's head.

Belinda had decided to do the opposite; instead of trying to escape Excariot she was attacking him by jumping on him from behind. He was now spinning around with her on his back. Val pulled herself up, just as Zac came flying past. He was also heading for Wendy. Shane came over the box following Jason, and a group of Hench men were heading for them. The fight was on to get to Wendy, and Zac was in the lead.

"Get them!" Excariot called as he threw Belinda to the floor. He also strode towards Wendy, his face set with determination..

The tear was getting bigger by the second, and flashes of light were darting in and out of it. Val was on the move again. Out of the corner of her eye she saw Shane scrum a man to the ground, as Zac leapt through the air towards what was still visible of Wendy.

She held her breath, but it was too late. Zac was thrown back by the holograms. Wendy's body was pulled into the tear and she was gone. They went from chaos to instant silence. The only sound was the book hitting the ground.

Val stood perfectly still only feet away from Excariot. His arms dropping to his side; he was clearly dazed by what had just transpired.

Val heard Belinda weeping behind her.

Excariot looked at Val. "You, why couldn't you just die? Why did you have to survive?" He looked ready to explode. Val reached out to grab his arm.

"Don't touch me, reject!" Excariot pulled his arm away from Val. "Someone grab them..." He didn't get to finish as Jason struck him from behind with the length of wood he had used on Val and Shane piled on him, pulling him to the ground. Val pulled her sleeve up to pull off her bracelet. She flicked it out and wrapped it around Excariot's wrist. He kicked out. She didn't quite know how to cope with him.

"I will kill you," he screamed before his face was shoved into the ground by Shane.

"Have you nothing more original to say," Val whispered into his ear.

The followers realising that maybe they weren't going to win had started to run in various different directions. In a matter of a few moments they were alone, somewhere in a hidden hanger, fingers crossed, somewhere in the UK! The question now was where was Wendy?

All of a sudden out of nowhere a red spark appeared about two feet away from Val. She knew what it was, but having never seen herself teleport it was mesmerising to watch. As the rip opened, in her heart Val wanted Wendy to fall through it, but it wasn't her. She watched quietly as Daniel appeared, landing perfectly.

He looked at them and then faced Val. "Where's Wendy?" he demanded.

"Gone, no thanks to you." Val wanted to blow him up. She didn't know if she had the power, but she was about to find out. Her hands came together and a sparking ball of energy, like nothing she had created before, began to form.

"Save your parlour tricks for the side show." Daniel looked at Shane and the others who were sitting on Excariot. "I asked you a question. Where's Wendy?"

"She's gone," Zac responded dryly. "And you should not exist. Your mother and father are evil and, as such, the Alchany prison rules state that you must hand yourself over to us now."

Even Val had to admit that what Zac had just said was embarrassing.

"This is your last chance to tell me, or I will have to take this into my own hands."

"Ask your daddy." Val lowered her hands. Her priorities were changing; she needed to be cautious; she didn't know what Daniel was capable of. However, she had a good idea that he didn't know which volume of the dellatrax Wendy had been using when she had been taken. She took a step towards the books.

"You and that thing will pay for what you did to me and my mother!" He pointed at them both, venom in his words. Val felt a pang of guilt. Seeing him in front of her made it hard not to want to say she was sorry.

"How did you know Eva was your mother?" she asked.

Anger spread across his face. "Delta is my mother and don't let her name cross your lips, freak, or I'll wipe them off your face."

Val took another step towards the book, "Look Daniel, we have all lost Wendy, but together we can find her I'm sure."

"Enough! You left me and my mother, and now you have lost the one person I cared about. I will now have my revenge." Daniel raised his hand and what resembled a bolt of light appeared in his palm. Val would have been more impressed if it hadn't been aimed at her.

She leapt to one side as the bolt came down. It still just managed to catch her side and she was knocked several feet along the floor. The pain was incredible. She looked up to find him instantly standing over her with another bolt ready to drop at close quarters.

"Daniel please, I promise together..." Val pleaded.

He had no time for her promises; the bolt was released. Val instinctively put her hands over her face. This was the best she could muster as the first strike had left her weakened. What she hadn't managed to see yet was the amount of blood spilling out her side.

Then there was a sound as if lighting had struck at close quarters. Val lifted her head and just got a glimpse of Sam. The funny part was he had his sword with him in one hand and in his other was what looked like a crystal ball floating in mid-air. Through her pain she marvelled at what that man could make. The noise had been so ear-splitting that she had been left slightly deaf, so the yelling of the others seemed muffled.

Val looked around her. There it was. She reached out for Wendy's book, pulling it close into her chest. Somehow she knew that the dellatrax would keep her safe. She felt a hand on her arm; it was Sam. He was lifting her off the ground into her arms. She was feeling light-headed, but saw Fran's face come close to hers, and she noticed instantly how shocked Fran looked.

"Are you ok?" she was mouthing at her.

"No, it hurts. Where are we going?" Val asked as Sam strode confidently. She felt herself slipping.

"Make some space, Shane," Sam ordered.

Shane shoved everything off the table. They could all see she was seriously wounded.

"You, who are you?" Fran asked as she looked at Sam.

"Now's not the time to ask." He smiled at her then concentrated on pulling at Val's top, exposing the place where Daniel's bolt had caught her. "You all need to move back."

"Why are you on Earth?" asked Zac.

"I will tell you everything in a minute; just let me help Val now." Sam pulled a piece of metal, about the size of a ten pence piece, from his pocket. Gently, he placed it onto the blood on Val's side. It started to fizz. The others watched in amazement as the foam built. When it eventually stopped, Sam used his shirtsleeve to wipe the excess away.

"That's not possible! It's healed." Fran covered her mouth with her hands in shock.

"You took your time." Shane patted Sam on the back.

"I'm sorry. I was trying to sort out some other issues when I got your call. You know this isn't what I wanted."

"I know, but life doesn't always serve you what you want," Shane said.

"Why aren't you freaking out, Dad?" Jason asked looking as bemused as the others.

"I told you son, me and Sam have been friends for a long time. I will explain it all to you later."

Val sat up and looked around her, pleased to note that her hearing was back to normal; the pain in her side had gone too. "About time you showed up," she said to Sam, "That ball thing you did was cool. I'm impressed. Has

Daniel gone?" No one answered. The others just stared gormlessly back at her. "What?"

"Well, I understand that you were wounded, but you seem oblivious to the fact that Sam here just appeared out of thin air." Fran shoved her hands on her hips. "Maybe this is all just a crazy nightmare. First Daniel's light show and now Sam's." She pinched Jason's arm. He howled in pain. "Ok, so I'm awake. Will someone please tell me what the hell is going on?" Her eyes were fixed firmly on Sam.

He signed. "Ok. I stepped, that's what we call it." Sam looked embarrassed just talking about it.

"Lovely, but since when have you been stepping?" Fran asked him, clearly on a mission. "And how do we know you're Sam and not a zombie body snatcher."

"Fran, I can vouch for the fact that Sam's not a Zombie," Shane said.

"Have I missed something here?" Val searched their faces for an answer.

"I think you and I have missed something massive. I was right; there is a judge on earth," Zac said looking pointedly at Sam.

"But that's Wendy, right?" Val asked, still looking directly into Sam's eyes.

"Sort of," he prevaricated.

"Samuel, my friend!" Excariot called from his spot on the ground. "How's about a hand for your old comrade?"

"Here!" Sam lifted his hand creating a mini ball of light, aimed it at Excariot and released it. They all held their breath. As it hit him, a force field was created around his body. Excariot screamed yet they could hear nothing.

"Explain what's going on. NOW!" Val demanded.

"I knew you would be like this." He shook his head turning to Shane. "I told you she wouldn't react well."

"I'm sorry, is Shane in on this?" She looked around the room. "Anyone else have anything they want to tell us while we're all at it?"

No one spoke.

Sam shook his head. "Shane couldn't tell you, Val, and neither could I. Now things will have to change."

"I'm sorry to break up the confessions, but is no one going to help me get my daughter back?" Belinda butted in.

Val held out the book to Sam. "She had this book when she disappeared. Get her back please. Then *you* can tell me what's going on."

Sam took the book from her. "There's a problem. If I bring her back from wherever she is, things will change. For everyone."

"What does that mean?" she asked.

"I can't control what Wendy has done. She has gone to a place where she feels safe, a place where she thinks everything is as it should be. I was sent here to guide her and I got distracted." Sam looked at the others. "For that I'm sorry, but if I bring her back here, things will have to change."

"Do it," Belinda pleaded. "Please. She's all I have." Tears started to run down her cheeks.

"Do it," Val and Fran chorused at the same moment.

"I need a moment with Val." Sam grabbed her hand and they were instantly transported away.

Val waited for the landing, but it never happened. They seemed to be suspended in mid-air. She felt stable, but there was nothing to support her. She held Sam's hand tightly for fear of falling. "What are you," she asked. "Who are you?"

"I'm Sam, the same Sam you met in sixteen forty-five. The Sam that has loved you from the first time he saw you. I had to let you go then and I'm going to have to let you go again now."

"But I don't remember being with you, even though I feel it. I'm so confused."

"This should help." He placed his hand over Val's eyes. Everything went dark, and then her memories started to return. She remembered Wyetta and the coven. And there he was: Sam. They had spent time together and however brief, it had changed them. She was very much in love with him. It was in every pore of her skin; every beat of her heart was for him.

Then the time came for her initiation. Excariot had arrived and she had fallen, as she remembered it so many times. With Wyetta's help, Sam managed to send her to the future. He had told her that it would be ok, that she would be safe in her new home. Val felt the intense pain of a broken heart. He told her that she would forget him, that it was for the best, that their love was never meant to be, not now, not ever. She had cried on his shoulder, but he knew what was best for her. They had kissed one last time and then he had placed his hand on her arm and led her to the future to be reborn with no memories of who she was, or why she was there.

Sam took his hand away. "I'm so sorry, Val, if I bring Wendy back, you will forget this all over again. You can't live with these memories."

Val's eyes stared into Sam's. "I love you, no memories will change that."

"And I you V."

For a moment she simply savoured the words. But then reality claimed her again and they were back with the others.

Sam looked around for any sign that anyone had noticed their exit or return, but they were completely oblivious. "Val, the outcome may be worse for you than anyone else here if Wendy does return."

"Look, Wendy's my friend. I can deal with whatever the outcome is. Just get her back." Val reached out for Belinda's hand.

"Let's do it," Zac said.

"Zac, you need to get Excariot out of here. Take him to Alchany." Sam moved his hand in a slow circular motion and a portal opened next to Excariot's temporary prison dome. "Twenty-three twelve you were never my friend," Sam told him, removing the light field that was holding him prisoner. "Zac, go."

Zac lifted Excariot up by his hands, which were tied behind his back. Excariot's head hung down, his imminent extraction obviously now weighing heavy on his mind.

"You have disappointed me," Sam said. "You have hurt and murdered innocent humans and if it you had been in my jurisdiction I would have dealt with you myself. You will have plenty of time to repent for your actions, because I will make sure you're imprisoned for a millennium."

He turned to Zac. "Zac, when you're finished you will return to Val and continue as her hunter and I will make sure the Warden hears of your bravery." Zac nodded then passed through the portal with Excariot.

Val was starting to realise how important Sam really was. He placed the book down on the floor. "Belinda, would you please free the people who are under Eva's spell?"

She pulled out the mirror she had in her pocket and held it up.

"Eva, with the power of three,

I send this magic back to thee,

take this mirror and reflect,

all the negative reject."

The mirror slowly filled with light that first appeared as a tiny, bright spot and spread. They all watched as the light started to spring out. It jumped from one unconscious henchman to another, and then a beam shot up towards the ceiling and out. "So be it done." She pulled the mirror down and put it back into her pocket.

"Is that it?" Jason asked.

"Yes, Jason. What's special about magic is it needs only the power of the individual's mind and belief," Belinda answered.

"Thank you." Sam smiled warmly at her. "Let's get Wendy." He put the book on the floor and opened it on the first page. Then they all waited for something as impressive as last time: holograms, rips in time, etc.

"Wendy, you can come out now." Sam spoke to the book.

Val gaped at him. "Are you being serious?"

Sam shot her a glare. "Wendy, it's safe. You need to come out; the others have gone."

The book started to shake. "No," a distant voice answered.

"I'm not coming in to get you, so you have to come out."

"I don't want to live there." It was like a surreal conference call.

"Please, Wendy, come home," Belinda begged.

"Shh!" Sam looked angrily at Wendy's mother, holding his finger up to his lips. She raised her hands in silent apology.

"What seems to be the problem?" Sam asked.

"I don't want to go with you," she said. Go with Sam? Why should she go anywhere with Sam? They all looked at him expectantly.

"It won't be for long and I will bring you back, you know why."

"I want to stay with Val and the others. I'm not special. I'm Wendy, Wendy Whitmore. The girl everyone loves to ignore, the one who always comes last. The girl no one sees when party invitations are being handed out. Leave me alone; I don't want to be a Judge."

"We all have to do things we don't want to do, Wendy." Sam looked over at Val. "Someday, we all have to face up to the fact that we make our own destiny, but some things are just in our blood, in our heritage and slap bang in our paths. Now it's time for you to do that."

There was silence. No one dared to speak in case she decided to never return. The book started to glow; it was a soft blue, the colour that Wendy created. The glow grew in size. It was glorious to look at, like the bluest sky, the one that makes you stop and look up and think that whatever happens today you could look to the skies for a speck of happiness. Then it started to fade away, revealing Wendy standing next to the book.

Belinda ran at her, throwing her arms around her neck, and sobbed with joy. Wendy returned her embrace.

Val approached, unsure how to tackle this new Judge Wendy. "So, you think you're special do you?" She said as Belinda pulled back.

Wendy's answer was to throw her arms around Val and burst into tears.

Val couldn't hold back her tears either. "I thought I'd lost you," she sobbed.

"I have been with you forever; there is no way you will lose me," Wendy reassured her.

"It's time to go," said Sam sounding very authoritative.

"What, what do you mean *go*?" Belinda's glare twitched between Sam and Wendy.

"Mum, it's ok. This is it, everything I have been getting ready for. I'm going to be what you wanted me to be."

"No, you can't take her away! Where are you going?" Val held tight onto Wendy's hand.

"We will return, when the time is right." Sam tried to reassure them.

"The time is right now! Don't you dare take her away from me. Do you people not grow tired of taking my loved ones away? Is this some sick joke that is all going to end in a minute, because you're in some serious trouble." Val was getting caught on her own tongue, her hands shaking with the pressure building in her body.

"Val, stop," Wendy interrupted. "I want this. I want to be what my destiny has mapped out for me. I have seen my future for the first time and it's good. Don't take that from me."

Val fell silent. She hadn't expected that. Belinda's sobs were all they could hear. Shane broke the tension by walking over to Wendy and kissing on her cheek, "Have fun and send us a postcard." He stepped back.

"Make sure they don't make you wear that stupid uniform that Zac wears." Fran hugged her and turned to bury her head in Shane's chest as she started to sob.

"I knew you were special all along." Jason punched her playfully on the arm, then threw his arms around her.

"I need oxygen!" she gasped and Jason let her go. Now it was Belinda's turn. She took Wendy's hands and wiped away her tears. "A mother should never have to give up her child. It's the sort of thing we push to the backs of our minds for moments in the night when we cry alone in fear. All your life I have pushed you, Wendy. I have made you do things that were never your true wish, and you did them, no questions. Now I want to know for sure, if this is what you want. If it is, I will let you go."

Wendy nodded. Belinda placed a kiss on her cheek as the tears ran down her face again. "Then blessed be my daughter, merry we meet and merry we part that merry we shall meet again."

"I love you mum," Wendy said as Belinda took a step back. "Val, I need to know that you're ok with this so I can go."

"All my days since I joined school you were there, lurking in the background and I did everything I could to get away from you. Then you saved me, told me you're my guardian and I still rejected you. It wasn't until I learnt to see who you were that I realised what a fool I have been. What sort of person would I be if I now stopped you having a moment of happiness, awesome powers and all the rest? I can't imagine anyone on this planet being a better Judge than you. You go, but make sure your mobile phone is on."

"We must leave." Sam started to open another portal for them.

"I'll be back." Wendy promised. A smile lit her face as if a huge weight had been lifted off her shoulders and she had finally found her own purpose in life.

Sam looked to Val. "I'll return as soon as Wendy is settled."

The little group stood, and watched as the portal closed, taking Wendy from them. Each wondered if they would ever see her again.

"So, we should try to get home? I'm not even sure where we are." Val broke the tension.

"So Dad, how long have you know about Sam?" Jason asked.

"Yes Shane, how long and why didn't you tell us? And what are you?" Val poked him in the side.

Shane laughed; she had obviously caught him in a funny spot. "I told you I have known Sam for a long time and, yes, I knew he was special, but I made a pact with him to keep his secret, and I did. That's all. There is nothing more to tell."

"I don't agree," Val shook her head. "What do you think, Fran?"

"I think I've had enough of aliens and teleporting, special powers and all that stuff for a very long time. Plus I need a wee and I'm very hungry."

Val let out a laugh. "You kill me sometimes." She grabbed her arm and they headed towards what they hoped was an exit.

"Did anyone hear that noise?" Jason looked around.

"Yes it was my mobile." Fran pulled out her phone.

"'Who is it baby?" he asked.

"It's Yass. She says she's at the bookshop and wants to know where we are. I told her specifically not to come here. Why does she never listen?"

"I can't imagine: twins." Jason raised one eyebrow.

"Well the henchmen will be gone so I'm sure it's ok," Val said. "I just can't say where we are and how long it will take for us to get there."

Fran was texting. "I've told her to go in and wait."

"Tell her to put the kettle on," Shane added.

Fran's phone beeped again. "I bet she can't find the kettle," she giggled, and then stopped abruptly.

"What's wrong?" Val asked.

Fran's face was now ashen. "She said it's ok, not to worry, she's with my friend, Delta."

CHAPTER 16

The Bookshop

Fran dropped the phone and turned to Jason. "Get me there now. She's not getting Yass." Jason nodded and they started to run.

"Wait, I'll teleport." Val grabbed her bracelet, but still nothing happened. "It's Eva's spell, it must still be working. Let's go." Val scooped up Fran's mobile and ran after them.

Delta walked around the counter as Yassmin put the kettle on. Her long strawberry blonde hair had a natural kink to it and fell like a lion's mane down her back. As she turned, Delta noticed how very blue her eyes were. She was a good height and weight for what they wanted and she had good dress sense. Yes, she would be perfect.

"Wow, I love your necklace." Delta moved towards her, lifting it up with her highly polished nails.

"Yes, my dad brought it for me, as a sorry." She sighed.

"Sorry for what?" Delta dropped it back onto her skin and stepped back.

"When I was born he chose my name, and he got so excited that he misspelt it on my birth certificate.

Look," Yassmin held up the necklace which spelt out her name. "It has two ss's which is wrong." She let it go.

"What a lovely story. Fran never mentioned you before. Are you very close?"

"Yeah, but she likes her time with Jason to be hers. So when she comes here to Arcsdale she tends to keep herself to herself. This time I thought she's been too quiet and I was starting to worry. That's why I came. She said something about this girl Val and that she was helping at some old bookshop, so here I am. Have you seen Fran today?" Yassmin poured herself a drink. "This coffee's revolting!" She added two sweeteners from her handbag and stirred.

Delta nodded in agreement. "I haven't seen them today, but I'm sure we will be hearing from her very soon."

Yassmin's phone started to ring and she pulled it out of her pocket. "Hi, yes," she looked up at Delta. "Ok, I will pass that message on." Yassmin's face said it all as she turned to run, dropping her coffee on the floor. Delta didn't bother to chase her. She knew what was coming; she had spotted Daniel in the shop doorway before Yassmin had even answered the phone.

"So, a distress call. That means that they know you're here, which also means we may not have much time!"

Val held the phone out in front of her. Fran's fears all came true at once. "They have her don't they?"

All Val could do was nod.

"We need to find out where we are," Jason said. They had finally made their way out of Excariot's hanger, but they were no better off. No one had any idea where they were.

"Can you see any signs? Shane, you're the tallest." Belinda asked.

"No sorry," he replied.

"Can't you witchy people tell by the sun or something?" Jason asked Belinda politely.

"No, you're confusing me with a compass," she replied.

"Look, he brought us in through some bushes from the edge of a street; it was like the building was cloaked. So no one could see it, and that was Eva's doing, so we know magic is involved. We need to stop running because I think we're going in circles." Val pointed to an odd-looking tree.

"Oh, I saw that tree five minutes ago!" Fran yelled in frustration. "Get me to Yass now. If she hurts her..." Fran was almost spinning in circles, trying to find the right direction.

"Hello." Val jumped, as a group of people appeared. It was Max and the others. They too had been walking in circles.

"Nice to see you're all ok. We're in a mess and we need to find a way out. Any input would be good," Val said.

"If she hid the building then she used a vanishing spell," Belinda said. Sarah nodded in agreement.

"So how do we reverse that?" Val asked, pleased that at last someone had an idea.

"To vanish you use the air element, so to return you must pull from the fire." Sarah said.

"Yes Val, you need to use your fire." Belinda knew what Val could do.

"Ok, if you think it will work." Val raised her hand, nothing happened. She focused hard, but still nothing.

"Do you think Eva has taken away my powers?" Val asked Belinda.

"She can't bind you without your permission; it's obviously a temporary thing."

"Val please, whatever this woman has done to you, fight it. I need to get to my sister," Fran pleaded.

Val tried again. She thought angry thoughts, about Delta and Daniel. She thought about losing Wendy, but still nothing. It was at that moment that it struck her, literally, across the face. Jason had slapped her! His blow was hard and it hurt, and it was enough. Her internal combustion engines seemed to rev up and in seconds her body was rippling with flames.

"I will let you off, today," Val said rubbing her cheek through her fiery aura.

"Normally tips you over the edge. Sorry, I would never normally hit a girl unless it's you or a prisoner from another galaxy." Jason blushed, obviously uncomfortable with what he had done.

"You're not making this situation any better," Fran pulled him back.

"Now what, and make it quick," Val asked Belinda.

"Now you burn everything you see."

"Are you sure?" Val felt slightly concerned.

"It's just an illusion created by the wind, like the shadows that aren't there in the corner of your eye. Now burn it," Belinda ordered.

Val took a step toward the odd-looking tree. "You first." She put her hands onto its trunk and she instantly felt that it wasn't real. The tree started to burn and as it did it began to disappear.

"If we have to do one tree at a time we will be here all day," Fran said, agitation giving her voice a shrill pitch.

"She's right." Shane could see this was going to be slow.

"Val, don't see one tree see the whole spell. See Eva closing a door; you need to burn that door down," Belinda instructed her. "Size is only in your mind; it's a mountain or a mole hill."

Val understood what Belinda meant. She could go at this, like the time she was trapped underground, one rock at a time, or she could go for the lot and rock that door down.

"Please Val," Fran whispered.

Her eyes surveyed the horizon. It was far too green for Arcsdale. She pulled in a deep breath from her stomach. Nothing could stop her doing this. It wasn't really there; it only existed in their minds.

The others could see how Val's focus had grown because the flames that had been clinging to her body were now starting to spread.

"Are we safe?" Shane asked Belinda.

"I've never known anyone with Val's powers, so we should maybe step back a few feet more."

Val could feel that she was as ready as she was going to be. She pushed her hands forward and a huge wave of fire emanated from her body. It was like an ocean wave against the beach. Everything in sight was now ablaze. As it burnt, like the tree, the illusion started to disappear. Within a few moments they could once again see the street they had entered by.

"Good job!" Shane said, jolting her back into reality. "Let's go save Yassmin."

Max grabbed Val's hand. "We need to go and find our families, so we are now on different paths." He pushed a tiny silver star into her hand. "Keep this. Thank you, and maybe one day we will meet again."

Val looked at it. "That would be nice." She waved as they moved off, pushed the star into her pocket, then ran to catch up with the others.

Daniel arrived as Yassmin was attempting to escape. He had no difficulty in catching her, and was now storming around the bookshop pulling her behind him by the arm, like a dog on a leash. "Wendy's gone," he said to Delta for what felt like the hundredth time in the past few minutes.

"She's dead." A woman's voice came from behind him. "It was Excariot; he killed her when she was trying to protect the witch, Val." Eva pushed Yassmin out of the way.

"What do you mean she's dead? Val said she would help me find her." Daniel looked annoyed.

"Son, if Eva says she's dead then she is." Delta tried to be sympathetic.

"She also said that Eva was my mother. Is that true?" Daniel was getting agitated again, and Yassmin's whimpering was getting on his nerves. "Well?" he demanded.

"Listen to me." Delta tried to calm him down. " Val left me and you alone in a very dangerous time and place. I brought you up and made sure you were safe. I looked after you and cared for you when everyone else had abandoned you. Eva was there to support us when we came home. Now stop asking irrelevant questions. And knock her out, will you? She's getting on my nerves. Where's Flo?" Delta walked off with Eva.

"I'll be quiet," Yassmin pushed her shaking finger against her lips.

"Do you promise?" Daniel released her arm a little and seemed to be calming down. "I have just lost the love of my life, and no one cares about it."

"I do," Yassmin said.

"She was so beautiful. We went to dinner in a restaurant." Daniel sat down and Yassmin had no choice but to follow. He placed his free hand over his eyes.

"It will be ok. I'm sure that woman is wrong. Why would this Val girl say she would help find her if she was dead? Surely there would have been a body or something and she would have been sadder. What do you think?" Yassmin asked.

"That does make sense. I'm sorry you're our prisoner. We just need a body and it seems like you're it."

"What?" Yassmin twisted, starting to struggle again. She had no intention of being a body for anyone. "Please don't do this, I haven't hurt you..."

"Now I'm going to have to silence you." Daniel put his other hand on Yassmin's arm and passed a small controlled volt though her, causing her to pass out. "You'll be fine, in a while," he said to the now unconscious body lying on the floor.

Delta pushed the door to the cupboard open to find Flo tied neatly to a chair with duct tape across her mouth. "Eva, I've found our little friend." She smiled walking in and swivelling the chair. Flo span around glaring at her with eyes of contempt.

"The job is done, Delta. Excariot has been captured and at last our revenge will be complete." Eva smiled at Flo who came spinning around for another time.

"Not yet. We still have to get her out of that place." Delta put out her hand bringing Flo to a halt. "And for that we need you." She pulled the tape off her mouth in one painful rip.

"AWW!!" Flo screamed as Eva untied her.

"Now go and help Daniel; make yourself useful." Delta pushed Flo out the door. "Look! How sweet. The gang has made its nest in a cupboard." She laughed and Eva joined her as she pulled the laptop crashing to the ground.

"What took you so long?" Flo shouted at Daniel, rubbing her sore lips. "I've been in there for ages."

"I was busy, get over it," he retorted.

"Take this," she handed him Zac's guard's bracelet. "Who's the blonde?"

"Someone for our guest." He put the bracelet on and picked Yassmin up off the floor. "Are you sure this will work?" Daniel asked as he carried Yassmin up the stairs into the flat.

"If it doesn't, you're dead, so why worry?" Flo patted him on the back.

"Very funny." He threw Yassmin onto the bed. "Let's get it done."

"Put Lailah in this vial to travel. She can't get through a controlled portal without it." She handed him a small glass bottle, which he shoved into his pocket. "Careful," she hissed at him.

Eva and Delta were standing by the portal waiting. "I'm telling you it's anti-clockwise." Eva pointed the rock towards Daniel.

"In the book it was the other way." Delta pushed it back at her.

"Look Mother, you know that you're not the best at magic. Maybe you should listen to Eva; she's the witch around here." He stroked her arm.

"Well, I think she's wrong and I haven't done all this for her to mess up the cloaking spell." Delta walked over to the bed, looked at it, huffed and sat down. "You would have thought Val could have bought some new bedding by now. This stuff is just disgusting." She placed her hands neatly on her knees so as not to touch the offending objects.

"Listen Delta, Lailah is as important to me as she is to you, so back off." Eva turned the crystal again. "Ready Daniel? Here's the map."

He nodded. "Let's do this." He entered the portal and Delta, Flo and Eva could only pray that their plan worked.

Val and the others were running down the road toward some signs. "This is a road my dad's worked on. We should go this way." Val pointed. As she started to run again, Shane grabbed her by the arm bringing her to a halt.

"Did you just say your dad?" he asked.

"What?" Val hadn't even realised what she had said.

"Yes you did." Fran was now involved.

"Not now, ok, I will tell you all about them when we have Yassmin back." Val pulled free from Shane and started to run again.

As they flew around the next corner Shane announced, "I know where we are now. If we keep going this way I have a customer who lives here. If he's at home maybe we can borrow his car." They all followed Shane to a nice looking semi-detached house. There were no vehicles visible on the driveway, but he ran to the front door and rang the bell, which proceeded to play the funeral march.

"Morbid." Belinda looked at Shane.

"I like to see him as a unique client." Shane shrugged.

The door opened and out came a fifty-year-old man with very little hair up top, but a huge caterpillar of a moustache on his lip. "Shane, what's going on? How come you're in my neck of the woods?" He greeted Shane with an American slap down of a handshake.

"Listen Brian, I need to borrow Bessie. I wouldn't ask but it's a life and death situation."

"Sure, she's out back. I was just giving her a bath. Come and get her and tell me about your lady friend?" Brian winked at Belinda as he and Shane walked into the house together.

Within a flash the garage door started to open and there was Bessie, with Shane in the driving seat.

"That has to be the most hideous thing I've ever seen," Belinda said her mouth gaping open.

"It's an imported Dodge Nitro. It's cool, Belinda, honest." Jason pulled her along. "Sorry, I'm with Belinda on this one, and what colour is that?" Fran followed.

"Canary yellow," Val said, joining the others as they climbed into the truck.

"Everyone got their belts on?"

They all chorused 'yes' and Shane pulled away, leaving Brian in the empty garage doorway waving.

Daniel's arrival went completely undetected; Eva's cloaking spell had worked. He was scared, but knew what was expected of him and now Wendy was dead he had no reason to care if he got caught or not. He watched for a moment as very short people scurried around him, oblivious to his presence, then he headed towards a wall. It only took him a few minutes to work out how people were accessing the next level. He swiped his bracelet and the door opened.

"So, what will they do with him now he's been captured?" one guard said to another as they passed. Daniel froze against the wall.

"Don't know. I'm just amazed that a girl caught him; after twenty-three eleven failed his daughter captured the elusive twenty-three twelve. That's one for the books," he laughed.

"What have they done with him?"

"Well, it seems that her hunter, the nutty one, has him waiting to go and meet with the Warden. I've heard they are going to extract him tonight without a trial. Someone is going to have to be very careful if that happens." They both nodded, then parted going in their separate directions.

Daniel pulled out the map Eva had given him. Two more corridors and he would be there. He heard more voices coming towards him.

"So she's real. Well, I'm shocked they have brought her here so soon. You know what happened the last time someone like that got all the way to Judge too early."

Daniel waited for them to pass before he stepped out towards the next wall. It was full of wispy lights and he recognised the prisoners from Flo's descriptions. She had also explained to him that as soon as he had Lailah, alarms would sound and he would be in serious danger. He had also been told it would be worth it. He made it to the end of the wall, glanced at the map and realised that the box he wanted was being guarded. He crept up as close as he could get.

"So, they want us to guard Lailah for our whole shift." The guard standing in front of her box seemed most unimpressed. "I was supposed to go and visit the Monahan planet today. That means that my arrests will be put on hold and those slimy creatures give me a terrible rash." The guard next to him gave his agreement just for a little peace.

Daniel would need to get them out of the way. He didn't enjoy hurting people. He pulled a ten pence coin out of his pocket and threw it towards the corner. One guard turned and started to make his way over to investigate. Daniel sneaked up on the stationary guard. He grabbed his arm, and as the volts ran through him, Daniel gently lowered him to the ground.

"Sixty-five, what's wrong?" asked the first guard, returning to find his partner on the floor. He crouched to take his pulse, but before he had time to sound an alarm he suffered the same fate.

Daniel knew from practise that this type of attack would give him on average ten minutes head start. He fumbled through the guard's pockets and pulled out a circular disk. He held in front of Lailah's cell. "Hi, my name's Daniel, and I'm here to set you free. You need to come with me. Delta, Eva and Flo are waiting for you on Earth." He flashed the disc and listened to the sound of oxygen rushing into a space that had been void. The wisp of light flickered in his face. He knew Lailah wouldn't take him; she needed him to escape, plus she was a female. "We need to leave now. Flo gave me this." Daniel pulled out the small glass vial; she said you could travel inside it." He pulled the top off and Lailah's spirit willingly entered.

He put her into his pocket as the alarms started to sound. Warning cries seemed to come from all over the building and all of a sudden it dawned on him, that he was on another planet, in another galaxy. He held the wall for a second, trying to get his bearings. Now wasn't the time to feel sick. "Ok, let's get out of here." He tapped his pocket making sure she was still there.

The alarms seemed to be getting louder. "Get the viewer, now. Someone is hidden!" a guard only a few feet from Daniel bellowed his orders. As he crept along the wall he wondered if this viewer was like night vision goggles. How wrong could one person be? Out of one of the doors came a guard with what looked like a large hairless dog. The difference was it had no eyes, not even holes for eyes. Daniel felt his breath catching in his throat. It was an ugly looking beast. No one had warned him about this! If he had to fight, he would, but these looked seriously vicious.

The guard bent down to the creature. "Find me something that I can't see. Now go." The animal snapped and growled with impatience. He let it off his lead and it began its search. Daniel knew this was extremely dangerous and ran, throwing himself at the nearest wall waving his bracelet frantically. A door opened and he fell through it, shoving it closed with his foot. He needed to get back to the portal and fast.

Delta was pacing the flat. "Please stop. Walking up and down like that isn't going to make him arrive any quicker," Eva said raking through the few clothes Val had in her room. "This girl has no taste. No wonder she's such a flake. You should have seen her with Excariot. They were all: *I'm the most powerful* and *no you're not.*

It was pathetic. I have to say I'll miss him; it was fun while it lasted."

"Shut up!" Delta shouted. "You know nothing about Excariot or Val. You were taken as a child and shoved into some crazy mumbo jumbo so that you could learn to use your inner powers for evil. You know nothing of what Daniel and I had to endure, what we had to do just to get back here, and when Lailah arrives you will see what real power is."

"I've missed her," Flo said from the bed where she was plaiting the unconscious Yassmin's hair.

"What's she like?" Eva asked.

"She's magical, more than that bunch of losers. She's a warrior and God help anyone who stands in her way." Flo laughed from her gut.

"Enough!" Delta wanted them to shut up. "Just be quiet. I can't concentrate. That spell had better have worked." She shot Eva a threatening glance.

"It will. I've been working on it for Excariot for over five years; it's perfect."

"Pray it does." She started pacing again.

Daniel found himself in a room filled with bodies. He jumped to his feet. He'd seen someone dead before, when they lived in the past, but this was different. They were piled high, stacked in clear boxes. It was like one of those toyshops Delta had shown him on their return. 'Very large dolls' he thought. They didn't look decomposed; they looked perfect. He walked around the room; it was endless. The boxes were mounted in rows almost to the ceiling. He headed towards the voices in the distance, if there was an exit he needed to find it. He knew his time was running out.

"So, which one do you think they'll give him." A large dirty-looking individual asked another equally dirty-looking man.

"I would go for a forty-three," he laughed, holding his belly.

"That's cruel. I think it would have to be a seventy-eight, he deserves at least that." They were now both almost on their knees.

"Whatever they do, we will have the pleasure of sticking Excariot the guard into a clone's body." They both nodded.

Daniel now understood what he was looking at. Flo had told him all about the prisoners and how they were removed from their bodies and placed into clones, but he could never have imagined the enormity of it until now. He pressed on, walking past the men and keeping as close to the wall as he could. A doorway opened and in walked a very small woman and the men instantly stood to attention.

"The Warden will need a number seventeen for tonight. This is confidential information and I will deal with you severely if this gets out." She said her piece, turned and walked out. Daniel was hot on her heels, just making it though the gap. He was back! He recognised the guards. "Just one more level, mate," he said to himself.

The sirens now started here. They weren't as loud as Daniel had feared, but the reaction of the guards was extreme. They all moved in an orderly fashion to the walls as the man who had released the Viewer came in, his eyeless companion on his heels sniffing everything. Daniel's heart was pounding. He had to make it out; that thing looked like it was ready to tear him apart.

"The viewer has made it here, so we know the person we're looking for is in this area. Does anyone have a clue how this has happened?" He walked up and down the rows, looking the guards directly in the eyes as the dog-like thing sniffed at their legs and feet.

"You!" he poked a guard in the chest.

"Yes sir," he answered quickly.

"Have you seen anything suspicious, heard any rumours about anything you want to tell me and my friend here?" He patted the creature on the head.

"I know nothing, Sir."

"Well, you had better find this thing because it has the princess of the Ranswar, and you know what will happen if she escapes!" His voice had risen to a scream.

Daniel wasn't sure if he had heard correctly, but he thought he had said *princess*. Delta had never mentioned that fact that she was a princess. He must be wrong. Then he spotted his break. One of the small people was going through a doorway, pushing with no obvious effort an extremely large odd-looking thing. It had what looked like a small head on top of an enlarged body. It was shocking, but he saw an opportunity and took it, sliding through the door.

The trail of stench the alien had left made his stomach churn. He heard the screams of the man with the Viewer to: "Shut the door, no portals in or out should be allowed to work until this hidden one has been found, by orders of the Warden himself."

Daniel needed to find his portal and fast. If they shut them down he would be Viewer meat for sure. He looked at them all, his height now an advantage. "All portals are to be closed. Please send messages to your designated guards and hunters; all portals are closing." A woman walked around shouting the message.

"Which one?" Now he was really worried. He pulled out his map. It had nothing to show which one it was.

"What about your precious, Val?" one of the small people said to a woman who was standing near a portal.

"She'll be fine. Zac's here with Excariot, so he can take the message to her on his return." She smiled and pressed a button to close her portal.

Daniel leapt for it. If there was more than one Val he would deal with it on the other side.

"You made it!" Delta grabbed him as he arrived.

"Yes, but only just." Daniel took a breath.

"Shut the door!" Flo hollered from the bed.

"Alright, keep your body on." Delta closed the door. "Wake up the girl."

Flo tapped Yassmin on the face. "Hello. Wake up now; it's time."

Yassmin slowly started to come round to find a little blonde girl smiling at her. "Who are you? Am I still in the bookshop?" She sat up.

"I'm Flo and yes you are. And now, after four hundred years of being a prisoner you're the one we have chosen to be a vessel for our beloved Lailah."

"I don't think so." Yassmin tried to stand up but Eva pushed her back down.

"This won't hurt."

Daniel came toward her with the bottle. Yassmin backed up the bed toward the wall. He pulled off the top and the wisp escaped. It closed in on Yassmin.

"Please don't do this." She looked at Daniel who for a second seemed to have a flicker of doubt, but then it was gone. The light danced in front of Yassmin's eyes.

She pulled away, but after a few spins it was as if she had been hypnotised. Yassmin's body slumped forward onto the bed and the light gently landed on her like a feather falling from the sky.

Daniel had been expected something more violent and was pleased that it seemed so gentle. That was until Yassmin's body started to vibrate.

"What's happening?" he asked Delta.

"Don't worry, this is normal. Everyone, surround the bed. I don't want this body to be damaged in any way. Her arrival must be perfect," she ordered as they all moved to surround the bed containing the shaking Yassmin.

It seemed to last forever, but Daniel was glad when it stopped. The body lay lifeless on the bed. "Is she ok?" Daniel leant forwards.

"I'm fine." Yassmin's body replied. She pulled herself up onto all fours then slowly she lowered herself onto her heels. Surveying the room, she took each person in. "Delta, I have missed you so much." She pulled herself up, placing her feet firmly onto the floor.

"And I have missed you," Delta replied. "It's been too long."

Yassmin's body then turned to Flo. "Still stuck hiding in the little girl's body. Shame on you, Sliyig," she laughed.

"I like this body; it keeps me safe, and my name is Flo." She put her hands on her hips.

"And who are these people?"

"This is Daniel, my son." Delta pushed Daniel forwards.

"You look familiar, but I'm sensing you're new to this world." She glanced at Delta for confirmation.

"He is the son of Excariot."

"Well, well, then we have a powerful ally." She lowered her head to him. "And who is this beautiful woman?" She pointed at Eva.

"I have been trained all my life in the art of dark magic and I have served your cause for many years." Eva bowed.

"Please, no need for us to be formal here. This is a new planet, a new opportunity and time for us to make plans. Let me see this body you have thought good enough. She stood, slightly unsteady on her feet and made her way to the mirror. She pulled at Yassmin's hair and touched her full lips. "Good choice, my friend." She turned to Delta. "I'm sure she will be happy to have given herself for me."

"Lailah, I don't want to rush you, but we need to leave here."

"Why?"

"Because there's a mighty guard coming here now to capture you. She wants to return you to Alchany." Delta held out her hand to lead Lailah.

"You say guard and female in the same sentence; tell me more before I run away." She seemed a little agitated by the idea.

"Her name is Val and she is the daughter of Gabrielle."

"Gabrielle had a child, with whom?" Lailah was now intrigued.

"A witch called Wyetta; it was when he came to capture Excariot."

"Oh that imbecile. Has he been dealt with?" Lailah asked looking around for confirmation.

"Yes, but did you never love him?" Daniel questioned.

"Never, Excariot was the only one weak enough to do my bidding, yet strong enough to cause a problem, and then he still couldn't get that right. I've been in prison for over four hundred long years." A look of distaste written across her face. "So tell me Delta this child of Gabrielle's, is she a threat to our mission here?"

"Yes and no. Daniel can deal with her I'm sure, but we are on her territory and you are still weak from your time in prison, so we need to get you to our home, your home now, to start our preparations."

"I trust your decision. So this is the girl's home?" Lailah looked around.

"Yes."

"Burn it to the ground," she said to Daniel.

"What?" he was confused.

"Boy, you do as I say and you burn it to the ground, and never question me again."

Lailah followed Delta, with Flo and Eva behind as they made their way down the stairs.

Daniel stood looking at the flat and the portal. Then he raised his hand as he created a ball of electricity and struck the bed with it. The seventies style cover leapt into flames. He threw three more onto the furniture, which also quickly caught alight.

"What about the portal?" Delta asked as they walked into the shop front.

"There will be plenty of opportunities to create one, but first we must gather our remaining brothers and sisters together. Does the boy do as you tell him?"

"Yes, he's just confused. He fell in love, but luckily she's dead now." Delta smiled.

"Good. You, Eva, are there any remaining spells in this building?"

Eva started to chant. "Yes, a memory spell, a powerful one. Do you wish me to break it?"

"Yes, it must be to protect the guard. The more trouble we cause her, the easier it will be to get what we want. Do it now," Lailah ordered.

Eva's eyes started to cloud over as Daniel came through the private door. He didn't like it when she did that. He felt uneasy around her. She started to chant words in a foreign language. That made him uneasy as well. He never knew who she was doing the magic on.

"Burn this down," Lailah pointed to the books.

"Yes," Daniel replied. He created more lightning from his hands. The old books caught quickly as Eva continued to chant through the smoke that was building in the bookshop.

The crackling of each book burned a little more of Wendy out of Daniel's life. These were the only memories he had of her, and he was destroying it one page at a time.

"It's done." Eva's eyes began to clear.

"Good. Let's leave here now." Lailah headed towards the front door and out onto the street.

As they emerged, a huge yellow truck skidded to a halt beside them. Daniel, recognising its occupants, throwing a few more bolts at the bookshop for good luck. There was no way they would be able to stop this blaze now.

Val was first out of the truck, as she ran towards the bookshop she wasn't sure what was worse; seeing Delta, Daniel, Flo and Eva all together or the fact that what was left of her world was going up in flames along with the portal.

"Yassmin!" Fran ran past Val towards the group. Luckily Shane managed to grab her.

"Stop." Val turned and faced the others. "Something's wrong."

"Hello," Delta greeted them. "Well, it's just so much fun to see you like this and I would love to stay, but we have other things to do?"

"Wait." Lailah stepped forward. "You are the daughter of Gabrielle; I can tell; you look just like him."

"Yass, please," Fran was desperately trying to pull free from Shane, but he knew better.

"This Yass, is this the body I have taken?" she glanced back at Delta.

"Yes."

"And is this Yass someone you love?" she asked Fran directly.

"She's my twin sister!" Fran screamed as an explosion rocked the bookshop.

"Then be proud. Your sister is now the vessel for one of the most powerful and worshiped princesses. She will be followed by the masses and cause chaos on many planets. Don't be sad. This is a time to rejoice my return."

"I'm going to..." Shane pulled his hand over Fran's mouth.

"Do you have nothing to say to me Gabrielle's daughter?" Lailah looked down her nose at Val.

"Yes. Now I know why my dad didn't want you. No wonder he ran a mile not to be with you. But then you wanted Excariot. Didn't work out too well for you now did it? Has anyone told you I've locked lover boy away?"

Lailah's lip twitched. "You are nothing. The inadequate Excariot meant nothing to me. Your father was weak and when the time comes I will make you the slave that cleans the feet of my slaves." Lailah turned her back and Val pulled out her sword, ready to at least defend her now blazing bookshop.

"Try this." She lifted her sword into the air, but one of Daniel's bolts struck it, knocking it smouldering to the ground.

"Back off," Daniel said, hatred for Val visible in his eyes. They all gathered around Lailah and Daniel teleported them out.

Shane released Fran who fell to the ground weeping. Val walked towards the bookshop. Now billowing black smoke came gushing out. She could hear Jason calling the fire brigade, but it was too late, her home was gone. Her doorway to hope was gone. How would she get help? She was lost, and now Fran's sister was possessed by Lailah. She hadn't been surprised to see Flo and Eva with Delta; it all made sense. It had been a very clever and elaborate set up from the start.

"What do we do now?" Belinda came up behind her.

"I don't know. I'm lost." She looked at her sword, mangled on the ground.

"Val, tell me something right now." Fran was up and grabbing Val's arm. "You said that people taken by prisoners can be extracted, right; that Lailah can be taken out of Yass's body."

"Yes, but the portal has gone. We have no way of getting back to Alchany."

"But Excariot opened a portal and Wendy opened a portal. Why can't you? Come on Val." Fran shook her arm. "Please don't give up on me, not now."

"Wendy's gone and so has Excariot; it's like last time, we played right into their hands. I can't carry on. I don't want to go on, Fran. I'm tired."

"No! Sorry, but you don't get to give up on me. I have given you all my trust. I have risked my life, and trust me I have no magical powers, and I'm scared. How will I tell my parents that Yass has just become the host body for the power of all evil from another galaxy? So no, you don't get to give up." Fran pushed her. It was as if she was looking to start a fight.

"Just give it a rest." Val turned away and Fran jumped on her. They were both down on the ground and Fran had her in a vicious grip. "Come on, Val, fight. I'm tired too, but I will still fight for you. You don't know my sister, I do, and I know Yass will be in there fighting with that thing, trying to get her body back." The sirens of the fire services were starting to draw near. "Please Val," Fran begged.

Val let her head fall onto the tarmac and took a deep breath. "Point made. Now will you get off me?"

"Yes, I'll do anything you say, just don't give up. Not today, not on me." Fran stood pulling Val to her feet.

Val's phone buzzed. She could tell it was a text. "Should I get it?" she asked the others. "It could be a clue to where Yass is." They all agreed. She pulled out the phone and flipped it open. She could instantly see she had three missed calls. There had been so much going on that she genuinely hadn't heard it. She opened the message.

I can't get you on the phone. I think you need to come home; you have some explaining to do. luv mum xxx

CHAPTER 17

Home again

Val looked down at the text message, her heart starting to feel all the pain of losing her parents. This was some sick joke Delta was playing on her.

"What does it say?" Fran asked.

"It's asking me to go home, that I have some explaining to do." She closed the phone and stuck it back into her pocket.

"Aren't you going to reply? I'm sure your mum will be worried about you. Oh dear God, you have a mother!" Fran looked shocked at what she had just said. "You have a mum and dad and they are called Susan and Mike, and why can I remember your parents if you're an orphan?"

"Yes, I can remember them as well; it's cloudy but they're real," Jason agreed with Fran.

"Are you serious?" Val had little trust for anything anymore.

"Yes, I can as well. Why would you make us forget your parents Val?" Shane asked her.

"Because Wyetta felt that they would be at risk if Excariot found them."

"Well Excariot's gone, so maybe that's why we can remember them?" Shane suggested

"I'm not sure, but Delta knows them as well. She said she wouldn't hurt them because they were kind to her, but I'm not so sure about Lailah. What do you think we should do?" She looked to the others for support.

"I say we go and find out if they're ok." Belinda insisted. "I would want to see my daughter if she was here." Val squeezed her hand.

"Right, back into Bessie then," Shane said as the first fire truck arrived.

"What do I tell them?" Val felt very confused; this wasn't supposed to happen.

"Tell her you'll be there in fifteen minutes," Shane said starting the engine.

"Ok." Val sent the text and sat quietly in the truck as they travelled. Everyone was tired. It felt as if they had been running for days without stopping, but now she was going home. Fran sat with her head on Jason's shoulder. Val knew she had to help her. She was right; she had walked into battle for Val without question and without power. She would get Yassmin back and extracted.

She actually felt sorry for Excariot. All that time, four hundred years, a prisoner on Earth, he had fought to get Lailah free and bring her back, yet she clearly despised him.

"Nearly there. Did you say it was the one on the left?" Shane asked pointing to Val's street.

"Uhu." She loved her house; it always seemed the brightest one. She was sure there was no need for quite so many lights, but who cared. Then she spotted her mum on the front lawn, waiting with her apron on, prowling the flowerbeds.

Shane pulled up and Susan stared at the truck now on her driveway. Val jumped out and ran, leaping across the grass into Susan's arms. She buried her head into her mum's shoulder, breathing her in.

"Mum." Val said the word and it was better than winning the lottery.

Susan kissed her check, and pulled her hair back. "Val what's going on? I feel confused. What's happened?" She took Val's face in her hands. "Your dad's on his way. He was at a building site when he suddenly remembered he had a daughter for heaven's sake."

Shane and the others were now standing together on the lawn, looking a little like party crashers.

"I will explain everything to you, but first, Mum, can we go in and sit down? It's been a very long day and I think I can vouch for us all when I say we're hungry."

She knew what to say to make things ok. Her mum instantly sprang into last minute *garden fete* action.

"Yes of course, come in" Susan opened the front door and they all piled in.

It didn't take long for her to whisk up some cup cakes and hot chocolate. Val introduced everyone to her mum with a little description about them and what they could do. She took it all in.

Then the front door opened. "I'm back," Mikes called from the hall. Val jumped to her feet, almost knocking Belinda off her chair as she ran to where he was removing his coat.

"Dad." Val waited. The last time they had spoken he still wasn't sure about her and her newfound abilities and friends.

"Val, where have you been? Come here." He opened his arms and she was safe. Mike's arms wrapped around her and the hard ugly world of a guard was gone. He smelt of aftershave and building site dust. He kissed her head. "I need to know what has happened. Your mum and I have been lost for days. Walking around like something was missing, but we couldn't put our fingers on it." He opened his arms to release her and the world didn't seem quite so bad anymore.

"Come and meet everyone, Dad." She pulled him into the very full kitchen. "This is Shane and his son Jason." Mike waved. "This is Fran, Jason's girlfriend and Belinda, Wendy Whitmore's mum." They all gave a salute back with their hands full of cake.

"I see your mother has been feeding them." He threw a smile in Susan's direction.

"Dad, we have a big problem. I don't know how you can remember me, but you're not supposed to, and before you give me the riot act just let me explain everything."

"Do I need a chair?" Mike asked.

"Two wouldn't be enough, Mr Saunders. I know you will find all of this strange, weird, unbelievable, but it's the truth and I just want to tell you what an amazingly brave daughter you have." Shane pulled back the chair next to him and Mike sat down.

"Please call me Mike," he said to Shane.

"So it goes like this..." Val would have told her mum and dad the story if there hadn't been an enormous smashing sound in the living room.

"Get my mum and dad out of here now," she yelled, grabbing for her sword them remembering it was broken. She raised her hand creating an instant flame.

"Oh dear Lord, you're on fire," Susan squealed.

"No, Mum it's ok. Just get out the back or something."

"Hello." A voice called. "Val?"

She lowered her hand. "False alarm. It's Zac." She walked into the lounge to find him standing in the middle of the new glass coffee table.

"Sorry. I was in with the Warden and Excariot and then I involuntarily teleported. What's going on? Sorry about this piece of your belongings." He raised a grin.

"Val, why is there a young man standing in my coffee table? How did he get in? Mike, if I've told you once I've told you a million times to lock the front door." Susan swiped at him with her free hand.

"I locked it," Mike defended himself.

"Mum, Dad, it's ok. Zac here is my hunter," Val said proudly.

"Well he found you, I suppose that's a good sign." Susan looked at him and smiled. "Would you like a hot chocolate?" Zac shook his head vigorously.

"Val's Mum it is an honour to meet you at last, but I do not eat your Earth food as it is poisonous."

"To him, Mum. He's not saying anything against your food. He's an alien."

"Oh, what does he eat then?" Susan asked.

"He takes tablets every couple of days and drinks this soup thing. It's vile." Val made gagging impressions at them. "No offence, Zac."

"I have information. I was with Excariot when I was sent here, but the Warden seemed very distressed. It seems that Lailah has been released and they aren't sure of her whereabouts."

"Right, yeah, slight problem there," Val grinned.

"Why are we here? I expected you to be at the bookshop." Zac stepped out of the coffee table.

"Right, yeah, slight problem there too." Val was edging towards the kitchen. "I think maybe you need to sit down and listen very carefully. I would like to say this just the once."

Val sat at the kitchen table surrounded by her friends and family and related their adventures of the last few days. Susan hugged Belinda as Val explained about Wendy, and Mike was impressed with Zac's sacrifices for Val. Then she told them about Delta. They didn't remember her and Val explained how she had become forgotten, and about Daniel, Flo and Eva.

"And so we get to Lailah, who is now here on Earth, readying an army as we speak." Val took a large sip of hot chocolate."

"She's here! We must get back; it's time to go," Zac grabbed Val's hand across the table.

"Slight problem. The bookshop is no more. Daniel burned it down."

"I'm sorry, but did you just say our portal to Alchany has gone?" Zac was visibly panicking. He studied his watch, and then looked up. "I still have a connection, but we can't get to Alchany."

"I'm sorry, Zac, plus I'm not sure how safe we are here."

"Don't worry, we can use the dellatrax to get back." He looked at them expectantly. "Where is the dellatrax?"

"Back at Excariot's hideout," Fran said in an attempt to take some of the attention away from Val.

"How could you leave it there?" Zac put his head down on the table.

"Look, we needed to try and get to Yassmin, but we failed. Sam said you would return to me. That's why you're here, and now you're as stuck as me. I think we need to move out. We need to go and make a base somewhere new."

"What about work, our lives, Val?" asked Shane. "They've taken too much from us already. That would be giving in to them. We can't let them win."

"I agree with Shane," Mike chirped up. "We have lived in this house, Val, since you were born and I'm not running away from a bunch of bullies just because they want to take over the world." Mike looked pleased with his speech, but Val knew better. She knew that this would never work, that's why Wyetta had asked her to protect them in the first place."

Susan's phone suddenly broke into song. She opened it up and looked surprised, and then worried.

"What's wrong mum?" Val enquired.

"It's a text message, from you." She showed it to Val.

"Oh my God!" Val said. Susan slapped her hand. "Sorry. Oh my gosh. I sent you this from Alchany. I never thought it would arrive. Maybe it re-sent when I came home, but if it did travel from there, then that means I can maybe send Sam a text to tell him what's going on."

"It has to be worth a try. I can still tell if a prisoner takes form, but that's about it." Zac was annoyed. "If we had the dellatrax it would be different."

"What does this deliatrixy thing do?" Susan asked, placing another plate of biscuits down on the table.

"It's the life force of the universe. It connects with its guard at birth and stays with them forever. Normally a guard is connected physically, but as Val has so many problems we couldn't do that for her, so we made books, which *they* left behind," Zac stated.

"I'm sorry, are you trying to say that my daughter isn't perfect in every way?" Susan questioned him.

"She can't help it. We have also given her symbols because she is a reject." Zac raised his hand. "Sorry, not a reject, she doesn't like this word. We use needy instead."

"Ok Zac, I think you have said quite enough, buddy." Val pulled her chair back. "We need to start making a plan to get out of this situation. If you want to stay here then, Belinda, we will need the coven to come in and make this place safe."

Belinda nodded. "Consider it done. As long as my Wendy is in your world I will be in yours."

"Right Fran, what are you going to tell your parents about Yassmin?" Val asked.

"What do you think?"

"Give us a couple of days to see what we can accomplish then we tell them everything."

Fran nodded in agreement.

"Shane, are you intending to go to work tomorrow morning?"

"Unless you have anything better for me to do?" He had a glint in his eye.

"Mum, you need..." Val was about the tell Susan to keep the troops fed when the front door exploded.

Susan screamed, throwing herself onto the floor; Mike followed. Val and Zac ran for the kitchen door. "Jason, protect my mum and dad!" Val called.

"On it."

"Zac, come with me." Her back was now touching the door. She was about to open it when it slammed inwards, knocking her across the floor towards her dad.

The door swung shut, and on the next swing Flo walked in pushing it open for Lailah to enter. "Well, all having a nice time I see."

"What do you want?" Val was openly hostile. Flo had just crossed a big line by coming into her parent's home.

"Why Val, that's not very good manners. I'm sure your mother would be very disappointed in you." Lailah bent down looking under the table. "Are you Val's mother?"

"Get away!" Val exploded. A huge gush of wind hit Lailah from the side making her skid across the polished floor. "Get everyone out," she yelled at Shane, turning the wind across the kitchen so it blew the back door off, accidentally throwing Zac against the fridge. "You will not touch my family!" Her body sprang into flames.

Daniel now came in, throwing a bolt at Val, which she deflected with a fireball.

"Stop children, please," Lailah called over the noise. "Val, all we want is the dellatrax. Just hand it over and we will go away and leave you alone."

"We thought you had it, so who's the loser now?" Val stood ready to attack anyone who took another step towards her family.

"She's lying." Delta came in behind Daniel.

"You said you would never tell anyone where my family were."

"Oh, did I? Sorry." Delta snarled.

"Enough. I want the books and you had better get them for me or else!" Lailah yelled.

"Have you heard yourself speak? You're like one of those really bad villains from the nineteen fifties. Do you remember the nineteen fifties? Oh no you were in a little plastic box. My advice would be you need to do a very deep mwahaha at the end, they all do it." Val knew she had given the others enough time to exit the house.

"Do not waste my time, guard. You are trapped on this planet just like me and you know the power the dellatrax possesses. So, if I don't have it, and you don't have it, someone does." Lailah said. "Let us leave. They have nothing here. Val we will be watching you and your family." Daniel was stood motionless, staring at Val, pure hatred in his eyes. "Daniel, now!" Lailah snapped impatiently. He grabbed her hand, teleporting them out.

"Facebook me, alright," she shouted into the empty kitchen.

"Well, they don't have the dellatrax; this is good news," Zac said as he pulled himself from behind the fridge door. Your powers are growing; just try to aim them at the right person." He brushed himself down.

"Sorry. We have to get out of here." Val stepped out the back door where the rest were waiting near her mum's potting shed. "We need to leave. Get Bessie. We can go to Sam's. If I know him, they won't be able to track us there. Dad we need to go to the house you have just built with the cherry wood front door and the glass wall." Val started pushing them through the garden.

"Mr Law?" Mike asked.

"You're joking. He called himself Mr Law and he's a Judge." Val laughed.

"Oh that's nice. Well at least we will be safe there," Susan said following the others.

"No mum, he's not that type of Judge, you know, but yes I think we stand a chance of being safer than we are here."

"How do you know Mr Law, honey?" Mike enquired as they all climbed into Bessie.

"He's a good friend." She didn't want to go into detail at this moment in time.

"Do you have a skeleton key, Dad?"

"Yes, but it's not appropriate to break into my customers' houses." Mike shook his head.

"Dad, a crazed psychopath from another planet just blew your front door off. I think now would be a good time to break the rules just a little."

"Yes, I suppose you have a point."

Shane drove while Mike gave directions. They arrived there within a few minutes. Sandy was sitting on the drive. Val's heart skipped a beat. Would Sam be there?

She watched, on guard with Zac, as they all made their way to the front door and Mike opened up.

"Come on." Zac signalled to Val when they were all inside.

"Coming." She followed and was pleased to be behind a door that, hopefully, no one knew about.

"Oh Mike, it's fabulous." Susan put her hand on his arm.

"Thank you. I think it's a good job." He kissed his wife on the cheek.

"Val, I think someone was expecting you." Jason came out the kitchen with an envelope.

Surely Delta hadn't been here. She took it with trepidation in her heart. The envelope read simply 'V'. She knew straight away it was from Sam. She tore it open and pulled out the letter.

"Fran, will you please get my parents a drink, I will be there in a second." She took the letter to the staircase and sat down to read.

Dear V,

If you are reading this letter, things have changed. My home is yours to use for as long as necessary. There are spare keys to all locks in the garage. I am guessing by now you know who or what I am. I would have told you sooner, but it wouldn't have helped either of us in our journeys. If things have gone to plan then Wendy will be

with me, and she will be ready to start her training as a Judge. We have been watching her for a long time. It's unusual for a Judge to be born out of our galaxy, but not completely unheard of.

The other day when you visited, I tricked you a little by imprinting your fingerprints onto the weapons room, so you will have no problem accessing it. This has all the equipment I have given you and a few extras. Jason should have some fun in there. If things have not gone well, then I hope the tools I have left you will come in handy.

V, I *will* return for you, I promise you that. My life is complicated and I have obligations to my people, but we have to complete what we have started. I think I owe you pudding.

Val laughed out loud.

Be brave until my return and remember that my love for you has no walls.

Sam

She stared at the letter for what seemed like an eternity. Then Susan came to her with a cup of tea. "You alright?"

"Yes, I think I am." She leaned on her mum's shoulder.

Her life was different now. She had her parents back and a new home. She had won a huge victory, made a few new friends and some enemies as well. So not everything was sorted or easy, but she was starting to understand that that was a side effect of real life. No one knew what was around the next corner - until they dared to look.

The End

Special acknowledgment goes to:

Chyna, Jason, Mum and John.
Niki Shakallis and Lyndsey Cooper for your support.
Jo Turner and all the staff at Waterstone's stores, for all your encouragement and advice.
Karen Waring for tirelessly dragging in those children to Lincolnshire libraries.
All the children and young adults I have had the pleasure of meeting on my travels.
Veronica for giving me a chance and Alison for not giving up so easily.
All the fans of *The Thirteenth* on Facebook, "Hi".
To Dom and Jess at the Advocate Arms Market Rasen (Hot Chocolate!).
Rand Farm near Wragby for the time to edit and the socket!
To all the WW ladies who supported me when no one else knew.
To the Carlton family for being so amazing always.
Miss Lockley and the gang; you know who you are!
To Chris, as always, for the Magic.
I thank you all xx.

Lightning Source UK Ltd.
Milton Keynes UK
10 December 2010

164141UK00001B/2/P